Jungle Lovers

Books by Paul Theroux

Waldo
Fong and the Indians
Girls at Play
Jungle Lovers

Jungle Lovers

Paul Theroux

HOUGHTON MIFFLIN COMPANY BOSTON

ISBN: 0-395-12107-8
Library of Congress Catalog Card Number: 70-144074
Printed in the United States of America

The author is grateful for permission to quote from the following:
"Rimbaud" by W. H. Auden, from *Collected Shorter Poems 1927–
1957*, copyright 1940 and renewed © 1968 by W. H. Auden, pub-
lished by Random House, Inc. "The Greenest Continent" by Wallace
Stevens, from *Opus Posthumous*, published in 1957 by Alfred A.
Knopf, Inc.

For Anne and my sons
Marcel and Louis

J'ai seul la clef de cette parade sauvage.

— Arthur Rimbaud, *Les Illuminations*

Now, galloping through Africa, he dreamed
Of a new self, a son, an engineer,
His truth acceptable to lying men.

— W. H. Auden, "Rimbaud"

Part One

1

On the day before Christmas — this was just a few years ago — in a dusty little dorp in up-country Malawi, which is in Central Africa, a young man sloped down the main road, alone. The dorp's name was Rumpi, and the young man's Calvin Mullet. He was from Hudson, Massachusetts. The quaint raffia suitcase he lugged could have passed for a picnic hamper, but he was no picnicker.

He had been dropped at the *boma* by a banana truck. The truck's dust cloud hung for a moment in the air, then was gathered into a murmuring whirlwind and hurried off the empty road and into the scraggy jungle, leaving behind a strong odor of fragrant patchouli. Rare patchouli grew wild in those parts. Calvin watched the whirlwind go.

Latterly divorced, Calvin was suffering the effects of paying alimony. He sold insurance (Homemakers' Mutual, Boston and New York, with fifty-six branches around the world) but all his goods and chattels so-called, and half his salary had been awarded to his wife. He roomed in a whorehouse in the capital, Blantyre, and hitchhiked to his several accounts: thus, the banana truck. He had sold his car. The marriage had been brief, unfriendly and faintly squalid, like the hunched-over gust of brown wind that had a moment before swept whispering past him. The divorce was a relief but something to regret.

He stopped walking. He wiped his face with a bunched hanky and read DRINK LION — YOU WILL INJOY. Under that sign slumped a larger-than-usual native hut which gave the appearance of being supported by some six or seven Africans who leaned against it for shade. Their heads were stuck under the eaves of the overhanging brooms of roof thatch. In front there was a smaller but more professional sign, GUINNESS FOR POWER — BIG DRUM BAR, bearing the motif of a black fist punching jagged cartoon lightning; a small scrawl on a pasted label warned *No Hawking.*

Ropes of hanging beads were strung over the doorway. Calvin pushed through them, dropped his creaking suitcase and after ordering a beer, fanned himself with his hat — once a fairly good Panama, now a wreck, with grubby crown and bitten brim. (It was turned down front and back like a spy's, but very dirty.) The bar was dark. When Calvin's eyes grew accustomed to the deep gloom he saw a row of Africans staring at him. Ragged and with unsteady heads, the Africans squatted on the dirt floor. They had wide machetes across their knees; each man balanced a pint of Lion on his knife blade. Calvin smiled at them. They nodded back, dark hellos.

Strangely, there was no picture of Dr. Osbong in the bar. He was the President of Malawi. It was against the law not to have his picture in a conspicuous place in every building in the country. Calvin had one in his office. There had been one in the bar; a nail and a rectangle of cobwebs remained. Calvin did not mention its absence; it was none of his business.

The bar floor gave off a ripe stable smell and was spread with looping rosaries of black ants. Almost immediately some ants located Calvin's suitcase. They swarmed into the mesh of the raffia, violating the contents. Calvin put his hat down. Leaning on the counter's sticky rings, one fist pressed into his cheek to aim his head at the ants, he gazed with that fatigued curiosity of strangers to hot climates. He was gasping for breath, trickles of sweat were running down the sides of his face, meeting at his chin and dripping onto his smudged shirtfront. A drop of sweat made its way like an insect down his breastbone to nest in his navel.

The temperature was in the mid-eighties, but there was no sun: it had risen and once off the ground disappeared into shapeless gray haze. A dull sky made the day throb with sunless heat, a kind of cookery worse than sunshine. The steamy air was a sickness; there was no fan in the bar, no electricity in the dorp.

A dusty bottle of beer was brought and opened, so warm it spewed suds. The bartender — wearing a paper party hat with a sweat-diluted Lion slogan on it — slipped a soda straw into the bottle.

"A glass, please."

"No want straw?"

Straws were favored, especially for drinking beer. Osbong said Malawi could take credit for the invention of the straw; in olden times it was a reed from a marsh, and still in the villages the common beer pot was drunk out of by a circle of men with four-foot reed straws. *He spits through his straw* was a local proverb. The row of squatting blacks sucking on straws, balancing their pints on their knives, lifted their eyes to Calvin.

"No want," said Calvin. Straws gave him gas.

The bartender lifted out the straw and emptied it of beer by blowing through it hard. He replaced it in the cardboard box. Pouring Calvin a glass of beer he said, "Happy Christmas, *bwana*."

"Somehow," said Calvin, "it doesn't feel like Christmas. No offense intended."

Propped on the counter a new ad from the Lion breweries showed a comical lion in a red stocking hat and white St. Nick whiskers; the ad was edged in plastic holly. A small tinsel

Christmas tree dangled from a twist of yellow fly paper in the center of the room. Dabs of cotton had been carefully glued onto the smeared mirror at the back of the bar: snowflakes. Calvin wiped the creeks of sweat from his face with his hanky. Snowflakes!

He tipped his glass and drank. He enjoyed drinking; he liked the bitter sting of warm beer on his tongue, the small bubbles needling his gullet, the taste of pickled nuts, a wash of foam, and so on to yeasty fullness; four pints was a square meal. He wasn't an alcoholic; he believed beer drinkers never were. But he was almost certainly a drunkard. It was his choice, not an affliction; it gave pleasure.

"How far to Lilongwe?" He smacked his lips.

The dozing bartender stirred. "Lilongwe. Three-four days on bicycle."

"How many miles?"

"Two hundred-so." The African shrugged. "You going that side?"

"Today, I hope. I want to get the night bus to Blantyre." Calvin sipped his beer. "This is my first trip north."

"You like?"

"Very nice," said Calvin. "You got a nice place here."

"Not like south," said the African. "No Osbong here."

"You mean no money?" Coins the value of a shilling were called osbongs, after the head they bore.

"I am meaning," said the African, "no *Doctor* Osbong bastard." He said it like the bird — "bustard."

Calvin went silent. He didn't talk politics; not there.

The African was staring at Calvin's glasses. "Good goggles," he said. "You buying here?"

"No, I got them from the States."

"American?"

"Yup."

"We hate Americans," said the African calmly. "They kill black Negroes. Start trouble. Spy on us. Hate us too much.

Just big gangsters and cowboys up to now. That their badness. Doctor Osbong say it good to trust Yankees. Myself I don't trust at all. Osbong is" — The African squinted — "how you say *fisi* in English?"

"Hyena," said Calvin. He put a ten osbong note on the counter. "Have a beer."

"Eh!" the African kecked gratefully. "Happy Christmas, *bwana*. You with those soldiers?"

"Which soldiers?"

"In the trees," the African said.

"I'm an American," said Calvin. "I sell insurance — or, as you say in this neck of the woods, *assurance*."

"God," said the African, "made everyone the same. I take Guinness." He got himself a brown bottle and inserted a straw; and slurping, his lower lip rolled down showing bright pink, he added, "For power, ha-ha."

"It's a good brew," said Calvin. He watched the African empty the bottle.

"Good goggles," said the African.

"Thanks."

He had six pairs altogether, the other five in his suitcase being trodden upon by ants. Calvin dreaded losing them, breaking the pair he was wearing and not having an extra. Being in Africa heightened his fear; he had bought three pairs since arriving in Malawi a year previous. (Don, the Hudson oculist, said it thrilled him to send the specs all that way.) But the glasses were all he had bought. The tan wash-and-wear suit he had picked up cheap in Filene's Basement; a year of dust and sun, rain and mildew had not been kind to it. It was wrinkled, it sagged, the cuff stitches had given away, the right elbow of the jacket was torn, the knees were swollen and the knee backs creased like accordians. The seat was dark and dead with wear, mainly the friction of sliding in and out of rides he thumbed. He wore suede shoes because they didn't need polishing; they collected stains like blotters. Calvin had a

7

habit, when drunk, of pissing on his toes. He had worn the suit on his trip north because he thought he might get a lift more easily; but the vehicles were few, the banana truck from the frontier to Rumpi was a stroke of luck. The suit had made little difference. If anything, in the heat and now-frequent rain, it made him look less respectable. In his Panama hat and grimy suit he looked like a stricken preacher. He was, of a sort: his belief was life insurance. He was pale, tall, a stringbean.

"Merry Christmas."

He turned. An African at the far end of the bar smiled a white mouthful of greetings. The African nodded pleasantly, revealing at his side the small head of a woman, and she was smiling too. Their clothes made Calvin feel faintly ashamed of his own. The man's shirt was clean, his collar stiff, the creases on his sleeves sharp. He wore glasses, but Calvin could tell they were fakes, the plain flat window-glass ones that were sold for five osbongs at market stalls. The young woman wore a pink dress, with ribbons and lacy borders. Man and woman crouched on stools, elbows on the bar, faces level with the straws that sprouted from their bottles: roosting postures of alcoholic unease.

Calvin smiled back, finished his beer, and then began brushing ants from his suitcase, preparatory to leaving. The bartender appeared before him with a pint of Lion. *"Bwana? That bwana and dona saying Happy Christmas to you."*

The African at the end of the bar shyly twiddled his straw and said, "Cheers."

Calvin walked over to him and said, "Look, Merry Christmas to you, pal, but I've got to get to Lilongwe. I'm bumming, hitching. The night bus leaves at — "

"African custom," said the man, waving Calvin to a stool. "Drink. Be happy. No worry."

The smile left Calvin's face. He looked straight into the lenses of the man's toy spectacles and said softly, "Friend, do you ever ask yourself, Where am I going to be in ten years or so?"

"No," said the man.

"But I'll bet there are plenty of times when you wake up at night and ask, What the heck am I going to do for ready cash when I'm too old to work?"

"No work," said the man. "After ten years pass I still here drinking, enjoying. Why not, eh?" He smiled at the woman. She nodded.

"Let me put it another way," said Calvin. Rephrasing had to be the insurance agent's forte. "How would you like to have a lot of money — about, say, five hundred pounds?"

"I like," said the man.

"You like," said Calvin. "Good. Now, look at this bottle of beer. It costs two osbongs. For *four* osbongs a week, the price of two of these bottles — " Calvin flicked the beer bottle twice with his finger " — you can take out an insurance policy that will guarantee you hundreds of pounds after ten years. Stick it out for twenty and you get five hundred, cash on the barrel-head. If nothing happens to you in the meantime. What do you say to that?"

"I get couple hundred quid," mused the man. "I have to work?"

"Absolutely not."

The man smiled, his lips stretching slowly, opening to reveal a set of hard clean teeth in a perfect row.

"All you have to do," Calvin went on, "is pay four osbongs a week. Now let's suppose that instead of buying this beer for me you had put two osbongs here. Go ahead, put two down."

The man pressed two coins on the counter next to the bottle. Each showed the President, Dr. Osbong, in profile, with a laurel-branch collar.

"All right, watch me. I'm putting an osbong down next to yours. You see?" Calvin stacked the coins. "That's the way we operate. For every *two* osbongs *you* put in *we* give you *one*. You can't lose. We help you, just like I'm doing here. It's creative saving, and the surrender value of the policy is high. Plus full protection. Are you interested?"

"In what?"

Calvin took the man hard by the upper arm and said, "Are you interested in getting hundreds of pounds at the end of ten years, yes or no?"

"Yes," said the man eagerly.

"Okay," said Calvin, "now you're talking. Put your John Hancock right here." He took a punched card out of his inside pocket and indicating the dotted line with an *X*, passed the card and a ball point to the man.

The man adjusted his glasses deftly, a precise but pointless gesture. He studied the card and then signed with a flourish, a large spiral, then a squiggle, several strokes and numerous dots above and below the squiggle. He underscored it boldly. It was a handsome signature.

"Now your address. There, right underneath."

The African's face went slack. He handed the pen back to Calvin. "Cannot."

"What do you mean? You've got an address, haven't you?"

"Got an address, sure." He told Calvin his box number at the dorp's post office.

"P.O. Rumpi," said Calvin. "Here's the pen. Write it down."

"Cannot write."

"Well, what the hell," and Calvin tapped the signature, "is that?"

"My name," said the man.

"That," the woman spoke up. She was very pretty, very young, with a small round head and a cap of short hair. She wrinkled her nose and smiled and continued, "That not name. That just — " She lifted long fingers and fluttered them to signify aimless writing. "It look like name. But," she smiled and dropped her eyes, "that not name. That *signature*."

"I see, I see, I see," said Calvin. He filled in the man's address and printed the man's name in block letters, Ogilvie Nirenda. He grinned at his client, Ogilvie. "Now you leave everything to me. I'll send you envelopes, reminders and the whole policy.

But for God's sake, remember," Calvin preached, "instead of buying that beer or that pack of cigarettes, or that new tie or whatever, put those osbongs aside. You'll be a rich man if you do. If you find yourself wanting a beer — *resist! Resist!*" Calvin grasped the man's hand and shook it twice. "Welcome to Homemakers'," he said. Calvin was pleased; and it wasn't the thought of the commission.

"Have a beer," said the African.

It was ungracious to refuse the drink. It was dangerous not to buy the man a drink in return; people were killed for less. The man insisted on filling Calvin's glass. Calvin, the man reminded him, was a guest, not in the bar, but in the country. Dr. Osbong was a socialist, and socialism was sharing beer. "So," Ogilvie smiled gently, "don't go away. Buy me a drink."

2

Two miles south of Rumpi a cool soldier named Marais watched the road through a pair of binoculars. He crouched hidden in tussocks of grass and dusty bushes on a high shelflike bluff of red laterite. Behind him a dozen soldiers, black men in khaki, were dug in, flopped in formation on their stomachs like a stranded school of fish. A car passed below on the road. Dust clouds pouring from the back wheels hovered just behind it in a high curling swell, threatening to engulf the vehicle.

"I give him a puncture, yes," said Brother Chimanga, who lay close to Marais. He peered seriously into the eyepiece of the telescopic sight on his carbine.

"Leave it," said Marais. "It's not him. It's the Indian. We know where he's going."

"Small puncture, so he not forget." Brother Chimanga locked a shell into the chamber and took aim.

Letting his binoculars fall, Marais grasped the tubular sight and used it as a handle to wrench the rifle from the African. With his right hand he hammered the African on the neck, forcing his face into the red dust; and when the African could not see or move — he was pinned to the ground — Marais took his knife away.

"No," said Marais, coughing on the dust he had raised, "don't be stupid." He let the African up.

They knelt before each other, breathing deeply. The African, Brother Chimanga, humiliated in front of the others, flexed his fists and spat. Dust was sprinkled on his long eyelashes and it powdered his cheeks. Glaring at each other in confounded anger they did not see the car disappear over a hill, though they heard the puttering engine shut out by the trees. Neither did they see that the sun was setting, the car plunging with a buzz distantly into it. It was half-past six, the spectacle of the sun rehearsing its disappearance usual in Malawi: the sun did not drop whole and round behind the earth, but rather broke like an egg low in the sky and slipped apart, making a fiery bloody omlette at the sharp rim of the sky's base. It was this wide thing — not the sun — that set, scrap by bright scrap.

Marais ejected the live shell from the carbine and tossed the empty rifle back to Brother Chimanga, saying, "Don't ever do that again."

Brother Chimanga did not reply. He brushed the dust from the oily wood of the stock with stiffened fingers.

"Brother George, you stay behind. If you see him, give us a whistle." Marais found his cap. He clapped the dust from it and put it on, pulling the peak down. And surveying the road again casually, he lit a cigar. "Let's go," he said finally. "Everyone up."

They trooped through the stunted trees along a sandy path, Marais in the lead wiping the dust from his binoculars with a red pocket handkerchief. Two men stayed at Marais's sides, the rest followed behind in a single column. They were all sizes, some very small, quick-marching to keep up with the long strides of the others, with shirtcuffs doubled over thickly and oversized trousers drawn together in bunched folds at their waists with knotted rope, like sack tops, and wearing clomping boots to their knees which fit only because they were padded with balled-up newspaper. The two soldiers near Marais were tall and powerfully built, in close-fitting uniforms, their rifles propped menacingly forward as they strode along the path. All the men wore red daisies in the buttonholes of their shirt pockets. Brother Chimanga's daisy drooped.

At the rough thornbush fence that marked the edge of the encampment they were met by a young sentry. He dragged his boots together, pounded his rifle butt on the ground and saluted, his forearm horizontal across his stomach, fingers touching the muzzle.

Marais stopped. He said, "Do that again."

The sentry saluted again, now with doubting slowness, sucking his lower lip as he did so. His large eyes were fixed on Marais.

"Who taught you to do that?" Marais walked up to the sentry whose arm trembled uncertainly and fell to his side. Marais spoke angrily to the men. "Who taught him to do that?"

"What he do?" asked one of the tall soldiers.

"He saluted, Goddamn it!" Marais rubbed his mustache with the back of his fist. He straightened his shoulders. "That man," he said, shaking his cigar at the sentry, "that man saluted to me! I want to know where he learned to do it."

"Is coming night and we — "

"Shut up," said Marais, "this is serious. Somebody here is teaching these men to salute, and I don't like it." Marais leaned close to the bewildered sentry and said, *"Don't salute!* Don't do this." He demonstrated a foolish salute. "You understand? Nobody salutes in this army. We don't have any officers. You're the same as him and him. If anyone tells you to do that you tell him *voetsak!* You hear?"

The sentry nodded uncertainly.

"I don't think he understands," said Marais. "Brother Mussa, translate what I said."

Marais walked on to a shelter at the center of the clearing, cursing the sentry under his breath and biting on his cigar. A hundred times he had told them: no insignia, no promotions, therefore no saluting. They were all equals; the fighting was done by everyone; everything was shared. It was a people's army, they fought together. Only loyalty mattered; the country was to be liberated, Osbong and his henchmen killed. The men needed no orders to shoot the corrupt, certainly no commands to act together. It was natural and inevitable that they should revolt.

On these principles three months previous in a camp on the Songwe River, in the far north of Malawi, Marais had armed his men and started marching south. The principles had proved assumptions: they needed correction. Unexpected things were happening, of which the sentry's salute was only one instance; Chimanga's impulse to shoot the tires of the Indian's car was another. And there were more, slight, but disturbing. The younger men reported bullying. The men who habitually marched beside Marais asked for special insignia, and they complained because they had to eat with the youths. As it was, at mealtime, they separated into age groups.

"This not happen in village," one of the older men said when Marais ordered them to eat together.

"You're not in a village now," Marais had replied. "If you want to live like that you have no business here." And Mussa had translated to them all.

They competed for privilege, there were quarrels, and some men tried to dominate. At the same time, possibly because these few sought domination, others disclaimed all responsibility and lately at night had begun terrorizing the villagers in Rumpi. There were beatings and thefts. Marais had found the culprits and had them locked up. But he was hesitant to order a whipping: giving the order indicated a degree of authority he did not want to assume. It was not his intention to boss them.

Terrorism was part of Marais's program. It was to be swift, selective, instructive — always against politicians and party hacks, never villagers, no matter how loyal to Osbong they seemed. They could be convinced. Local villagers were invited to join the terrorism with his men; they were welcomed in the camp. But the policy of violence, which was an extreme measure, was as difficult to explain to the villagers as to his men. Violence for them was a problem's complete solution; it had no limits. They saw it in terms of an ordeal: death was the proof of guilt, and was its own punishment.

In the first month Marais mistook their recklessness for courage. They had seemed brave: ignoring all risks they had rushed police stations, capturing weapons and a stock of gelignite, and they had sacked and burned the customs post at Fort Hill, on the northern frontier. A truck was commandeered and so was one party chairman's new French car. But that, Marais decided, was far from courage: it was simple thoughtlessness. It was the confusion of the shy egomaniac, one who is paralyzed by reflection. Their strength was subject to changes of mood. Marais had seen them ponder a move and then shrink back. They refused to fight alone; they would only scout in numbers. They took no conscious risks. Acting out of ignorance they ridiculed the discipline of strategy; without meeting resistance their attacks had deteriorated into fanaticism, nothing more.

That they had overrun the entire northern province as far as Rumpi had made them irresponsible, the possibility of power had intensified their bullying. Some had taken lovers at knife point. Others had looted shops and cached the goods for themselves. Their whims with this new power became obsessions and, ungenerous, they killed or crippled. The guilty were traced and made to explain. But they had not been punished severely. It had been enough, Marais had thought, for them to see their wrong. He had hoped to awaken the slumbering conscience. He had come a long way by a painful route to set these people free. He found it intolerable that all the risks were his.

He pumped and lighted his pressure lamp and carried it across the camp to a low hut. A soldier sitting cross-legged at the locked hut door stood when Marais spoke to him.

"Open it up," said Marais.

Inside, a wick burned in a dish of kerosene, illuminating the faces of the thieves on the floor. Marais beckoned them out.

The men were barefoot, their uniforms were wrinkled and stank of kerosene. Their belts had been taken away. They stood before Marais holding their trousers in place with their hands. Marais raised his lamp. They squinted at its brightness, then glanced at the guard and at Marais suspiciously. Two weeks' detention in the hut hadn't changed them much. One yawned into his shoulder like a cat, still holding his trousers. Far from punished, they looked fed and content and, though stupefied by the fumes, well rested.

"Give them their rifles," said Marais. He walked away quickly, leaving his lamp and avoiding the cooking fires so that no one would see his anger.

3

Drink was traded for drink. The African had begun it, only the African could end it. Calvin was a guest. In the evening, in smoky lantern light, Calvin became uneasy, and his unease, his impatience and panic, made him rude. Ogilvie was talking to him, blah-blah-blah, but Calvin wasn't listening and wasn't even looking at the fellow or his wife. He drank desperately, quickly, looking into his glass and at his watch and into the little cotton blizzard on the mirror at the back of the bar, his tired and drunkenly lip-smacking face showing through the phoney cotton flakes like a sick phantom perspiring in a snowstorm. He missed his turn buying the beers, Ogilvie paid twice in a row; and then in what was simple panic he turned his back on Ogilvie, threw the bead strings aside and looked out the bar door.

He felt woe deeper than dread.

He saw blackness, pure jungly blackness, thick and woolly. It did not stop after a mile or two. It extended for two hundred miles where it was pierced by a few lamps in Lilongwe; it continued for another hundred to Blantyre and a few more lamps, and it wasn't interrupted by light again until somewhere in Mozambique or Swaziland. Night had fallen while they had been drinking. The darkness was a net, flung over willing victims. Somewhere near the bar the dark night was being celebrated with a thumpy-thumpy of drums. But no one bothered to disperse it with a bulb. There was no juice.

And there was no place to stay in the dorp. It was Calvin's second night on the road. The first he had spent on the frontier, which was a burned-out shambles, not a soul in sight. He had slept under a table, wrapped in a big canvas wall map, and had shivered until dawn. Calvin still stood with his back to his hosts; he peered into the darkness. There were huts beyond the road, he knew. There always were. He knew those huts: windowless, stuffed with urchins, and stinking of woodsmoke, old food and damp clothes, worm turds and dog hairs littering the earthen hut floor between the crush of sleeping places. In a country filled with sun in the daytime and cool air in the evening, people crawled into huts and decrepit little bars, curling up in the dirt. It was not a recent impulse. These places were cool, but that was not the point. It was resignation; they were uninsured.

Calvin sensed his panic leave; the bird which had been flapping on his shoulder took wing. He felt eased, lighter, unworried all of a sudden. His nerves had been rinsed by the warm suds of the beer. He was fully drunk now (he tottered in the doorway): anxious reason left his hands and feet; they felt like large turnips. Now he was out of the bar, swaying in the middle of the main street of the dorp, under the stars, pissing on his toes. He did not have the foggiest idea of what was going to happen next, and plastered, he did not care. He went inside, then thought, parted the bead strings and spat. He was happy. He loved being in a place where you could spit where you pleased and piss by the door.

With silly vigor he clinked Ogilvie's glass with his own, hitting unnecessarily hard and shouting "Merry Christmas, Merry Christmas" much too loudly and finally smashing his glass to bits. He stood there in the half gloom of the bar, sweating booze, holding only the bottom half of his glass, a little crazy cup of up-turned teeth while all the beer ran down into his sleeve and collected in a slurpy puddle inside the elbow of his jacket.

"Oh my God, I'm sorry," said Calvin, so drunk and so polite that he sounded like someone new to English and so extremely attentive to his slow apology that in his contrition he stepped on Ogilvie's foot and knocked the lady's glass into her lap.

"Christ Almighty, look what I've done to your wife!"

Ogilvie insisted it was nothing and signaled to the bartender to bring another bottle.

Abjectly, Calvin put his finger into his mouth and bit down hard, all the while uttering hurried apologies through the fingers as if through a flute. This calmed him and he said, "I'm sorry about this, Ogilvie, but I'm drunk as a skunk. I should have been out of here hours ago." He picked up his suitcase and began dragging it to the door. "Don't worry about a thing. I'll be sending you reminders about your premiums and so forth. Tell your wife I'm sorry. I couldn't look her in the eye after what I've just done to her, really I couldn't —"

"Please," said Ogilvie, "wait."

Calvin gently fought him off with his free hand, but it was no good. He was in the road outside and Ogilvie was still with him, hugging him and being dragged along, bumping against the raffia suitcase. Calvin tried to run; it was like struggling underwater.

"Get off, sir," said Calvin, hitting Ogilvie gingerly on the shoulder with the flat of his hand. "You got your insurance. You're all set. I'm going now — good-bye and good luck."

"You cannot," said Ogilvie. "You have to stay. Lilongwe-side too far, and listen," he said earnestly, snatching at Calvin's hand, "that lady not my *dona*. That my sister, same mother, same father, and —"

"Yes?" Calvin stopped. He saw that he had gained only ten feet with Ogilvie attached to his leg.

"She *like* you, sir."

"She does?" Calvin put down his suitcase and turned his back on the jungle.

"Oh, yes, too much! She want you come home with her, enjoy and what-not. You like, sir?"

Calvin looked up. She was standing there in the doorway, holding the bead strings open. The lantern in back of her, just that feeble light, shone through what could only have been a very thin dress, for Calvin could see the girl's dark uncluttered shape sharply defined, with a light frock thrown around it. One hand was on her hip which was slung sideways in a pose of impatience, and her feet were apart.

4

Calvin stepped on a soft pillow-shaped thing. It let out a little squawk of protest and shifted sideways. The girl said it
was her brother and that there were more in the room. She did
not say how many more. But Calvin discovered there were
three little boys sleeping on the floor of the room: after a short
time one asked in the darkness why his sister was making so
much noise and if she was all right. And when the sister, at
that question, became quiet — held her breath, in fact — one
boy struck a match. He held it, his eyes goggling, in Calvin's
white face even after his sister screamed for him to blow it out.

In the morning when Calvin woke the little boys were gone.
There were three stained flour sacks where they had been.
The girl snored beside him on the narrow cot, curled up, sleeping with her arms folded across her breasts, her legs poised like
a cyclist's. The room, half the hut, was a low oven of musty
odors, crammed with broken crates and poor blankets and mis-
shapen clothes. A small prison window which was not square
had been cut high on one wall; a rag was tacked over it. Calvin
shifted himself to a sitting position. The girl groaned, stopped
snoring, but did not wake. On the far wall was a calendar, a

year out of date, with a highly colored picture of a little blond girl in a party dress playing with a fluffy kitten in a studio garden. The calendar advertised Jaganathy's Madras Bazaar and listed provisions.

That calendar picture on the mud wall of the hut annoyed Calvin even more than the other picture in the room, Dr. Osbong nailed to the door. It was the official picture of the President, the kind missing in the Big Drum Bar; it was sold by the local party branches. It showed Osbong in a fur hat bristling with rat tails, a carefully beaded collar, tinted glasses and his old school tie (Fort Hare, '21). The business end of a fly whisk was visible in the lower left of the picture. One side of Osbong's mouth drooped in what seemed to be a snarl. It was not a snarl, but a facial tic caught in a wild contraction by a quick camera, the side of the lower lip drawn down to reveal a sharp yellow tooth. It was the picture taken in the States on the occasion of Brandeis University's awarding him the honorary degree of Doctor of Humane Letters. Before then he had been called *ngwazi*, conquerer, because he had negotiated Malawi's independence. After Brandeis he was doctor. He was the country's first and only president. He was seldom seen except through the thick windows of his Rolls. The legend under the picture read: *They call me a Dictator! If I am, then I am a Dictator for the People, by the People and of the People — Hon. Dr. Hastings K. Osbong.*

In a year Calvin had seen him twice, once speeding past his office behind a raucous sound truck and a truckload of police, once at a political rally. Calvin had heard him often blustering over the radio about foreign aid ("I would go to the devil himself to get help"), about Malawi ("What did we Africans do to deserve such a poor place to live?"), about the whites ("One white man can do the work of ten Africans as you know very well, my people"), about a cabinet minister who attempted a *coup* two months after independence ("I want him brought back alive. If not alive, then any other way"). Any success, a big peanut harvest or a generous loan, pleased him to the extent that he would sing five verses of "Bringing in the Sheaves" over Radio Malawi. Failure made his facial tic very severe. Local settlers called him "the twitch doctor." He was an elder of the Church of Scotland and hated by every other African president; he knew his way around Debrett's *Peerage*, and in the group photograph at the annual Commonwealth Conference he was always seated next to the Queen.

The face in the official photograph suggested a man eating. But it was black and battered, and it seemed appropriate in the little mud room. The chubby little blond girl on Jaganathy's calendar offended Calvin. He felt pity for the Africans, the little black boys crouching on their flour sacks in the hut looking up at it, probably envying her and her fat pet. He pitied them all in their huts, snoring on their dusty beds, crawling tediously through a rubble of damp rags in a little jungle slum. Only the thought of insurance kept him from despair, as it would keep them.

He swung his legs over the side of the cot and looked for his trousers and shoes. It was only a little after eight, but already he had broken out into a heavy mucky sweat. His neck ached, his ankles were stung with mosquito bites. When he stood and stretched the girl woke up. She looked sleepily at him, then shook her head and said fiercely, "Where you going?"

"Outside," said Calvin, picking his undershirt from his sticky skin. "What's wrong with that?"

The girl shouted something to the door. There was a knock. The door creaked open and one of the small boys entered on his knees. Drawing the sheet across her nakedness, the girl spoke to the kneeling boy in a bark, incomprehensible to Calvin. He knew few words of Chinyanja, the language used in the south: mostly greetings, and the words for *money, good* and *beer*. The girl said to Calvin, "Go him."

Calvin found his trousers knotted at the foot of the cot where he had leaped out of them; and under them his shoes. One sock was missing. He felt too sweaty to grovel around looking for it. He slipped on his suedes without socks but with great care: once in a hut he had found mice nesting in his shoes. And there were stories of scorpions.

The little boy beckoned him outside and led him to a narrow stall of bamboo secured with bits of string. Calvin entered; the little boy stood outside. The smell in the latrine was so powerful that in the blast of early-morning sun Calvin felt faint. He slapped at the large flies which, strafing the rocky floor, were making a buzz as loud as an electric shaver. Calvin left with his bladder still full and he headed for a clump of high grass. Again the little boy stood guard, his back to Calvin.

The boy's presence inhibited what was usually a pleasure, but with determination Calvin let fly, bending the blades with his jet. When he finished he said, "Do you speak English?"

"Yes, *bwana*."

"Don't call me *bwana*."

"Yes, master."

"How are you?" Calvin spoke slowly.

"And I am quite well, sir, and hoping you," said the little boy in a hoarse nervous voice.

"I don't believe you know English," said Calvin.

"I do know and speak," said the little boy.

"All right then, what's your name?"

"My name," said the little boy, "is Richard."

"And what's your sister's name?"

"My sister name Mira."

Calvin repeated the name and thanked the boy; he had found out what he wanted, the name of the girl he had made love to.

Later he was brought an enamel bowl with a cake of yellow soap in it. He tried the name; it was not challenged. Mira poured tepid water from a pitcher while Calvin splashed his face. It was ritual washing: the water was brown, the process turned grit into slime. Calvin felt filthy when he was done. He wiped his face with his shirt and without preliminaries asked, "Why did you tell your brother to follow me?"

"Bad people here," said Mira.

25

"So what?"

"My English not —" She smiled and called Ogilvie.

"Bad people here?" Calvin asked Ogilvie.

"In the trees," said Ogilvie with authority. "It not good walking here alone. Make trouble and noonsense."

"Soldiers?"

"Some soldiers. With *bunduki,* pistoli, what-not. They are saving us," said Ogilvie.

There had been talk in Blantyre; Calvin had been warned to take care. But he had checked with the Ministry of Information and they had denied everything. The *Time* magazine was late; it was hard to know what the rumors were without it. Trouble, some people said; and one man had said, "The north is a complete shambles."

"What are they saving you from?"

Ogilvie did not know.

"They kill people?"

"Sometimes," said Ogilvie.

"Their leader," said Calvin, "he's an African?"

Ogilvie smiled and winked through his fake glasses. He wore a striped sarong, which he adjusted as he spoke, and an undershirt and plastic sandals. "He is a white man, like you. Tough. Eats fruit from the bush and small animals and sleeps just under trees or anywhere. But he can go with no eating food or sleeping. Bullets do this, *pung!*" Ogilvie slapped his chest imitating a bullet bouncing off. "He is going to kill Osbong. People say. He will kill you, too, anybody."

"Well, that's too bad," said Calvin, "because I'm leaving here."

"And me," said Ogilvie, "I am leaving here. It is a nice place to leave."

"Not live," said Calvin, "leave. I'm going."

"No go," said Ogilvie, becoming truculent. "You stay."

"I have to get to Lilongwe —"

"No bus. It Christmas. Stay here."

"He no like us," said Mira, pouting.

"No!" Calvin looked at her and shook his head. "That's not true. I like you both, but I can't stay. I have business to do."

"It Christmas," said Ogilvie.

"I *know* it's Christmas," said Calvin. But he hadn't until Ogilvie reminded him. He said angrily, "Merry Christmas."

"Give us Christmas present," said Ogilvie.

Calvin was being watched by three little boys, another taller goofy-looking one standing at the side and taking licks at a dish, and an old woman who seemed to be wearing two or three long dresses, one over the other. All their heads were shaved. They stared at Calvin, with Mira and Ogilvie.

Calvin took out his wallet. That was a mistake, but it was too late to conceal it. They watched him flick off a beetle; they watched him part it to reveal folded bills. Calvin attempted to extract a single bill without disturbing the others; they seemed to understand. Calvin tugged impatiently to get it over with. But too hard: all the bills came loose and fluttered to the ground at the feet of the Africans like the dead petals from a large blossom. The dish-licker dropped his dish. The boy called Richard knelt, gathered them up and still kneeling before Calvin, crumpled them into a ball and handed the ball to Calvin.

They settled for one apiece, although Mira and Ogilvie thought they should get more. Calvin tried to be firm; Ogilvie insisted on more; Calvin promised him another gift in the afternoon. The whole operation cost four pounds, ten osbongs, or roughly (Calvin figured rapidly) thirteen bucks. He had never spent that much on his wife on either of the two Christmases they were together. That thought pleased him: it was a charitable way of getting even with her.

And they gave Calvin a present: a fur hat, much like Dr. Osbong's, but with fewer rat tails (the number denoted rank). Calvin wore it for their Christmas drink, a yellow quart-sized Shell Oil can brim full of local beer. They passed it from mouth to mouth. The beer was thick, soupy, very bitter, an alcoholic porridge which could have been consumed with a fork. Calvin was allowed to finish it, after everyone had a swig. He did so with a leaden feeling in his feet. Then had another.

They all drank. They drank for breakfast and lunch. They drank, they said, because Calvin had arrived and given them cash and it was Christmas. Calvin, sweating in his fur hat, remarked on the heat but said, "It's a dry kind of heat." They drank on that. They drank to make themselves sleepy, and slept. They awoke and drank to alert themselves. They sang and drank some more. Other villagers dropped by and drank a good deal out of nervousness for the white man who was quite drunk and pretty dirty, but friendly. They drank out of the common beer pot drooling through their straws.

The local brew was gone in the afternoon and they switched to local gin, *kachasu* unrefined, which (poisonous, colorless, viscous) looked and tasted like witch hazel. It passed down Calvin's gullet like razor blades, leaving slashes in his throat. Calvin's belly had been sourly filled by the beer; now it was on fire with the gin. Gulping the gin in tots from a tumbler they praised drink, America and Dr. Osbong. ("To Hastings!" Calvin said incautiously.) There was an argument about Osbong, and a fight. Two men rolled on the ground, kicking and punching wildly, but soon they rolled away and the drinking went on. Late in the afternoon the drink was gone. Ogilvie appeared beside Calvin; he grinned and pulled the cork out of a bottle of crimson cough mixture.

"What I need," said Calvin, "is a couple of pints of Lion to fix me up." Mira and the old lady were sent to the Big Drum Bar for some bottles. Drunkenly wagging his finger in their faces Calvin said they should buy the beer with his Christmas present. They hurried off with baskets.

Calvin faced Ogilvie and discovered himself speechless and slightly panicky. Without a drink there was nothing to say. Calvin felt as if someone had ripped out all his bones, leaving sick flesh. It would be dark soon, another day gone. The feelings of pity he had experienced in the confined hut, in the narrow cot, were being crowded by thoughts of flight. He felt captive and watched; they apparently did not want him to leave. It could go on for days. His wallet was almost empty and he had few valuables. They thought he was rich. He had little more than his six pairs of glasses.

"I have a present for you, Ogilvie," Calvin slurred.

The raffia suitcase was shoved under the cot. Calvin rummaged through it and found his darkest pair of prescription sunglasses. Perhaps suspecting a trick, Ogilvie lingered in the doorway. He grunted and sat heavily on the ground when Calvin leaned toward him.

"Merry Christmas," said Calvin, grinning, "straight from the U.S.A. Here it is." He offered the glasses in an imitation alligator hide case, snapped shut. "Have a look, you lucky dog."

Ogilvie thumped and bashed the case, but found it impossible to open. There was not much time. Calvin pulled it away and fought with the little button.

"Beautyful," cooed Calvin, finally popping the case open.

They were expensive ones, with French frames and dark lenses for the equatorial sun, and thick for Calvin's astigmatic eyes. The lenses had cost thirty dollars alone, the frames with the wide bows another twenty-five.

"Nice goggles," said Ogilvie. He caressed them and put them on, and stumbled.

"Look in the mirror," said Calvin.

Ogilvie entered the hut by the door on the right. Calvin sprang through the left-hand door, snatched up his Panama and his jacket, grabbed his suitcase and dashed outside.

Ogilvie was also outside. Calvin had not counted on a portable mirror. But there it was, Ogilvie was holding it before his sightless eyes.

"Cannot see," he murmured.

"Hold it closer," said Calvin, tiptoeing to the edge of the clearing. Cupping his hands around his mouth and loudly, thinking it would make him sound near, he called, "*Closer!*"

The mirror was against his captor's nose.

Calvin ran, the suitcase banging against his legs. He charged headlong into dense bush, crashed against trees and lost his hat. He changed direction. He crossed a little bare patch, a compound with two tired huts and a dozing family. Their dog tore after him. The family awoke to see in the twilight a tall *mzungu* in a grubby suit and goggles flinging himself past their hut.

The bush thinned out. Calvin was certain the road was close and with the road, a bus, a car, another banana truck. Or he could walk. He wanted only to be away, and he knew that in a matter of minutes (his bejesused mind whirred) he could be. He found a path and followed it. Running became easier. He jogged, and all at once his glasses steamed up.

He slapped to a halt, took them off and wiped them with his sleeve and his fingers. When he put them back on he saw through the streaks two figures standing before him on the path. One was Mira. She had a pint of Lion in her hand which she raised. Calvin could not lift his arms quickly enough to stop her; they were drunk and slow. He said no, softly.

Mira was not tall. She could not reach the top of Calvin's skull. She slammed the bottle against the side, just in back of his ear and he fell, sat rather, on the path. The bottle didn't break, but it knocked his glasses off. Mira whispered, "We want you," and he was defeated.

5

Today," said Ogilvie, lowering his head through the doorway and peering over the top of his new sunglasses, "it Boxing Day."

"Who's fighting?" asked Calvin. He was groggy, barely awake; he felt the painful throb of his pulse in the bump behind his ear. He rolled over onto his side, nearly shaking the cot to pieces and squeezing the other sleeper — she who had raised the bump — against the mud-daubed wall.

"No one fighting," was Ogilvie's answer.

Calvin looked up. Ogilvie's hand was out, palm upward, fingers scratching the air avariciously.

"Give him box," came a whisper from the wall.

"I'm leaving," said Calvin without feeling. "Have to get that bus." He yawned and rubbed his eyes.

"Boxing Day. No buses on Boxing Day," said Ogilvie. "Give me box, *bwana.*"

"I gave you a Christmas present — *two* Christmas presents!"

"For Christmas. But today," Ogilvie smiled, "today Boxing Day. Give." His scratching fingers beckoned.

Calvin shook a pound out of his wallet and handed it without rising from the cot to Ogilvie, who saluted his thanks by touching a finger to the side of his sunglasses. Before he left, Ogilvie smacked Mira's ankle and said, "She pretty, eh? She like you too much. And me I like English people."

"I'm not English."

"No? Too bad." Ogilvie's good humor was renewed by the money. He became helpful. "You want to pass water? I go with you to the latrine. You want?"

"Get out," said Calvin. "And close the door."

Ogilvie smiled, saluted again, and was gone.

"Give me," said Mira, "give me."

With speed, his head rapping, Calvin turned Mira onto her back, lifted and parted her legs, cupped her cool bottom and entered her snugness in a single thrust. Mira arched; her slim arms reached in a praise gesture for his hair, as if she were making an offering to a hut spirit. Calvin took her by the wrists, rode her for seconds, until his loins sneezed and he fell. She had scarcely realized what was happening when Calvin handed her twenty osbongs and asked her quietly to go. She did so, dazed, wrapping herself in a long cloth and shutting the door after her.

Word got out that Calvin was distributing cash. The rest came and got theirs, the three little boys, the tall goofy one, the old lady: they entered the hut on their knees and took their money, heads bowed, with two hands. Calvin told them to stand up. They wouldn't; each left shuffling backward haltingly, still kneeling. Calvin bolted the door when the old lady left.

There was more knocking, villagers, relatives perhaps, looking for presents. But Calvin had paid off the immediate family; he did not feel obliged to pay the whole village. He wanted desperately to leave. For the time being he knew he could not. Before he had assumed that to do so would have been impolite, offensive to their hospitality: they would be hurt. Now he knew it was dangerous, he would be hurt: they would savage him if he tried to leave.

He could stay. Lying in the cot he had a vision of how it would be if he did stay a few more days. He would drink with them, learn a little bit of their language, settle into their life. After weeks passed in this way his clothes would fall off his back and he would change those rags for a sarong, his suedes for plastic sandals. Mira would work in the fields. If the crops failed they would force him to buy bags of mealies. He would father a few children, not as black as Mira nor as white as he, but probably the color of Mister Bones, the minstrel, a browny glow. He would insure them all and set up an agency in Rumpi for Homemakers' Mutual. All the while the whole extended family would be extracting money; but they would consult him on village decisions. He would die there, of drink or fever, and they would scrape a shallow hole under a tree, roll him in and heap up the mound with rocks and plant a little cross. Later they would spin yarns about him, in their homely droning fashion, making that long visit a simplicity: *Once there was a white man who passed this way. And he gave us much money and fell in love with the beautiful Mira who bore him three strong . . .*

Or were they making him their slave?

Calvin was not sure. He was positive he wasn't exploiting them. They seemed to need a chief very badly. They were treating him well. But he was paying, and they were making up excuses for him to stay: holidays, villains in the trees. A chief was at the mercy of his subjects; their pain was his suffering.

He dressed, went outside and was accompanied by Ogilvie and Richard to the high grass. Then he drank, sitting with his fur hat on, in the place of honor, in the only chair (a stuffed but badly bruised settee) while the others squatted around him and sat at his feet. They stole for him: a glass from the Big Drum Bar, an umbrella from a neighboring hut (it rained at noon), a hen because he asked for something to eat and they had nothing. They found his Panama hat and returned it. Mira had washed his shirt in a wifely way. She buttoned it on him.

Calvin, with the Shell Oil can full of beer in his hand, watched her fussing over him and decided it was cruel to stay. He would escape and leave no trace. It was enough to insure and go; he had done them some good; staying would undo it. His presence misled them: he didn't want to be their chief.

With more drink the mood that afternoon became by turns polite and threatening, one embarrassing, the other scary, for they made no bones about demanding money from him. They put their hands out and bulged their eyes at him in a belligerent way: and they began calling him *nduna*, chief. Twice during the afternoon of Boxing Day Ogilvie promised Calvin bodily harm; once he did so with a rusty dagger. He swished at the air blindly with the weapon, his sunglasses obscuring his vision. Calvin was terrified and ran to a tree. His mind knitted the several possibilities of escape; the question of being an ungrateful guest no longer troubled him, their anger would have to be faced. It was dangerous to go, but it was death to stay. Ogilvie clung to his dagger. Calvin decided to duck out at nightfall.

"Wait!" Calvin called out from behind the tree. He fully intended to climb it if Ogilvie's aim improved. He forced a ghastly laugh. "I have an idea. Let's all celebrate — get back Ogilvie, put your knife down — celebrate Boxing Day at the Big Drum. I'll buy some beer, we'll get some straws — "

Ogilvie dropped his dagger.

"Go Big Drum?"

"Why not?" said Calvin. He held his breath; his eyes asked for assurance.

"Why not, why not," said Ogilvie. He kicked off his sandals and ran into his side of the hut to change his clothes. Mira did likewise. Somewhere in the hut mice and mildew did not reach. There Ogilvie and Mira kept their Sunday best. Ogilvie's shirt was spotless, his collar stiff, his silk tie in a thick neat knot. Mira's dress was the same, the pink wrapper with lace which in sunlight gave glimpses of her body's angles. She wore a turban around her head, a gay one, with enough pink to match the dress. Her gold earrings were large gypsy hoops which jangled and promised pleasure. Calvin noticed her eyes were hooded, almost Chinese. She held her slim neck perfectly straight, her excellent posture from a girlhood of carrying hefty objects on her head in marked contrast to Ogilvie's. He had carried nothing, and slouched.

Calvin's suit was in an advanced state of decay; on his sockless feet were mildewed suedes; the weaving raveled on the brim of his Panama; his lenses were specked. He had not shaved for three days. His hands were clean because he had eaten wet, rather abrasive food with them. In one trouser pocket he had the price of three beers, no more; in the others his remaining pairs of glasses, a toothbrush, five nicked antimalaria tablets. His shirt was stuffed with insurance leaflets, some brochures and the details of another new account, whose quarterly premium had been extorted over the two holidays. He knew he could not flee encumbered. He left his raffia suitcase behind and in it a twisted tube of toothpaste, a hairy razor, one sock, some dirty laundry and a very dirty Michelin map of central and southern Africa.

There was trouble at the Big Drum when they arrived. A tall African who had been standing outside under the eaves of the building followed Calvin in and demanded a Boxing Day present. He put an empty glass in front of Calvin. He said, "Fill up."

"You no give him," said Mira.

Calvin wanted to calm the man. He started to fill the man's glass. Mira knocked the bottle away, spilling the beer down the front of Calvin's suit jacket. She turned to the man and told him sharply in the vernacular to get stuffed.

And: "You noonsense," said Ogilvie to the man.

The man leaned over and spat into Mira's beer glass.

Calvin quickly exchanged glasses with Mira. He said, "He didn't mean it," hopefully.

The man growled.

"Hit him!" said Mira to Calvin. "He did spit! Beat him!"

"I couldn't do a thing like that," said Calvin. He tried to smile at the man, but his smile was that squinting grimace of a person swallowing hard: it threatened. He put his hand out in friendship. The man gripped himself about the stomach where he guessed Calvin was going to land his punch, and he backed away and out of the bar.

"Tough guy," said Ogilvie.

Calvin nodded and then uttered the sentence he had been rehearsing since they left the little hut, "I have to pass water."

The sun was dropping. Every evening, just after sunset, there was an hour of complete darkness; it ended when the moon rose and the stars blinked on, but while it lasted it was perfect and hid even the ground beneath one's feet. Calvin planned to flee into that darkness and hope for the best; he could crouch in it until the night bus passed. As long as he had an extra pair of glasses he needed no bus fare.

"Okay," said Ogilvie. "I go with you."

Calvin could not look Ogilvie in the eye. His trick was a cheap one; Ogilvie was a sucker for theatrics. He looked instead at Mira, so lovely, here in a place where love was simple. What had he done to her? *We want you,* she had said; how was he to explain that it was not fair to them, that he had business?

"Listen. I am going to pass water," said Calvin. "Alone."

"Go him," said Mira to Ogilvie. It made Calvin uncomfortable to hear two foreigners speak to each other in poor English for his benefit.

"There are people here," Ogilvie said to Mira. "They kill him."

"I'm a tough guy," said Calvin, removing his jacket. "Just going out back, you see? To make water." Calvin pointed through the beaded doorway to a black tangle of trees in which the last of the sunset was snared; an orange beam lingered. "And to prove it, here's my jacket." He shook the jacket out and folded it on the bar. Then he took off his glasses. "And my glasses. I can't run away without my glasses, ha-ha, can I?"

"Watch too," said Ogilvie.

"Not the watch," said Calvin quickly. "But how about a nice toothbrush?" He placed that with his glasses on the jacket. He was glad to be rid of the toothbrush, a Portuguese one he had bought in Blantyre, pig's bristles set in yellow bone.

Ogilvie grunted.

"This is what we call security in the insurance game. You keep this stuff just to make sure I'm coming back. I have to come back to get it, see?" Calvin spoke, backing to the door. "And when I come back you have to give them to me, right? So don't think you can keep them. Bartender, three more beers! I'll be right back!"

Calvin went outside and listened to the bottles being opened. He walked to the corner of the building, zipped down, turned to see if anyone had followed, zipped up, and ran.

6

Single, commuting from Hudson to the Worcester branch of Homemakers' Mutual, Calvin had not been able to look at any girl without idly considering marriage; and thoughts of marriage produced more serious ones of divorce. This had made him shy with women; but his behavior seemed to him natural for an insurance man concerned with risks. A bad investment was worse than none. Marriage was a risk. A married couple could be an awful thing, with two heads and eight limbs; a monstrous octopus really, with a huge appetite and a short life.

In the leatherette album titled "Wedding Bells," a volume Calvin had often browsed through in unbelief, and now in his ex-wife's keeping, there had been a professional photograph of the woman, taken before he married her. She gazed out of the pebble-grained picture through large unfocused eyes, her little fingers lightly twined, making a gentle support for her chin, her face forward, as if at an open window. She was cute, her earrings small pearls, the tiny buttons on the front of her thin blouse neatly fastened — they could only have been fastened by those dainty fingers. The posies on her fancy bra showed faintly where the blouse was snug. She pouted slightly, the lips ripely full and dewy. Pert little curls, the sort that are seen only in good photographs, wound toward her cheeks in springy tendrils, suggesting that she was gay and, probably, vivacious.

Lies. That album (it had cost a fortune) was mostly lies, with the exception of one snapped on the front steps of the Hudson Baptist Church, too soon for a pose, and yet capturing all the truth of the marriage: his wife with wide-open lips berating the flower girl, Calvin looking wildly in the opposite direction, toward the Assabet River, his hands crossed over his groin.

He preferred his own candid shots of the woman. He grimly considered these in the joyless solitude marriage had imposed on him, in the distracted regret of his divorce. His were mental pictures no court could award to his wife, with ironies, for they were what a single man might think of as sexy, showing a young woman naked, making unusual gestures. But they spoke to him; the malicious speech lived to infuriate. In Calvin's favorite, a memory that justified everything he had done and consoled him in his distraction, his wife stood before him stark naked; she cupped a breast lightly in one hand and with the deft fingertips of the other stroked the rosy nipple, watching its color closely and harping in a voice that could have belonged to the crazy or cruel: "Anyone who's not interested in me and my problems is a Goddamned egotist."

A fearless, bossy little woman, the instant they were married (they had met on a hayride organized by the sexton of the church; she said insurance fascinated her and that she was a college graduate; "A small college in upstate Vermont — you've never heard of it," she had said, laughing gaily, with the expressive poise that the thirdrate grants as compensation) — the instant they were married she possessed everything she had ever wanted, and in that grasping she lost Calvin forever. It did not matter very much to her that he was unhappy and not hers. She expected marriage to be unpleasant; she was not moved by what Calvin (who fancied bliss but would have settled for peace) came to think of as an unbearable swindle. Marriage had arrested him in his adventure, deprived him of companionship; he had never felt so lonely, so captive as when married.

He had been shy with her and explored her gently; she mocked his pajamas and flung off her nightie. In passion her personality altered for good, the sex masks were off, her face was hard in an expression of greed: she sought him the way a cloven monster might seek its lost half, and in seconds they were a thrashing octopus. Disengaged she was cold, her four limbs outstretched, and she developed the disquieting habit of referring to his penis in the third person. She spoke with such conviction that Calvin, hearing for the first time, "He's getting a run for his money," covered himself hastily with a pillow and turned to see if some stranger whom she was addressing had slipped into the room.

She knew so much; she bought paperbacks and manuals with explanations so clinical they chilled Calvin into temporary impotence; her euphemisms appalled him. The word *screwing* had implications of torture for him, *fornication* was Biblical, but *fucking* had a finer edge, hinting as it did at a mutually enjoyable assault. Her phrase was *having sex,* a precise emphasis characteristic of her need, with a convenient balance of associations, suggesting appetite and regularity and a smattering of passion but not love. When it was over she leaped from the bed, dashed to the toilet, fitted herself with a hefty nozzle and a rubber bulb, and squirted a fatal concoction on Calvin's seed. Convinced she was purged of the slime, she returned to the bed and talked of the hell of having kids and how they would never have any. Calvin had at the first been impressed with her handy grasp of sexual matters. She liked to discuss it, sometimes using the sex manual euphemisms like *foreplay, heavy petting* and *penetration;* at other times hardly beguiling phrases like *erectile tissue, erogenous zones, oral manipulation.*

She could talk this way at breakfast, chewing toast and spooning egg, and think nothing of it. She even thought they were well matched; she encouraged Calvin to break a state law in bed. Calvin rued the hayride and the passivity he had felt at twenty-eight. And childless, he felt the marriage a lonely conspiracy, almost as if he and his wife were a couple of queers.

And she was small souled. Calvin could have put up with everything else if she had not been. She was bossy and demanding, his jailer; but millions of other men were in the same boat, Calvin knew. The fact of his marriage inspired discussions at lunchtime in Worcester with other salesmen. They compared agonies; one always claimed his wife was worse than the others'. Calvin, they said, had it easy; they winked and nudged. Marriage got worse: he would see. But Calvin had not told them everything.

Once he had tried. He began, "The thing about my wife is she hates everybody. I know women are supposed to be more conservative than men, but my wife is anti-Semitic. She hates Jews, she hates Negroes, she hates — "

He stopped speaking. The others' silence was an interruption. They gaped at Calvin, lowering their drinks. One, after a long pause, worked his face into an expression of total incomprehension and said, "What's wrong with that? So what if she hates yids? My wife *likes* them, she's always inviting them over. *I'm* the one with problems!"

Calvin never mentioned his wife again to anyone. He had known she was stupid, that her small nameless college was a fiction; but he had not expected her to be cruel. Stupidity humbled many people; it made them good listeners and easy to please. For her, stupidity was privilege: it licensed her arrogance. She could be blameless because of it. She took advantage of it and talked loudly about the people Calvin insured: what she lacked she imagined had been thieved and hidden by the minorities, each of which she knew by a one-syllable nickname. Calvin's defense of each, at her attack, was ignorant

41

simplicity, too; he saw her bigotry make him stupid. She said yids were crafty, he said intelligent; she said wops were greasy, he said jolly; she said coons were savages, he countered with jazz and baseball. He knew it was not so simple. In ramshackle parlors, falling-down piazzas and yellowing kitchens in wooden duplexes, Calvin had seen them studying the small print of numbered paragraphs on the back of a policy. He knew more about them than their closest relatives, their wonky lungs on X-rays, their explanations on health reports and the reports of investigators and underwriters. *I have dizzy spells. I shit blood. My eyes not so hot. Arthuritis in joint. Cold makes my knee pain. Lump in my breast. Bridgework makes my gums raw. Three doses of clap during the first war because I was young and didnt know no better. My blood is tired and I sleep bad.* On the long insistent forms they set down the pathetic details of their lives. They were honest, most solemn when they were challenged. They were shy. Most were black. No company on earth would insure them. Calvin's heart twisted with their misery. They trusted him.

She hated them. Calvin did not hate even the customers who tried by various means to defraud Homemakers' Mutual: the insured who poured gasoline on their furnishings and set their homes alight, the ones who bombed their paid-up mothers out of the sky or who complained of an undiagnosable back injury after a minor accident and then made a deal with the garage mechanic, or the ones who lied on their forms or wrote to the general manager claiming compensation for bad service. The acts were mad, sometimes murderously backfiring; it was too desperate to hate. Calvin wondered how, if she hated so many, she could love him; but he saw hope for himself: if he could love that small-souled woman he could love anyone. He tried. She misunderstood. She thought he meant something else.

"I want to love you, I want to make it work out," he said. "I really do. We have a whole life left, but sometimes I get the feeling it's over. I don't think I like you now. But still."

"What do you expect?"

"A baby, a divorce," said Calvin, "but not this."

She replied in a voice she usually saved for minorities: "Anyone who doesn't like being married to me can get the hell out."

Calvin was given a new assignment at Homemakers' Mutual. It was, in a sense, the baby he said they needed, and for a while it looked as if it might save his marriage, not yet a year old.

He was called to the main office in Boston and spoken to by a director, a man whose name appeared on the letterhead. He said, "I've been hearing good things about you from Worcester." Calvin thanked him and the man said, "Well, I like to hear good things from the branches."

His name was Wilbur Parsons. He wrote poetry which he sometimes included in the firm's newsletter. He also endowed poetry magazines and published in those; and he gave readings. He wrote about rustic things. He did a sonnet sequence about Cape Cod and then made a film of the Cape and hired a famous actor to speak his poems on the soundtrack. He showed the film at his readings and sent prints of it to all the branches to be screened for employees. The Worcester branch had privately jeered at the old man. Calvin stayed silent; he liked the poems, but even more liked the impulse in Parsons that made him write them, a civilized boldness, like playing the violin. And he did not despise Parsons's vanity. It was true the verse was not as ambitious as that of the late vice president of the Hartford Accident and Indemnity Company; nonetheless, it proved to Calvin that there was nothing in the insurance business that prevented anyone from setting down his thoughts in verse, and in his spare time Calvin often thought of writing himself. There was, in the process of insurance, a way of knowing what worried people: the insurance agent was as near to people's misery as a doctor or undertaker. And it was an encouragement to work for Parsons, a published author; it seemed to make the event of his own publication more likely. He imagined writing a warning novella, informed by what he had seen in shabby parlors, narrated by a man lamed by poverty, one only insurance could help. That, rather than poems about sugaring off or fishing shacks.

Parsons said, "I've got a dream, a kind of vision, call it anything you want." He beckoned Calvin to the window.

Fifteen stories down was Boylston Street, aswarm with shoppers.

"Look there, Mullet. Look at them. *People.* Thousands and thousands of them. They're in a hurry. No one stops to pass the time of day. They're all going, going. But do they know where they're going? Do they know where they've *been?* Sometimes I stand here just like I'm doing now, and I look down at all those people. I say to myself, good God!" Parsons sighed in amazement and looked at Calvin. "You know why I say this?"

"I think so, sir."

"Tell me."

"Maybe those people you see out there aren't insured."

"You put your finger on it, Mullet. *People* — that's what insurance is. It's people, their hopes and dreams. And I'll tell you something: some of those folks don't have a dime's worth of coverage." Parsons put his arm around Calvin, awkwardly — Calvin was tall. "I'm sending you out there."

Calvin nodded seriously. "I'm out there already, sir."

Parsons smiled and said, "Not where I'm going to send you. How's your geography?"

But his wife said, "If someone wants to sell insurance to black people why doesn't he go to Roxbury and do it?" Roxbury was Africa for Massachusetts.

Knowing her mind, Calvin said nothing about market possibilities or rising expectations. He told her he would be getting a hardship allowance, twenty percent more than in Worcester, plus two round-trip air tickets. And he showed her brochures of Mozambique, Victoria Falls and one from Malawi which claimed it was "the Switzerland of Africa." Strangely, there were no black people in the pictures.

She agreed to go. Calvin was eager, and pleased. It would save the marriage; that was important, but not fundamental. Calvin was not escaping. On the contrary: it was a positive step, a mission, and though he said before he left (speaking of the cynics he worked with in Worcester and the wasps in Hudson), "I've had enough of those birds," he was not fleeing an outrage or a weakness, not announcing defeat by going away. He was going to help.

The night before they left his wife said, "The tropics — isn't that where everyone's marriage goes on the rocks?" She seemed almost giddy at the thought.

The plane stopped in London, but transit passengers were not allowed to get off. Calvin looked out: small yellow vehicles and little blue men were busy in the mist. At Rome they changed planes and had a *cappuccino*. It was one in the morning. They asked a man in a faded brown uniform where Gate Five was; the man replied, *"Cosa?"* and smiled. So much for Italy.

Calvin's first view of Africa was from Benghazi, Lybia, where the plane was delayed for an hour. It was dark, his wife crouched asleep on her seat. In the airport building Calvin drank a cup of heavily sugared tea, served by a shrouded male Arab, and then walked outside. A cold wind snatched at his jacket, the bright moon lighted the arid blasted place, the cactus and sharp stones. But Calvin was excited: he had arrived in Africa and felt, in an unlikely place to make promises — the edge of a desert — he would be staying a long time.

They arrived in Malawi in late afternoon, in time for tea at their hotel. Buttering scones at a verandah table they noticed a beggar walk out from a hedge and stand near, like a terrible angel. He wore rubber clogs cut from automobile tires, and wings of rags, and a filthy skullcap.

"Tell him to go home," Calvin's wife said.

The beggar stared; he made no gesture. His gaze penetrated to Calvin's innards. Calvin felt very white. The beggar looked fierce, strong even, a muscular man, capable of savagery. He could kill with his hands. Calvin knew the man hated him; he wanted to help him or at least tell the man that he was there to help. Calvin raised his hand, a timid salute. But a waiter took this as an annoyed signal and shooed the beggar away.

In the room they argued about the official photograph of Dr. Osbong. It was hung over the bed, but Calvin's wife said, "Even if it was in the john I'd take it down."

"The President," said Calvin. "A nice way to talk."

"Uncle Ben's rice," said his wife, and giggled mirthlessly.

"You insensitive bitch," Calvin said. He took down the picture of Dr. Osbong and banged it into a bureau drawer.

His wife locked herself into the bathroom and washed noisily. Calvin went to the window and threw back the curtains. It was still light, and it was cool. He peered down two stories to the street, which was a side street, bordered by Hudson-like foliage: bushy-boughed trees, high hedges and even several tepees of pine tops showing. A man in a wide felt hat pushed a bicycle out of sight. There were no more people. But Calvin knew there was a beggar in the hedge, and there were odors, of fresh grass, of flowering trees, of sweet decay; there was a high whine of locusts building to tea kettle pitch, and a sky so blue he could have cried.

7

During his marriage Calvin had been able to look at any girl without worrying about marrying her. He stopped staring up the skirts of seated women or down their blouses waiting for a bus; he could watch their shadowed parts, package firm in tight clothes, and be tempted by no mystery or little challenge. It made him calm and gave him poise, useful to a young man who was too tall and too skinny, who sold insurance, who met strange women all the time alone in their homes. So many wives lounged half-dressed in parlors dreaming of laying the first salesman who knocked. Before his marriage Calvin had felt uneasy about confronting a housewife, lazy breasts loosely aswing in a flannel robe, giving his trousers a big moo-cow wink from inside the doorway and offering coffee. They seated Calvin on sofas and then sat beside him and leaned over the policies balanced on his knees; they squeezed him playfully and said their husbands were out of town and what bastards they were when they were home. Married, he was indifferent to what the flapping robes showed. His hesitancy had once been due to a guess; now, his wife a reminder of the dreary urge, he knew the risk. His was a frigid caution that made him a faithful husband and a good insurance man, all business; and he had stopped bumping into furniture and fumbling with his brochures when a lady idly drew a stocking up and hooked it.

And so it came as a shock to Calvin, after arriving in Malawi and moving into a Blantyre bungalow in the district called Sunnyside, to walk into the kitchen for matches one day, see the newly hired African girl fussing at the sink in her green uniform, and feel the old dread waking in him. But with this difference: his thought of marriage did not produce one of divorce. He could not keep his hands from plucking at that uniform. It seemed to have something to do with being so far from Hudson, at a great distance from anyone who would frown, in a place which was so green and simple, everything, even the risk of indiscretion, seemed possible and safe. The housewives in Worcester would have welcomed it; Calvin had been unwilling. He was prepared to loosen up for the Africans; they might appreciate the favor and receive it with gratitude. But he restrained himself.

He set up an office in town, on the top floor of a yellow wedge-shaped building, the only one of size, owned by a Goan named F. X. Agnello. His office window faced the clock tower and the railway station. Downstairs was the British Council Library and a bar, the Highlife, at street level. Over on Fotheringham Road he bought office equipment, an adding machine, a typewriter, files and ledgers, and a ream of foolscap because he liked the name. He registered the company and had stationery printed with the Homemakers' letterhead.

For a month he stuffed envelopes, enclosing the Homemakers' Mutual brochure, the information about the easy payment plan (quarterly premiums) and a stamped postcard reading, "I would like to have full details about your family coverage. Let's talk about it at your office/my home (delete one). I understand that I am under absolutely no obligation to take out a policy. My address is —————" Calvin got names of potential clients from the slim Malawi phone book and the voters' roll.

48

His mailing, plus multilingual ads in the *Malawi News* and little taped inserts, with music, on Radio Malawi, produced eleven replies. Three of the replies asked for details but appended no names or addresses. Mr. Agnello, who wore a rosary around his neck, told Calvin that it was a mistake to enclose stamps: people steamed them off and stuck them on their own letters. Calvin said it took time. He was only trying to sell them on the *idea* of insurance.

The second month he spent up-country, in the villages near Lilongwe and the lake shore. Again, he had no plans to sell; he just wanted to get acquainted. He brought mechanical pencils and ball points, little desk calendars and paperweights, letter openers and keyholders — all stamped in gold with *Homemakers' Mutual* and *Your Agent: Cal Mullet,* abbreviated for the friendly sound. It was "remembrance advertising," and it was accepted with thanks by people who couldn't write, or had no keys, or counted moons.

He would drive down a dirt track in his Austin and park before a collection of houses, and immediately begin handing out ball points to the children who greeted him. The village men would follow and Calvin would order some warm beer for them if there was a shop nearby. And he chatted.

"That's a fine house you've got," Calvin would say. "Very nice little bundles of grass on the roof, too. You do that yourself?"

"Wife," the man would say, and take a pull on his bottle.

"It'd be a real shame if it burned down, wouldn't it?"

"This hut, it will fall down I think — " pausing the African would count on his fingers, " — next year. Two rains will finish it. Then I think we move maybe that side."

"But you could fix it up, put some more mud on and insure it."

"Oh, yes, we mud it, but once in a blue moon only." Calvin noticed they used phrases popular decades back: *blue moon, blue lies, hot jazz, tough guy.*

They expected their huts to collapse and so did not maintain them. They did not own anything worth insuring, except bicycles or radios; they denied possession of these in case Calvin asked to see licenses they had never bothered to get. And they showed no interest in life insurance: "But I still die, isn't it?" one had said.

One day at the end of that second month he lost himself in a labyrinth of roads near the lake. He drove and drove, trying to stay on cleared tracks, but always the tracks narrowed into a single path too small for his car. He reversed and was stuck in sand for hours. Toward nightfall, having used bundles of twigs for traction, he freed the car and climbed a hill on foot. He saw through the trees the brick steeple of a church.

It was a leper colony run by Dutch priests, who greeted Calvin warmly and gave him a bed. In the morning they showed him around the buildings, all of weathered red brick, some with ambitious arches and windows, and they invited him to mass. The altar was decorated with shards of broken glass set into cement: crosses and fishes and Latin mottos. They pointed with pride to their generator, run by a paddle wheel, and their dispensary. Draped everywhere, sleeping under trees and in the shade of round huts and even in the back pews of the church, were the lepers, dusty dozing souls with bandaged hands and feet.

The priests persuaded Calvin to stay for three days. He ate their food and found it unpalatable; he played whist; the lepers drummed. By candlelight (the generator was shut off at nine) Calvin read tattered magazines. An old priest, Father Euthyme, helped Calvin find his car and get his bearings on a map. Calvin offered him insurance. Father Euthyme smiled and touched the crucifix pinned to his stained cassock. "Do I need more insurance than this?"

"I guess not," said Calvin, and went on his way.

He should have been discouraged, but he was not. His was the only Homemakers' agency in Africa: it would take time to catch on. His fear was unconnected with insurance. It concerned Grace, the house girl. He didn't trust himself. He was inclined to fire her, give her several months' pay and the sack, and hire a man. His wife wouldn't hear of it. She felt safe in Sunnyside, no black families lived there, and she refused to have a black man in the kitchen. She had started to call them *Kaffirs* (which she pronounced "car-fares").

Ignoring the girl was out of the question. His wife criticized her, argued with her, claimed she couldn't understand her. Calvin, after nearly three months, was still finding his feet as an insurance agent; his wife in the same period of time had become a proper *memsahib,* a *dona,* a *missis,* and knew a dozen orders in the vernacular, a lingo known in Blantyre as Kitchen Kaffir.

Grace knew English cooking: boiled cabbage, fried pasty fish, stewed fruit, limp Yorkshire pudding and mince curry. "Garbage," said Calvin's wife. Grace used the English names for utensils: *serviette* for napkin, *drying-up cloth* for dish towel, *fish slice* for spatula, *cooker* for stove, *geyser* for water heater. Her pronunciation was not perfect, and Calvin's wife took her speech to be a kind of pidgin which she mocked, saying, "What's your problem? Don't you speak Eng-lish?"

Calvin would look up from his chair and see them framed in the kitchen door. It wasn't as simple as black and white, one nice, the other awful, though that would have been a convenient contrast. Certainly the girl seemed innocent and pretty; but when Calvin was near her and alone and thought of marriage it was in his mind a sort of insurance, a good intention, to protect her ever after; it was one way of saving a poor person, hardly love. Which was why it was so hard to fight the urge: it seemed inhuman not to give her everything he had. And, alone, he didn't hate his wife. He felt let down by his marriage, but that he knew was his own fault, at least half the blame had been his. Seeing them together, his wife bullying Grace ("Don't just stand there like a bump on a log — *say* something!"), he was not inspired to hate one and love the other. It was something out of joint, something unfair and indecent he felt impelled to correct, even at the risk of being misunderstood. Not lust or a political attitude, his was a fragile sympathy, asking nothing in return, honest because it was not love, but kindness. He offered it to Grace in the same degree as his wife offered insult. When his wife was cruel, Calvin tried to be kind; his wife shrieked, he murmured apologies; Calvin gave private consolation when his wife humiliated Grace publicly. He did his best to reassure; he took pains to be gentle; and had his wife simply left her alone and not slapped her Calvin might have spent months more in the bungalow, muddling along, and never attempted to make love to Grace.

There was nothing to eat that evening when Calvin came home. The cruets and sauce bottles that Grace habitually arranged on the table were not there. His wife did no cooking, did nothing in fact; she had been made redundant in every way except one by Grace, and spent her days leafing through South African women's magazines, in a chaise longue on the sunny lawn.

"Pickle?" She fished a gherkin out of a narrow necked bottle with her fingers. Lights burned in the kitchen, but Grace was not there.

Calvin looked at the label and recognized the language as Afrikaans. He refused the pickle. He never used South African goods; it was a private embargo that deprived him sometimes of nutrition — the corn flakes, peanut butter and ketchup in Malawi were all imported from South Africa. His wife who declared no such embargo said they were almost as good as the real thing and made life bearable; she went through a bottle of Koo Ketchup in a week.

"Where's the food?"

"Don't ask me." She munched pickle.

"Grace?"

"I wouldn't know."

Calvin found her sulking at her quarters, holding her stung

cheek. She sat on the low steps of the hut. He sat beside her and talked softly to her, "I know what you think. You think all white people are like my wife. I don't blame you. She's hateful. But please don't go away thinking that we're all exploiters. Take me for example. I sell insurance. I could have been pulling down a pretty good week's pay back home, but I figured . . . You don't understand, do you?"

Calvin moved closer and put his arm around her; his other hand trembled on her knee. "We're not all like that," he said, "really we're not. Some of us are lovers." He kissed her; it was a child's kiss, bumping heads, brushing lips. Grace tried to get away.

"No," said Calvin. He held her; she tried to stand, and toppled into the hut where a candle flickered. "Listen," said Calvin. Grace resisted, kicking. The kicks made a loud thumping on the floor planks and hiked up the skirt of her uniform. Around her naked waist was the loveliest beaded belt. Calvin touched it; it had the detail of wampum.

Grace whimpered, and squirmed out of Calvin's loose clasp. She leaped to her feet, her back to the wall; her hands were over her mouth, muffling her murmurs, and there was a look of mortal terror in her eyes.

Calvin left the hut and started back across the grass to the bungalow. On the rear verandah, her hair swarming with a corona of moths and sausage flies, stood his wife. She did not speak until Calvin did. She silenced him with, "You fucking bastard." She repeated it and, unused to saying such a phrase, gave it a special clarity lacking in the slurred abuse of the experienced.

Later that evening Grace disappeared. Calvin's bedroom was barred to him. He spent the night on the floor of his office.

At nine the next morning Calvin was awakened by a knock. He thought it might be the police. It was a tall man with a briefcase, sucking an unlit pipe.

"I wonder if I might have a moment of your time," asked the man. "Saunders is the name. I'm a lawyer."

Calvin stood barefoot in the doorway, in wrinkled trousers and undershirt. "Having a little nap," he said, gesturing to a blanket mussed on the floor.

"Right you are," said Saunders. "I'll come straight to the point. Your wife is suing you for divorce."

"Go on," said Calvin.

"The grounds seem to be adultery. The correspondent's a Miss . . . a Miss . . . confound these names."

"Adultery? It must have looked that way, but I never — "

"English law applies here, I'm afraid. The only grounds for a legal divorce are adultery and nonconsummation. It's very sticky."

"I'll take adultery," said Calvin.

"You will? Good. In actual fact, the only matter I'm concerned with, as your wife's lawyer, is whether you plan to contest. It's awfully complicated, but you're entirely within your rights if you do. Now," said Saunders heartily, "are you in the picture, so to speak?"

"She's serious, I guess," said Calvin.

"Hell hath no fury, et cetera, et cetera," said Saunders.

"I won't contest it."

The hearing a month later was brief. Saunders had got Grace's signature (an X, a thumbprint, a witness), and Calvin was served with a summons but told he needn't show up at the hearing. His wife was there and so was much of Blantyre's white community. The details appeared the next day in the *Malawi News,* where, when, how many times Calvin had been adulterous. He had connived in the fabrications, but when he read them in the paper he felt warm toward Grace: he was stimulated to give them reality by marrying her. She was nowhere to be found. Calvin's goods and chattels so-called, and half his salary, had been awarded to his wife. The day after the hearing she boarded a plane for Boston, and Calvin moved to Auntie Zeeba's Eating House, a brothel on the upper road, near the bus depot. He sold his car to pay for packing and shipping, and hitchhiked to his several accounts.

8

Calvin dragged himself wheezing for a mile, his arms extended before him into the night like antennae. He stopped. Walking, he decided, was safer, if not a great deal healthier. His lungs could not keep pace with running strides, and his throat harried by beer and gutted by cigarette smoke gushed with deafening breath, constricted and burned. Going slowly he would be able to hear other sounds, those of Ogilvie for example. He was sure that if Ogilvie was chasing him, Calvin would hear and would have time to take cover. He heard locusts and owls and certain shrieks he could not identify — from a hyena? a swindled host? There were no quick noises of pursuit, though, no leaping steps; this was especially unnerving and made Calvin turn again and again from the darkness he was penetrating to face the darkness he was fleeing. Each time he turned he suspected Ogilvie of having crept swiftly after him on muffled feet, the angry man about to leap out of the ink to claw his face.

The repeated turning made him dizzy and once in the silliness of lost balance he stumbled into a ditch, believing as he fell that it was a booby trap and letting out a yell. The yell died in the trees, silencing the night sounds. After the fall he shuffled backward. It was slow work, and heartbreaking, for Calvin knew that if they caught him he would go back: he owed it to them for the dirty trick he had played. ("Hold my jacket — I'll be right back!") The poor things needed him, they had no chief, they didn't know any better. They were Africans: for years people had been bamboozling them.

It grew chilly; Calvin shivered without his jacket. He sniffed and for a minute or two thought he was crying. He felt the way he imagined the uninsured did, a sense of falling, falling, and getting colder and sadder as he fell. But he wasn't crying — it was the night chill, the goose flesh on his arms — not sobbing but shuddering with cold. And the sadness — he had let so much slip through his fingers; no one had ever known him or his plans, his hand extended in friendship was taken for a punch, his height was a threat. Anticipating cruelty, no one had seen his kindness. If they had let him alone, let him get on with his insurance, if they had paid their premiums on time and trusted him and not expected his whole attention from a casual encounter, he would not have hurt a soul. But they had made him.

And then his back hit something cold with a clang. Calvin stiffened; it was smooth, dew-covered steel. He turned. The moon was rising, a neatly pruned orange peel, the color the last splotches of sun had been. In this feeble light he could see the outlines of a low car, the sleek hood facing him.

A Citroën: Calvin could tell from its shape, the protruding beaklike hood, the slanting roof, the low foreshortened rear. He struck a match, but saw only the flare: nothing was illuminated for him. There did not seem to be anyone in the car, there was no one around it. To steal it one had to jump the wires; car thieves could do that with bits of silver foil from a cigarette pack. Calvin knew only the simple phrase *jump the wires*. One of the rear doors was unlocked. Calvin jiggled the door handle, then lifted the door slowly open. A light went on inside; it was empty.

"Don't move!"

Something hard and blunt pressed against Calvin's back, the nostril of a revolver snout, he was sure.

"Put your hands up and turn around."

A powerful flashlight was switched on. It shone in Calvin's eyes. He heard boots crunching pebbles in the road, but saw no faces, heard no voices. There were more flashlights on him, playing on his baggy trousers, his shoes, over his shirt.

"Empty your pockets."

Calvin pulled three pairs of glasses out, placed them on the ground, and heard a familiar word from behind one of the flashlights, "Goggles."

A black hand stretched out and tried to grasp them. A boot interfered and stomped on the glasses, grinding them into the road. The light had wavered and revealed a glove, an inch of white wrist.

"Take your shoes off."

"Can I keep them?" asked Calvin, hating his pleading. "They're the only ones I have. I lost my socks."

"Tie the laces together and carry them around your neck." That voice was American, the one giving all the orders. "Blindfold him!"

9

The rag across Calvin's eyes stank, and the path — if it was a path — was strewn with boulders. They had taken a further precaution of tying a rope around his ankle which one man held and from time to time jerked, tripping him. When the blindfold was removed Calvin wondered why they had put it on in the first place: the night was still dark, his vision was no better with the rag off his eyes. He saw little more after his last pair of glasses was given back to him. He stood in skyless dark. A lantern was lit. He was towed inside a hut and left alone with the man who had done all the talking.

"Sit there," said the man.

Calvin seated himself. He had never found it easy to be comfortable sitting upright in a straightbacked chair: he arranged his long arms and legs slowly, ineptly, as if he was folding the wooden lengths of a carpenter's collapsible ruler.

The man took a length of rope, and spoiling the careful arrangement of Calvin's limbs, tied his hands behind the chair back, his ankles to the legs. Knotting the rope, the man heard a rustle of papers, the sweaty bundle of policies and brochures filed away in Calvin's shirt. The man tore open the shirt and peeled the papers from Calvin's hollow belly. He finished the knots on Calvin's wrists then stood and said, before he began to read the papers, "We've been expecting you."

He was not tall, but he had an impressive compactness, broad shoulders and a solid head set on a thick sunburned neck. He was dressed like a soldier on bivouac. He wore military sunglasses, tinted green with gold bows; he removed these to read and Calvin saw his bright quick eyes. His khaki shirt was creased twice down the front where it had been folded for a suitcase or a pack; his peaked Castro cap was tinged with a dark band of sweat. His mustache drooped dramatically into two carefully waxed points, setting off his sunburned face, a young face with an eager muscle in the jaw. There were large flapped pockets on the sides of his trousers; the trousers ballooned at the knees where they were tucked into the tops of combat boots. Hooked to his wide belt was a bluish pistol in a shiny black holster. On the other side of the belt hung a machete in a canvas sheath. He wore no insignia except, in the buttonhole on the flap of his shirt pocket, a bright red African daisy, the wild variety. That flower gave Calvin curious hope.

Still reading, the man walked to a table beside Calvin and flipped open the lid of a cigar box. The box was gaily trimmed in green and white and stuck with an ornate stamp, a kind of seal the size and color of a dollar bill. It read *Republica de Cuba*. On the end of the box in tall white letters was the brand name, ROMEO Y JULIETA. The man took out a blunt aluminum tube, pulled off the cap and shook out a cigar and a thin slice of wood. Calvin expected a man with a pistol like that and in such a uniform to bite off the end and spit a chunk of tobacco into his prisoner's face. But the man simply tapped it and drew out a small silver object which clicked open lengthwise. Thoughtfully, he circumcised the cigar, and with the long flame of a gas lighter, puffed it, turning the cigar in his mouth.

"Keeps off the mosquitoes," he said and went back to the papers. "You want one?" he asked after a while.

59

Calvin swallowed and pulled an appreciative face. "No, thanks, they give me a sore throat. You wouldn't have a beer around the place, would you?"

"Whisky?"

"Firewater," said Calvin. "Never touch it."

The man grunted, puffed, and said, "All I see here is insurance."

"Homemakers' Mutual," said Calvin. The man stared. Calvin tried to point, but his hands jerked on knots. He went on, "Fifty-six branches around the world, including," he nodded at the papers, "Malawi. That's my baby."

"Like I say, we've been expecting you. What took you so long?"

"You knew I was coming?"

"There isn't much that goes on here that we don't know. But you were easy. One of the men gave you a ride. Don't you remember? He dropped you in Rumpi. We like to keep track of strangers."

"The banana truck?" Calvin shook his head. "Can you beat that."

"Bananas on top, dynamite underneath. If you had run into something you would have been blown sky-high."

"Dynamite," said Calvin. "What for?"

"There's a war on," said the man. He puffed and twirled his cigar. "We've liberated this area."

"Oh, you have, eh? Well, you might tell the people up the road that. They'd be pleased to hear it."

"They know it. We've been here a month."

"Taking Osbong's picture down," said Calvin. "Whose are you putting up?"

The man did not reply. He looked at his cigar and picked off the slim brown band that circled it. "It's a funny place," he said. "People here still have reactionary tendencies."

"For shit sake!" said Calvin, sputtering. "Who the hell gives you the right to come in here and throw your weight around?

Yes, they know you're here. Soldiers in the trees, they keep saying. As if you ass-kickers really matter! Why don't you leave them alone, huh? Haven't they got enough to worry about?"

"We leave them alone," said the man. "Osbong's the one who squeezes them."

"Osbong," said Calvin, and laughed, recalling the official picture of the baffled snarling chief.

The man leaned toward Calvin, the peak of his cap almost touching Calvin's glasses. "What's your game?"

"No game, just insurance. I told you. Read for yourself. You think I carry that stuff around in my shirt to keep myself warm?"

"Don't snap at me," said the man slowly.

"Well, Jesus, what do you think I am, a spy?"

"You could be."

"I'm not. Anyway, who would I be spying for?"

"We have enemies."

"I don't doubt that," said Calvin, looking around the room. A map was spread on the table. Near the cigar box was a steel case of bullets.

"You spent two days in that village. Why would a person like you stay there all that time?"

"Selling insurance. Look — "

"You travel pretty light. Where's your suitcase?"

"It's a long story," said Calvin. The man was silent; he went on, "Stopped for a beer up the road. I met a couple of people. They invited me to their house for Christmas, after I sold them a policy. Then I left. Without my suitcase. I guess it's not such a long story." He felt the weight of fatigue on him, and the itch of dirt, the frailty of three days of hard drinking.

"Sounds as if you were exploiting them."

"That's a laugh," said Calvin. "*They* were exploiting *me!*"

"We'll look into that," said the man. "The villagers around Rumpi have instructions to report strangers. You weren't reported."

"You don't mind pestering people, do you?" said Calvin. "They were very nice to me, those folks. And I fixed them up with a policy. I don't see why you should interfere. Are you going to do anything to them?"

The man blew smoke and watched it rise. "We expect cooperation from these people. We got Osbong off their necks."

"Yeah, sure. But they're Africans — "

"What have you got against Africans?" The man spoke through clenched teeth; it was his first show of anger.

"Nothing," Calvin protested. "What I mean is, no one ever gave them a shake. You know what I mean? They're kind of confused."

"They're less confused than you are."

"I agree," said Calvin readily.

"You ethnocentric son of a bitch." The man's mouth was clamped malevolently on his fat cigar. He strode to the other side of the room and seated himself on a crate. He puffed billows of smoke.

Calvin did not say anything for five minutes. He didn't feel, having been called an ethnocentric son of a bitch, there was any handy reply. He looked at the cigar box. On the lid the romantic couple embraced on a balcony, Romeo in blue tights on a rope ladder gazing into the white expanse of Juliet's bosom. There seemed to be much more in the picture, but in the bad light Calvin could not make out anything more. It was a warm little scene: it gave Calvin comfort, as the daisy in the soldier's pocket had done.

"Funny, the Cubans still making cigar boxes like that, isn't it? You don't expect it somehow."

"They're for export," said the man.

"I guess you're right."

The man grunted. He seemed to be avoiding knocking the large ash from the cigar; he was gentle with it.

"Can I ask you a question?"

The man gave a barely perceptible nod.

"If you don't mind my saying so," said Calvin, "you're in a risky business, shipping high explosives, camping out and so forth. Now this is your business, don't think I'm crabbing — it's not for me to say you're right or wrong. I don't know anything about politics and I don't pretend to. But tell me something, did you ever stop to think what would happen to your loved ones if you suddenly passed on? Suppose your gun went off accidentally. What then?"

"What the hell are you talking about?"

"People that depend on you. Wife, kids, girl friend — your mother, maybe. To put it in a nutshell — it would help if you untied me — do you ever ask where you're going to be in ten or fifteen years?"

The man smiled.

Calvin persisted. "What about your men? Do you know that for a few dollars weekly you can take out an all-inclusive Homemakers' Mutual policy — don't let the name scare you, you don't have to be a homemaker to insure with us! When the policy matures you're guaranteed a very large sum, as much as fifteen or twenty grand if you reach the age of fifty-five. In the unfortunate event of your death, anyone you name will get the money as beneficiary. You know how it operates. Think it over. You can buy a hell of a lot of dynamite with twenty grand, and don't think you can't. Or look at it this way: you're not going to be here forever — "

He was drowsy, he continued to speak without effort; the sales phrases came, they always did, like funky music out of a hand organ. And then Calvin was awakened by panic; he realized where he was, where he had been for days. In a voice woozy with fatigue and kerosene fumes he pleaded, "For God's sake, untie me! Let me go, please. I'm no spy, I haven't got a cent to my name. Have a heart! Spies don't hitchhike! They kept bumming money off of me, they wouldn't let me go, I wanted to. You don't know what they *did* to me. Don't you have any feelings?"

And went to sleep, his head down, his shirt torn open, his chin on his bony narrow chest.

*   *   *

Calvin's ropes were being loosened. It was still dark, the lamp low, the room close with cigar smoke. The man was undoing the knots, his daisy was wilted.

Calvin stood, immediately bending, a tall man's instinctive stoop. He was unsteady on his feet. He rubbed his wrists and said, "You must think I'm a real jerk, crying like that. But you don't know how it is. I know you're an American. Where are you from? I'm from Hudson, Mass. Small world, eh? Who'd ever think," said Calvin, stamping to get the circulation back into his legs, "that in a place like this — "

"Don't you ever shut up?"

"It's my nerves. Normally I'm very quiet. When I'm balled up I talk a lot," said Calvin. "I'm balled up now. Well, you should know."

"Follow me," said the man. He held the rope attached to Calvin's ankle and keeping it taut led him outside. The moon was bright, the sky a deep blue dotted with clusters of star buds. It was light enough to walk without a lantern. "See those tents? Fifty soldiers. Fifty killers sleeping. Ammo there under that canvas, rifles, grenades, blasting powder, small arms."

"Why are you telling me that?"

They passed low wooden buildings. "Our kitchen. Blackboard for tactical instruction. Water supply. Workshop."

Calvin asked for a drink of water. The water was cold in the tin cup. It revived him. He poured a second cup over his head.

"There isn't anything we don't have. See that tall tree? Radio transmitter at the foot, antenna up above."

"It's very impressive," said Calvin.

"Tell them that in Blantyre," said the man. "Tell them what you saw. Tell them you met Marais."

"Any other name?" asked Calvin. "Or — "

"Just Marais," said the man.

"Like Mantovani," said Calvin. The man didn't respond, and Calvin added, "You know, the conductor. One name. Like Liberace. Like — " He gave up. "My name's Mullet, Calvin Mullet. I take it you're letting me go."

"You're clean," said Marais. "Stupid, but clean."

"Thanks," said Calvin. "If you point me in the direction of the road I won't take any more of your time. I'll light out of here just as tight as I can jump. They say that back home."

"Put on the blindfold. I'm driving you to Blantyre."

Marais drove the Citroën like a maniac. Calvin forced himself to sleep, but woke on hairpin bends, sliding across the seat to see red laterite walls, scored with erosion, fly past. Marais went by a devious route, for Calvin had woken at regular intervals but did not see Lilongwe, or any town or roadblock. He mentioned insurance again.

"This is my insurance," said Marais. He held his pistol in Calvin's face.

In the morning, outside Blantyre at the junction where the tar road began, Marais said, "Know the name of that road?"

"Yes," said Calvin. It was chilly; a light rain had started. He hugged himself and yawned. "Isn't it Queen Elizabeth Drive or something like that?"

"No, it's Osbong Drive," said Marais, "all the way into town. But someday it's going to be Brother Jaja Drive. Tell them that. Now screw."

10

Auntie Zeeba's Eating House — (*More than a bar . . .*) — a rambling tin-roofed brothel, had a wide covered verandah and deck chairs where, in slack hours, the girls sat, hooting amiably at passers-by.

Tonight it was raining. An elderly Englishman and two of the girls stood at the verandah rail, mutely watching the empty street awash in the rain. It had been raining most of the day, steady drizzle in the morning, windy beating in the afternoon, and now a straight heavy shower which poured ceaselessly from cold night. The dry season had been wet, and so the wet season was uncertain. For days the sun would shine, and then came the reminder that it was December. In other places rain gave life; this rain swelled rivers and washed out bridges, turned dust into muck, and moistened crumbling turf and made it slick; it inconvenienced and killed.

Major Beaglehole, the elderly Englishman, warmed a whisky soda. The girls leaned on the rail; he stood some distance from it, as if watching an erupting ocean from a ship's bridge. He was stout, though dignified, and had a sparse square of mustache. His baldness emphasized his overlarge ears. He wore a hearing aid, a bulky cream colored plug in the right ear, with a wire looping down his starched bush shirt to a small metal box hung from his neck on a harness. For the first time that day there was thunder. Major Beaglehole tuned his hearing aid low and continued to gaze. A lightning bolt split the sky very near in a blue electric crack. He yanked the plug from his ear. He believed the contraption would attract a bolt and knock his head off. He claimed sometimes to hear Morse code through the device, military messages in cypher. He liked that, and listened for the beeps, but he had the quaint fear of storms and machines of others who lived in Malawi.

Below the verandah, at the street's edge, the open drain frothed full of rotten water and flotsam. A cat, floating on its back, paws aloft, shot past, rigid in death.

"Bad luck," said Major Beaglehole, "a black cat crossing your path."

The girls said nothing. The superstition was not theirs: their version was a snake on a path. They leaned and watched the street blister with the big raindrops.

"But it was dead, so that doesn't count, I should say. Possibly it only *looked* black. The fur was wet." Major Beaglehole smiled tentatively and waited for a reply from the gods.

Another lightning bolt rent the sky, three pronged. Even before the thunderclap reached the verandah the electricity failed. All the lights went out. Major Beaglehole took his whisky soda to one of the chairs. His curse was a very small voice in the thunder.

The girls groaned and slapped the railing. There were more groans from others within.

Pressure lamps were pumped, their cloth mantles lighted. In the overbrightness of one of these lamps an old woman appeared at the bar door. She hung the lamp she was carrying on a hook near Major Beaglehole.

"There you are, Major," she said. She was chewing decisively; she nibbled as she spoke. "Don't know what we pay our light

bills for. Never any bloody lights. Gets my back up, it does."
She walked to the railing. "Ain't it beastly?"

Major Beaglehole was retuning his hearing aid. He caught
her last words and replied, "Makes me want to spew, Bailey."

"It would bloody well serve them right if we all went back to
U.K. I don't know why we keep on like this." She shifted
slightly into the lamplight and saw that only a peel remained
of the banana she had been eating. She tossed it into the darkness. "What I'd give for a half of draft Guinness." She looked
into the night. It was totally dark, crackling with rain. Bitterly
she said, "The filthy sods."

Several times a day Bailey stood on her verandah, looked at
what she could see of Malawi and threatened to leave. She had
come to Malawi at the age of five with her parents, who were mis-
sionaries. They were buried up at Monkey Bay, "A fitting end,"
as she said, "for a mish."

"Makes me want to spew," repeated Major Beaglehole.

Bailey seemed to take it as a hint. She began coughing, desperately, gasping for breath. She had a terrifying cough, fruity and
full; she brought up juice and sauce and fragments of banana;
she gagged, ruining the appetite of anyone within earshot.

Major Beaglehole hated her appearance, but enjoyed her
rough moods; she was a good old stick. What was disconcerting
about her was that while she did not smell bad, she looked as
if she did. A diet of sodden fish and chips which she ate lustily
with her fingers off a copy of the *Malawi News* had made her
pox-pitted face fat and free of any expression. She blamed her
bad complexion on the weather. She wore faded men's socks
in hairy felt bedroom slippers. Over her shoulders was a shawl,
greasy from her habitual clutchings. Overworked veins stood
out on her calves. She had a heart condition, often went pale
and flopped in a chair, looking horrible. She had diagnosed
this as indigestion and, after a seizure, dosed herself with liver
salts. She owned one dress; several buttons were missing from
the front. She was Auntie Zeeba. In any other country she
would have been jailed as a bawd.

Major Beaglehole burred at her. "The wind's up," he said. "I'll have to get my U.K. woolly out one of these days. Didn't think I'd need it till May."

"Ain't this weather a menace," said Bailey. "Had a shocking dry season, the *chiperoni* gave me my rheumatism back, then the thunder rains were late. It's the atom bombs." She made a move for the door, tugging at her soiled shawl. "I've got the old wrap."

Major Beaglehole looked away and spoke loudly, as if to a multitude, stopping Bailey in her tracks. "This rain reminds me of a fearful storm we had in Alex in forty-three. Came hammering down in great buckets. My batman was pissing his bags with fright. Useless chap. Asked him for my handgun, and the damned fool," Major Beaglehole turned again and raised his eyes to Bailey, "the damned fool shot me in the leg."

"You've had a life, Major."

"I have indeed. The rain reminded me of that tale." Major Beaglehole drank, and said, "It's a pity I've forgotten all my Arabic. I used to speak it like a native."

Bailey lit the butt of a cigarette she had put out earlier and kept in the pocket of her dress. There were not many more puffs in it. She screwed up her face, pinched the butt to her lips with her inefficient fingers, sucked twice and burned herself.

"Bugger it!" she said, tramping on the fag end with her slipper. "Think I'll go inside and put my feet up. It'll be quiet as a bloody grave tonight with no lights."

Major Beaglehole said, "My batman was a gyppo."

"A black," said Bailey.

"A gyppo," said Major Beaglehole.

"They're all nig-nogs," said Bailey, "with arses for faces."

"They're laughing at us now," said Major Beaglehole. "They're putting the Union Jack on their knickers. We're down and they're laughing. But we won't be down much longer. I tell you, Bailey, we're coming back in numbers and God help them then. You'll see a Union Jack flying over Government House."

"They can have this bloody place, I say. It don't matter to me what happens, it's not my lookout. I got my house to see to."

But Major Beaglehole had switched off his hearing aid. "We'll have it all back, from the Cape to Cairo. We may have been wog-bashers, but by God we were fair." He finished his whisky. "Get me another peg, will you Bailey? The damp's getting into my bones."

Bailey took the glass.

"Where's the Yank?" asked Beaglehole, turning the volume knob.

"Still sleeping," said Bailey, "I haven't seen him about."

"We might have to take it away from the Yanks, from the looks of it," said Major Beaglehole to himself.

Bailey went inside. The rubber blades of the ceiling fans drooped; the pressure lamps, pumped by the girls, sputtered and hissed, the glow of the mantles made giant shadows of the men standing at the bar. There was the tick-tick of the metal plungers, the hiss of the lamps, the sweep of rain on the tin roof. The only other sound was that of an Arab in an ankle-length *galabia* and sweaty skullcap, who fed osbongs into a one-armed bandit fruit machine. He had chin tufts of an Abe Lincoln beard and held a glass of untouched orange squash in his left hand. He played the machine with his right, taking a lucky tango step backward and averting his eyes from the spinning symbols each time he pulled the crank. The rest of the gambling machines, the electric ones which on a normal evening would be buzzing and flashing lights, were silent.

Bailey handed Major Beaglehole's whisky soda to a fat waiter with a tray and directed him to the verandah. She took her usual place in an easy chair at a door near the back of the bar. Beyond were rooms, some rented for an hour or two, others for weeks or months, for she also took boarders. The room keys were on labeled hooks on a little board at her elbow.

The Arab kicked the fruit machine in disgust and walked over to one of the girls. He offered her his orange squash. She refused it and, seeing Bailey's eyes on her, asked him to buy her a beer.

"No beer! Beer bad!" He took the girl's hand and said amorously, "If my penis could speak he would say 'I love you *habibi.*'"

Bailey collected twenty osbongs. She passed a key to the couple and let them through the door.

Around nine there was a particularly intense flash of lightning. It illuminated the whole place, each beam, every cobweb, the broom in the corner, the official photograph of Dr. Osbong, the amazed faces of the girls; it made a dog, driven indoors by the pelting storm, stiffen and Bailey check a belch; it bathed in bluish light a sleek plump-backed rat making for the kitchen door. Every chair and bottle glowed, the tablecloths were crumbfree, for seconds all things were new, all the squalor gone, the spots gone from Bailey's face. Then just as quickly, in the whoosh of sudden darkness, there was an earsplitting crack of thunder.

11

In a back bedroom of the eating house, Calvin Mullet salt bolt upright and listened to that last thunderclap fading, a thudding rumble, like a big piano being shoved on wooden casters. The rain drummed on the tin roof, the louvered shutters knocked together, clinking where they were loosely hooked. Calvin rattled the switch of his bedside lamp and saw there had been a power failure. He lit a candle.

By candlelight he took inventory. He examined his face in the dresser mirror. (The dresser occupied a third of the small room, which was a cheap single of the sort the girls lived in when they were off duty.) He wore a mask of shadowy blue stubble; his face seemed more pinched than the last time he had looked critically at it, his skin too white, a ghostliness that was sickly if not downright nasty. He had grit in his hair, and dust in his nostrils. The strain of the trip north showed. Tall people suffered more than most in an ordeal, and the suffering was conspicuous.

Marais had given him his papers back. The important ones were there, two do-not-spindle-or-fold cards with names and addresses, some damp brochures and monthly report forms which, folded carefully, became envelopes, needing no adhesive and no stamps if mailed in the United States or its possessions. Five pairs of glasses were missing: one to Ogilvie for Christmas, one in the maneuver at the Big Drum Bar, three under Marais's boot. The sixth pair sat cross-legged on the dresser, mildly tinted tortoise shells. On the floor where early that morning he had pulled them off were his baggy pants, his mud-caked suedes, his shirt — laundered by Mira, torn by Marais, dirtied by Calvin. And here in a stack his books: *Teach Yourself Chinyanja,* with a dog-ear at Chapter Two ("The rifles are rusty," "My good bow has fallen"), the *Information Please Almanac,* ten *Time* magazines, *Principles of Selling,* a book of Parsons's poems (*The Muse and Mammon*) and two by the vice president of the Hartford Accident and Indemnity Company. And five novels, three in translation. He had brought the unwieldy paperbacks of these great works of fiction in the belief that Africa was the sort of place where among other things one had plenty of time for reading the classics, as on a sea voyage, a long illness or a summer vacation. He hadn't touched the novels, though paradoxically they had the look of having been read: the pages thickened by the dampness, the bindings curled and cracked. But he would read them eventually. Calvin had that sense of inadequate education, common among American graduates; that obsession to supplement what he felt sure must have been imperfect. He had continually bought dull difficult paperbacks in drugstores and forced himself to underline passages in them with a felt pen. He had attended night classes on (was it?) The Disadvantaged Child, and still wished he had done more sociology, less sales and management.

In the top drawer of the dresser were odds and ends, can opener, nail file, Band-Aids, string, paper clips, mosquito repellent, playing cards, mosquito coils, after-shave, passport and health card, one cuff link, a tin of tightly rolled safes and an exhausted cigarette lighter. In other drawers bargains from Filene's, string vests from Jaganathy's Madras Bazaar, marriage certificate, divorce summons. This, plus a fifty dollar bill thumb-tacked to the underside of a bottom drawer, a kind of primitive insurance, was all Calvin had: a small accumulation for thirty years on earth. There had been as much in Ogilvie's hut.

Standing skinny-legged in damp underpants, smoothing the stubble on his chin with one hand and fingering his worthless possessions with the other, Calvin felt a certain justice had been done; he did not feel guilty about Ogilvie and Mira; the only wrong was misunderstanding. The man whose insurance premium he had spent would never know. Calvin would make good the amount. He was no better off than any of them, and maybe worse. But shortly after, having gorged himself on what was called in Bailey's menu, *Spaghetti Bolognaise* — a large knot of sticky noodles doused with ketchup and cheese — and two pints of warm Lion, Calvin was visited again by pangs of craven remorse. The pleading faces of Ogilvie and Mira ("We want you") and the smile of his own deception ("I'll be right back") scared and saddened him; even with his pistol stuck in Calvin's back and his leash tugging on Calvin's ankle, Marais had not affected him half so much. On a full stomach the memory of the Africans pained him terribly, particularly Mira, who at this distance seemed frail and very lovely. He could have been kinder; they hadn't wanted much. He had insured Ogilvie and slept with Mira, and run off. No wonder they hated whites. She lingered in his mind like a small bird circling.

"Power cut," said Major Beaglehole, joining Calvin. He looked at the empty plate. "God, how can you eat that stuff?"

"It's very filling," said Calvin.

"You should ask for the rum omelette. Bailey does a good rum omelette. But you Yanks. Cranberry sauce. Marmalade on ham. Did I ever tell you about the Yank in Cairo who plastered marmalade on my ham?"

"Yes," said Calvin.

"I could have fetched him one, I can tell you." Major Beaglehole stopped speaking; he squinted, listening intently, with his head to the side. Then straightened his head and said,

"Thought I was getting a message. They come about this time. But the storm gives me static. Been arsing about up-country?"

"So to speak," said Calvin.

"You look a proper mess. Dirty weekend in the native quarter, what?"

"I went where you told me. There wasn't much traffic. The border post was burned down. I got stuck in Rumpi."

"Saw you pitch up this morning, looking like the wrath of God. Bailey thought you were a burglar. I was up splashing my boots. 'Go back to bed,' I said to her, 'It's only the Yank.' "

"It was me all right." Calvin wished Beaglehole would go away. He wanted to concentrate on Mira, in the lamplight, have a marrying reverie. But the bar had emptied, Bailey was asleep in her chair, snoring with her mouth open; she coughed without waking. Several girls lounged on chairs, Ameena, Rose, and a new one.

"Was that public house still there in Rumpi?"

"There was a bar," said Calvin.

"The Izaak Walton. Run by a fat old chap, Dirty Dick. I know the place well. Dick's a rogue, he is."

"I didn't see him."

"Maybe he packed it up," said Major Beaglehole. "I could tell you stories about the Izaak Walton."

"It's called the Big Drum Bar now."

"*No!*" said Major Beaglehole, astonished. "Why Dick must have flogged the place to a black."

"There seemed to be an African running the place."

"What about the dart board, the bar billiards? Dick had everything laid on. Even a paraffin refrigerator. It was always ice cold at the Izaak."

"They must have got rid of all that," said Calvin. "All I saw were ants." In his confusion, trying to make the deaf Englishman understand, he said *aunts*.

"That's a shame," said Major Beaglehole. "But that's the blacks for you. Disaster. You meet any of the locals?"

75

"I made a couple of sales," said Calvin.

"Used to be my old parish. Oh, almost forgot. A letter came for you." Major Beaglehole drew a large white envelope out of his pocket and handed it across the table to Calvin.

The postmark said HUDSON, MASS., and MAIL EARLY. It was a Christmas card from his wife, of the sort New Englanders liked to send: Yuletide on the farm, a red barn, snow-covered fields, a log fence in the foreground, a wreath on the farmhouse door, a hunter trudging through the snow with a rifle and a brace of pheasants.

Calvin ripped the card into little squares.

Major Beaglehole leaned forward and twisted the knob on his little metal box. "Bad news?"

"Christmas card," said Calvin. "From my former wife."

"Oh, her," said Major Beaglehole. He had gone to the hearing. How many times had he told Calvin what he had seen? Dozens. *You remember his case* was the way he introduced Calvin to strangers.

"I think I'll go back to bed," said Calvin. He yawned. "I still feel crappy. What a Christmas."

Major Beaglehole tilted his glass and saw that it was empty. He looked Calvin squarely in the eye and said, "I killed my commanding officer, as sure as you're sitting there."

Calvin had moved his chair back and had started to rise. He sat. "What did you say, Major?"

"You heard me."

He had. It was a familiar cue, Beaglehole's way of demanding a drink, startling revelation delivered with enough sincerity to be urgent, usually violent enough to make anyone pause. Only the heartless ignored Beaglehole's openings. He let these idlers pass on: they seldom refreshed him. The price of his candor was a whisky.

Calvin had not known Beaglehole long enough to be called a friend. For his friends Beaglehole abridged the stories, giving only the highlights and little dialogue. The tale he had told Bailey earlier in the evening, about his batman shooting him in the leg during a downpour, was with all its details very long. Likewise the one about the American soldier slapping marmalade on the ham.

"A whisky for the major," Calvin called to the waiter.

The drink was brought, Calvin signed the chit, but Major Beaglehole did not speak.

"Now what's all this about?"

"I beg your pardon," said Major Beaglehole. He was switching off his hearing aid. He was unlike most bores in that in his cadging of drinks he did not really enjoy listening to his own stories. Being stone deaf and a flawless lip reader, with the gift of total recall, were advantages: he heard no interruptions or complaints; he spoke in a silence so fine that his shattered eardrums did not admit even the booming noise of his own voice.

"Your killing your C.O. What about it?"

"That," said Major Beaglehole, "is the truth. I'm not ashamed of it. He deserved it, the rogue." He toyed with his drink and told the story at his own speed. "It was in Cairo, just after the war. I was invited to a sort of officers' do over at Shepheard's. Now, among my own friends I was known as a character. I was famous for sleeping in my chair at important staff meetings. When called upon to speak I would open my eyes, make a trenchant remark and go promptly back to sleep."

Calvin impatiently guzzled beer.

"I was not so well known to the other brass, and so it came as something of a surprise to me, being introduced to one very tall colonel, to hear my name spoken by him. He interrupted the man introducing me and said my name. Then simply stood there, smiling at me, looking very pleased with himself.

" 'I knew I should meet you sooner or later,' he said. He had a double-barreled name which I shall not divulge.

" 'You know me, Colonel?' I asked.

" 'Of course I do,' he answered with a sneer, 'I've seen your photograph on the mantlepiece many times.'

77

"And with that he walked away, joking with the other senior staff and flexing his riding crop. It goes without saying that I had a suspicion as to which mantlepiece he was referring to. But to confirm it I wrote directly to my wife and put the question to her. Pointblank, you see. I thought I should never get a reply. A month passed, two months, three. In the fourth month I got her letter. She was not contrite. She admitted everything. The mantlepiece the colonel referred to was my own, in my house at Broadstairs. Somehow this randy old colonel had met my wife, and while I was fighting in the Western Desert that chap was tupping my wife!"

"Have another drink," said Calvin.

"Cheers," said Major Beaglehole. "It was crystal clear to me what my duty was. I was after all an officer in His Majesty's Own Fusiliers. I was a gentleman. What is more important I was among people of color, in a foreign land. I felt an especial responsibility. On Saturday mornings we had a full-dress parade, all the regiments out, the band playing. We did it partly for the gyppos — showing the flag, as it were — and also for our own morale.

"I waited for one of these parades. It was one of those incredibly bright, sort of terribly Egyptian days. Blue sky, a slight breeze lifting the flags. And I saw the colonel, strutting about, and then standing, slapping his boot with his riding crop, watching everything in that rather sly way of his. The order was given to present arms. That was my signal. I stepped out of line and marched straight up to him. He looked a bit confused for a moment — what I had done was against all regulations, of course. Then he saluted."

"What did *you* do? You shot him, right?"

Major Beaglehole saw Calvin's eagerness, and drank. "I simply looked at him at first. I did not return his salute.

" 'You're no gentleman,' I said at last. Every eye on the parade ground was upon me, soldiers from every corner of the Empire. The band had stopped playing, but the drum roll for the present arms was still going, and that steady beat heartened me.

" 'You're off your chump, man,' said the colonel. 'Get back to your regiment.'

" 'You swine,' I said, 'You filthy swine.' I didn't take my eyes from his panicky face. Not for a second."

"Then you shot him." Calvin was nodding.

Major Beaglehole glared. His eyes were watery, his ears stuck out like jug handles. But his jaw was set. He made no move.

"Another drink?"

"Light on the soda," said Major Beaglehole. With the drink in his hand he continued: "Dash it all, I thought to myself. I've come this far. If I don't go through with it I won't be able to go near the Officers' Mess. I drew out my handgun and shot him twice in the face. He fell. The drums stopped. I threw the gun on his corpse, did a smart about-face, and marched off the parade ground."

"Where did you march to?"

"To jail, you fool. Where else would I go? I had just killed my commanding officer." Major Beaglehole swished his drink. "They gave me life," he said. "After two months in the lockup in Cairo, I was sent under guard to Gibraltar, and then to His Majesty's military prison in Kent, not far from my home. I was a model prisoner. Six years later I was released. They knew it was a *crime passionnel.* I was granted a full pension and came here to retire. That was in late fifty-one. I had aged ten years. They were surprised that I chose the Colonies. They thought I was going to kill my wife."

Beaglehole emptied his glass in one swig. Calvin did the same.

"I suppose I could have done," said Major Beaglehole. "Killed her somehow and collected on the insurance. But a gentleman doesn't do that sort of thing."

"Depends on the policy," said Calvin.

"You're mad. Of course I wouldn't."

"If she had a comprehensive, with you as beneficiary, you might have."

"Rubbish."

"Or a double indemnity that she countersigned."

"Balls," said Major Beaglehole. "How do you know?"

"I've come across cases," said Calvin. "Homemakers' has had a few like that."

Major Beaglehole attempted to shoot Calvin a withering glance. But he was too drunk; in the best of times his eyes were crapulous.

"I'm an Englishman," said Major Beaglehole. "Englishmen don't murder their wives. Wops, dagoes, Yanks do that. We don't. We have a code and we obey it. It kept the Empire together. Damn it, it made these blackies respect us. They loved us for it, because we were British and stood no nonsense. Ask them, ask any one of these beggars. They'll tell you. That waiter there. If there's a jot of honesty in him he'll tell you that the British — "

"Why don't we just go ahead and ask him?"

Major Beaglehole thumped the table. "Mark me, he'll say the British were our rulers and they cared. He'll say the British didn't keep us down — we kept ourselves down, he'll say. Which is the truth."

"Let's ask him to choose," said Calvin. "The British or Doctor Osbong. If he says the British I'll buy you a whisky. If he says Osbong you buy me a beer. It's only fair."

"Boy!" shouted Major Beaglehole.

The waiter stood at Major Beaglehole's elbow. He was a big man of about thirty, with a hunted look in his bloodshot eyes, and furtively hunched shoulders. His shirt was ventilated with long slashes, his shorts tattered. He was barefoot. He wore the red sash Bailey required of all her waiters. He was nearly as tall as Calvin, and uncommonly fat, the size of an old-time jazzman posing by an upright piano or holding a bugle, but without the jazzman's grin.

"Now," said Major Beaglehole to the fat waiter, "I want you

to tell me who's the best ruler for this country. Tell me the truth, what you feel deep down. Take your time. Is it Osbong or the British Crown?"

The African looked at Major Beaglehole, then at Calvin; the hunted look left his bloodshot eyes. His jaw became defiant, his eyes wild; he straightened to his full height. "They all exploit us," he said.

"Go on," said Major Beaglehole, "choose one."

"Brother Jaja!" roared the African, opening his mouth very wide and raising his fist in a stiff-armed salute. The sudden ferocity of it startled Calvin, but before he could respond, the African had downed his tray and marched to a corner where he continued to stare at Calvin and Major Beaglehole with that black half mask of sullen defiance over his bridgeless nose.

"What did he say?" asked Calvin.

"I don't know," grumbled Major Beaglehole. "He's around the bloody bend like the rest of them. No different from you Yanks, flogging life insurance."

"Insurance is what they need," said Calvin.

"There's where you're wrong. The black doesn't need anything. He's not like you or me. He's happy with whatever he's got. That waiter over there — if I gave him a bicycle he'd stop his nonsense right enough. That's the limit of his wanting, a bicycle, but he knows as well as I do that he doesn't *need* it."

"They don't plan," said Calvin. "With insurance they begin to think about the future, they have something to look forward to. It's important."

"It's a lot of cock," said Major Beaglehole.

"You're a colonialist," said Calvin.

"You're bloody right I am," said Major Beaglehole. "And this territory's going to be a colony again. We'll be back, just you wait and see!"

Calvin got up quickly and walked to the doorway, where Bailey dozed. He turned and shouted, "You're a murderer! You killed your commanding officer!"

"You're just a fucking Yank who ran off with his black slut of a house girl!" yelled Major Beaglehole across the room, wincing because he had not been able to see Calvin's lips and had turned up his hearing aid too high. "What I did was for King and Country!"

At the word *king* another bolt of lightning restored the lights, and during the ensuing thunder — a very mild crepitation this time — the fruit machines buzzed, the refrigerator behind the bar hummed, the fans started to spin, quacking crazily. Ameena, Rose, and the new girl hid their eyes, and the fat waiter put his broad hand over his brow, like a warrior watching for enemies. Major Beaglehole cursed as sincerely as he had when the lights had gone out. Bailey awoke, breathless, hacking and whinnying, and seized a black-handled switch on the wall. She swung it to *off*, killing the lights. It was midnight, closing time.

Part Two

12

The morning after the storm, Blantyre was cool and had a sweet breath; it sparkled, the sun was gigantic in a cloudless sky. Brown kites and pied ravens swooped on the storm's leavings, and other birds soared so high they appeared motionless. All the dusty trees of the town had been renewed by the rain, the leaves washed green, the withered blossoms knocked off. The fresh branches still dripped. Overnight, the gray moss on the shady side of verandah posts had become lush and spongy. But there was a casualty. At a shopfront some children shoveling twigs — swept into twisted nests by the torrent of water in the storm drain — came upon the dead body of a man, apparently drowned.

On his way to Barclay's Bank on Victoria Street to collect his pay, Calvin had seen the crowd of people poking sticks at the corpse. It crouched in the narrow drain on all fours, as if it had drowned searching for something. A bystander took a mangrove pole and levered the body upright. It remained in the same stiff posture, its tongue sticking out of bared teeth. It was a gray-faced African, wearing a suit and a government necktie with the rooster motif, black cocks crowing at rising suns. The grooved handle of a bayonet protruded from the lower end of the tie like an awful black cross.

It was the closest Calvin had ever been to a dead man. He felt sick to his stomach, and a peculiar deadness dried his throat. But it was not the woeful look of horror on the corpse's face that bothered him; rather, the unfair surprise of being murdered, the indignity of dying uninsured in a dripping drain and being found, and poked, by a crowd of strangers.

He hurried away as the police arrived. At Barclay's the nausea left him. A cable authorizing his December salary had come in that morning. In a corner of the bank, at a high desk, Calvin dunked the scratchy bank pen into an ink bottle, shook a drop from the nib and made out the alimony check. At Jaganathy's, on the corner of St. Andrew's Street and Osbong Drive (it *was* Osbong, as Marais had said, but when had they taken down the Queen Elizabeth sign?) Calvin bought a shirt of Japanese make, a razor, a toothbrush (not pig bristles this time) and the rest of the essentials he lacked, including a new bottle of malaria pills.

"Time for new gap?" asked Jaganathy, smiling at Calvin's dirty Panama. Jaganathy, a pin-headed Tamil, had close-set eyes, a huge nose and chin, and looked to Calvin like a Spaniard in blackface. He was as black as his African sweeper. He showed Calvin a plastic snap-brim hat.

"Not today," said Calvin.

"Gristmas gards?" Jaganathy drew Calvin's attention to a dusty stack of festive Christmas cards, which he said Calvin could have cheap, Christmas being over. Calvin was on the point of refusing when one caught his eye: a card printed at the Stella Maris Mission in Kasupi. It depicted a nativity scene in a grass hut, with a black infant Jesus, black Mary, black Joseph, black wise men and, in the background, jungle foliage. He bought it, and sent it with the alimony check to his ex-wife.

Calvin wanted to avoid the crowd still gathered around the corpse at the upper end of Osbong. He detoured up Victoria Street, stopping at the bookshop next to the American Embassy for the new *Time* magazine. Back at the eating house he washed,

86

shaved, changed into his Japanese shirt, and had a coffee on the verandah, reading the shortest letters to the editor, then the pictured items in the section headed "People."

One more detail remained before he could go to the office. He called the fat waiter.

"Sir?" The fat waiter sauntered over to Calvin, wiping his tin tray with a cloth. He was round-shouldered again, hardly defiant; this the man who had shouted and raised his fist in an aggressive salute!

"Anyone in the *chim?*"

"No," said the fat waiter. He looked very tired; he wore his expression of fatigue with uncomfortable eyes, as if the heaviness was a poor fit.

"You're sure?"

"Sure."

Calvin glanced at "Milestones" and lit a cigarette. He sat very still. This first smoke of the day, and his quiet pause, made his heart patter and his breath short, but it helped to purge: it had a gently mollifying effect on his bowels. In the *chim* at the leper colony he had been cheated out of it. The wooden privy bench there had a splintery oval hole where two bats hung by their feet. He had not seen them immediately, but after he sat they had taken flight under him. They had flapped in circles in the deep cess pit, beating their wings, constipating him. He might have stayed at the leprosarium longer, but for that annoyance.

He inhaled the cigarette deeply. Everything hinged on that first dump of the day. If it was a success he was all right until the next morning. If not, he could not get the failure off his mind. It ruined his appetite and funked his digestion. It either happened at nine-thirty or not at all.

Calvin stubbed out the butt and locked himself in the toilet at the back of the bar. For the next fifteen minutes he sat, with the *Time* magazine on his knees, pleasurably crapping in spurts: the sound of beads spilling into a dish.

To complete Calvin's pleasure there was a short piece in *Time* about Malawi, titled *"Eminence Noire?"* Calvin read with interest.

In Malawi, Africa's peanut capital (half a million tons a year), the current slogan is "Nuts to you!" So says dandified President and *éminence grise* of this pint-sized Republic, Doctor Hastings Kanyama Osbong, pooh-poohing the ugly rumor that the house of his government is being shot out from under him by 100 Cuban-trained guerrilla soldiers.

Black mischief is an old African story, of course, but Dr. O. has shown remarkable staying power for a sub-Saharan head of state. Malawi's per capita income is nothing to rave about: $20 a year — the lowest in Africa. But Osbong isn't alarmed, in spite of . . .

The story went on to speak of rural unrest, "parts of the country in turmoil," "fear gripping the blacks who toil in peanut patches," and it finished: "So there could be, after all, an armed *éminence noire* lurking in some jungle encampment."

He's no more *noir* than I am, thought Calvin.

13

Marais? Never heard of him," said Major Beaglehole. He had dropped in at Calvin's office unexpectedly at noon, something he had never done before. He was not wearing his usual bush shirt and starched shorts, knee socks and ox-blood brogues. He wore khaki breeches and puttees, a hound's-tooth jacket and a tweed peaked cap. He gave Calvin one of his very rare smiles, his old face like a loose cloth drawn up at the corners, making dozens of cheerful wrinkles.

"I think that's what he said. I was scared. He had a gun — did I tell you that?"

"Yes," said Major Beaglehole. "A gun. You didn't see what *sort* it was, did you? Type of weapon a man carries tells masses about his character."

"Well, he stuck it in my guts. It was dark. Just a pistol I guess. I don't know anything about guns."

"Of course," said Major Beaglehole. "I told you before you left that the north was a shambles. My advice is don't say a word to anyone about it."

"There was an article in *Time* magazine," said Calvin. "It's funny. When you read about a place you happen to be living

89

in, it never sounds like the same place. It still sounds . . . I don't know, *foreign,* somehow." Beaglehole wasn't listening. Calvin shuffled papers. "You're not interested in taking out a policy by any chance?"

Major Beaglehole shook the merry wrinkles out of his face and became apologetic. "No, nothing like that. I just popped in to say that I was a bit under the weather last night. Rotten of me to call you an effing Yank, old man."

"No harm done," said Calvin, and grinned.

In a low serious voice Major Beaglehole said, "You're quite mistaken there. Don't you realize we were jawing in front of those African girls. And that waiter. That's very bad form. Encourages them to cheek us. You saw how that fat waiter got shirty with us. That's what happens."

"He seemed okay this morning."

"Oh, he's a nasty one. But Bailey won't hear a bad word about him. You know how it is: my *Kaffirs* are different from your *Kaffirs.*"

"That's a word I don't like," said Calvin.

"Infidel," said Major Beaglehole. "Means infidel."

Calvin saw that Major Beaglehole was staring at the mess of papers on his desk. Calvin clawed at them. "Lots of work to catch up on," he explained. On top were two policies, Nirenda Ogilvie and Mambo Goodson. "New accounts."

"I understand. Wheels of progress and all that, what?" Major Beaglehole drew out a gold pocket watch and pressed a button on the winding stem. Up popped a slim round lid, revealing the dial. "Lunchtime," he said. "How about lunching with me at the Club. No hard feelings, eh?"

"Suits me fine," said Calvin. "I was just going to have a beer."

"My bike's downstairs," said Major Beaglehole.

Major Beaglehole had brought his motorcycle. He drove; Calvin sat on the rear saddle, his feet dragging on the road.

*   *   *

The Moth's Club was on the Chikwawa Road, at the end of town, a whitewashed building with a roof of red tiles, set in a

clump of trees, in the center of a ruined field. A Union Jack
flew on a flag pole, hidden by branchy camouflage.

A man stood on the verandah, watching the motorcycle
bump up the driveway. He held a walking stick in one hand and
in the other a drink. He shook the stick at Major Beaglehole and
said gleefully, "I *say*, Bunny, going ratting?"

"Aubrey, old man!" Major Beaglehole bellowed. He dismounted, with Calvin, and walked up to the verandah.

"What sort of kit is that, Bunny? I haven't seen a pair of
those in donkey's years."

"My old regimental puttees," said Major Beaglehole lifting a
leg. "Keeps the mud off. I always wear them when I'm using
the bike. Where are the chaps?"

"Not a soul about. I came down for a game of darts. Had to
settle for a whisky, ha-ha!"

"Aubrey, Calvin Mullet. You remember his case."

"Pleased to make your aquaintance," said Calvin.

"Case?"

"The house girl," said Major Beaglehole. "You remember."

"Well, actually — " Calvin began.

"Pleasure's mine," said Aubrey. He winked at Calvin. He
had two beaver's teeth sticking out from under a small immobile
mustache. "Well, I must press on. Wife waiting. Hip, hip!"

"Hip, hip!" said Major Beaglehole. Aubrey struck out
across the ruined field.

"Seems like a nice guy," said Calvin.

"Aubrey? Oh, he's frightfully good value," said Major Beaglehole. "How about a drink?"

"Beer for me," said Calvin.

"Willy!" Major Beaglehole yelled, making Calvin jump.
"Beer for *bwana*, the usual for me."

An old scarred waiter in a red fez brought the drinks. He
flinched when Beaglehole reached for the whisky soda.

"Frightfully good value," said Major Beaglehole reflectively.
"But he's had a rough time of it, poor old chap."

'Aubrey?" Calvin poured his beer. "He seems very cheerful,

and very, you know, very English." He lifted his glass to his mouth which was puckered into a chorister's *O* to receive it.

"Yes, well, I suppose he does," said Major Beaglehole. "But his brother was carved up by the blacks. Then he had quite a time of it when his wife died. We reckoned here at the Club that he was taking it rather well on the whole. But — "

"Didn't he say," said Calvin, "his wife was, um, waiting for him?"

"Yes, dash it. Pathetic, isn't it?"

"She's not waiting?"

"She's dead," said Major Beaglehole. "How could she be waiting?"

"Then why — "

"One of Bailey's girls," said Major Beaglehole. "He takes them home."

"I do that now and then," said Calvin.

"Yes, I know," said Major Beaglehole, and made a face into his glass. "But Aubrey — well, you see, Aubrey takes them home and gets them to dress up in his wife's old clothes. Makes them stand in the scullery, you see, facing away from him. He talks to them, as if he's talking to his missis. Then he pays them, and they go. It's all very curious, very curious indeed."

"He just talks? He doesn't do . . . anything else?"

"No," said Major Beaglehole. "He just talks, the poor beggar. Very upsetting really."

"The last thing I'd do is have one of those girls dress up as my wife," said Calvin.

"And me," said Major Beaglehole. "Still, Aubrey's quite a colorful character."

Quite a colorful character, thought Calvin. It was what everyone said about Major Beaglehole. In Malawi it was the highest praise, and it was the reason no settler would take up arms against Osbong.

"Want to have a look around the place?"

"It's okay with me," said Calvin. "Where'd you get the name Moth's Club?"

"Memorable Order of Tin Hats," said Major Beaglehole. "This is Shell Hole Thirty-nine. See this badge?" On his lapel was a small gold helmet, the flat sort. "Only the Old Bill is allowed to wear this — the president, you might call him. This year it's my privilege. Aubrey's the Wee Bill, the vice president, and there's also a Pay Bill and some others." He explained that there was a British cartoonist who during the Great War immortalized the character Old Bill, a Tommy with a tin hat. Thus the names, thus the club. They met on the first Tuesday of the month.

"What if I wanted to join?" asked Calvin. Homemakers' encouraged its agents to be clubbable.

"Have you been fired at in anger?"

"In anger," said Calvin. "Let's see. What about that guy in Rumpi?"

"Did he take a shot at you?"

"No," said Calvin.

"Bad luck," said Major Beaglehole. "You have to be shot at. In anger."

Now they were outside, in the field, and between sips of his whisky soda Major Beaglehole pointed out the crumbling brick squash court, the cricket pitch bursting with weed clusters and stacked with rotting beams. "And over here," said Major Beaglehole, "is the garden where we debagged Bobby Stallybrass back in fifty-four."

"What's that big thing?" asked Calvin. It seemed a large decrepit barn; branches billowed from a gaping hole in the roof.

"Stables," said Major Beaglehole. "For our ponies. Started with polo — that was the polo ground, beyond the tulip tree. Fever took most of the ponies. Switched to fox hunting. Enough ponies for that. Aubrey was Master of the Hounds."

"I didn't think there were any foxes around here," said Calvin.

"There aren't. Not one. But we had a fox pelt — a very nice one indeed. That steward you saw inside, that black chap, used to fit the pelt on his back and hare off through the bush, if you see what I mean. He was the fox, Old Willy, and very fast he was. It was a devil of a job catching him, I can tell you."

"You chased that African," Calvin said, "on horses."

"Oh, we had hounds, too. Can't have a proper hunt without hounds." Major Beaglehole sipped his whisky soda and glanced sadly around at the rubble of broken buildings and the weed patches he had just identified as playing fields. "All this was ours once. They took it all away from us." He finished his drink, pursing his lips. "No matter. We'll have it back soon."

Lunch began with tepid chicken soup, topped with yellow oil slick. A narrow wedge of fish followed. The main course, served in a quarter inch of warm water, was a hunk of blackened meat, two boiled potatoes and pale soft peas.

"Choice of desserts," said Major Beaglehole, who had eaten with obvious relish. "Have the apple crumble. Old Willy does a marvelous apple crumble."

"Just coffee for me," said Calvin.

"Two coffees," said Major Beaglehole to Old Willy.

Calvin scraped his chair back and looked around the room. On the wall were group photographs of men in cricket flannels, a large framed photograph of the Queen and one of a man holding a rifle, his boot on the mane of a small lion. Another showed a man hoisting up a fish nearly as big as himself. Nailed across one wall was a faded tiger skin, brown and striped with gray, with popping glass eyes and massive teeth enclosing a red plaster tongue. Calvin rose, and went over to the skin to examine it. It was dusty and very shabby at the edges, but unmarked.

"That's *some* tiger."

"Mine," said Major Beaglehole. "Shot him on a *shikar* in the Punjab in thirty-two. I was born in India, you know. Spoke Urdu like a native. But I've forgotten it all now. Pity."

Calvin brushed the pelt. "Where'd you shoot him? I mean, I don't see any holes in the skin."

"You won't find any bullet holes in that tiger," said Major Beaglehole. "I shot him in the eye."

After coffee, Calvin said, "Did you hear about that man they found in the drain this morning — the African fellow?"

"Minister of defense," said Major Beaglehole. "Knifed during the storm."

"Terrible, isn't it?"

"It doesn't surprise me in the least. A few years ago we were getting knifed," said Major Beaglehole. "Someone's getting his own back."

"Who? That's the question," said Calvin.

"We ran this country once. It was taken away from us by the arse-creepers in London and handed over to the blacks, after Osbong made a fuss. I could quote you chapter, line and verse of that operation. It's only a matter of time before we have the whole place back. When I saw that dead black in the drain I said to myself, *this is only the beginning.*"

"I wonder who he was knifed by," said Calvin.

"I can't say," Major Beaglehole said very slowly. "But remember, he wasn't knifed in the back. Only blacks do that. On the face of it he was killed by a gentleman."

"The poor bastard," said Calvin. He passed his hanky over his face, thinking of the dead man.

"That your first corpse?"

"Yes, I guess so," said Calvin. "And I hope it's my last."

"I've seen masses," said Major Beaglehole. "And not blacks either."

Calvin was folding his napkin. "Duty calls," he said. "Look, Major, thanks for the lunch, but I have to — "

"Ever see a man hacked to death?" asked Major Beaglehole loudly.

"Can't say that I have," said Calvin. He knew the opening; he ordered the whisky soda.

"*I* have," said Major Beaglehole. "Hacked to bits. Thanks." He took his drink. Calvin poured his beer.

The day, only half gone, was already wholly wasted. Calvin knew the progress of such days. It seemed that in the lifting of a glass, the staring at a tide of foam, the day flashed past: by the time the glass was set on the table, darkness had fallen.

"It was Aubrey's twin brother, Nigel," said Major Beaglehole. "Nigel was a prison governor on Livingstone Island in Lake Nyasa, a prison colony for the hard cases — rapists, murderers, what-have-you. But he was just like Aubrey — a wonderful *raconteur*, a fast bowler. Held his whisky like a gentleman. And Nigel had vision. He used to say, 'What I want to see is a prison without bars or walls, warders without firearms, no flogging, no messing about.' He was on that island for years, built a recreation hall and a cinema — very swish. Good quarters for the men. He even had classrooms put up. Started cottage industries. Everyone knew that Livingstone Prison Island sewed the best mailbags in the territory. First class."

Major Beaglehole grinned. "But, you see, one can't treat them with kindness, can one?"

"That depends," said Calvin.

"One can't," Major Beaglehole said. "They take advantage if they think you're weak, take the mickey out of you. Well, they tried that with Nigel; had a bit of a mess up. Oh, the things he had to endure! One chap refused to work and started a sort of strike, you see. Said Nigel was overworking them and rot like that. Chap started a rumpus. Nigel handled that chap very well.

" 'Don't want to work, is that it?' he said. 'Off you go then.' And he had the chappie transferred to another prison. Take the rotten apple out of the barrel, very sensible. But the others, being very largely bush types, thought that this chap's disappearance meant he was dead. Simpleminded, of course, but something Nigel hadn't reckoned on." Seeing that his glass was empty, Major Beaglehole stopped speaking.

"Another whisky?"

Major Beaglehole closed his eyes, the subtlest of yeses. "All the best," he said, when the full glass appeared. "So there was

96

a riot on the island. All of them cock-a-hoop, screaming their heads off and waving sticks. Nigel came out of his quarters and saw them, all three hundred of them, black as the Earl of Hell's waistcoat and making a god-awful racket. Incredibly off-putting.

"Nigel watched them closely. He understood the native mind, you see. Oh, he was a frightfully patient chap. He knew just how to handle them. He harangued them a bit from his verandah and said, 'You have bad leaders who want to get you all killed. Don't believe these men. Go back to work — these men are misleading you!'

"Then quite unarmed he walked into the middle of this frightful mob of natives. He was cool. As tall as you, Mullet. He towered over them.

" 'All right now,' he said, 'Rag Day's over — you've had your fun. We've all had a good laugh out of it. Now sort yourselves out, chaps, *sort yourselves out!*' "

Major Beaglehole put his empty glass on the table. He looked at Calvin severely. He said, "And the bloody beggars hacked him to bits."

Calvin whistled softly.

"I went with Aubrey to the island. Had to scoop up Nigel with a shovel. We put the bits and pieces in a mailbag. Naturally all the blacks had beetled off. Aubrey hasn't been the same since."

"So you think Aubrey might have killed that African in the drain?"

"I can't say," said Major Beaglehole. Then he gave Calvin an evil wink.

14

At teatime Major Beaglehole suggested a game of darts but, angered by whisky, directed most of his darts at Old Willy and two or three at Calvin. The no-longer-nimble waiter ducked behind the bar. Major Beaglehole swore at him, dared him to show his face: "Up with you! Defend your country!" Old Willy stayed out of sight; Major Beaglehole peppered the shelves and supporting posts above the quaking fez. Some darts stuck in the wood, others made tinkling glances off the bottles arrayed in rows at the back.

Fearing the public-spirited bravado that came over him in times of semidrunkenness — five pints — Calvin cursed Major Beaglehole, staggered out of the Moth's clubhouse and walked back to town. He chose the south sidewalk of Osbong Drive with the intention of drinking himself into a safe state of inertia. He stopped at the Goodmorning Panwallah, the Zambesi Bar, the New Safari Drinkhouse, the Victoria Club, the Highlife, each in spite of its name exactly alike: a damp musty-smelling room with a small fan, a few hard stools, Cinzano ashtrays, Lion beer ads, and not more than a handful of customers — men with banana knives. In the latrine enclosure at the back of the New

Safari, a little girl of about fourteen, possibly out earning her school fees, tapped Calvin on the leg (nearly knocking him, out of fright, forward into the pit), greeted him formally and asked, "You want jig-jig?" She waggled her little bum. Calvin said, "No thanks, sweetheart," and gave her an osbong. Later, feeling perfectly drunk, fat and nerveless, he glided to his office to examine Ogilvie's policy.

He stared at the policy for a long while, holding it under the dim bulb. He was motionless, the paper trembled. He smoothed it flat on the desk and bent over to read it closely. A heavy yo-yo of drool dropped slowly from his gaping mouth on a string of spittle, and plopped on the policy. He brushed the droplet down with his sleeve, but it had already made a round wet blister on the page.

In handwriting unfamiliar to him Calvin made out a check covering the first three payments on Ogilvie's annual premium. He entered this amount beside Ogilvie's name in the ledger and saw that of the five other accounts listed there, two were about to lapse, the period of grace gone. They were barely covered to begin with. Calvin wrote another check for these two.

Ogilvie had neither filled out a medical report nor named a beneficiary. A thorough medical wasn't necessary because of the small premium. Calvin got the proper forms from the file cabinet — so empty it thundered at him when he rolled out the steel drawer — and scrawled what he knew of Ogilvie, naming Mira beneficiary in case of death. In drunken candor, Calvin forged the short medical report, ticking boxes up one column and down another: *To the best of your knowledge and belief, have you ever had or been told you had or been treated for* ———. In the space marked *Any additional Information? Attach Extra Sheets If Necessary* Calvin wrote, "I have dizzy spells, I shit blood, My eyes not so hot, authoritis in joint, I sleep bad . . ."

And before he could stop himself Calvin slid over the stack

of foolscap paper and wrote passionately in his unfamiliar hand, *Would you insure me? I have been beaten, robbed and nearly killed a thousand times. I live at the worst end of a bad world where people drop dead every day from sickness, disease, tiredness, bugs, misery and drinking, and I live in a dirty hut without beds and food and it amazes me when I wake up alive but what do I see more misery more sickness leprosy that crucifixes can't help and a hut that leaks on me, like our proverb* [here Calvin thought a moment] *under the cabbage leaf of life we hang like hungry worms. The white man who we called Master and Bwana just threw darts at us and put us on prison island and beat us and made us wear clothes and took our land and the number one reason for this is I was born black and invisible because I am the color of night.*

No, you would never insure me. I am a risk and I die easy. You say I am the color of shit because my face is black, but you sit in the sun and read magazines from Nazi South Africa and get a tan and you think you are lovely brown, but you are the color of my old granny who wears three dresses and shaves her head.

Someday soon I will rise up . . .

Calvin wrote until the muscles in his hand stiffened, until he could not wag his thumb. At midnight he took a clean sheet of paper and in capital letters wrote THE UNINSURED. Underneath, he wrote *by A. Jigololo.*

15

Calvin had been drunk and sad; he had begun the book, *The Uninsured*, on an impulse of fuddled despair; he had felt as misbegotten and slighted, as wasted and deceived as he pictured his jungle narrator, Mr. A. Jigololo: squat, black, near-sighted, underfed and relentlessly screwed. Calvin had believed he was content until he had started writing; then on the page his anger was apparent. He had rushed into the book at night, in blackout and panic; but in sunlight and sober, days later, he was no less eager to continue.

He continued in his own handwriting, sometimes altering the rambling paragraphs for effect, sometimes conveying the sense of oppression by using half-educated phrases, changing tenses and generally scrambling the grammar of the plea. The book's first pages were written in confusion, but the rest were thoughtful: it was a deliberate act — creation, rather than a valve for his idle misery. A. Jigololo had a past. Born in a small rural village, he had never known his mother and was unsure that the man who drank and shared the hut and beat him regularly was his father: the man's paternity seemed essentially a rapist's, a mixture of pride and violence. A. Jigololo married a selfish girl; she was cruel and barren and he left her. He traveled, he met abuse at every turn; at thirty he was a houseboy, watching his white employers from the kitchen door, sweating in his uniform.

The Uninsured occupied Calvin's night hours, it was part of his daily routine. Each morning he awoke to the twittering of birds and the clang of pots being shifted in the kitchen at the back of the eating house. After a coffee, a few items in *Time* and the four-page *Malawi News* (the minister's stabbing was mentioned in neither) and the glorious dump that followed upon his carefully timed smoke, he went to his office to type envelopes for the Homemakers' Mutual brochures. At one he knocked off for lunch, had boiled cassava and fish kedgeree at a market stall, and started the day's drinking with a cool shandy, ginger ale slopped into beer. He gradually made his way, via the bars, back to the office, where he continued drinking, sending down to the Highlife for warm quarts which he gulped from a cracked coffee mug. For the remainder of the afternoon he dozed on his arms, drank, and typed envelopes.

As the afternoon wore on the clack of the typewriter slowed, and later, usually after dark, remembering he had but five clients, three of whom he kept up to date by paying their premiums out of his own pocket, he dragged out the pile of handwritten foolscap sheets and continued with his book. A. Jigololo was beside him, haranguing; he hung at the edges of Calvin's dreams; he was tireless, he could be eloquent, he quoted Scripture. The pages, written in black ink, were numbered in pencil for easy expansion of a thought by an added page (page counting and renumbering was an obsessive activity, like the miser's alone with his gold). On page two there was a morbid, depressing, but nonetheless true epigraph, from a poem by the late vice president of the Hartford Accident and Indemnity Company. It began, "Death, only, sits upon the serpent throne: / Death, the herdsman of elephants, . . ." and ended, after speaking of endless pursuit, "And Africa, basking in

antiquest sun, / Contains for its children not a gill of sweet."
There were possible titles in it: *The Serpent Throne, Endless
Pursuit, Not a Gill of Sweet.* But something austere was
needed, the barbarous age demanded it. Calvin was going to
use the word *black* in the title, but decided against it as too
stagey, too common (it abounded in American book titles) :
black was losing its associations, like the word *naked*. *The Uninsured* described the heart of the problem which was, after
all, rooted in simple finance. Money made men.

He wrote until he was tired, then numbered the pages,
punched holes in them and clipped them into a loose-leaf
binder. Then he read, and corrected. Around midnight, flying ants and sausage flies found their way in noisy swarms to his
lighted office. They came through the window and made for
the light and the bright sheets of paper; they stuck on Calvin's
arms and crawled up his leg. He could not kill one without
making a mess, the white paste of insect guts on the swatted
page. He went back to the eating house, ate some bananas and
had a beer spiked with a soporific half of stout, took a reflective
piss, slashing a tree in the night air, and went to bed.

There were few replies to the mailed brochures, and some
of his extra hours were taken up by the book, which gave him
a sense of purpose and accomplishment, greater even than that
afforded by making entries in a ledger or filing do-not-spindle-
or-fold cards. But there were hours more, and still some
loneliness.

It seemed a loneliness imposed by the solitary activity of writing — not during, but after: as if leaving the book was leaving
good company, a crush of silence he had felt, single in Hudson
and leaving a party alone, or that sense of falling he had experienced outside Rumpi after he had said, "I'll be right back!"
and had run into the chilling darkness, the night against his
face.

So nearly every night at the eating house, but always with the
red eyes of the fat waiter upon him, Calvin took a girl to bed

with him. They were the dregs, either school girls or badly mauled hags, ignored by the regulars, the most lonely. If there was more than one in the bar when it closed for the night they quarreled over Calvin, gabbling and pushing each other, holding to his arms, feebly protesting. They inspired dread and pity, they were awkward and fat and loaded with poisons. Some had ridiculous nicknames — Essy and Kitty — and others Biblical names — Abishag and Zipporah (Abby and Zip) — or names of troubling irony — Comfort, Grace, Chastity — the missions' legacy. All of them had bruises on their shins, a badge of the profession; their hands were lizard textured. They were very shy; they giggled monotonously, they smelled, they snored. Calvin had seen men drag out their breasts and begin biting them.

"I love you, mister," one whispered continually to Calvin. She was homely and had a cough like Bailey's. But if she seemed comfortably plain late at night in the frothy light of the bar, in the morning dead asleep in a faded dress, with sun streaming through the slit shutters, she had the alarming sadness of the very ugly. And her dry dusky arm was usually thrown across Calvin's narrow chest. On those mornings Calvin rose early, driven out of bed by the neck. He left money for them and hid outside under the window until he heard groans, bedsprings, water being slapped, a sigh, a banging door. He hated himself for ducking out: if anyone was uninsured it was them.

He felt responsible for these stragglers in the bar who turned his stomach with their guileless caresses. They said they liked him, in so many words ("You — me — bed," was what they said). They had nothing. They were failures as prostitutes. And Calvin felt responsible; he wanted to help them. But there was little he could do except take them to bed and pay them, or make what sounded like wild promises, tell them to save, plan, beware, insure. Calvin tactfully defined the cause of their misery. They did not seem to care: they behaved as if it was his own misery he was describing. Calvin watched them with increasing dread. They killed time as heedlessly as queens, smoking *dagga* and *bhang* in newspaper tubes, making anonymous jungle love ("I love you, mister") ; they lived hand-to-mouth oblivious of risk, as if deathless. But they would die.

Some, not many, were lovely, and they eased Calvin of his loneliness. But what had begun as an exercise in ridding himself of loneliness became, after a time, an extension of selling insurance and writing *The Uninsured,* part of the activity of both. It was not a religious impulse. It bordered on guilt and made him ache, but it was not a sense of sin that drove him. What he felt was concern and, frustrated in his concern, acute regret. He would never be struck down blind on the road for going with the girls; he was not ashamed of his impulse. Vice was spending desire on the unworthy; but the objects of his desire were honest, they deserved kindness. There was no guilt.

Calvin wasn't offering salvation, as others had done in Malawi — only simple comfort, the possibility of a future with children, a little cash. The girls took their fees, but they did not seem interested in what Calvin said to them: the talk of bewaring and insuring. Even the Africans Calvin was personally insuring weren't interested. They never replied to Calvin's letters, they didn't seem to give a damn. Calvin continued to pay the premiums, and the longer he paid the clearer it became that to stop paying would be punishing them. And while all of this — the preaching, the wenching for charity, the paying of strangers' premiums — while all of it filled Calvin with a useful fury in adding to *The Uninsured,* it likewise depressed him, greatly; these additions, slanting with his mood, were a feverish polemic. Now, *I hate you* pulsed in every line. Jigololo, a pseudonym chosen casually from a glossary of common nouns, became flesh-and-blood, a scary being (not nearsighted or weak). Calvin discovered impatient resentments in his narrator and gave them voice; he felt less a writer than a captive protector, helpless before his charge who, disguised as an orphan, had strayed into his life, and only at the moment of fond attachment did Calvin grasp that this was a soul-sucking child in whom it was impossible to eradicate the urge to growl and bite. Calvin was forced by fear to describe it. Such was the creation's cunning in revealing the creator's weakness. The oppressed brayings turned abusive. A. Jigololo raged.

* * *

And at last, indignantly, so did Major Beaglehole. He had watched Calvin throughout with growing disapproval. He had hoped to recruit the young chappie from Boston. (For simplicity — who had ever heard of Hudson? — Calvin had given Boston as his hometown; everyone from Massachusetts did when he was abroad.) He believed Calvin to be a colorful character in small; he regretted calling him a fucking Yank and had confided, "They say Bostonians are more English than the English," which was a measure of Major Beaglehole's suspension of disbelief. He had lunched Calvin, the only American he had ever taken to the Moth's.

Major Beaglehole knew nothing of *The Uninsured*. And Calvin's beer-drinking habit didn't bother him, though he considered it working class. Calvin's filthy clothes amused him, like Bailey's coarse threats. Major Beaglehole had one objection, but it loomed: he saw the makings of dementia (a humiliating and ineradicable blot on the copybook of every white man in Blantyre should the news get out) in what he took to be Calvin's mindless passion for the ugliest girls at the eating house. A character was made colorful by tasteless practices, but he had to understand the limits of excess.

He instructed Calvin with a story of a trek he had made his first year in Malawi through the wildest bush. He had many such stories: he was the adventurer, setting out alone in bush jacket and topee. Each time, Calvin saw a solitary white man wrapped in jungle, and then Beaglehole would say, "That day I lost thirty porters . . ." and dimension was given. Calvin would see the trek anew, not a little man alone in the green, but a huge caravan, half a mile long, hundreds of men with cases of whisky and kippers and H. P. Sauce on their heads, marching behind the major.

And now Major Beaglehole was saying, "At the first sign of a spot of bother all my bearers did a swan. We had sighted tribesmen on the road, certainly rather fierce, standing starkers, with their enormous great John Thomases hanging to their knees. I was left with only a knapsack, some tins of bully beef, my Webley revolver, field glasses and so forth. I offered those savages tinned food and spent some days among them.

"Weeks later I headed south, hacking my way through the thick undergrowth. And later one afternoon I burst into a clearing. There were scores of natives on their haunches muttering and dancing, a drinking party in progress — going full bore.

"They ceased their merrymaking as soon as they saw me. They looked at me: fear was written all over their black faces. They were dead scared, of course. They had seen white men before, but never that close. I fancy I gave them a turn. They didn't know quite what to make of me.

"Well, I didn't pause. I've forgotten all my Chinyanja now, but at the time I spoke it like a native. I walked up to their chief, who was sitting in the center of all those frightened fuzzywuzzies — he was on a throne, a sort of gilt toilet bowl. I greeted him cordially. I told him I was a traveler and would not harm them.

" 'I am British,' I said, 'I will share your drink.'

"One thing led to another. Before I knew it we were chaffing each other and exchanging gifts. I gave the chief the last of my tinned food, drank myself silly and made a jackass of myself in front of the whole village. I had to be carried to bed.

"Late that night there was a knock at the hut door. It was the chief's envoy. He bowed low and said, 'It is the chief's wish that you should have a woman.' And I saw her there, standing shyly behind him, a woman with very full breasts and a blue stipple of tattoo, so to speak, around her eyes.

"If I could live through that moment again I would have shot that man and run. But I didn't.

" 'Tell the chief I am grateful, and I will use her well,' I said. Which, to my eventual disgrace, I did.

"A month passed. There were holidays and festivals, and masses of drink. I told them that I really had to press on, but they wouldn't let me. I tried to bribe the chief with my pistol — I gave it to him with fifty shells. But all that came of it was that he shot one of his subjects to see if it worked. He said he would shoot me if I tried to go. I kept on with the black woman."

Calvin knew the rest of the story: the casual encounter, leading to capture, had to end in escape, and its final feeling had to be regret. Major Beaglehole's disappearance was a more brutal matter than Calvin's ("A guard stopped me, but I told him quite plainly that if he continued to annoy me I would kill him, and with that I came back to Blantyre"), but it was a story so like his own. The principal difference was in emphasis: Major Beaglehole's shame was in going to the village, Calvin's in having deserted; Major Beaglehole spoke of the woman's ugliness ("but it's true that you don't look at the mantlepiece when you poke the fire"), Calvin thought of Mira's beauty: the hooded eyes watching for him to return. Beaglehole's was a colonial tale; and so, Calvin realized, was his own. It was not fair to insure and go. Insurance wasn't a business: it was a whole way of life.

Major Beaglehole's story should have been enough; but it was Calvin's fright on the street that decided him. It was an indulgence in terror Calvin did not believe possible in a person with as much coverage as he had. It was late. He had just left his office; he was drunk and felt the weakening effects of A. Jigololo's intimidation. He stepped off the sidewalk, holding tight to his briefcase, and vaulted the storm drain; then he paused.

The main road, once Queen Elizabeth, now Osbong, had

been made broad enough (this, in 1910) for a large horse-drawn wagon to make a complete turnabout on it without having to back up. It was a long crossing. Fugitive cars whickered down it with the small pupils of their parking lights aglow. People snoozed at its edges, next to the drains. Calvin had to cross it: Auntie Zeeba's Eating House was on a back street, beyond the opposite side. But, unlit, Osbong Drive seemed to have no opposite side.

Calvin began to pick his way across, his heart sinking with each step. Bats menaced him; he waved his free arm to beat them off. A rising whicker signaled the approach of a jalopy. Calvin dashed, and felt the jalopy's breeze at his back. But he still had not gained the other sidewalk; he was breathless. Boozed, burdened by a case of envelopes to be posted, and slowed by the night heat, he wondered if he would make it. He could be run down in the darkness, flattened in an instant — and none of the girls at the eating house would lament: they didn't know his last name. He struggled toward the sidewalk. He felt like an enfeebled pensioner, a widower with no kin, caught out on a wild street at night, in his baggy pants, humping a heavy briefcase. It was not complicated fright; it was a drunken glimpse of jungle dark as he inched across the open street with the slowness of a dream cripple. He felt overwhelmed by his intentions. He didn't want to die childless, on all fours, alone in a monsoon drain.

Here was his simple hope: Mira had left bird prints on his mad heart, funny fragile tracks stitched all over it. The illiterate black girl had left her X on him; he had run from her, but still she touched him. He made it to the far sidewalk with the kind of vow on his lips that men make in storms at sea: as soon as the rains eased off he would go back to Rumpi, to the little dorp, to remind Ogilvie that he was safely insured, and to persuade Mira to come to Blantyre and live with him. He needed her.

16

Eat!" said Mr. Harry. "Go on, eat! It's good for you."

In the garage behind Auntie Zeeba's, a rough table — a door across two sawhorses and covered with a checkered cloth — was laden with plates of food. A Tilly lamp hung from a rafter, lighting the meat and the two diners' eager faces: the fat waiter's and Mr. Harry's. The fat waiter wore collarless black pajamas and heavy boots to his knees. He watched Mr. Harry expectantly. Mr. Harry's pomaded hair glistened; he had a thick black brush of a mustache which twisted as he spoke. He picked up a whole roast chicken and passed it to the fat waiter.

The fat waiter gathered the chicken up in his hands and tore it in half. It oozed grease where his thumbs gripped it. The bones splintered, making the sound of a basket being rent.

"Now," said Mr. Harry, tugging at the tablecloth with his damp fingers, "eat it."

Holding the chicken breast in one hand, sideways, like a harmonica, the fat waiter raised it to his mouth and lapped at the crisply varnished skin. Then he nibbled, loosening an underdone piece of skin, which shook as he ate. He put the whole piece in his jaws and tore at it by jerking his head back.

Mr. Harry listened with satisfaction. The fat waiter was grinding bones and meat in his mouth.

"Excellent," said the fat waiter, one full cheek a gleaming bubble. He smiled at Mr. Harry; the black twig of a burnt bone stuck out of a notch in the fat waiter's front teeth. He plucked it out and used it as a toothpick.

"You like?" asked Mr. Harry, eying a block of beef. "Eat," he said, "you deserve it."

"You take good care of me," said the fat waiter.

"It is an honor, believe me," said Mr. Harry, opening his jack-knife with a black thumbnail. He began slicing the beef. As soon as he pierced its crust it bled into a puddle of juices, ovals of brown blood in warm grease. He sliced deftly, holding the free end of the limp slice between thumb and forefinger, and working the knife up and down in short strokes. He cut four thin slices of beef and folded them on his plate.

"Such an honor," repeated Mr. Harry. He felt the sinewy plug of meat scrap tight in his back teeth. "What I like is the texture. That's the best part of eating. The nice . . . chewy . . ." He chewed. ". . . texture of meat." He swallowed and smacked his hand on his heart.

"In the Congo," said the fat waiter, "they cut out their enemies' hearts and ate them. It makes you strong. They said that in the Congo."

"I have lived in a lotta countries," said Mr. Harry. "But not in the Congo. It is one thing I don't like, eating people. In some places they eat dogs. That's my idea of disgusting."

"What does Marais eat?"

"He doesn't eat much. I asked. It threw me off," said Mr. Harry. "He worries about other things. Watch a man eat and you know a lot about that man. That's what *I* say. The soldiers eat like pigs."

"Maybe they're hungry," said the fat waiter.

"You're going to leave those chicken bones?" The fat waiter

shrugged. "There's a whole meal there. You're leaving the best part." Mr. Harry selected a long pale bone from the fat waiter's plate. He bit off the knob and blew it onto the floor; then, he placed the bitten end in his mouth and crunched it, and sucked. "Marrow, soft and nice, like chicken paste," he said, tossing the shattered bone over his shoulder. "Try one."

The fat waiter did as Mr. Harry suggested.

Harry said, "I like to hear the little snaps when the bone breaks."

"Good food," said the fat waiter.

"Rice," said Mr. Harry. "Didn't I see some rice — ah!" He found the rice bowl, put his hand in and squelched some into a ball. He popped the white ball into his mouth. "You need that. Plain food with greasy."

They continued eating, saying little. Mr. Harry amused the fat waiter by opening a plump green bottle of Tuborg and holding it upended in his teeth with his head thrown back. He drank it all, no hands. He smashed the bottle by flinging it to the wall with his teeth. The fat waiter opened the next bottle for Mr. Harry: he lifted the bottle cap off with his teeth.

"Wonderful," said Mr. Harry. He stuffed his mouth with greens. "Nice texture. Crunchy radish. Crunchy lettuce. Onion. Nice."

Slowly the food disappeared and was replaced by sucked bones, rinds, knots of masticated gristle. Rummaging through a plate of bones, Mr. Harry came upon a whole fish. He picked off the belly flesh, leaving the head and tail joined by a spiny backbone.

"We eat the head," said the fat waiter, and showed Mr. Harry how.

"You can have it," said Mr. Harry. "The best thing is to get soft meat from a cracky shell. Lobster. We had them in Angola. You open their claws with a nutcracker, *crunch*. Then you pick out the soft meat. Delicious."

. . . *pick out the soft meat. Delicious.* Calvin listened at the door, with his eye against a crack. He stood in the early morning chill, his trouser cuffs fixed with bicycle clips, his arms folded.

"Later on today I have to go up there again," Mr. Harry was saying. "But when I come back I'll try to get some nice lobsters. You'll like them. But you can do the same with a sheep's head. *Crack, crack,* you knock the skull with your knife handle. You take away the bits of bone and, la-la, there is the soft jelly of the brain, still cool. You eat with a spoon. *Very* nice."

Mr. Harry found a dish of oranges. He peeled one and began eating the juicy segments, spraying the seeds onto the table.

The garage door creaked open.

The fat waiter was saying, "By the end of July, every part of the country will be — " He stopped and rose to his feet.

Calvin squinted in the bright light. He could not take in the whole table. It looked like a pile of garbage; the edges of plates showed beneath the heaped leavings.

"Drink, sir?" asked the fat waiter, wiping his hands on his black pajama suit. He picked up a napkin and folded it over his arm.

"At five in the morning?" Calvin laughed. "You must be out of your mind." He noticed Mr. Harry.

Mr. Harry tilted his head politely and, still seated, made a sort of bow.

Calvin smiled. "You eat a big breakfast."

Mr. Harry guffawed, very loudly. "That's good!"

"It is Ramadan," said the fat waiter. "We are Moslems. We fast all day and eat at night."

"Ramadan, true," said Mr. Harry. "You might not think I'm a Moslem, but of course I am, of Lebanese origin."

Calvin was drawing on a pair of gloves. "I won't be a minute," he said. He walked to a corner of the garage and threw a large tarpaulin off Major Beaglehole's motorcycle. He wheeled the motorcycle to the door, saying before he left, "I sure wish I had your appetite."

Mr. Harry bowed again as the door closed. He listened to the kick starter. Once, twice: the engine fluttered. A third time: it scraped and roared. Its puttering died away. "He always gets up so early?"

The fat waiter watched the door Calvin had just passed through. He said no.

"This is the first time. Interesting. I find that interesting," said Mr. Harry, biting into the last orange segment. Juice dribbled down his chin. "You find that interesting?"

The fat waiter said, "Maybe."

Mr. Harry tore a hunk of bread from a long loaf. He chose a likely plate and scrubbed it with the bread. He ate the bread, with his eyes on the fat waiter. "You should," he said, chewing, "keep a close eye on that skinny fellow. You never know do you, brother?"

17

It was a beautiful old Matchless. Major Beaglehole said he had ridden it through the Battle of El Alamein; he had loaned it to Calvin for a quart of whisky and had said, "Don't disgrace us, Mullet. Be a man. And don't scratch the machine."

Olive green, it had a wide, well-soaped saddle slung low between the large wheel humps and suspended on springy coils. The coils oinked pleasantly when the motorcycle jounced. Three dials with lazy needles were clamped to the handlebars, their cables trailing past a profusion of spokes to the chrome hubcaps. The fenders were trimmed with looping gold tracery and curled up, front and rear, like the visors of antique helmets.

Calvin snuggled down on it, hugging the curves of the gas tank with his elbows and knees. He shot up Osbong Drive, rattling the shop windows and waking the night watchmen. Then skidded around the flowerbeds at the base of the clock tower, and down the Chileka Road, past Henry Henderson Institute and the Flamingo Bar.

A signboard at the crossroads outside town listed the following choices: POWER STATION, MOZAMBIQUE, SOUTHERN RHODESIA, and on a single arrow pointing down a dirt road, at right angles to the three choices, the one word North. Calvin turned on to the dirt road, settled into one of the deep ruts of the car tracks, and gunned the engine. The refined *bap-bap*, the sharp pistol crack of backfiring when he decelerated down the dirt hills, made his pleasure greater. He flew. An hour passed: the cool low clouds of early morning veiled the grass and the flat-topped trees with draperies of silver mist, and long before the sun came up the sky was streaked pink and yellow, with faint sequins of stars.

He had bought a new Michelin map, but a map was hardly necessary. Malawi was finger shaped, with mountains for knuckles; Mozambique was on one side, Lake Nyasa on the other; at the top was southern Tanzania. There was only one road north, a bad one, and at regular distances there were white posts with the name of a town abbreviated to two letters on them and its distance in miles. Near a town called Dedza the road veered around a mountain into Mozambique for several miles. Here was a collection of square white shops at the edge of a precipice. Their signs read Associão Portuguesa, A. DaSilva, Gomez Motors, and there were several cafés. Calvin stopped, frightening some feeding goats, and had a pint of Manica Beer — it was good *tipo de exportação* from Beira — and two hard-boiled eggs on a café verandah.

Calvin, salting an egg, watched the sun rise over low hills at the farthest end of a yellow plain. In the foreground dusty cacti grew as tall as trees, and behind them were huge single boulders with the beginnings of sculpture at their edges. Scattered between cactus and boulder were large mounds, the shape of wormcasts. For a moment a feeling of deep contentment settled on Calvin; he watched the emptiness of the desert with the same calm he had felt outside Benghazi, a peaceful aridity of soul from the vast unpeopled stretch. He was about to say, "Another *cerveja*," when it struck him that the wormcasts were huts and kraals. There were stirrings of goat flocks at the boulders' sides and near the cacti. There was movement, so slow he had taken it for stillness; he felt sad to have misunderstood it, and remembered that he was delaying.

The Portuguese shopkeeper, a short square man with the face of a Sioux, sold Calvin a pack of brown cigarettes from Lourenço Marques, thin sticks called Pueinte-Cinco, wrapped in sweet-tasting paper. Calvin decided against having one: he knew it would bring on a shit and he feared being led to an enclosure with a hole in the floor. One had to accept the constipation of travel. He bought a bottle of Casal Garcia, a near-sweet sparkling wine; the shopkeeper obligingly loosened the cork and packed it in the saddlebag so that it would not break. The man signaled, through his African servant, that he had something important to tell Calvin.

"He ask are you going that side?" The African pointed north.

"*Si*," said Calvin to the Portuguese shopkeeper.

The shopkeeper spoke directly to Calvin, a flood of gutterals squeezed intermittently into sibilances.

"He say keep careful," said the African.

"What's wrong?" asked Calvin.

"African dere," said the African.

The shopkeeper spoke urgently to the African for a few moments.

"They stopping car. Troubling and beating. Maybe you buy a *kisu* here — " The African continued to speak; the shop-keeper drew out a knife and nodded.

Calvin laughed.

The Portuguese man's Red Indian face creased. He muttered and went back into the café, kicking the door shut.

"What did he say?"

"It bad to trust African. They chop you maybe."

"Forget it," said Calvin. "I don't need a knife." He set off again on the motorcycle.

Riding down a long slope he had a view of thirty miles ahead, the narrow brown road winding into a thicket of bush to reappear, a thin shaved streak, two balding hills later; and showing again beyond that, a narrow thread at the horizon. He saw smoke trailing up from packed clusters of huts, the greeny quilt of vegetable gardens and, above it all, a black witchlike cloud dragging a gray skirt of slanting rain from the east to the road.

Closer to the rain there was a fertile earthen odor in the air, damp grass and turf; and an odd breeze which blew in circles lifting the leaves. He knew he was in for a heavy storm. He increased his speed, keeping his eyes on the rain's hem which was fast approaching the road. After half an hour, in one of the thickets he had picked out earlier, thinking he had out-distanced the rain — though the earthen odor was still powerful, and the air was cool — a dozen boys in red shirts, carrying rifles, jumped out from wind-lashed trees.

They aimed their rifles at Calvin's head.

"Alt oo go dere!" shouted one wearing a beret. His lower jaw was fearsome, big with teeth. He shouted again and set his gunstock against his shoulder. He peered down the barrel at Calvin.

Calvin braked. The rain roared on leaves, out of sight, like the rushing feet of riotous peasants, voices in the jungle: this rising sound and the chill darkness of the cloud-eclipsed sun always preceded a storm. The rain was now near; in the jungle one could hear it approach; it soughed and breathed.

The red-shirted boys surrounded Calvin, each of them only a barrel length away. On each shirt was pinned an Osbong badge, like a campaign button: the official photo, the snarling one. They were Youth Wingers, though not all were young. Curiously enough, the smallest were very old, the biggest looked youthful; the one with the beret was not more than eighteen.

"What," said Calvin in a voice not his own, "can I do for you?"

"Dis loadbrock," said the one with the beret, still with his face against the rear sight of his gun. "Where you coming?"

"Blantyre," said Calvin. His trembling tongue gave it four syllables. He twitched before the gun muzzles, blinking fiercely:

he could see their fingers crooked around the triggers. "Take it easy," he said. "Be careful with those things."

The beret growled an order; a frizzy head appeared at Calvin's chest; he felt his pockets being slapped, the buckle on his saddlebag tinkling. Calvin still held the handlebars of the Matchless. He said irrelevantly, "I'm a resident of Blantyre," and attempted a smile.

One boy reached over and unscrewed the chrome gas cap.

"Don't think I'm being nosey," said Calvin, "but what are you looking for? Maybe I can help you."

"We looking," said the boy putting his eye against the greasy hole to the gas tank, "for a certain gentleman." The gas fumes stung his eye. He wrenched his head away.

"What your name?" asked the boy, wiping his eye.

Calvin told him.

"It not you," said the boy with the beret. None of the older wizened men had spoken; but they looked impatient to Calvin and still steadied their rifles on his face. The beret moved the muzzle of his gun to a spot just below Calvin's nose. The noise of the approaching rain grew very loud, the road turned black. The beret shouted: *"You Chinese?"*

"No," said Calvin trying to raise his voice. "I'm not, I'm — "

"He Chinese," said a high voice at Calvin's back. Several rifles rested on Calvin's spine.

"Sure, *he* Chinese."

"I think he Chinese too," said the beret.

"Look at me," said Calvin. "Go ahead." He took off his glasses. "Do I look Chinese?"

"Do not know," said the beret. "I never see one. But I *think* you Chinese."

The bottle of Casal Garcia blew its cork, soaking the red shirt with his hand in the saddlebag. The rest broke into mocking laughter, seeing bubbles on the boy's face and his soaked shirt. As they laughed — the laughter made their rifles shake and poke Calvin — the rain came, drenching them all and putting a stop to their merriment. They turned their wet faces up to the low spitting sky; their shirts were black.

"Take this bottle," Calvin said, handing the wine to the boy with the beret. "Drink-drink! Very good!"

The rain slapped the road.

The beret took a swig and grinned. The others mobbed him, cracking their rifles together, pleading for a drink. The beret swigged furiously, swinging the bottle up with one arm and holding the others off with his rifle butt.

Calvin saw a straggler standing near him, watching the others; the straggler slouched, idly licking raindrops from his lips. Calvin hissed to him: "This," he said, tapping the Osbong button on the boy's collar, "for this" — he showed the boy a handful of coins. It was raining so hard Calvin's cupped hand splashed full of rainwater.

The boy smiled and quickly unpinned his badge. Seeing that the rest had run into the trees he snatched the money and followed them.

Calvin pinned the badge to his own collar. He tromped on the kick starter and took off into the driving rain.

For a mile the road was slippery but passable. Then the soil loosened to a soft porridge of muck. Gobs shot into Calvin's face, layers of the sticky stuff accumulated on the heavy tire treads, rubbed at the fenders and slowed him. He could barely see through his spattered lenses. His toes plowed the mud. He dismounted and pushed the motorcycle up one hill, but at a second, very long hill, he gave up halfway and, leaning the motorcycle against a tree, put his head down and ran for shelter.

He found a dry spot in a grove of peeling blue gums, he cleaned his glasses. He wrung the water from his cuffs. Then he looked up and sighed.

Ten yards away, huddled under a leafy fig tree, were more red shirts. Two braved the heavy sheets of rain that separated them from Calvin.

"Alt oo go dere," said one, casually sticking his rifle into

Calvin's stomach. Calvin's whole body went instantly numb. Another rifle muzzle rested in the hollow at the small of his back.

"Is this a roadblock?"

"Is," said the voice at the rear.

"Well, the damn road — "

"Load over there," said the one in front. He motioned with his rifle, sliding it across Calvin's belly to point to the road.

Calvin looked at the boy's face. The boy was staring at the badge on Calvin's collar, and smiling.

A moment later, with the blessings of the two red shirts and the eager approval of the others wagging their rifles from the dry spot under the fig tree, Calvin crawled back through dripping forest onto the road. He didn't want them to change their minds. The rain fell with no less vigor than before. Calvin found the motorcycle and labored up the hill, pushing the motorcycle, walking beside it, but keeping the engine running in first gear. He worked the throttle, the engine griped and strained. Calvin's shoes were huge with mud.

It was worth the struggle. At the top of the hill Calvin passed through a wall of rain onto a dry sunlit road. It was like leaving a rainy room; the rain was just behind him, pelting on a dark road. He stood in light red dust, in warm sun. After an hour his clothes were dry. But his shoes stayed soggy: they slavered bubbles when he flexed his toes.

There were no more roadblocks, though Calvin expected them and prepared for them by slowing down at blind leafy bends — good ambush spots. Closer to Marais country he took off his Osbong badge, for he knew that if he was stopped again it would be by Marais's men: they would make trouble if they saw him wearing it. On the other hand, he was not afraid of Marais: he had passed through that ordeal and lost only three pairs of glasses. If Marais stopped him, Calvin planned to say, "I told them everything you said, about your soldiers and your radio transmitter. You've got them scared shitless."

What a place, thought Calvin. In what could have been the simplest country in the world, nothing at all was simple. Drunk, he had expressed a similar thought to Major Beaglehole: "You always think it's going to be cheaper here, but somehow it's always more expensive." He was not sure what he had meant by that, though Major Beaglehole said he agreed. "It's a fine place, Mullet," the major had said. "I've spent some happy days here, and some bloody awful ones. I can't say I like the natives, but there are some damned colorful characters here. It's just as you say, one doesn't expect it."

Bumping along the road on the motorcycle Calvin had a more lucid perception: Malawi was not a country, not in the most generous definition of the word. He had seen the figures; Homemakers' Mutual showed more of a profit with its insurance than Malawi did with a bumper harvest of peanuts. Even Osbong admitted it: "What did we Africans do to deserve such a poor place to live?" Most countries had factories here and there sending up smoke, an occasional election or riot, paved roads and stoplights. Most countries made a little money. But Malawi was a political accident, an attempt at order foiled by lusty jungle; it was bankrupt. Its one factory, Chiperoni Blankets Ltd., had to import rags from Italy to make the blankets. Calvin had heard it with astonishment: *You have to import rags?* When Wilbur Parsons told Calvin where he was being sent, Calvin hadn't been able to locate it on a map. It seemed not to exist.

It had a president, a clownish Papa Doc defended by a *Tonton Macoute* of giggling Youth Wingers who, during the day or when it wasn't raining, put up roadblocks and searched for spying Chinese. It had a seat at the United Nations, a national flag, and a national anthem. But no, it wasn't a country. Calvin thought of Mira's words: "That not name. That *signature*." It was something like that; not a country, but a situation, a patch of jungle in central Africa, so little a man on an old motorcycle could travel most of its length in one day, and in doing so, see no dwelling higher than one story and, except for the Dodge City place of Lilongwe, no town larger than ten huts and two shops — see nothing in fact more significant than bags of peanuts decaying in uncollected mold-green stacks by the roadside, the one roadside.

Yet so much of it was lovely: the air charged with ozone, the fields of wild flowers and wide jug forests of baobabs, the sky's serious blueness, the faces of rocks; it was a dense beauty that made everything seem edible, the jungle was a salad, the bamboo looked succulent, the mountains were muffins.

Its prettiness was circumscribed by poverty, and though there was nothing newsworthy in either, the *National Geographic* had once taken photographs in color: crocodiles and dik-diks, toothy and titsome black ladies carrying bundles of sticks on their noggins, ballocky black men paddling hollow logs down a coursing river. But that could have been any nameless jungle. *Time* magazine's notice was particular; it spoke of riot and intrusion, an infant war: it named Malawi. So Malawi was important. Murder, the equatorial commonplace, mattered to the world; a rumor of death had put Malawi on the American projection of the map, as tulips had done for Holland. That was its claim to statehood: the possibility of its being attacked. Though it had never existed seriously in print before, now it had a name; and the use of the name seemed to burden it with an importance it never needed and couldn't pay for.

Calvin arrived at the Big Drum Bar late in the afternoon. He decided to stop for a drink, hoping he would meet Ogilvie and Mira. That would be appropriate: he had kept his word about coming back. The Christmas decorations were tattered, the bar was empty. Calvin called out, "Anyone here?"

The bartender showed his head. Scaly bruises on his face were painted purple. He had a square of gauze taped over one ear.

"Remember me?" asked Calvin. "The guy selling insurance?" He put money on the counter. "A beer — and have one yourself. You look like you could use one."

"No beer," said the bartender. He touched at a purple bump. "They took it away."

"What do you mean? *Who* took it away?"

"Soldiers. In the trees."

"The ones with that *mzungu* leader?"

The bartender said yes, them.

"What a bunch of bastards," said Calvin. "When did they do it to you?"

"Last night they come, drink beer, whisky, just taking like that. Beat some people here. I hate them too much." The bartender looked at Calvin, as if he had just recognized him; he said with force, "Your friends! Yes, yes — they troubled your friends!"

A dying fire smoldered in front of Ogilvie's hut. The compound was empty, the aimless trickle of smoke and the unimpeded shafts of sunlight giving it an aspect of abandonment. The two hut doors were closed. Calvin killed the engine and propped the motorcycle on its kickstand.

"Mira!"

His voice sounded helpless in the silence. It stopped the birds chirping and made a fluting locust pause. The place seemed deserted. Near to the fire, pots had been overturned; they leaked stiff gruel. The Shell Oil can was on its side.

Calvin tried the left-hand door. To his surprise it swung open, exposing the dark room where he had made love to Mira on that first night. It was so still and shadowy it appeared empty. But flies buzzed, and a figure lay on the little cot, in a stained undershirt and sarong, and wearing one plastic sandal. Calvin started forward with a greeting; but he quickly checked himself and turned, fanning at the flies, when he saw that the figure — it could only have been Ogilvie — had no head.

He did not open the right-hand door as he had the left. He rapped on it, holding it shut, afraid to see what was inside. He went on knocking persistently, in anger; and after a while, between knocks, he heard someone inside burst into tears.

18

Here he comes," said Marais. "And she's with him. What did I tell you?" He lay on his belly, his elbows dug into the soil and he squinted through a heavy pair of binoculars. While he spoke, he spun the grooved focusing wheel, beckoning into sharpness with his forefinger the image of the two people on the motorcycle, the insurance agent, the village girl.

Marais moved to a sitting position and watched the motorcycle disappear, leaving a red dust cloud on the brow of a hill. Marais was impressed by the fast driving, by the guts it took to start on a long journey at nightfall. He pushed his dusty cap onto the back of his head. In his left hand was a plump cigar: a jewel of a glowing spark was set into the coal of the blunt black tip. "He didn't waste any time. I was right, wasn't I?"

The African soldier next to Marais was silent. He worked the bolt on his rifle, preoccupied.

"Wasn't I?" Marais insisted.

The African muttered and slid the bolt, slapping it down.

"Maybe you'll listen to me now," said Marais. "Let's get back to camp."

In the babble of the camp at dusk a group of men stood

around two prisoners tied to posts. Although the two men were tied, they spoke loudly and laughed often; the conversation was a relaxed one.

Marais had started toward them when he heard this note of cheerfulness in the talk. He paused momentarily and thought, they only understand pain. They had to be hurt themselves. Pain taught reliable humility. In the art of revolt there were more lessons in failure than in victory, and if the enemy was not strong enough to make a man beat a retreat into discipline, the punishing would have to take place in his own camp.

That morning, after the prisoners had been caught, Marais had searched through his books, and he had copied into his notebook:

The punishment of putting a soldier in jail for ten days constitutes for the guerrilla fighter a magnificent period of rest; ten days with nothing to do but eat; no marching, no work, no standing the customary guards, sleeping at will, resting, reading . . . From this it can be deduced that deprivation of liberty ought not to be the only punishment available in the guerrilla situation.

They were not his own words, but they were justification enough for what he planned.

"Get away from the prisoner," Marais said. He never shouted; he didn't have to: his voice had an edge that was always heard. "Make a circle, and bring the first prisoner forward."

An African was released from his pole and led over to Marais. He stood before Marais unsteadily, wearing only a pair of khaki shorts, and in an exaggerated posture of attention, for his hands and arms were tied tightly behind his back. Roped as he was, with his chest out, he appeared smugly defiant. He picked out a friend in the crowd of watching soldiers and broke into a chuckling smile. It was for a few seconds the only sound in the camp, this assured cluck.

There had been four previous trials. Marais had always spoken eloquently. He had listed the qualities of a good guerrilla soldier and then asked the prisoner to explain what he had done. It was a public confession. If the confession and apologies came too readily, as they often did, Marais humorously ridiculed the offender, and allowed the others to jeer. His words were translated by a comical soldier named Brother Yatu who screeched the mockery like a mad bird and worked himself into a frenzy of abuse, as Marais's words became his. The others shouted, "Shame!" "No, no!" and laughed. And after a week in jail the humiliated prisoner was released and allowed to rejoin his patrol. It was no punishment at all.

Brother Yatu took his usual place, next to Marais.

"We won't need you tonight," said Marais, waving him off. Marais looked at the prisoner's bare feet: they were like roots ripped out of the ground, dusty, tuberous, with small yellow nails on the mangled toes.

The prisoner was still smiling into the circle of men.

"For murder," said Marais.

The prisoner uttered a wordless yes; he closed his eyes and thrust out his lower lip.

"Yes! Yes!" shrieked the others. "He's a dog!" They stopped abruptly to let Marais start his harangue.

Marais said simply, "Where are the witnesses?"

Two boys, each about fifteen, with large eyes and long adolescent legs, marched over to Marais. They yawned nervously. Their cloth caps sagged over their ears, the peaks askew; their shirt-sleeves were pushed up, bunched under their arms. They rocked back and forth in their large boots. They were dressed absurdly, but they were not absurd; their faces were small, fragile with childish concern; their hands were fine, their wrists almost feminine. They plucked at their trousers with their fingers.

"You are to punish the prisoner," said Marais. "You were brave enough to report to me what happened last night in the village. Take this pistol."

The prisoner bumped his head questioningly at the translator, Brother Yatu. Brother Yatu shook his head; he understood English, but he did not understand what Marais was doing. He shrugged and folded his arms.

"This is how we forgive a murderer," said Marais, motioning to the boy with the pistol. "You are to shoot him through the right foot, the top of it." Marais demonstrated. He took the revolver and pointed it at his own instep and said, *"Pah!* Here, you see?"

The prisoner saw Marais's demonstration; he threw his head back and yelled horribly. He continued yelling as he was tied to his post and wound with rope from his neck to his ankles. The young boy approached, the revolver so heavy in his small hand that it aimed down, testing his wrist. The prisoner rolled his head from side to side and, when the boy aimed the revolver, picking out a spot on the naked veined instep of the rootlike foot, the prisoner tried to dance. The muzzle was an inch away.

In fear the African's nose grew very small, his open mouth quite square, his face tight and slick, like a striking snake. He spat clumsily on the boy's uniform.

A loud report, a ringing bang, silenced the prisoner's screamings. Blue smoke mingled with a puff of dust. The prisoner's mouth was stretched open, his eyes shut, his face tensed in the expression of a scream; but the face did not relax into simple horror again or utter another noise. The second boy, holding the revolver awkwardly in two hands, fired a bullet through the left foot. The prisoner fainted, went limp on his ropes. He was dragged to a tent to be bandaged. At the base of the post was a scuffle of shifting footprints, and most of those hollows were bloody.

The second prisoner had already started to cry. It was Brother Mussa, the Yao translator, the rapist. Over the sound of Brother Mussa's blubbering Marais ordered a hole to be dug, just in front of the post. Marais had not finished speaking, but already the men had started to dig. He was indicating the size of the proposed pit with a vague circling of his cigar; he

was saying, "Right here, at his feet. You see what I mean — "
Five men stripped off their shirts; they hacked at the spot with
mattocks and spades.

The face of Brother Mussa was taffy, pulling and stretching. His mouth and eyes widened as the hole widened, the
wails grew shrill as the hole deepened. With each gravelly
crunch of the mattocks, stray pebbles flew up at Mussa's face,
making him gulp and shout at the hole in broken English, for
Marais: ". . . big picture Osbong in the room. They spies!
I know spies! . . . These women are ever liars . . ." He
denied the rape, he accused several of the watching men of
doing it, he battled with his knots; and he wailed his appeal to
the scrape of the spades in the hole.

Now two men stood back to back, waist-deep in the hole,
shoveling dirt cakes into baskets and bumping each other with
hurrying elbows.

It had gone dark, moonless; night had obscured all the landmarks of the camp and made the diggers invisible. But they
could be heard: they gasped, hacked, chucked dirt in a steady
three-beat rhythm. Brother Mussa whimpered; he could hear
the hole being dug at his feet.

"Lights," said Marais. Instantly, lamps were brought, and
the clearing filled with light, making it seem the dusty chamber
of a high-ceilinged cave. A grim soldier's face showed over
each lantern; the face of Brother Mussa shone.

Marais regarded the tamed faces of the men; they obeyed
now, he had not been wrong. Discipline had to be one of the
bases of action of the guerilla force; even Che had said, *Punish
him drastically in a way that hurts.* Brother Mussa was still
shouting; the shovels obediently scraped the bottom of the
hole.

"That's enough," said Marais. The men stopped digging
after Marais repeated it. Brother Mussa was making a racket; he
had been a trusted man, the chief translator — what had he
said to the men? It had to be worse for him; Marais had valued

him. And the rape: *drastically in a way that hurts.* Marais
pointed a finger at the shouting man, held it a moment, then
let the finger bend and fall slowly, the nail describing an arrow's
path into the hole. The men understood: it was the order chiefs
gave when they wanted subjects to kneel.

Brother Mussa was trundled into the hole up to his armpits
and held in place. The loose earth in the baskets was dumped
back and tamped around his body. Only Brother Mussa's head
and arms were free; the rest of his body was sunk into the
ground. His breathing was troubled, his lungs were pressed by
the earth. It was an eerie sight, Brother Mussa's large angry
head with two limbs attached, like a piteously beached sea animal — head fitted neatly to arms — making fish mouths, scrab-
bling and clawing at the sandy soil.

Marais turned and looked around. He saw what he wanted,
an egg-sized stone; he picked it up and weighed it thoughtfully
with a bouncing hand as if he was considering whether to bite
it. For a minute the only movement in the circle of men was
Marais's filled hand, rising and falling, the arm shadow trun-
cated and made numerous by the hissing lamps. Worried into
silence, Brother Mussa watched Marais with anxious curiosity,
arms flat on the ground, his head back, no longer a stranded sea
animal but a man in quicksand.

All at once the limp hands of Brother Mussa rose and produced a yellow palm-and-finger butterfly; it clung and fluttered
before his squawking face. Marais was winding up, crooking
his arm behind his head. He pitched the stone thirty feet, con-
torting the butterfly in a spasm of panic (here a smack of stone
on bone) into two black fists. Brother Mussa hammered on his
eyes.

The lamps were set down, a clamor of light. With a shout
the men stooped for stones and began to pelt the head and arms
rooted in the center of the clearing. The men bumped each
other, as if they were relearning an old ritual and were practic-
ing it in a poorly lighted place.

"What if he dies?" whispered a voice in back of Marais.

"If he dies," Marais said — but he did not have to take his eyes from the torn face and whirling arms of Brother Mussa to know that the voice was Mr. Harry's — "if he dies, then it means he's guilty, doesn't it?"

19

This beece of gloth," said Jaganathy, bumping the bolt along the counter and snapping a few feet of material with deft fingers, "it was brinted in Holland. Observe golors: so bright. Battern: so glear. Nice imported style all ladies want." Jaganathy regarded his two customers, Mira and Calvin.

Filing a claim for a bereaved family, Calvin had often wondered where the money went. It was no substitute for grief, naturally death made people cry. But Calvin had guessed that the cash, now where mournful loss had been, gave their lives a hopeful nudge and helped them start all over. It was not the insurance agent's job to go back and make sure the money was well spent; Calvin knew that nothing blotted tears like money. All insurance could be reduced to that. Calvin had always computed the amounts due and sent them with a note offering his condolences. He had given Mira Ogilvie's endowment when they arrived in Blantyre and had said, "I don't know what to say."

"Six-seven yards this," Mira was saying to Jaganathy.

"Think of Ogilvie," said Calvin.

The first item had been a coffin for Ogilvie: mahogany, with chrome handles and lined with cushions of black silk. Jaganathy was frank in his disapproval; he recommended cremation. "It is better to burn. Cheap, quick, no trouble." But during the course of the morning the coffin proved useful. Jaganathy put it on the floor of his Madras Bazaar and filled it with Mira's purchases.

Calvin stood to the side, watching the coffin fill: a pair of sunglasses in a sequinned case, a dozen Portuguese bras, a crate of scented soap, two pairs of gold quilted slippers, ten yards of raw silk, a clock.

"And what else?" asked Jaganathy, totting up the amount in the margin of a newspaper.

Mira ran her eyes over the shelves. She smiled. "Comb and blush."

"*Nice* gomb and brush set, *matching,* made in Great Britain." Jaganathy tossed it in the coffin and turned to Calvin. "You are very lucky chap, Mr. Calvin. Our brices they are still modest. But next week they will be — " He closed his eyes and threw his head back, a crafty agony.

"That's what you always say."

"Pomade," said Mira.

"Quart jar, year's supply." Jaganathy leaned forward and cupped his hand over his mouth. "We are getting nationalice," he whispered hoarsely. He grinned, but there was no pleasure in the grin.

"Tea caddy."

"Nationalized?"

"*Collapsible* tea caddy. I throw in nice tea cosy half brice," said Jaganathy. "Nationalice. You have not heard? Osbong is taking over all retail businesses in town, dry-goods shops. Just" — he pulled the tassels of the tea cosy with his long fingers — "like that."

"He can't do that. It's against the law."

"Blandy bottle."

"South African, one case V.S.O.P., aged on the train from

Capetown, ha-ha!" Jaganathy wedged the case into the coffin, groaning. He straightened his back. "The law, the law! He will nationalice law, too! They will nationalice our backsides and tax our shit." He turned to Mira, "Wireless from Japan? Radiogram?"

Mira said yes.

"Nice tunes with these," he panted, heaving them. "I tell you Osbong has no money. Trouble all over. Chaps want to kill him. He is vexed. What to do? He needs cash so he takes over my trading gompany. I am obliged to work for him. I am baid—" Jaganathy gave Calvin another mirthless grin "—a *salary,* if you blease." He spat.

Mira bought a Jim Reeves album, a Mildred Mafuya record, a watch made in Hong Kong, five Indian bangles, a book.

Jaganathy wheezed. "Watch out, Mr. Calvin. They will nationalice your business, too."

"They won't make any money on me," said Calvin. "I'm running at a loss." As soon as he said it he thought of Ogilvie's endowment and looked at Mira.

Mira bought a tennis racket, some earrings, five headscarves, a nickel-plated fountain pen.

"Osbong can do anything. Farmerly, it was difficult. Now it is, *ptah,* simple," said Jaganathy. "Super handbag made of blastic. Bocket mirror."

"Two," said Mira.

"If they tried that in the States there'd be trouble," said Calvin. "They'd never get away with it."

"This is not States, thank you," said Jaganathy. He wrapped two handbags, two pocket mirrors.

"Well, I don't know anything about politics. I suppose they've got some reason for doing it."

"Reasons! Of course, blenty reasons! They need money so they steal from us. Bathing towels? Shower cap? Ladies' gloves?"

"They're not stealing—they're nationalizing your business."

Jaganathy looked angrily at Calvin. "You Europeans give these blacks such big words. I speak Chinyanja very well. In this language there is no word *nationalice*. They get from you. Tomorrow you give them another one, and they will rob us another way. They are goons. Girdles fresh from Liverpool? Sockings?"

"So you're blaming us for your problems?"

The coffin was full. A tea chest was brought, and the items for which Mira had nodded assent — the girdles, the stockings — were dropped in. Mira took out a stocking and started to examine it. Jaganathy took it from her and stretched it before her face as if he was working a concertina. He spoke to Calvin. "I blame no one. But I tell you one thing. At one time, not many years before this, beeple here were so timid. They stole nothing. They liked to smile at we Indians. Hello, *bwana*, good morning, *bwana*, cheerio, *muli bwanji*. You leave the door to your go-down unlocked. Your house. Bantry, larder. Many imported goods inside, wireless berhaps. These Africans see no locks, but they do not blace a finger on anything. This is true. They were mice. Little mice. Now," said Jaganathy, "they want to kill us. I ask you one question — why?" He snapped the stocking into the tea chest.

"Big teddy bear."

"Look," said Calvin, "whose country is this?"

"I agree it's not mine," said Jaganathy. "But is it theirs?" He wrapped the teddy bear and put it in the tea chest.

"Of course it's their country," said Calvin.

"Necklace, with gold beads."

"Excellent choice, madam," said Jaganathy. He turned to Calvin. "Monkey swings on tree. He eats nice fruit there. He is jolly. He sits on branches. He likes tree very much. But," said Jaganathy, poking a sharp finger into Calvin's face, "does tree *belong* to monkey?" He shrugged, sheathing his finger in his pants pocket. "That happens in countries also."

"I think you're being pretty rotten," said Calvin. "Pretty rotten."

135

"It's true I am a simple man, just a foolish trader. I am sorry to upset you and your wife, but — "

"She's not my wife," said Calvin. "She's an African! And she's got as much right to be here as you do."

"She is welcome," said Jaganathy. "I thought she was your wife."

"Me wife," said Mira. "This *mwamuna wanga,* my husband."

"Not yet, sweetheart," said Calvin. "In a week or so — "

"No," said Mira.

"I take your word for it, Mr. Calvin. She owes me pounds one hundred and twenty-one, osbongs sixteen only." He smiled at Mira and added, "Gash."

Calvin had filed the claims before. But he was unprepared for what had happened in the three days since Ogilvie had been beheaded in Rumpi. Here was Mira counting bills into Jaganathy's open hand. Virtually a waif, Mira was paying half of Ogilvie's endowment to the doomed Indian for a load of junk. Calvin could not look. There was no wisdom, nobody prospered; there hadn't been much grief, only fear, for Mira refused to tell Calvin why the soldiers had killed Ogilvie, and now she didn't remember. The event was lost, like any event that takes place in a jungle: Ogilvie was turned into money, and the money into junk and discarded. Perhaps that was what all insurance could be reduced to.

*   *   *

Witnessed by Major Beaglehole and Bailey, the marriage between Calvin Mullet (condition: divorced) and Mira Nirenda (condition: spinster) was performed in the office of the government agent, Blantyre, in the last week in February. The dingy office was decorated with faded views of the lake and some of wild obtuse-looking animals, a mop-maned lion staring at his paws, a glabrous hippo kneeling at a puddle's edge, his bristly chin resting in the water, his armored buttocks aloft.

Calvin and Mira stood; Major Beaglehole and Bailey sat on camp chairs, tacky things with woven plastic backs and seats.

A worn blotter on a dented table was imprinted with an almost Arabic configuration of reversed signatures, one over the other, spidery and black, all sloping the wrong way. The ceremony was performed by an aged African in a threadbare double-breasted suit with broad winglike lapels. He read out of a leatherbound law book, turning from dog-ear to dog-ear. In ten minutes it was all over, the signatures were appended to the perforated marriage certificate. Beaglehole prefaced his name with three initials; Bailey licked the ball point, stifled a whiffling belch, and wrote her name laboriously, smudging the certificate with her thumbs.

It was a dry legal ritual, brief, ordinary, final until divorce. The bride and groom did not kiss; the elderly black man shook them by the hand and wished them good luck. He had a kind smile. Calvin smiled back. This was joy. Love required a kind of genius Calvin knew he did not have. It was a vertigo of mortal loneliness he had felt. Fortunately it was loneliness and not desire: her simple presence was a satisfaction. It was all he needed; she was safe. He had once desired the tender knowing body of his small-souled former wife. But they had not shared anything; they had only conspired to live together and she had made him more lonely, for desire, like appetite, was temporary: it was whisked away with a grunt. Loneliness endured without desire's hungry initiative; it was weak, it whined, wanting company. This, with black Mrs. Mira Mullet, Calvin had. Married, Calvin felt as if a warm sunset had been gathered from the black branches of a distant grove of trees and cleverly squeezed into his belly.

Part Three

20

Marais was dead. He had been gunned down on a city street, shot in the back while crossing the wide Rua da Boa Vista in Beira, Mozambique. The Portuguese secret police had pounced on him; his capture was announced in a thick headline in the *Noticias da Beira*. He was placed immediately in solitary confinement; torture was rumored. The South African government asked for his extradition, to stand trial for the post office bomb in Johannesburg. But he was not extradited. There was a brief closed trial in Lourenço Marques. Marais was found guilty of treason and condemned to death. He was swiftly hanged.

As the days passed, detail was added. The authorities said he had pleaded for mercy and died a coward's death; he had given the names of all his lieutenants. An unmailed letter was found among his effects, in his own handwriting, in which he said that every man, woman and child of Portuguese origin would be killed, and that at night you would hear their blood running in the drains and choking the sewers. Much was made of the phrase *hear their blood*. Privately it was whispered that Marais had been brave at the moment of death, his last words,

"Now I will show you how a man dies." He had leaped on the rope and broken his own neck before the hangman could mask him or spring the trap.

In his name a farm was attacked and burned, the owner murdered. Five Africans were picked up; they readily confessed, were sentenced and put to death, and their last words were that they would die as Marais had, bravely. They were shot, in public, in a bullring just outside Beira.

Marais heard of the execution of the five men in September. He was in a café in Vila Cabral, wearing a brown Franciscan cassock and fingering a rosary; a helpful planter translated the Portuguese article into French, bought Marais a glass of port and asked to be blessed. Marais made the sign of the cross at table level and piously moved his lips. Then he raised the cowl of his cassock and pulled it over his head; he boarded the train for the lake.

He had reason to doubt the story of the five Africans, for he had read of his own hanging three weeks before in the *Noticias,* and he knew the PIDE had faked it. But he was heartened by the power of the lie: he was now convinced that when he did die it would matter. The planter had believed both stories and so, he said, did his tenants and their Africans.

The shooting was true. Three or four hard inches of his spine still gave him pain. Using two mirrors he had looked at the scar where the bullet had gouged muscle and nicked several vertebrae, a roughened purplish bruise on an awkward part of his back. He felt the wound tugging at him when he ran or lifted something; he imagined it would hurt if he made love, but with the Franciscan habit he had taken a vow of celibacy. He looked at the scar only once; the one look killed his interest. But others could see it. It had silenced the mission priest who cauterized it and sponged it with alcohol. It was important to Marais that others were moved by it. It was proof he had been shot. And he knew what people would say: "Marais was shot . . . in the back."

Sheepishly he went first class, intending disguise, not comfort. But when he got out at Metangula he saw three white-clad priests emerge from a third-class compartment. At the railhead he took the lake steamer to Karonga where he set out on foot for the prearranged spot on the Songwe River, at the northern frontier of Malawi, where he was to meet his men, who were marching from Dar es Salaam. He wondered if they had read of his death; they were already a week overdue.

Hope came unexpectedly one night, eight days after his arrival. He saw some nearby hills burning: snakes of tropical flame wriggled sideways to the summits of the hills, and the low forest around him also took fire. Where the stems were thick and the blades below dry there was a crackling like the rattling of muskets. Some old trunks of trees slowly lit and continued to burn all night. The fire passed on behind his camp and along the ridge parallel to the river. All around him the flames devoured old grass, with the violent appetite of passion. It was the burning season he had read about; everything in Africa was burned once a year or nothing new would grow. Marais watched with excitement; his clothes, his face were heated by the flames. He was alone, the only witness to the fire, and soon the shelter he had made of branches burned. All night he stood on the road, watching the flames, like the eager poet in love who waits sleeplessly for dawn. He threw the hooded cassock and the rosary beads into the flames. He saw himself a fire raiser bringing his own torch to decay.

By morning the fire was out; Marais woke to black hills and fields spiked by charred tree trunks. It was through this, across the smoldering turf of a black meadow, that his men came, a file of fifty, in sooty uniforms. They stopped when they saw Marais. The white man at the head of the column brightened and came forward with his hand out.

"They think you're a stiff," the new leader said, offering Marais a clammy hand.

The men looked at Marais as if at a zombie, a walking corpse

— a familiar demon to them, but nonetheless scary: it was deathless and drank human blood and could assume the shape of any animal. Nothing could kill it. None of the men would speak to Marais. They stood uneasily in the black meadow, with their rifles and packs still slung over their shoulders.

"Dead, see? We read about that business in L.M. You're the last person I expected to see, but I'm goddamned glad you're here. It's been sheer fucking hell. The food is lousy. I've got things in my hair, I've been *walking* ever since Mbeya. And you can't get a cold beer in this banana republic either." The man shook his head and smiled gratefully in relief. "Anyway, this is your show now. They're pretty stupid but they're itching to taste blood. You won't have any trouble. Oh, by the way, my name's Harry."

"Where's the van?"

"We ditched it," said Mr. Harry. He pointed behind him, without looking back at the black hills, the black tree spikes. "Somewhere back there. They ganged up on me, wouldn't let me drive. Jesus, are they stubborn! One of them drove. I said take it easy, but they drive like loons. They knocked the sump off somehow, probably on a sticking-up rock. The engine seized, the radiator got disconnected, everything went wrong, don't ask me how. It's a Czech van or, I don't know, maybe Bulgarian. No spares. Don't talk to me about the van. Believe me, it was a problem."

"You were supposed to be carrying ammo and blasting powder in it. And guns — what about the extra rifles that were in the van?"

"Some we took with us," said Mr. Harry. "And some we left." Mr. Harry smiled. "I thought you didn't need anything fancy like that. In Dar they say, 'Oh, Marais. He can make a bomb out of an old alarm clock and a couple of boxes of match heads. Too bad they knocked him off,' they said. So what's the problem?"

"You left live ammo in the bush," said Marais. "You know

what will happen if someone finds that stuff? Did you think about that?"

"The engine seized, they were all bitching and moaning. I told them to take what they could carry and leave the rest. I wanted to stick to the schedule."

"You're two weeks late."

"The fires held us up. These people burn everything! And I was sick, I didn't feel — " Mr. Harry broke off suddenly and looked around. He saw that the soldiers were still in the field, out of earshot, watching. He put his face close to Marais's. "Don't talk to me that way," he said in a rapid whisper, twisting his face. "Understand? I don't like to be talked to like that. I get crazy. I hate it, see? So cut it out! If you want to give orders you can hustle over there and give them. But don't give *me* that crap. I busted my ass getting down here. They told me to come. 'Marais's dead,' they said, 'it's your show, Harry.' I started getting crazy with all their do-this and do-that. I'm in the political section, I said. We don't walk in the political section, we don't camp out in the rain, we don't eat shit. But they told me to come. So I came. So fuck you and get off my back."

Marais stared at Mr. Harry whose shirt was unbuttoned to the navel, whose boozy gasping and low-slung paunch indicated a heavy drinker. He looked hungry, and glumly out of his element. His boot laces were in knots, his neck burned red, his dark loose lips threatened drool. His hair fell in straight oily blades, parted in the middle, to frame his sweating face. He was obviously suffering, but Marais did not like the craziness of his feeble panic.

"You lost the van," said Marais coldly.

"I'm telling you I didn't lose no van," said Mr. Harry. "It's there, in the boondocks. We put it in a hut. Ask them where it is, they're a bunch of geniuses. They'll tell you."

"Okay," said Marais. "Now you listen to me. I don't know you. I don't know where they found you. I've never heard of you. But let's get one thing straight. This is an army. As long as you stay with us you take orders, just like everyone else. If that doesn't suit you, you can clear out."

Mr. Harry smiled. He nodded and examined Marais's face. Then he asked, "How old are you, sonny?"

"What difference does it make?"

"You ashamed of it?"

"No," said Marais. "I'm twenty-seven."

Mr. Harry laughed loudly, opening his mouth in Marais's face. He had a cracked laugh; he pumped it, then said, "Twenty-seven! Twenty-seven years old! Jesus Christ, do you know how old *I* am? Go ahead, wise-ass, take a guess."

Marais shook his head at Mr. Harry's white-flecked mustache, his dirty shirt, the loose slick neck, the clotted nostrils, the dead gray eyes. "I don't guess," he said. He walked past Mr. Harry and went over to the soldiers, watching them fade back as he approached. He told them to line up, but as soon as he opened his mouth two men broke into a run.

"They think you're a stiff!" Mr. Harry called, and he laughed again. Marais sprinted after the men and coaxed them back. Mr. Harry was in the road taking off his boots when he looked up and saw all the men standing in the black smoking meadow, in files of ten. There was not a green thing anywhere, and even the sun was hidden in smoke haze.

After dinner that evening Marais explained in detail his three-month journey, from Leopoldville to Luanda, to Johannesburg and Beira. Angola, Mozambique and South Africa all had to be fought; but there were better ways than Mondlane's. Osbong was collaborating with these racist governments; he had captured Mondlane's men and locked them up because he wanted to stay on friendly terms with the Portuguese who let him use the port of Beira, and the South Africans who promised financial aid. Malawi was a crucial country, a corridor into all the white-controlled countries. Once it was in sympathetic hands the other places would be easy. Malawi gave access to Tanzania; it had a railroad, a big airport outside Blantyre, planes. And Malawi was the easiest place to take; the landscape was mountainous, heavily forested, excellent terrain to hide in. There were only three points to capture: the border post in the north, Lilongwe, and Blantyre.

The men listened in silence; they sat rigidly, staring as if at a ghost. None had spoken.

"You're wondering how I got away from the Portuguese and how I came here. Okay, I'll tell you." Marais explained the shooting in the Beira street, how he had scrambled into a tenement and eluded the police, staying for weeks in a township of half-castes and then disguising himself as a priest. "They lied about catching me — they wanted to demoralize Mondlane."

He could not tell if the men accepted his explanation; he was not sure they spoke English. Later, Harry brought Marais a box. Marais removed his shirt to prise the cover off. He caught sight of the men staring at his strangely lunar bruise in the firelight. They whispered.

Marais removed the contents from the box, a .45 caliber pistol, greasy clips of shells, a first-aid kit wrapped in cloth, a stack of neatly folded shirts, eight boxes of cigars, a coil of green fuse.

"There was a bottle of whisky in there. I put it in myself," said Marais. "Where is it?"

The men looked down. They had seen the scar and now, with Marais close to them, asking about his whisky, they saw the collar of raw skin around his neck where the hangman's rope had strangled him. He was dead. Their leader was a *mfiti*, a demon.

"What happened to that bottle?"

Mr. Harry spoke up. "We didn't know you were gonna be here, did we? You were supposed to be dead, right? So we drank the whisky. I mean, *I* drank it. I didn't want any drunks around the place. They were bad enough when they were sober."

"You opened that box," said Marais. "I gave orders that my box should be brought from Dar *unopened*."

"You don't look like a drinking man," said Mr. Harry. "What are you worried about?"

"I don't care about the whisky. But I wanted that box kept shut."

"We thought you were dead," said Mr. Harry. He appealed to the men. "We didn't know he was alive, did we? We thought he was dead, didn't we? Go on, tell him."

The men stared. For them he was still dead.

"What else did you touch?"

"Nothing. The whisky, that was all. Have a look for yourself."

Marais felt in the bottom of the box and took out a plastic bag with notebooks sealed inside, three slim copy books.

"So that's what you're bothered about!" laughed Mr. Harry.

"Did you mess around with these?" asked Marais. The edge of his voice was intimidating.

"What would I want with them? I'm no bookworm." He wiped his mouth. "I wish there was a drink around this place. I'm leaving for Blantyre tomorrow."

Marais peeled off the tape which sealed the notebooks. He asked for a lantern. With the men before him, reluctantly squatting close, near the embers of the fire and the remains of food on tin plates, Marais opened one notebook to the first page and read in a slow reasonable voice, "A revolution is not a dinner party, or writing an essay, or painting a picture, or doing embroidery. It cannot be so refined, so leisurely and gentle, so temperate, kind, courteous, restrained and magnanimous." He paused and said, "Magnanimous — it means bighearted." The men watched him white eyed, knotting their fingers. Marais stopped reading in a teaching voice. He exhorted now, in a voice tinged with excitement, "A revolution is an insurrection! It is an act of violence by which one class overthrows another." He snapped the book shut and placed it on the ground.

Mr. Harry squinted at the neatly printed label on the cover. It read *Principles of Revolt*. He nudged Marais, who was looking from face to face for a reaction, and he whispered, "I used to write stuff like that, when I was about your age." He smirked.

"Do you understand?" Marais faced the men across the fire; their faces were lighted by the flames.

"You gotta do better than that," said Mr. Harry. "They don't speak English too hot. I used a translator."

Marais stood up and peered at them. He punched his palm and said, "I'm asking you, do you understand? A revolution is an act of violence! It means killing!"

The men were startled by the sudden change in his voice. They looked around. One began to clap, slowly, with cupped hands. Another took it up, and another, in the same rhythm; and soon they were all clapping. It was not applause; it was the slapping of respect that was accorded to chiefs and elders. Now it was very loud, and several men gave an approving tongue-yodeling howl. The clapping increased its rhythm to a quick cracking, and with such loudness that Mr. Harry slid back from the fire into the shadows and unsheathed the black bayonet that was strapped to his belt.

*   *   *

That was their first meeting. Marais did not see Mr. Harry again until the slaughterous day in February when the two men were tortured, the murderer, the rapist. In four months Mr. Harry had become fatter, his loose flesh had filled, he wore a flowered shirt; in his trouser pocket there was the obvious bulge of a pistol. He had knelt behind Marais, watching Brother Mussa struggling against the hail of stones; he had seen Marais give the order to stop, which was unheard by the men, forcing Marais to run over to Brother Mussa and cover him with his arms, ending the torture. Brother Mussa was dragged out of the hole.

Marais supervised the bandaging and ordered the hole to be filled in. Mr. Harry waited for Marais, and later in the evening, when Marais returned to his square tent, Mr. Harry showed him a bottle of whisky. "I owe you this."

"Come inside," said Marais, entering the tent and hanging a lantern from the center pole. The walls of the tent were stacked high with crates of liquor. "We have plenty. They've looted every bar from here to the border."

Mr. Harry eyed the crates and swallowed thirstily. He whistled, the old way of showing surprise, and said, "It looks okay to me. You could have a real booze-up if you wanted. But you don't sound too happy about it."

"They stole this stuff," said Marais. He looked at the wet rope end of his cigar and added, "I wish that was all they had done." He sighed and looked again at Harry. "You saw the punishments. I was trying to avoid that, but they had to be taught a lesson."

"Tough lesson," said Mr. Harry. "All I did was pull a knife on them when they got out of line."

"I had to show them that I meant what I said."

"Don't explain to *me,*" said Mr. Harry.

Marais threw the damaged cigar on the floor and shook a new one from a metal tube. Lighting it he said, "They had to be punished."

"Maybe so," said Mr. Harry. He found a glass and wiped the inside of the rim with his finger, then settled into a chair and polished the glass on his sleeve. He poured some whisky in, sloshed it, and sipped. With a wet half smile he said, "They'll kill you for that."

"They'll be lucky if they can walk."

"I don't mean the guys you tortured — "

"Punished," said Marais.

"Punished," smiled Mr. Harry. He sipped again and licked his lips. "I mean the others. Now it's you against them. They hate your guts for that. Someday, when you think everything's rosy they're gonna surprise you. They'll jump all over you and *wham-o.*" He drank again. "I seen it happen before. Jungle bunnies," said Mr. Harry. "Jungle bunnies."

"How did you get up here?" asked Marais.

"I got me a nice car now," said Mr. Harry. "There was a lot of dummies on the road. I've marked the roadblocks on my map. They tried to give me lip. They didn't reckon on old Harry pulling rank on them. I brought them some crates of food, cans of stuff, cookies and crap like that. I'm your mess officer, I says, just delivering this to you boys — you're doing a fine job. Naturally they believed it. They believe anything. They don't even have passwords. It's pathetic."

"You hate them, don't you?"

"Me? I don't hate anyone. I got a wife and kids," said Mr. Harry. He said it with feeling, as if claiming a disability, like a gimpy leg. "I just don't trust people like you do. But I think you're learning. I watched that poor bastard getting the rocks on his nut and I said to myself, yup, Marais don't trust them either these days." Harry grinned. "You think I'm an old fart, but I'll tell you something. The trouble with you is you trusted them before. So when they let you down you hate them. Me, I *expect* them to let me down. I keep an eye on the loyal ones, the ones that are always doing what they're told. I figure they must have an angle or why would they be so nice? Anyway, I suppose it don't matter."

"It matters," said Marais. "They know when you don't trust them. They can sense it."

"They can't sense shit," said Mr. Harry. He poured himself another whisky. "As long as they get theirs they don't care what we think. They care if you kick their asses, though. Like you just did. Call it punishment if you want. We used to have other names for it. Whatever you call it they don't like it any better. So don't say I didn't warn you, okay?"

"We can't have them pushing people around," said Marais.

"I heard all that before. It's natural. Who cares?"

"I care. I'm not going to be here long. As soon as we take Blantyre I'm moving back to Dar. I gave myself a year and I'm sticking to it. It's their show after that."

"The Lone Ranger," said Mr. Harry. He pushed his hair

back, accentuating the white part down the middle of his head. "So what do you want me to do?"

"What you've been doing. Sit in Blantyre and keep smiling. We hit Lilongwe in six weeks and bring it to a halt. We'll try to recruit some more men there to hold it. Then we'll move into Blantyre."

"Like shit through a tin horn," said Mr. Harry. "It sounds nice. But I figure you're a little behind schedule."

"We'll make it up. What about your end?"

"We got it married. You could crash into Blantyre tomorrow if you wanted. I know my job. Everything's staked out."

"Just remember, we do it quick. I don't like sloppy revolts. They don't work — you make enemies that way. If you can't do it quick, then don't do it. That's what — "

"They're still fighting in Angola," said Mr. Harry, patting his mustache.

"I talked to Holden in Leo. I told him he's wasting his time."

"I got some buddies there," said Mr. Harry. "They've had some terrific strikes in the mines. They know what they're doing."

Marais snorted. "They don't know the first thing about it."

"Says you."

Marais put his arms on the table and leaned toward Mr. Harry. "They don't know the first thing about it," he said, drumming his knuckles on the map. The map was spattered with cigar ash; inked crosses, marking roadblocks, ran where they had been splashed with whisky.

"But *you* know, don't you?" said Mr. Harry. "Twenty-seven years old and you got all the answers. It's lots of fun, isn't it? All the glory boys marching in and beating up the simps at the roadblocks! You make me laugh. A tin-pot little place like this with a tin-pot dictator who doesn't know his ass from a hole in the ground. It's a pushover! I've seen places like this taken in a week, a lousy *week!*"

"We're doing it right," said Marais.

"Don't give me that," said Mr. Harry. "You're enjoying yourself the same as me. Only you make a big deal out of it and I don't."

"We're both in this together," said Marais.

"You think so. But there's a difference between you and me, pal. For one thing, I do it for the money and you don't. As long as they pay up I'm working. But you — you make it into a big scientific study. Sure, I heard all your Chairman Mao bullshit. That's the way they talk in Dar, passing out books, having meetings, this and that. It's enough to drive you nuts. Give me the plane fare to Blantyre, I told them. I'll find a trigger and get Osbong knocked off. Then we see what happens. No, they said, we're doing it Marais's way, as if you have all the answers. They almost pissed their pants when they read about your bomb in Jo'burg. He just messed up some letters and killed an old lady, I said. They wouldn't listen. So I come all the way down here and see you bouncing rocks off your own men. Wow, do you give me cramps."

"I know what the score is," said Marais.

"Sure you do," said Mr. Harry. "But I'll tell you something. To those jungle bunnies out there you're just another fucking *mzungu* bastard looking for a little action."

"I think you've had too much to drink," said Marais. He took the whisky bottle off the table and placed it beside his chair. He smoothed the map and said, "Now give me a rundown on the roadblocks from here to Lilongwe. What kind of rifles do they have? What kind of cover?"

Mr. Harry glared at Marais. "You're writing some kind of book, aren't you?" He spoke with contempt.

"That's my business," said Marais.

"Chapter One," Mr. Harry mocked, holding his glass up. "How we beat up the simps at the roadblocks and raised the flag — "

"It's not like that," said Marais.

"Yes, it is," said Mr. Harry. "I read all those books. I know what you're doing. Big scientific Chairman Mao bullshit, with bells ringing and all the flags waving. Nobody gets dirty — "

Marais reached quickly across the table and pinched Mr. Harry's windpipe, shutting off Mr. Harry's gagging voice and making his eyes pop.

"Revolution is rape," said Marais. "I don't enjoy it. It's vicious, but it's quick, and no one ever forgets it. You won't forget this one, Harry, I promise you."

Mr. Harry pushed Marais's hand away from his throat. He swallowed painfully and rubbed at the spot Marais had pinched. "You'd do that to them," said Mr. Harry. "They're gonna kill you, sonny."

"No," said Marais. "They're going to thank all of us, because when it's all over they'll realize that we've been raping a whore. That's what revolution is."

Mr. Harry started to reply, but voices outside the tent stopped him. He listened and crooked his head. Marais got up and flung the flap of the door back. Three men stood before him.

"What do you want?"

"*Achimwene* Mussa," said one. "*Wafa.*"

Marais walked over to the table again and sat. The three men remained at the door, waiting for an answer.

"What's up?" asked Mr. Harry.

"The man we stoned," said Marais softly. "He's dead."

Mr. Harry closed his eyes in concentration, studied forcefully for a few moments, pursed his lips, and then brought up a honking belch. He directed it at Marais as if it was a reflection, and when he finished he said, "That's one son of a bitch who's not gonna thank you."

21

The wedding presents were two: Bailey gave the couple her
best double room, rent free for two months; Major Beaglehole
gave them his Matchless motorcycle and a full tank of gas. And
no one at the eating house found it unusual that the day
after his marriage Calvin slept late and didn't go to the office.
There were jokes in the bar; as witnesses to the ceremony, as
the only gift givers, Bailey and Beaglehole took a kindly pro-
prietorial interest in the couple and spoke for them: "Honey-
mooners," said Bailey; "Not wasting a minute," said Beaglehole. "He'll be back to the office soon." After a week there
were no more jokes, but there was talk. Calvin was seen every
afternoon on the verandah, with his long legs braced against
the rail, with a bottle of beer clenched between his knees.
He had stopped going to the office. Major Beaglehole wondered if something wasn't, as he put it, "profoundly the matter."

"Nothing's wrong," said Calvin to the major. "I just don't
sell insurance anymore, that's all." Calvin did not tell Beaglehole, but his interest in insuring people had died with Ogilvie
(fully protected and paid up); he resolved not to delude any
more Africans by offering the false hope of a policy.

But his concern for Africans, undiminished, took other forms. Instead of calling attention to the future he repeated the Chinyanja proverb "What comes doesn't beat a drum" and reminded the Africans of how lucky they were to live in a simple country where poinsettias grew wild and no one starved. He pointed out the greenery of the jungle salad, and indicated (from the verandah, where he sat and drank) the dozens of people stretched out in the free shade of the trees. He warned against complication, he smiled at their alarm.

The alarm was recent, and not more than a month old, acute. For some reason the Africans in Blantyre were plagued by intimations of disaster. In a chaotic way they petitioned Calvin for help. The Homemakers' Mutual brochures, sent months previously and all but forgotten by Calvin, were having a marked effect: many people wanted policies.

"Wanting inner-surance," an African would say, with a new worrying wheedle in his voice and a stammering of the body, hand-wringing and glancing around the verandah where Calvin sat with Mira and a bottle of beer.

"What's the rush?" was Calvin's usual reply.

"Wanting money," the African would go on, then pausing as if to single out the worst verb, "to achieve wireless set."

"Simple as pie," Calvin's new formula ran. "Instead of paying us four osbongs a week, put that money under your bed. In a couple of months you'll have enough to buy a very nice radio. Now, how about a beer?"

It was soon the end of March; the rains were less frequent, there was a good breeze. Calvin's marriage to Mira was completion, he was convinced of his happiness, and only once since his marriage had he agreed to insure someone: a very old lady.

She had come to him with a paper bag full of money. She could not bank it — the Barclay's Bank had recently been nationalized and all the strongboxes in the vault emptied by Osbong's men.

"Go," said Calvin, "and dig a hole in the ground, inside your hut. Put the money there. It will be very safe."

The old lady did as she was told, but after a few weeks she disinterred the paper bag to count the money again, and she discovered that ants or perhaps termites had chewed the bills to shreds. Calvin insured her, accepting the confetti of her cash. But he ended her policy when he had a remedy for the termites. He refunded her money, giving her new bills for the shreds, and told her to sprinkle the bills with goat piss before she buried it. This would, he said, repel all insects and keep the money safe.

The sort of insurance Africans needed, Homemakers' Mutual did not sell. Ogilvie was dead, the minister of defense was dead; there were rumors of worse. Extra money wouldn't help anyone — it would only make him more liable to theft. A person who appeared the least bit prosperous was nationalized and burgled; if he refused he got his skull cracked by the Youth Wingers. Insurance: there was no future in it; Africans needed it like a hole in the head. And the country (not a country, more a wild little parish) was bankrupt, underpopulated and shrinking like a cheap shirt. To Calvin it wasn't foreign anymore: usually it was a broiling hot nothingness, sometimes it was unaccountably cold, it was doused occasionally by rain, a heavy mist obscured it in the early morning. The phenomena were friendly, the clouds of dust sifting back to the road in the wake of a jeep, the startling sameness of glorious sunsets, the flowering trees always in season: all very routine, usual, familiar — the beauty had a trustworthy permanence.

Understanding everything, Calvin was not contemptuous of the place. He stopped comparing Malawi to Massachusetts — though Malawi came out well in that comparison. (There was no Mafia in Malawi, there was less graft on Chichiri Hill than on Beacon Hill, and the Brahmins in Blantyre were real ones, not descendants of bootleggers as in Boston.) Calvin stopped sizing up the Africans. He was concerned about them, but this was no special feeling. Provoked, he defended them. The girls at the eating house were black, the customers never were. Calvin was seldom provoked: in whorehouses there was complete integration. For this Calvin was grateful. He had begun to realize that the defenders of the underdog were in that pose an unpleasant minority all their own, but more vocal than the genuinely oppressed. Calvin had been touched by their apparently sincere accusation; he had once indulged in this himself. Now he was unmoved by them: with their bugles out and in their screeching simplicities they were a type of underdog themselves. But unworthy, they were unbearable, like the beggar who has more coins in his outstretched hand than you have in your pocket. They were always foreigners, they were big bores. It was a relief to be rid of that impulse to preach, that yen to save lives. For what?

The arrival of Mira seemed to sweeten Major Beaglehole's disposition: he stopped mentioning blacks with malice, and Bailey too exhausted her curses. They often drank together, inviting Mira inside to join them at their table. Calvin heard them from where he sat, the old man's voice rising to the climax of a story: ". . . seen your picture on the mantlepiece . . ."; ". . . had to scoop him up with a shovel . . ."; ". . . forgotten all my Urdu now . . ." There was always a fourth at their table, a man named Jack Mavity, who was married to an African woman and who dragged three bushy-haired yellow children with him wherever he went. The eldest was only six, the others much younger. They pissed on the bar floor and took turns slapping it.

Mavity always had news. It was he who reported seeing Mr. Harry in town. He reported it in a way that caused Major Beaglehole discomfort. Mavity reached over one day, interrupting the old man in a story; he switched on Major Beaglehole's hearing aid and turned it to loud. Major Beaglehole, hearing the thunder of his own voice, stopped talking. "There's a new face in town!" shouted Mavity, not into Major Beaglehole's ear but into the small enamel box which hung on the harness around Major Beaglehole's neck.

"Good God, Jack, don't do that!" Major Beaglehole winced at the ferocity of his words. He retuned and said, "What new face — who?"

"In the Zambesi," said Mavity. "He looks a drinker, he does."

"He's bound to turn up sooner or later," said Major Beaglehole.

"We'll make him feel welcome when he does," said Bailey.

Mavity watched the door, hoping the man would stop in for a drink. But all Mavity saw was Calvin, sitting in what used to be known as the major's chair, with a bottle of beer in his lap and his legs propped against the verandah rails. Sometimes Mavity would stand near Calvin and stare at the street, and he would sigh and sigh until Calvin asked him what was wrong.

"Oh, God," Mavity would say. "I could tell you stories."

"About the Africans." Calvin disliked Mavity, but he could not refuse to talk to him. They both had black wives: Mavity took this as something like kinship. But because he was married to an African Mavity felt free to abuse them.

"Yes, about the Africans," said Mavity. "They wear bandages and sticking plasters on their legs. They all do. But the queer thing is — *there isn't a thing wrong with their legs.* Them bandages are for decoration. Yes, it's a fashion. Can you believe it?"

On occasion Mavity would be reading about Americans in the paper, the *Rhodesia Herald* or the *Bulawayo Chronicle*. He never explained what he read; he smashed the paper to the floor and walked out to the verandah and said accusingly to Calvin: "Now you're giving them rockets" or "So you think ten million quid isn't enough for a jackass of a dictator?" or "You and your flipping computers!" Once Mavity said, looking over the top of the paper he was reading on the verandah, "It says here you're going to the moon."

Most of the time Mavity watched the door for the man he had seen at the Zambesi. And one day Mavity said, "There he is."

Mr. Harry was being carried by two Africans, one on each

arm. He was blowing through his lips and spattering his mustache. The two Africans steered him up the stairs and through the swinging doors to the edge of the bar counter. Mavity watched, fascinated. The fat waiter eyed Mr. Harry and poured out a tot of whisky. When Mr. Harry raised his head and reached for the drink, Mavity recognized him, and winked.

"I think I know that man," said Calvin, who had wandered inside to watch the drunken man supported by the two Africans. Everyone — Mira, Bailey, Major Beaglehole, the girls — watched.

But Mr. Harry was guzzling whisky and did not see them; the drink was running down his chin. He had several more. He tottered and threatened to fall. The Africans gripped him and held him straight. Mr. Harry cursed, and tried to focus on the winking Mavity. The fat waiter poured another drink. Mr. Harry picked it up and touched it to his lips. But the little tot glass slipped through his fingers and smashed. He was drowsy, his head heavy.

"Time!" shouted Bailey to the fat waiter.

The fat waiter corked the bottle.

The two Africans held Mr. Harry tightly under the armpits and gently steered him out. They had trouble getting him through the door. One took him through, and Mavity went to the verandah and watched him being carried down the street, like an injured footballer, his ankles dragging.

"He didn't recognize me," said Mavity. "I don't think he saw me."

"I've seen him someplace," said Calvin, but gave the fat Mr. Harry no further thought. Calvin swigged his beer and watched the street and learned to prefer rainy days. The weather report on Radio Malawi never changed: mostly sunny, scattered clouds, the possibility of showers in the afternoon. They said that every day of the year, and most days were like that. But Calvin preferred the rain. Africans could smell the rain coming, sense the wind shifting; they ran in all directions as the sky blackened and the far-off patter of raindrops started. The rain was an event: it made steam rise from the heated street, and it flooded the drains. Often, trees were blown down in the storms. And it was during the storms that murders were committed and shops broken into. But the rain's sound was not what Calvin had thought of on the trip north: not the sound of riotous peasants or crying voices in the jungle. It was a thin regular patter of drops, small talk at a beer party, with a number of rising amused moments, wind-inspired, a kind of laughter. It made a change, and gave Calvin something to look forward to, for nowadays he never went to his office.

It was cruel to make those people there with plastic bags pulled over their heads, peddling their bicycles out of the rain's path, or sitting under the eaves of shop houses, much like Calvin, and like Calvin waiting for the diversion of a crashing tree or a boiling flood — it was cruel to make them think that they could be saved by insurance. The Africans sat; they were clumsy and perishable; they had a very old but very narrow culture. Nothing could or did happen to them, except death. Only storms diverted them but briefly, for the sun always returned to heat their heads. Nothing changed, not even a death in the family altered them, insurance never could. Some giant would have to snatch up the country like a clogged ketchup bottle and smack it violently on the bottom for it to change; but that would never happen either. And besides, the bottle might turn out to be empty.

In any case, it was not crucial. People missed the point about Africans. The alien hurried past, clucking at the Africans hunkered down in a bit of shade. All the goals of wealth and position, even the memory of slavery, and certainly the idea of so-called progress was the alien's own. Strangers upset the African by making him ashamed and calling his harmonic sense of peace laziness. What the stranger never saw was the blank smooth shrug on the face of the hunkered-down father, the jaunty twinkle in the eyes of the wood-carrying crone, and the delight of the naked black children flinging mud and jumping in puddles, or sailing reed-woven boats along the soapy plops of gray sewage in the open drain.

"What's going to happen to those children?" Calvin had once asked. The Africans had no answers. It was not their question.

The plague of flying ants convinced Calvin.

After a heavy rain they pulled themselves out of the ground, and crawled and flew in a pulsing swarm around the verandah rails and wooden steps of the eating house. They had done the same at the bungalow in Sunnyside Calvin had shared with his first wife. "Creepy-crawly," she had said. She hated them. She thought they carried disease. There were too many to kill. They could not fly straight. They were fat, their wings dropped off in shiny flakes on the floor, they exhausted themselves pelting against the lights.

Mavity said, "You're sending planes to dust the country with DDT." It was not only flying ants that were a menace, but also sausage flies, locusts and green grasshoppers. Calvin watched them swarm and waited for the planes. Sometimes the verandah was alive with them: they shinnied through the seams in the planks and held to the posts and banisters; they wiggled their bodies, and shook off their shiny wings; the coated wood rails seemed to move. The ants flew into Calvin's beer glass. It got so bad that he considered moving inside whenever the flying ants came.

On that day in March when there were so many flying ants on the verandah that Calvin skidded on them and forsook his insect-upholstered chair, he wondered whether instead of escaping into the bar he should go to the office and see what he could do about getting the ants destroyed. The U.N. might help; perhaps he should ask Mavity about the planes. A plague of insects was a Biblical punishment, but a little planning could wipe it out. It occurred to Calvin that for the first time in weeks he was thinking like an insurance man.

"Why you no sit on *khonde?*" one of the waiters asked.

"Ants," said Calvin, who was standing just inside the door, still in two minds about going to the office. "They're all over the place. I don't know how you put up with it." Several ants clung to Calvin's sleeve.

The waiter closely observed Calvin picking them off.

"Where you find?"

Calvin motioned toward the verandah.

But the waiter had already started out of the bar, and now he was gathering them up in his hands, bending this way and that. Calvin watched. Pausing at Calvin's feet the waiter looked up and nodded with enormous gratitude. Later the ants were fried and eaten; Calvin shared them, eating them with his hands off a square of newspaper. And the planes never came with the insecticide.

The flying ants, yellow beetles, the locusts, the sausage flies and *ngumbi* were not a plague, but a blessing, welcome as food and for the sport they afforded — the thrill of the chase. After that incident Calvin began noticing greasy sacks of them at the market; they had been there all along: but why had he not noticed them before? They were a treat, they had a nutty taste, not disagreeable at all.

From his shady verandah and primed with beer, Calvin saw angels in the black men's minds. He had spent more than a year trying to sell insurance. It was, like any stranger's, a charitable but deluded eagerness to help, like crop spraying or reporting on literacy or asking solemnly, "What's going to happen to those children?" Worse than simply pointless, it was in a word, corruption. Industry polluted, crop spraying made people hungry, tin roofs were hotter than thatch. And literacy simply frustrated and crazed: *The Uninsured* was proof of that. But did any stranger stay long enough to get the hang of the place? It was not that Calvin did not care; it was because he cared that he saw their angels and left them in peace and only spoke to alert them of a swarm of delicious insects. Calvin was married, complete, and happy; he was thirty; he felt jungle vibes in his skinny legs; he was (munching toasty fried ants) practically an African.

Eventually he had another look at *The Uninsured.* He was shopping with Mira (the endowment had dwindled to five hundred osbongs, but with all the shops nationalized there was little to buy) and looked up and saw the yellow wedge-shaped Agnello building and the Homemakers' Mutual sign. He sent Mira on her way and hurried upstairs. On the floor, amid dusty applications and empty ledgers and a progress chart neatly recording sales on a rising black line and stopping abruptly in the middle of February, Calvin found the manuscript.

It was thicker, bulkier than he remembered it. What a lot of work was in it! The pages were carefully numbered to 83, with some pinned in or glued over messy paragraphs; it was a secure much-labored-over bundle of foolscap in a loose-leaf binder with the title and *A. Jigololo* showing in a window on the spine. There were ovals of green mold on the covers of the binder. It had a quaint charm, like a newly discovered book, in the unknown author's own handwriting (cramped, concerned), found decaying in a trunk in a dusty attic, the Mullet Manuscript of the Jigololo Variorum, a credible forgery. If it had value it was the curiosity value that all irrelevant antiques have, washstands and flatirons: something bizarre rather than beautiful. But it embarrassed Calvin. What embarrassed him most was that no honest African could have written it. Only a fearfully unhappy white person could be the author of the distressed phrases Calvin saw as he flipped through it: . . . *My heart is heavy, my face is dirty, I hate everybody . . . I am slavishly aping the people who chained up my grandfather and sent him to Alabama . . . I suffer, I worry . . . I am the color of night, just a little voice in the jungle . . . We have an old proverb . . . Someday we rise up and kill the white man who . . . Would you insure me?*

Calvin's answer to that last question was no. Not you or anyone. Sentiment permitted him to put the manuscript into the top drawer of the desk. But he would add no more to the narrative. Now he knew the narrator.

22

The real narrator, in mood if not in fact, was not himself or the imaginary A. Jigololo, but that fat swart man, the waiter, whose name Calvin discovered was Jarvis Moore.

Calvin at first tried to avoid Jarvis. He was happy with Mira in the large room. But Mira was not the carefree person she had seemed at Christmas; she was more serious than the girl who had waved her hand in the Big Drum Bar and said, "That not name. That *signature*." She was for weeks after the marriage afraid of strangers, especially soldiers; and she jumped at loud noises. Calvin had once reached for a light pull and she had drawn back and covered her face, as if she expected to be struck, like the bully at the Big Drum Calvin had cowed at a handshake. She was quiet, catlike, purring beside him; he heard the fast thump of her heart. She would not leave Calvin's side.

Trust was harder than love, and Calvin was grateful for her loyalty; but he scarcely knew her. The few details he did know could not matter — that she had done two years of primary school and knew hymns and sums, that her parents were dead and now her brother, that she oiled her legs and cared about clothes, that she had, in the Hudson, Massachusetts, expression, a nice ass. She was still a girl, maybe seventeen, but in an even less recent youth she had learned what love was and not to trust it. It was plain that she had had lovers, for she knew how to be attentive to Calvin's passion: she looked on with feline wonder at Calvin's jungle antics, and did what she was told. It was also plain that her role had been victim, for she was indifferent to her own pleasure, apprehensive about his. To inquire anymore into that was to be pitying, and pity was a mood of contempt Calvin tried now to avoid. In the village, at Christmas, she had said, "We want you." Calvin translated the want as need, and though part of her interest undoubtedly was his type of color, the notoriety of being white in that place, she meant him, she began to trust. In the jungle, safety was more urgent than love, and had to be love's beginning: they began not by knowing but by needing.

He knew her temper, but in his ignorance of everything else he could not predict anything in her: a bonus, the promise of surprise giving its own special glamour. To have known just one of her jungle lovers would have been to deprive him of any surprise: the lover and the loved tattooed each other with the same marks, as Calvin's ex-wife had affected his sense. Lovers might be opposites, but duration always turned them into twins. What Calvin didn't know of Mira, all that soft darkness, drew him on. He was secure in that mystery; she was slim, busy with his body, and without any malice; she tasted of jungle, and she knew him as a protector.

That Calvin was kind in his possession was nothing new. He had been gentle with prostitutes to whom most men were brutal. He had pined away for little schoolgirls in shrunken uniforms and plastic sandals who passed by the eating house, and been jealous, too, when a bar waitress he had once slept with sat in another customer's lap a day later. He was made miserable by a girl who claimed that she had learned a particularly pleasing trick from an Italian tea planter in Cholo: it was a reminder of her use.

Calvin drank with gusto. Purely for the sake of appearances

he kept his office sign up: HOMEMAKERS' MUTUAL — FULL
PROTECTION — INSURE & SAVE THE CREATIVE WAY. But he
refused to sell anyone a policy. It was a racket, the worst on
earth. People only bought insurance for good luck: if you were
insured, so the folklore went, nothing bad happened to you.
That was a big load of crap; Calvin was sure that insurance cor-
rupted the next of kin. He told interested customers to save
their money, and when they had a fair amount to spend it in
one splurge. Eat, drink, get married, Calvin advised. Have
kids, enjoy yourselves. "Insurance? Don't waste your money!"

He rose late these days. He stopped buying *Time* magazine. It insisted too cynically on the terrifying, with hundreds
of labored puns, scores of shrill stories, riots here, revolutions
there, wars somewhere else, rigged elections, political strife.
Calvin read the *Malawi News* instead. Everything was fine on
the four over-inked pages of the unbleached *Malawi News*:
Osbong praising the Women's Brigade, Osbong repeating that
he was a dictator by the people, for the people and of the people, Osbong being referred to as "Our Great *Chirombo*, Savior,
Messiah, Founder and Father of the Republic of Malawi, Life
President of the Malawi Congress Party, Doctor . . ." There
were lovely little misprints: MESSIAH PLANNING STATE VISIT TO
EAT AFRICA, one headline ran, describing Osbong's visit to
Nairobi. There were poems, too: "I sing of Doctor Osbong
. . ." or "O Africa! O Malawiland! Let me taste of your boun-
teous . . ." There was no foreign news in the paper, except
for the odd scrap from a wire service about fifty reindeer crashing through some Finnish ice during the early thaw. It was all
perfect for the can. Calvin sat with his elbows on his knees, bent
over, the *Malawi News* spread on the floor and held in place
with his feet. He read and he shat; he was happy.

But Jarvis Moore, the fat waiter, sulked. Large and black,
he entered the bar or lingered on the verandah, and just like
the evil-favored narrator of *The Uninsured* he cast a grouchy
shadow over all. He was huge, the color of raw liver, with powerful shirt-splitting shoulders and a thick neck. His horny

fists suggested cudgels, and he had a zombie's insomniac eyes, set close and deep in his head. He could, and often did, pull the caps off beer bottles with his teeth. Once Calvin saw him spit a clam of dribbling saliva into a small child's face.

Calvin saw the cheerless man brooding over a beer crate, working his angry jaws on a cud. "How about a smile?" Calvin said.

Jarvis Moore told Calvin to drop dead.

"Just being bolshie," said Bailey, when Calvin told her. "Oh, he's a shocker, he is." She smiled.

"I never did anything to him," said Calvin.

"Course you didn't," said Bailey. "That one's a lad, though. Dresses up at night, he does. Fancy black suit, Teddy-Boy boots. Carries a knife now and then."

"Doesn't it worry you?"

"Just acting savage and bloody-minded. They all do it," said Bailey. "They don't mean any harm. Jarvy's very good with the accounts."

"He does your accounts?"

"He's very clever, is Jarvy."

"I think I'll buy him a drink," said Calvin. "That might make him brighten up."

"Don't you do any such thing! I don't want him arse-creeping around. Don't take any notice of him."

"He told me to drop dead," said Calvin. "He dresses up at night and carries a knife. He sulks, for God's sake."

Bailey replied by saying she liked Africans that way. Politeness in anyone was a challenge to her; in an African it was a threat.

Calvin kept his distance. He saw Bailey encouraging the fat waiter to be beastly. She snarled at him; he snarled back. She swore; he took to stropping a meat cleaver on an oiled piece of leather tacked to the bar. He refused to serve Calvin. When Calvin asked for a drink Jarvis twisted his face, flashed his knife and stropped. Calvin got his own drinks, made out his own chits, initialed them and pressed them on the spike.

169

In the first week of April Jarvis was especially moody, strop-ping and spitting, kicking chairs and growling as he did so. He had tremendous feet. In the evenings the girls strolled in twos on the street or draped themselves on the verandah, shouting and hooting to passers-by; Calvin sat on a barstool (Mira turned in early) and drank a beer. Usually he watched the progress of the fruit machine players, but this evening he looked through the delicate lace of dried froth at the top of his glass at the fat waiter fretting.

Seeing that Calvin's eyes were on him, Jarvis grunted and drew out his meat cleaver. He began slapping it, rocking from side to side as he swiped at the grease-dubbed strop.

Calvin moved three stools down the bar, across from Jarvis. They were so close to each other the blade passed back and forth under Calvin's chin. Jarvis gave off a strong vinegary smell that might have been sweat.

"What seems to be eating you?" asked Calvin.

"Bloody white men," said Jarvis. "Big so-called *bwanas* killing Africans. I am fed up of it."

"So what?" Calvin grinned good-naturedly.

"I know you despise me. I don't care about that," said Jarvis. "I have traveled around. My father was a chief. You can see I speak English. Booker T. Washington — I have read his book."

"A very impressive man, Booker T. Washington."

"A sellout," said Jarvis.

Calvin smiled. "Where'd you come across a word like that?"

"Lumumba. I have read Lumumba."

"No offense," said Calvin, "but big deal."

"Osbong is a sellout, a big stoogie for the Boers. He uses Ambi-Special."

"Why worry about Osbong? All politicians are like that. Re-place Osbong with someone else and you'll have the same thing all over again. I don't know anything about politics, but I know that's the way it always is."

170

"You don't know anything about politics. Lumumba was murdered."

"By Africans," said Calvin. "I read it in *Time* magazine."

"Some Africans behave like white people," said Jarvis. "They are stupid."

"Sure, but some white people behave like Africans," said Calvin, and he thought of A. Jigololo.

"They are good ones if they do." Jarvis stropped faster. "I know very well you bloody foreign devils want to steal this country."

Foreign devil? Calvin was crushed. He did not think of himself as a foreigner. He was surprised to hear Jarvis name him so. He thought of himself as a sincere friend; he had sold insurance and, finding it inadequate and bogus, stopped selling it. He cared. He liked the Africans and trusted their idleness; he had thought the feeling was mutual, for his own idleness was no different from theirs.

"I'm your friend. I'm no foreigner."

"You're a white bloodsucker. You want to kill us."

"I don't want to do anything," Calvin protested. "Besides, my wife is black."

"You're stealing our women."

"I'm married," said Calvin, "to one of them."

"You want to take Malawi away from us, like Osbong."

"Look," said Calvin, picking a shelled peanut out of a bowl on the bar and cradling it in a wrinkle on his open palm which he held near Jarvis's face. "See this? *This* is Malawi."

Jarvis stared at the peanut.

"No offense intended," said Calvin, "but who wants it?"

Jarvis plucked the peanut out of Calvin's palm. He opened his mouth, put his whole hand inside, deposited the peanut on his back teeth and crunched it. "You want to eat us like this," said Jarvis, swallowing. "Many people want to crush us."

"I hate to disappoint you," said Calvin, "but I don't know any. Oh, I know how you feel — "

"I know them," said Jarvis quickly. He smacked his cleaver. Saliva brimmed in the dark little trough behind his slack lower lip. "Spies! Spies!"

"But who would want," said Calvin nodding, "to spy on you?"

Jarvis tested the cleaver's edge with a moist thumb. He raised it high, then slammed it into the bar an inch from Calvin's fingers. The whole surface of the bar rang with the vibration of the blade. He glowered fiercely at Calvin. "Plenty of people want to spy on us! Maybe you. I can't stick you."

Now that was not so strange. It was always the ugly neglected spinster who was obsessed by the thought that she was being followed by a man, and who was always being exposed to fugitive genitals. Calvin wanted to reply to Jarvis's abuse, but he didn't want to hurt the man's feelings. Calvin found it odd to hear such things from a man so fat. The sentiments were all those of A. Jigololo, the narrator of *The Uninsured,* one of the browbeaten oppressed. Somehow Calvin had pictured the oppressed as very small and sick, like the unemployed in Worcester, not Jarvis's size. Calvin decided to say nothing. Some people just didn't want to be happy, but why give them another excuse to be miserable?

Jarvis gave Calvin a wintry sneer. He yanked the cleaver out of the splintered wood and resumed his stropping, a caricature of A. Jigololo, who was himself a caricature of one wasp's unhappiness. Jarvis would, Calvin was sure, give that up and perhaps he would be as embarrassed by the memory of his fruitless anger as Calvin was by his own. Calvin understood Jarvis; he knew what made him tick, better than he knew Mira's worries or wants. That was the saddest part. And because he talked that way it showed Jarvis wasn't being honest. Jarvis's was a white liberal pose. He would change, of course he would; as Calvin had. It was only a matter of time before he would find out that life was worth living. He would meet a nice girl — maybe a white girl, what was the difference? — and give up his griping. Underneath it all Jarvis was probably a very sweet guy.

23

Kill them all, Brother Jaja had written in the tall narrow loops of his graceful mission-school hand, his last gruesome dispatch to Marais. It was insane. It reminded Marais of the demented killer who lingers to riddle his victim with bullets, or keeps stabbing a corpse. Perhaps Brother Jaja was exaggerating; Africans often did, but Marais had Harry's word that Jaja was unusually bright: he had been educated in Rhodesia, had received military training in Algiers and had fought in the northeastern Congo with Gbenye Christophe. He had been born in Malawi but was unknown there, for he had left for Salisbury when he was fifteen and had assumed a number of different aliases. In Dar es Salaam, Gbenye had said to Marais, "It wasn't Jaja's fault we lost. But if we had won Jaja would have been the first man I killed. He's dangerous." It intrigued Marais that Gbenye intended to kill his best man, and it was then Marais decided Brother Jaja should head the new government.

But Brother Jaja's latest dispatches sounded madder than the first Marais had received from him. Even if it was not madness it was very bad judgment: the impulse was revenge — excited, irrational, easily detected. The revolutionary put one bullet in his enemy's head and let that kill him. Vengeance was wasteful, and not a revolutionary's motive but a cannibal's. *Kill them all.* Marais decided otherwise. Encircling every village and attacking every flimsy compound was unnecessary and inconvenient, and with only fifty men and no dependable supply lines, probably impossible. A show of arms might persuade; it never convinced; at best it frightened. Marais knew he did not have Brother Jaja's instincts — that much was clear from the stack of bluntly worded dispatches. But he avoided giving a direct reply.

Marais's strategy could be explained in a sentence: three key places in Malawi were to be either controlled or neutralized, the way Marais had seen the brush fire in October. A torch was thrown on a dry mountain, and soon a whole province was ablaze. Malawi was small, arms were concentrated in one customs post and in two large towns. The first tactical objective had been the customs post at Fort Hill on the northern frontier. It was attacked and taken one day in November. It was burned to the ground, but the position was not held. It would be retaken when the *coup* was announced. The two towns, Lilongwe and Blantyre, remained. Marais was camped a day's march from Lilongwe.

Holding Brother Jaja's dispatch in his hand, Marais wondered whether he should give a candid reply to the order *kill them all.* But he hesitated to describe the attacks in terms of a brush fire. He was about to write that the key places once taken would spread and enlarge like a brush fire. *Like a brush fire.* He didn't like that: it sounded as poetic and inexact as Brother Jaja's order sounded cannibalistic and exaggerated.

Marais's perceptions had not changed, but his imagery, with the action of one violent siege and the fatigue of many marches, had sharply altered. He noticed the change in himself as a practical, almost puritanical insistence on order and necessity. This was new. It was disturbing how, earlier, in thoughtful essays on revolt he had taken refuge from concrete detail and worked on imagery which ignored such necessities as drastic punishment. He had never thought that he would ever have to torture anyone — Harry was right: it *was* torture. Torture worked.

He was colder now. The image of the brush fire rubbed at him: it was unclear, it lacked detail, it was romance, convenient but misleading. It made the whole operation sound too easy. He had seized on such images from habit — a habit consistent with the spirit of the early chapters of his *Principles of Revolt,* where he had described tactics in parables. There he had spoken of weeds being uprooted, insurrection's vulcanism cracking open the landscape, the rotting corpse of the middle class stinking in the marketplace. It was a beginner's impractical rhetoric. The images had come to him in a closed room in a hotel in Bagamoyo, a slave port north of Dar. He had not been hurried — that much was evident in the style of the book. Here was the neat desk, and beyond a stack of copybooks the sea front framed by a carved window: a dhow moving noiselessly from one side of the frame to disappear at the other; at the quayside, boys in beaded caps sloshing small fish into tureens. Above Marais a steady fan beat, and there beside him a loaded pistol weighted loose notes and scribbled drafts; before him a clean sheet of paper, an ink bottle. In such a room he had written of revolt.

He flicked the pages of one copybook and was disgusted. All the wasted time, the pretense of ambiguities. His tactic of occupying strategic positions he had described with easy lyricism: *A stone is dropped into a pool; it makes rippling waves radiate from the place of impact, which splash the sides of the pool. Every action is felt.* It was not a poem, but it was trying to be. The aim was all wrong. Poetry was a clever reply, an illness of the ear, a lying substitute for a coarse truth. The subject was obscured by the poet's self-importance, and there were always symbols, in themselves primitive statements: symbols were bubbles, falsifying, making brutality into a lyric. The little pimpled man wrote of love, the coward of battle. But not even a soldier's image could represent a broken man crying and pleading for his life, the shock of a bullet, the stink of a jungle camp. It was no wonder Rimbaud chucked his poems to come gun-running in Somalia. Only the unloveliest of textbooks could describe how to win a war.

Marais regretted all his earlier attempts to describe revolt at a distance; he was haunted and mocked by how wrong he had been. Abruptly his style changed. Now, camped within striking range of Lilongwe, he was writing.

All guerrilla bands minimize the importance of suburban struggle. This should not be so. A proper maneuver of this type is worth a hundred rural battles. The target should be the center of a strategic city. The attack must take the people by surprise, at dawn, and ideally should end at sunset the same day. (In Lilongwe on April 27th sunrise is at 0620 hrs., sunset 1935 hrs.) It can, if completed with thoroughness, totally paralyze the commercial and industrial life of the city and place the whole urban population in an atmosphere of unrest. Bringing everything to a violent halt it will make people impatient for the development of more violent events, to relieve the period of suspense.

Weapons must be light carbines, sawed-off shotguns, pistols, machetes.

For sabotage: dynamite, picks and shovels, apparatus for lifting rails, crowbars, gasoline . . .

"Everything will stop so suddenly — it will be so quiet — that people will get nervous and want something more violent to happen," Marais was saying. He stood before a street map of Lilongwe chalked on a blackboard nailed to a tree. His men squatted on the ground and watched him closely. "But we will be in charge. They will do anything we say."

There was no response from the men. No one had volunteered to act as translator in Brother Mussa's place. Marais now spoke slowly, choosing his words; he repeated and asked questions. But out of impatience or fear the men were sunk in a restless silence. They had behaved strangely ever since they had broken camp at Rumpi and marched south. Marais had skirted all the roadblocks and traveled at night over secondary roads, leading his column of men in the fully loaded Citroën. To attack the roadblocks would have been to alert Lilongwe of their progress south. For over a month not one shot had been fired, and the only casualty was Brother Mussa, the rapist.

"All right," said Marais, "now let's go through the whole thing again." He pointed to a man at the front with his cigar. "At the signal, where are you?"

The man got to his feet, walked to the map and pressed his finger against a white chalk line, leaving a moist dark fingerprint. He said, "Heah."

"And you?" Marais pointed to another man.

"Power plant," said the man, leaving a wet mark on the left side of the map.

Marais spent the next half-hour questioning the men about their duties, making them describe the sequence of the attack by showing their positions on the map. When he finished, the map was obliterated; all the chalk lines of the landmarks, the roads, the carefully drawn positions and converging arrows were smeared and rubbed with the damp fingerprints of the men. Each had touched it; it was destroyed.

"Fine," said Marais. "Now what's the signal? Brother Eddy, when are you going to begin tearing up the railroad tracks?"

"When I heah a big bang," said Brother Eddy mechanically, "I take jack and lift up tracks."

"Okay, you," Marais indicated another man. "What's the big bang?"

"Da big bang," the man recited, "is da car esplodin."

"Right. I park it on the main street, here — " Marais referred to the map and chalked an X over a faintly marked line. "It will be filled with dynamite. The timing device is set for seven. By then you should all be in your places. When you hear that dynamite explode, get to work as fast as you can." Marais looked at the men. "Brother George, where is the car parked?"

"Police headquarters," said Brother George, speaking as he rose.

"Brother Chimanga," said Marais, "why am I parking the car there?"

"Cause at six-something police reporting for duty. They line up at seven near door. We blow them," said Brother Chimanga.

"And at the same time we blow the front of the building," said Marais. "There's no cover, they'll be confused — very easy targets. Once we capture the building we have all their guns — " Marais stopped. He noticed that Brother Chimanga was still standing.

"Do you have a question?"

"Yes," said Brother Chimanga. "I am wanting to know why you ever drive the car. You driving car from the north. You driving the car into Lilongwe. You driving. We all the time walking, footing. I am wanting to know why."

Marais was surprised, not so much by the question as by Chimanga's tone of voice. It was a challenging, aggressive complaint, too loud, almost as if no reply was expected. Marais was unprepared for it. His driving the car seemed so trivial. But an attentive pause hushed the camp. Marais felt he was being judged. They watched him. They were not with him.

"Do you know how to drive that car?"

"Eddy is knowing," said Brother Chimanga.

Marais glanced over at Eddy. Eddy busily scratched his ankle. "Yatu is knowing," said Brother Eddy.

"But what about you, Chimanga?"

"You can teach me," muttered Brother Chimanga.

"I am asking you," said Marais, in the tone Chimanga had used in his own challenge, "do *you* know how to drive that car?"

"Nuh," grunted Brother Chimanga.

"Brother George," said Marais, "put the dynamite in the car. In the back seat."

"How many leebs?"

"Put in a hundred. Four cases of sticks."

Brother George went to the sandbagged enclosure for the cases of dynamite. He carried the boxes slowly, picking his way to the Citroën, holding the boxes as one would hold a small infant. He slid each along the back seat, closing his eyes as he did so. The men watched nervously, in silence.

Marais walked over to Chimanga. "Here are the keys. Let's have a lesson. I'm teaching you how to drive." Marais swung the keys on his finger. "Take them."

Brother Chimanga's eyes moved with the keys, but he made no other move.

"You want to learn, don't you? I drove that dynamite down from Rumpi. Now it's your chance. But just remember, you only make one mistake in this lesson. If you hit something — *boom!* — "

Brother Chimanga flinched.

" — the dynamite explodes. You die. And without dynamite we can't attack Lilongwe, can we?" Marais smiled. "Take the keys."

The expression on Brother Chimanga's face said nothing. The muscles were slack. Marais said, *"Take the fucking keys,"* and slapped the keys onto Brother Chimanga's palm.

The keys did not rest on the palm. Brother Chimanga tilted his hand and let them slip down his fingers, and there was an innocent clink as they hit the ground. Brother Chimanga's head had not moved; he had not looked at the keys in his hand. He stared past Marais to the scrub jungle where locusts whined.

Marais stooped over and picked the keys out of the dust. The hush of silence subsided to a babble of relaxed voices. To show he meant what he said, Marais drove the car loaded with dynamite three times around the camp. The men cheered him when he parked it and got out, but it struck Marais with a force that made his spine throb that in the stretched seconds of that challenge he could have fumbled and lost them all.

179

24

In the last week of April, on a Saturday night in Blantyre, the Miss Malawi Contest was held. Sponsored by Ambi Creams Ltd., a Rhodesian skin-lightening manufacturer, it was an annual affair: every year Miss Malawi won a cash prize and several cases of Ambi, and was flown to London in June to compete against Miss Gambia, Miss Pakistan and the other contestants for the Miss Commonwealth crown. There was always the possibility, though it had never happened to a black girl, of being sent later to the Miss Universe Contest in Miami. But that eventuality was so remote it was not spoken about, and locally the contest was seen as a political struggle. It was invested with all the authority of folk tradition: "What will happen when the old man goes?" was answered with "Who was Miss Malawi last year?"

Before anyone had heard of Hastings Osbong, the girl who was crowned Miss Nyasaland Protectorate was seen being squired around Blantyre by a talkative little man with a facial tic and always in a natty suit. The white settlers took no notice; they had their own beauty queens, elected at the sports clubs and agricultural shows, Miss Rugger and Miss Groundnut. But most Africans guessed that, at Independence, the Homburgwearing companion of Miss Nyasaland Protectorate would be the first president. This augury confirmed, a tradition was born, and many of the cabinet ministers used the Miss Malawi competition to test their influence. Entering their girl friends in it was regarded as something like fighting a by-election in a stubbornly mute constituency.

That was the talk. It was what Major Beaglehole told Calvin. Major Beaglehole went on to say that three former Miss Malawis worked at the eating house. To look at them was to be certain the contest was rigged. But Calvin was bored by the thought of beauty contests; Homemakers' Mutual had one at their annual outing at Nantasket Beach, and Calvin told Beaglehole, "I didn't come nine thousand miles to watch a beauty contest." He would have ignored the Miss Malawi Contest altogether had Mira not brought him an application form and asked him to fill it out for her.

"Come off it," said Calvin. "What do you want to enter that thing for?"

"Miss Malawi," Mira pouted.

It was wrong. There was not the faintest bit of African culture in it. It was a reversal, offensive to Calvin. Africans were a proud race: why should they let themselves get involved in the publicity gimmick of a Rhodesian skin-lightening company?

"What's the point? African countries shouldn't have beauty contests. It's not right. It's not — " Not *traditional,* he thought. She didn't know the word. He said, "No good."

"Is good," said Mira.

"No," said Calvin. "You don't want to be Miss Malawi."

"Do," said Mira.

"Mullet, you're talking like a black," said Major Beaglehole. "Of course it's a fiddle, everyone knows that. Osbong's favorite popsie won it back in sixty-three. It's always the same, but that's no reason to talk like a black."

"I'll talk the way I want," said Calvin. "I won't have my wife entering any beauty contests, and that's that."

"Don't you listen to him," said Bailey to Mira. "I always say,

181

just having them up there with their bums showing in their cute little frocks is good for trade."

"It's a waste of time," said Calvin.

"You're a fine one to talk about wasting time," said Bailey. "Stop nattering and fill in the form. There's a love."

Grumbling, Calvin filled in the application and pinned a fifty osbong note to it as a deposit. Only then, delaying and snapping the bill, did he notice that the dark face in the watermark was Osbong's.

Calvin was angry, because in spite of what everyone said about the contest, he was sure Mira could win. The winners of beauty contests were driven foolish and they always seemed to end badly, as whorish starlets or hostesses in nightclubs. In Malawi their pictures were used on the Ambi posters.

Mira received the application with a smile. She flung her arms around Calvin's neck and kissed him. She was wearing one of her flowered headscarves and a length of silken sari drawn close to her body. One arm jangled with a whole sleeve of gold bracelets. In her, jungle genes were threaded on black necklaces of Central African chromosomes. She was hard and slim, her mouse ears were slightly larger than most women's ears, or perhaps seemed so because they were not hidden by hair. She had a long graceful neck, and hooded slanting eyes; she was not black, but a deep brown. From the waist up she was gently molded, like the handle of a dagger; her breasts were small. Her legs were long for her size, and straight as two stiletto blades. She was his blackbird, his cat; she had sharp little teeth.

When she was dressed in smooth silk, the soft fabric slipping over her curves, Calvin desired her. He tantalized himself by sliding his hand under the silk sheath and caressing the flesh of her gloriously firm edges, so many angles and surprises. It verged on the perverse. She obliged Calvin by dressing this way, baited him by draping her bareness which, masked, provoked him, drove him wild. He groped up her thigh. She showed her teeth and helped his hand.

She was pretty, and though he had not married her for that (he would have settled for the company of her simple presence) it was welcome. She had her secrets, but her loveliness was unhidden. Of this, Calvin was positive. A week after their marriage they had had a little quarrel about washing. She washed a great deal; Calvin did not. He had washed and shaved for the wedding and had glued his hair down, but after that he lost interest. He was not trying to impress anyone. He said that like an African he was happy dirty: filth relaxed him. There was something cozy and familiar in an undershirt that had been worn for a week or two. Mira told him to keep clean; she gave him soap. Calvin was hurt. And scared: obsessive washing reminded him unpleasantly of his other wife. Now Mira, black Mira from a little dorp in Central Africa, was starting the same business. Calvin said it was stupid to spend so much time under a dripping barrel suspended in the air while Jarvis lugged buckets of hot water up a ladder, attempting to keep the punctured barrel filled. Mira caught at the word stupid and cried. But this was not the end of it. That night she lay flat on the bed; Calvin bent over and spread his hands on her, one hand on the full boneless dumpling of a breast, the other fishing in the fuzzy nave of her thighs. He was first a blind man lightly translating the body's Braille; then, with desire, an organist feeling for chords. Calvin crouched to pick her open with a kiss.

"Peeg!"

She jackknifed and slapped his face.

Calvin fled from the room, tumescent, and walked the streets searching for a girl to pick up. The eating house bar was empty. Calvin walked down St. Andrews Street to Osbong where he found the bars closed and shuttered. A girl in an alley off Henderson Street clicked her teeth at him. Calvin stopped and went closer to her. She was drunk, she held his sleeve and pursed her lips, trying to kiss. Calvin pulled away and ran up to Victoria Street, where at Barclay's Bank and Kandodo Supermarket, night watchmen huddled around fires or were slung in charpoys in the doorways with bedclothes of newspaper. Two blocks up Victoria a pack of Youth Wingers appeared, armed with truncheons and knobkerries, and started toward Calvin. Calvin ducked down Fotheringham Road and saw several girls dispersing. He followed one, then another, back down to Osbong, avoiding the Youth Wingers, and almost reached Agnello's building and the junction when he saw a figure he first took to be a lithe young Sikh boy in a sarong. It was a girl. Calvin followed, led on by the busy bobbing of her likely bum. In Chinyanja there was a specific word of eight thumping syllables for the rotating movement of a woman's bottom when she walked. The girl moved swiftly, sixteen syllables to a step, and had almost reached the clock tower when Calvin, drawing close to her and on the point of making a kissing sound — the way one calls a cat: all the girls responded to it — and saying *muli bwanji*, saw the girl's face in the helpful blaze of a watchman's fire: Mira, yes.

So pretty, even from the back, in the dark, late at night, as a stranger. They hugged and brushed lips: jungle lovers. Mira plunged her hand down the top of his trousers and held his quickening shaft. She steered him back to the eating house, and much later she bathed him, soaping him by lantern light in Beaglehole's clawfoot bathtub.

*　　*　　*

"Lays and german!" called the master of ceremonies on the stage of the Rainbow Theater, in a slurring attempt at an American accent. "Wid yer permission, lays and german, lemme interduce these luffly, luffly chicks!"

They were under the Ambi banner LOOK LOVELIER, LOOK LIGHTER — AMBI IS FOR YOU. The Ismaili brothel had sent a very thin one, the Groundnut Marketing Board sent two, the *Malawi News* one of their girl reporters, the League of Malawi Women one, and two each from the Goodmorning Panwallah, the Zambesi Bar, the New Safari Drinkhouse, the Victoria Club and the Highlife. There were three (Grace, Abby, Ameena) from Auntie Zeeba's Eating House. Five in special finery (feathered hats, trim dresses and long white gloves) were unsponsored: these were assumed to be the cabinet ministers' girl friends. There was Mira in silk. And there was another.

"Look at that," Major Beaglehole said. "A ruddy Hottentot."

She was a fat black woman with streaks of red ocher on her face. She wore a leopard skin, a necklace of yellow lion fangs and a civet cat peruke. Strings of little bells were tied around her ankles and wrists. She stamped and made swimming movements with her arms, sounding these bells. She was armed, a quiver of arrows at her back, a bow slung over her shoulder. In her hand was a limber spear, a trident, popular with the lakeshore tribes. A carving knife with a beaded handle, and a stone hatchet, were crammed into her belt. She was introduced as Zanama.

Each girl on being presented by the master of ceremonies had winked or salaciously adjusted her dress. Mira had smiled toward Calvin. Zanama had called out in a coarse village voice; a whole section of the audience had replied. Encouraged, Zanama hopped to the center of the stage, shook her bells and waved her spear. Calvin thought she might nock an arrow and zing it into the audience: he slumped down in his seat. But no arrow was shot. The master of ceremonies persuaded Zanama to return to her place in line. She did so, scowling.

Only Mira and Zanama appeared to be their natural color; Mira was chocolate, Zanama molasses. The rest, rubbed with Ambi, were shiny-faced in hues of glowing blue, the difference in shade due to the strength of lightening cream each had used — Ambi-Regular, Ambi-Extra or Ambi-Special. All the girls' arms were brown, and all their mouths were clowny with lipstick.

"Les give da judges time to look dese luffly chicks over and pick da nex Miss Malawi," said the master of ceremonies. "Now a little music to brighten things up!"

A penny-whistle band from Johannesburg, led by a man

named Spokes (a short *tsotsi* in a porkpie hat), played two numbers. Spokes danced an extravagant *kwela*.

Elvis Masooka followed with "Jailhouse Rock" and "Ooby-Dooby," accompanying himself on a cracked guitar.

Jim Malinki sang a pious rendition of "This World Is Not My Home."

The girls' choir from the Stella Maris Mission harmonized, to the tune of "Santa Lucia," the Hastings Osbong song; they finished up with *"Zonse Zimene Za* H. K. Osbong" — "Everything Belongs to H. K. Osbong." Doctor O.'s picture was right above the Ambi sign, and tinted blue, giving credence to Jarvis Moore's charge that the President used it.

A judge in a white smock went among the girls at the back of the stage with a tape measure. He shouted numbers to a serious-faced judge who jotted in a notebook. Another judge examined the girls with a magnifying glass (upstaging the girls' choir) when the measuring judge was finished.

Calvin sat between Major Beaglehole and Bailey. Jack Mavity had also come along; he sat next to Bailey with two of his children. Mavity said, "You see that magnifying glass? Well, the Africans like shiny objects like that —" Major Beaglehole looked at Zanama and said, "Makes me think of a rogue elephant." Bailey coughed, and ate from a parcel in her lap, and coughed. Calvin chain-smoked. He was embarrassed on behalf of every performer and contestant; he tried to avert his eyes. There was something unnatural about it. It was wrong: he had known that as soon as Mira had shown him the application headed *Ambi Beauty Search.* He felt discomfort, he wanted to leave.

One perception held him. It dawned on him that he was watching a minstrel show in reverse, a negative rather than a photograph. Instead of Al Jolson in blackface — popping his eyes and crooning "Mandy, is there a minister handy?" — black people wearing skin-lightener were cavorting around dressed as *bwanas, memsahibs* and white showgirls. They weren't making asses of themselves: they were reacting against years of mockery and insult. Calvin had never seen Al Jolson, but he had seen the Hudson Baptist Men's Club dressed as darkies — that was their word *darkies* — balling the jack in 1951 at a church gala. It made his flesh creep to recall that sorry decade, when dreary people tried to strut, and middle-aged men in striped golliwog jackets tipped paper derbies and said, "Hel-lo, Mistah Bones! Who was dat lady I seen you wid last night?"

"That was no bloody lady — that was my wife!" was the reply by Spokes, fifteen years later on the stage of the Rainbow Theater in Blantyre, Malawi, Central Africa. Time had stood still. There were the Ambi-whitened girls instead of the burntcork blackened men; there was Elvis Masooka, Jim Malinki, and even his own wife, and it was still the fifties. That other era sputtered back in gray haphazard recollection like an old TV warming up: the Andrews Sisters, Perry Como, Julius La Rosa, Ed Sullivan's "Toast of the Town," Dave Garroway, all the cool hepcats in Hudson, Mass., barfing on a six-pack of Carlings and listening to Symphony Sid. It was the Miss Malawi Contest in Blantyre; but it was also the Sunday afternoon variety show on a Boston TV: "Community Opticians" with your genial host Gene Jones singing, "Star of the day, who will it be . . ." Talent time in snow flurries on a twelve-inch Muntz.

Fond memories at age thirty, effortless reminiscences. Africa permitted such insights. No one could be nostalgic in America, the country was not designed for it: with gusto the past was erased. But here in Malawi the world had not turned. Here for Calvin were ghostly voices and signature tunes: The Green Hornet, Inspector Keene Tracer of Lost Persons, Mr. and Mrs. North, The Shadow, Lamont Cranston, the Quiz Kids, Twenty Mule Team Borax, Quaker Oats Shot from Guns, Jack Armstrong the All-American Boy, Tonto, the Rosenbergs and Guildersleeve. For twelve cents at the Hudson Roxy you could see Jane Russell (a torn blouse, a haystack) in *The Outlaw*, Edmond O'Brien in *The Barefoot Contessa*, Jane Wyman (whatever happened to her?); Lex Barker was Tarzan. Those queer gray years you were a liberal if you had seen *The Jackie Robinson Story*, and there were minstrel shows, millions and millions of (Toot-Toot-Tootsie, Good-bye . . .) minstrel shows.

"Here is another musical sandwich to munch on. So gird up your loins and let this squeeze-box knock you off your feet!"

On stage, out of the Rainbow wings, came a nervous accordionist, a gangling man with a bad haircut. His black face was neutralized with Ambi-Extra. On "Community Opticians" he would have said, "I'm a busboy at the Chelsea Waldorf, Gene — been playing this here thing since I was ten-eleven years old — I guess you might say I'm waiting for my big break — " But the gangling man with the bad haircut when asked, "What are you gonna play for us?" said nothing in reply. He shook his bulky instrument, felt for the keys and chords, and swaying in the way all the accordionists used to, played — *My God*, thought Calvin, *am I dreaming this?* — "Lady of Spain."

Singing "Old Black Joe" and "Suwannee River" the Hudson Baptist Men's Club must have known how ludicrous a spectacle they were, and so probably had Amos 'n' Andy known: "Let's unlax, Brother Andy. Get dose feet up on de desk and unlax yo'self til Kingfish come from de Mystic Knights of de Sea Lodge." But did *they* know, up on the Rainbow stage — Elvis, Jim, the Ambi girls, the "Lady of Spain" accordian player, his wife . . . *his wife?* For their sakes, and his own peace of mind, Calvin fervently hoped they did, and that theirs was mockery in the same manner, getting even with their white-faced minstrel show, a form of revolt. It was awful to consider that other thought, that if they believed in the mimicry of their names and masks it was a sad terrible dereliction.

A dereliction, that is, for everyone except Zanama. She had no business there. She stuck out like a sore thumb. She was not trying to be white, she was not mocking: her black integrity did not permit her to play along with the others. If she had a counterpart in Hudson it was the white soprano from the church choir who every year sang "Alice Blue Gown" and reminded those present that there existed under all that war paint a Jew-less master race. But what about Zanama?

The music stopped.

"What in bloody hell is going on up there," grumbled Mavity.

The judges were at a small table, doing arithmetic and comparing sums. Most of the girls smiled through running Ambi. Zanama beetled her ocher brows and looked fierce.

"Will they announce the winner right here?" Calvin asked.

"Always do," said Bailey. She ate from the parcel in her lap, licked her fingers and said, "But they take their time about it."

"I don't know why I came here," said Major Beaglehole.

"You could have stayed back at the bar," said Calvin. "No one forced you to come."

"What's that?" Major Beaglehole squinted at Calvin.

Calvin allowed his lips to be read.

"I meant to Africa," said Major Beaglehole.

"Ain't it beastly," said Bailey.

"They wear bandages on their legs," said Mavity. "And there ain't a thing wrong with them."

"The sods," said Bailey. She coughed.

"I'm the one who should wear bandages," said Mavity.

"This place," Major Beaglehole looked around and winced, *"ponks."*

"Like a bleeding rubbish dump," said Bailey.

"It?" Calvin looked at Bailey.

"Stinks," said Bailey.

The doors of the theater were shut, there were no fans, every seat was taken. The body odor was overpowering, an acidic old fruit smell which, taken in a whiff, groped into the nose and burned; humid and dark, the noxious air sat on them. But Calvin was sure that it was the fact that he was sitting between Bailey and Beaglehole that occasioned the comment. He knew he smelled worse than anyone in the place.

"Then you shouldn't have come," said Calvin. He meant to Africa.

The audience was in milling disarray. People had left their

seats. There was a general hubbub, some were singing "Ooby-Dooby," others "This World Is Not My Home." At Calvin's feet a woman in a knitted stocking cap suckled a kicking infant; other babies, bound up and slung like haversacks on their mothers, yowled. Groups of angry boys slouched around the theater blowing through paper cones.

"Lays — "

The drone of voices, the shuffling of feet, the *yip-yip* of laughter, the stray shouts, all these mob noises drowned out the master of ceremonies.

"Lays and german — "

The woman huddled on the floor at Calvin's feet stopped suckling her child. She turned him over her knee and clapped him on the back.

" — your attention, please."

But most of the attention was focused on Zanama who, mumbling aboriginal static, a rising and falling *wah-wah-wah*, rocked on her heels, swelling forward and back. Calvin expected a war whoop, some kind of scream. But hers was a sullen menace, and all the more scary for the suspense it created. At first Calvin had thought she was smiling; now he knew it was a snarl, it had never been anything else.

" — great pleasure to announce the winner of dis year's Miss Malawi Contest — "

The master of ceremonies glanced down at the piece of paper in his hand. His expression was that of the man who after blowing his nose examines the wadded contents of his hanky before folding it into his pocket — satisfied, but slightly apprehensive. He took a breath and spoke. The name was not heard.

An arrow thwacked a roof beam. Another. Another.

With the first arrow half a dozen girls fled on wobbly heels, and the second sent Elvis Masooka and the accordion player scurrying for their instruments. Others pushed toward the exit. The third arrow stopped the master of ceremonies.

Zanama threw down her bow and, with her speartip jabbing

at the M.C.'s bowtie, snatched the handmike from him and cried, "Black! Black! Black! I am the winner!"

Calvin gnawed his thumbs.

"Call the police," said Bailey, gathering up her parcel of fried potatoes. "Get a constable!"

"It's the Hottentot," muttered Major Beaglehole. Even with the plug of his hearing aid torn out he heard the moan of the mob tickling the dead drums in his ears. He winced.

"Why doesn't Mira — " Calvin began. He was drowned out by Zanama shouting into the mike.

" — Bloody nonsense! This is all lubbish! I am an African. I am fat and strong! I have spaces between my teeth! I am black, *black!*"

For seconds while Zanama shouted, Calvin was on her side. It was only right. She *was* black, she should win. He had been wrong about the others. They weren't mocking; they believed in Ambi and Elvis and pale hourglass loveliness with ironed hair and big boobs. They needed to be prodded into sense with a spear. Calvin would have sat in his seat except that Zanama was beginning to terrorize the contestants, one of whom was his wife. Zanama slashed with her spear.

Calvin vaulted onto the stage and took Mira's hand and led her out of the theater. At the same time, Mavity passed one of his yellow children to Major Beaglehole and, holding the other in his arms like a football, retreated through the crowd with his head down.

The rest of the contestants, the master of ceremonies and all the performers left. Zanama had the stage to herself. She continued speaking. She proclaimed herself winner in the name of Brother Jaja and all that was black. She said in a loud voice that Africans were here to stay. The disruption was enjoyed by everyone, as if, after being deprived of such pleasure for so long, at last they were allowed it, the quaint activity of furious hollerings. It went on much longer than anyone expected. The police, it turned out, were somewhere else.

25

The object had been to bring Lilongwe to a halt. They had given themselves twelve hours; but by noon on Saturday the attack was over, Marais was on the flat roof of the Great Northern Hotel, a wooden five-story structure with a large clock on the front. The town was theirs: a column of black smoke rose from the telephone exchange. A dozen policemen were padlocked in their own jail cells. A fleet of trucks had been taken over, the party headquarters burned, stocks of food and ammunition found. There were no casualties. By any reckoning the attack had been made with classic speed. The several things that had gone wrong Marais had turned to his advantage, and Lilongwe was taken in only a morning. It was a market day. The streets were packed with tipsy stalls and goat flocks; hens squawked in cages; fruits and vegetables were piled on mats. Most of the shops were open. People milled around, haggling and buying, seemingly oblivious of what had happened a few hours before. The town had been brought to a halt, and earlier some people had been terrified; but now it seemed as if no one cared. Except for the smoke, it could have been an ordinary Saturday in Lilongwe.

The men had brought furniture up to the roof of the Great Northern; the hotel served as headquarters for Marais. Marais told the protesting manager, a Scotsman, to get lost. The hotel was the highest building in town, and the roof afforded a view of miles around. Marais could see the activity, the roadblocks to the north and south of town being manned by his soldiers, gun emplacements being set up on some hills above a road junction in the southwest. To the west the aerodrome was visible, a light green patch of meadow with a small hangar; like the rooftop of the Great Northern, the hangar at the aerodrome flew the black and red flag of Brother Jaja on the pole that held the windsock.

The table on the roof was sheltered by an umbrella taken from an ice cream stand. *The Principles of Revolt* notebooks lay on the table, their pages turning and riffling in the breeze. Who would believe that a place could be captured so easily? Marais sat, found his place, and began writing: *27 April. Lilongwe is ours. The operation got underway at 0500. The patrols headed for their positions by a circular route. I took the car and drove from . . .*

*   *   *

Marais drove slowly down the main street in the Citroën with only the parking lights on. It was cold enough for the windshield to be fogged with his breath; the rest of the windows were painted black to conceal the four crates of dynamite sticks wired to a clock and two dry cell batteries in the back seat. He was riding in a bomb; it lurched on hard corrugations in the road, the loaded springs groaned with the weight of the dynamite and the drum of gasoline that sat next to him like a passenger. Twice, without warning, the car bumped into potholes, and Marais shut his eyes and held the steering wheel with numbed fingers, expecting to be thumped by an explosion. Both times the dynamite was jarred, the gasoline drum shifted. There was no explosion, though Marais passed those moments in a sudden fever, the air from the side window chilling his drenched face. They would never piece his body back together; it would be scattered all over town. But they would know who it was. "Marais," they would say, "riding a bomb. He was once shot in the back."

It was a cowboy town, a set for a western movie even if such towns did not exist in the wild west; only stage coaches and hitching posts were missing. One wide treeless street ran into jungle at either end; the street was crowded with shops, and except for the hotel and the police headquarters, all the buildings were one-story affairs, with false fronts and roofed verandahs.

At the police headquarters, a cement cube of two stories, most of the lights were on, the only lights in town. The sign in front was illuminated. Marais smiled at the thought that he had committed the map to memory. He pulled into the compound and shut off the engine; he rolled up the windows, covered the gasoline drum with a blanket, and locked the car. Zipping the front of his jacket he entered the building, noting the movement of three of his men in the shadowy alley next to the hotel, diagonally across the main street.

The duty officer snored face down on a canvas cot behind the high reception counter. The walls of the room were dirty, there were papers on the floor, a cat pawed at an overturned wastebasket. It looked as if it had already been attacked, the inert policeman one of the victims. A roster was chalked on a wall blackboard just above the sleeping man, thirty names, and beside them a schedule with assembly noted for 0700. Mr. Harry's information was correct, the timing device on the bomb did not have to be reset. Even the clock in the room synchronized with Marais's watch, ten past five, the wrong time, just as Harry had said. Chained to a rack on a side wall were twenty rifles; in a glass case mounted beside it a dozen pistols, some handcuffs and leg irons and a row of knobkerries.

Marais rapped on the counter.

The policeman awoke with a start, groaning and rubbing his head.

"Are you the duty officer?"

"Yes, sir," and he added sheepishly, "just fell asleep this minute." He got up from the cot and came over to the desk. He found his cap and put it on. He smiled. "It's quiet tonight — this morning. I must have been sleeping — "

"That's all right," said Marais. "I'm just passing through and — "

"Can I help you, sir?"

"My car," said Marais. "It's probably the generator. It keeps stalling. You see — "

"Oh, yes, sir. You want to park it here? No problem."

The policeman seemed relieved the matter was so trivial. Marais's long explanation, carefully rehearsed for the policeman's possible refusal, was unnecessary; and the bribe Harry advised him to carry stayed in its envelope. The policeman was helpful, polite and even — unexpected in that filthy littered room — efficient. "You parked it already? Very good. Leave it right there, it's quite safe, sir. The garage opens about nine. They'll take care of you."

"Nine?" said Marais. "I thought it would open earlier than that."

"Maybe earlier. Nothing happens on time here, ha-ha. Just a very small town. Not to worry. You can leave it unlocked, sure."

"It won't be in the way?"

"Oh, no, plenty of room, plenty," said the duty officer. "You're coming from Blantyre?"

"That's right."

"Going north?"

"As soon as the car's fixed."

The duty officer shook his head. "There's some trouble in the north, didn't you hear?"

"They said something about it in Blantyre."

"Yes, some of our men reported shooting in Rumpi District. If you're going that way you need a special pass."

"I do? Where do I get one?"

"Not to worry. I can issue one. Here," said the duty officer. He wrote numbers on and dated a printed sheet of paper. He asked for the car's registration number and Marais's name, passport number and address. He stamped it and initialed it. "Show this and they'll let you through. Up to now they haven't been troubling Europeans." The pass was headed FOR TRAVEL IN OR THROUGH A DISTURBED AREA.

"I suppose I can wake them up at the hotel?"

"Yes, yes. They will wake up, there is a night watchman."

Marais thanked the policeman and started out of the building.

"Sir?"

Marais turned and put his hands in his pockets, one on the pistol, one on the bribe.

"Do you have — " The policeman laughed quickly.

"Yes? What is it?"

"I ran out of cigarettes."

"Have a cigar," said Marais. "Here, just a minute, I'll light it for you."

The explosion came precisely at seven, several blasts, one after the other, as the Citroën blew apart and was flung in flaming chunks all over the street. The attack on Lilongwe had begun.

"Right on the button," Marais said, fitting his pistol into a gunstock. He was with three of his men, under the back fire escape of the Great Northern. He waited a moment for the flaming gasoline to settle and then dashed with the men around the building, four rifles level, ready to pick off the scattering policemen.

They halted at the front of the hotel and looked across the street.

"Where the hell — "

The blaze crackled in the empty early morning street. There was a powerful smell of cordite, there were clouds of blue powder smoke; gaudy orange flames engulfed the compound of the police headquarters, but no one, not even the duty officer, was there to be killed. At that moment, after the blast, the street was as silent as it had been at five. Pieces of cement facing had been knocked off the front of the building, and all the front windows were broken; but the front door, which was to have been blown off its hinges, had been open at the time of the blast. The chain link fence was torn and stretched open; a sizable crater had been dug in the compound. In the crater was lodged the black underchassis of the car.

Marais waved his men back.

The exploding car had the opposite effect from the one Marais intended. It was to have killed the policemen when they assembled at seven, the day shift for inspection, the night shift for filing their reports; but at seven ("Nothing happens on time here") the compound was empty. Instead of killing them, it put them on the alert, waking them in little huts all over Lilongwe. It made them sit up and yawn and remember that they were late for assembly; it made them wonder what all the noise was about.

It woke everyone up, for at seven-fifteen, as Marais and his men were ripping the rifles down from the wall and smashing the glass case that held the pistols, a score of market women gathered outside to look at the ruined building and the big hole in the ground. Marais told two men to stand guard out back. He took one man upstairs where, in a toilet, they found the duty officer cowering. From an upper window they watched the crowd gather. Everyone went to see where the bomb had gone off: the staff from the power station, the radio operator from the aerodrome, the night shift from the telephone exchange, the Youth Wingers who were supposed to be manning the roadblocks outside town, some guests from the hotel, and a bus full of people from Blantyre. And there they all stood, until the police arrived, marveling at the big hole and the damage.

At the sound of the explosion a patrol of Marais's men had seen the whole telephone exchange empty, and the people run toward the blast. Two of the men entered the building, sprinkled it with gasoline and gunpowder and set it alight. Several switchboards sounded futile buzzes in the flames, but this cricket echo was soon gone.

The power station, the pump house and the aerodrome, deserted by curious employees at the sound of the explosion, were easily occupied and left intact, though water and electricity were shut off for the day. The bus depot was taken over by one man, the hotel by two. At the roadblocks Marais's men simply changed places with the Youth Wingers who had run off.

The police tried to restore order in the ruined compound. The ground floor of the building was still burning, while Marais watched from the upper window. The police saw a mob of people and, unable to fight a fire but trained to deal with mobs, they joined hands, encircled it and pushed it into the street; then the police dropped back and threatened the people with batons.

Three of Marais's men leaped from the still-smoking front entrance of the police headquarters, surprising the police at their rear, and yelled for the police to lie down. The police turned, saw the rifles, and sat in the dust. Before the crowd of delighted people they pulled off their shoes and let themselves be handcuffed. They were led to the cells and locked up.

"Look! Look!" The smoke rising from the telephone exchange was noticed, the flag on the hotel, the flames at the party headquarters. The crowd dispersed. It was just after eight o'clock.

Before noon the excitement had died down. A few people lingered around the crater in front of the police headquarters, a small crowd watched the last of the telephone exchange burn. Stalls were set up, and goats were tethered to the blasted fence. Children played with fragments of the Citroën, door handles and ornaments. Most people shopped.

Marais, at his rooftop desk shaded by the ice cream umbrella, was writing: *The elements of surprise and dispersal in a largely undefended town must never be underestimated. A bored populace watches the attack with interest, the fires fascinate them. And, as our experience has shown . . .*

Marais heard steps. He put down his pen and saw Brother George covered in sweat, panting toward him. Brother George's bootsoles squelched the softened tar of the roof, making a gum-chewer's snap.

"Come," Brother George said. "They are shooting. Come quick!"

Marais shut his notebook. He did not rise. He hooked his elbow on the chair back and crossed his legs. He nodded for Brother George to explain.

Blurting phrases between gasps, Brother George told Marais what he had seen. Just after eleven he heard shots at the railroad station and had gone over to have a look. Entering the railroad yard he saw a man face down in some cinders, bleeding from his back. The station appeared empty, but when he called out the code word several men came to the windows and shot at him. He was not close enough to see who they were and, alone, did not dare to return fire. He found cover and slid away.

"How many men altogether?"

Brother George's eyes were pickled in fear. "Three, four. Maybe five."

"Not more?"

"Maybe more."

"They might be police — we haven't got them all. They might be anyone."

"They have guns. They shot at me."

"You said that already. Don't get excited, George. Round up a few men. I'll be waiting for you downstairs."

A main-line station, it was roomy but low, of sooty brick, with a weathervane cupola and tiny black spikes along the ridges of the brown tiled roof. To the left, just across the tracks, stood a water tower, its slack canvas cock upraised on a pulley. It should have been the easiest place to capture, Marais thought, watching with three men from behind a coal pile. There was much more cover than had been shown on the map, and Harry had said there were only two rifles in the place. There was no sign of the men he had sent to take it, no evidence that the tracks had been torn up.

The dead man was still on the ground between the station building and the goods shed. Even at that distance Marais could tell it was not one of his own men; he wore the white shirt and black trousers of a petty official, a ticket agent or a telegrapher. One of his shoes was missing.

There was cover everywhere. Two coal piles were conveniently placed, and a flatcar was overturned in such a way that it was a natural barricade. There were many stacks of oily ties and lengths of track, pyramids of steel drums, all bulletproof and affording good access to the station.

"You could have done this alone," said Marais. "Here, Brother George, go back to the hotel. Get the camera, the sawed-off shotgun and a bottle of gasoline."

Brother George repeated the items, questioning the camera; he backed away.

"We can get pictures of this," said Marais. "We'll make copies and send them to Osbong."

There was some movement in the building. Two men peeped over a windowsill, and another watched from a doorway. They did not show their faces long; they looked at the dead man and then disappeared inside.

"Keep your eye on me," said Marais to Brother George when he returned. "I'm crossing over to that pile of logs, then to the flatcar. Take a picture each time I move. If you see them shooting back, take one of them. When I'm up to the building, move close and keep clicking. You got it?"

"Who going with you?"

"I'm doing this alone. Watch me — you'll learn something.

The three of you stay put." Marais slung the carbine over his shoulder, and taking the shotgun in one hand and the bandaged bottle of gasoline in the other, he ran, keeping his head down, to the pile of railroad ties.

Brother George raised the camera and clicked.

Marais did not make a move to shoot. There was no target; the men were out of sight. He ran to the overturned flatcar. Just as he ducked behind it, a bullet banged it and ricocheted into the air. Marais got onto his stomach and aimed the carbine from ground level through a clump of grass at the far end of the flatcar. A spray of shots burst from the station window nearest to Marais. Marais did not shoot back immediately; he waited, studying the window. The squashed head and shoulders of a man appeared, hunched over a rifle. Marais shot at the lump of rifle; there was a cry.

At the sound of the man's voice — it was a surprised groan, unusually loud — the shooting stopped for a few moments. Marais sprinted to some steel drums. He was positive there were only three men in the station. If there had been more there would not have been a pause when one was hit.

Brother George snapped a picture of Marais fixing the bottle of gasoline to a cylindrical stick extending from the muzzle of the shotgun: a catapult for his Molotov cocktail.

The firing started again. The bullets rang on the flatcar. They had not seen him move to the drums.

Marais lit the soaked bandage on the bottle. He stood, took aim and shot. The bottle was an ungainly missile; it sailed, spinning wildly in a smoky spiraling arc, end over end, a trajectory which led through the near window of the railway station. The smash was barely audible; it was a gentle pop. Flames shot up, making rippling heat waves, and the building became plastic and seemed to shudder.

A dark figure flashed before the window. Marais had rested his carbine on the steel drums; he fired, and instantly there was a shout of protest. It was a healthy deliberate yell, not from the man Marais had hit but from the remaining man who, still grizzling loudly, chucked his rifle and a belt of ammunition through the fiery doorway. He staggered out with his arms over his head in surrender. Once in the sun, he stopped his protest and began coughing violently.

Brother George raised his camera.

Marais aimed his carbine.

But neither did more than that. The man coughing on the cinder path of the railway station was Brother Chimanga, wearing sunglasses and a tan wash-and-wear jacket.

Marais leaned his carbine against the steel drums and signaled for Brother George to come over.

"Tie him up and tell the others to put out the fire. If the ones inside are dead, bury them here. If not, bring them along. Get the tracks torn up and," Marais put his hand out, "give me the camera."

"Yatu and Eddy are inside," Marais heard Chimanga saying. Marais walked behind the overturned flatcar. He stripped the leather holder from the camera and pinched open the back. He pulled out the length of bright yellow film and showed it to the sun.

26

Calvin, I want you to meet my mate," said Jack Mavity. "Here he is, Harry, the chap I was telling you about. Where's the missis, Calvin?"

"In bed," said Calvin. "Pleased to make your acquaintance."

"Hi," said Mr. Harry. "Call me Harry."

"You American?" asked Calvin.

"That depends," said Mr. Harry. He looked around, sniffed, then halfheartedly hiked up his trouser tops with his wrists, a fat man's gesture.

"The reason I ask," said Calvin, "is *I* am."

"Go ahead, Harry," said Mavity, "tell him what you told me."

"How about a beer?" asked Calvin.

"I like a man who drinks beer in the middle of the morning," said Mr. Harry. "Cold one for me."

"Well," said Calvin, "it's Sunday. There's nothing else to do except drink on Sunday. Or any other day." Calvin looked at Harry and added, "I'm not complaining."

"Tell him," said Mavity. "He'll be interested."

"Okay," said Mr. Harry.

"Two beers," Calvin called to Jarvis.

Jarvis, at the doorway to the verandah, fanned himself with his tin tray. He shrugged and looked away.

"Two beers," growled Mavity. "And step on it."

Jarvis brought his shoulders together again and dropped them. He fanned faster. The meat cleaver hung on a thong from his leather belt.

"He doesn't like us much," Calvin explained to Mr. Harry. "I'll get the beers myself."

"Sit where you are," said Mavity. "I'll boot him up the arse if he doesn't — "

"Jack, for Christ's sake," said Calvin.

"You're using the wrong approach," said Mr. Harry. "You gotta know how to talk to the jungle bunnies." Mr. Harry waited for Jarvis to turn. He said, "Two beers," to Jarvis.

Jarvis nodded and went to fetch the beers.

"See?" said Mr. Harry.

"Tell him now," said Mavity. "Go on."

Calvin squinted at Mr. Harry. "I've seen you someplace."

"Ever been to Rio?"

"Never," said Calvin. "You?"

"Twice," said Mr. Harry. "Manila?"

"No," said Calvin. "It was somewhere around here. I could almost swear I have."

"I've never seen you," said Mr. Harry.

"I didn't say you had," said Calvin. "I said *I've* seen *you*."

"Smart guy," said Mr. Harry. "Ever been to Algeria?"

"Harry's quite the traveler," said Mavity. "You name it, he's been there."

"I'll think of it," said Calvin. "It'll come back to me."

"Tell him what you told me," said Mavity.

"The Algerian story?"

"No, no. Lilongwe," said Mavity. "Wait till you hear this, Calvin."

Jarvis returned with the tray of beers. He poured into dented pewter mugs.

"Oh, Lilongwe," said Mr. Harry. "Yeah, well, Jack here tells me you sell insurance."

"Not exactly," said Calvin. "I used to. But people aren't very insurance conscious these days."

"That's news to me," said Mr. Harry. "Anyhow, Jack said you make trips now and then up-country. And I said to him, that guy better watch his step if he knows what's good for him. Sure, I said — "

Mavity caught Harry's attention. He darted his eyes sideways at Jarvis, then rolled them ominously back. Harry puckered his mouth and shook his head. He said to Calvin in a loud voice, "Don't go near Lilongwe."

Mavity glanced at Jarvis and winced. "Well, there it is," he said quickly. "You told him the important part. You can tell him the rest later in private."

"Why? What's going on in Lilongwe?" asked Calvin.

"Not much," said Mavity with another glance at Jarvis. Jarvis stared at Harry.

"Plenty," said Mr. Harry. "Rebel soldiers captured the town yesterday. People dead all over the place, buildings burned down, bombs going off — "

"It probably don't mean a thing," said Mavity. "That's the way I see it." He tossed his head in Jarvis's direction and rolled his eyes again.

"Oh, it's serious all right," said Mr. Harry. "I figure if you sell insurance you better sell it around here and forget about Lilongwe. There's some mighty strange things happening there."

"Was one of those soldiers a white fellow with a funny mustache and sunglasses? About so high?" Calvin demonstrated with his hand.

This information of Calvin's seemed to surprise Jarvis and Harry. They stared, Mavity fidgeted.

"I couldn't tell you," said Mr. Harry. "I didn't get close enough to see. I took one look at the smoke and all the dead bodies, and got my ass out of there."

"Imagine that," said Calvin. "There wasn't anything in the paper about it this morning."

"You must be kidding! You think they'd put *this* in the paper? There'd be a full-scale revolt if they did."

Mavity stamped one foot, and cursed, and tugged his ear.

"I suppose Osbong will send in the troops and mop up the whole mess. They've got a pretty good army, you know."

"Not a chance of the army doing anything," said Mr. Harry. "They might surround Lilongwe or something like that, but they'd never attack it."

"You never can tell," said Calvin.

"I can tell," said Mr. Harry. "Those rebels in Lilongwe are sitting on the water supply for Blantyre. The water pipes from the lake, see, run straight through Lilongwe."

"So if they want they can shut off the water," said Calvin. "Is that it?"

Mr. Harry smiled. "Blow up the pump house," he said. "They can blow those water pipes to Kingdom Come. Or they can poison the water."

"I don't drink it," said Calvin. He thought a moment. "Osbong's Youth Wingers can't get in?"

"Nope."

"Well, how do the rebel soldiers get *out* then?"

"I hadn't thought of that," said Mr. Harry. "Anyway, Jack thought you might like to know. I've got a wife and kids myself."

"Thanks," said Calvin. "I appreciate it. But I don't sell insurance."

"Just thought you might be interested."

"I'm interested," said Calvin. "But it doesn't matter. I'm not going anywhere."

"You should watch what you're saying when there's locals around," said Mavity reproachfully. But he was more fearful than angry.

"Which locals?" asked Mr. Harry.

They looked around. Jarvis had gone.

"There was one here just a minute ago," said Mavity. "You should have told him to eff off."

"That fat guy?" Mr. Harry laughed. "Forget it." He turned to Calvin and said, "Well, if you don't sell insurance, what *do* you do?"

"Nothing," said Calvin. "What about you?"

"Nothing," said Mr. Harry. "So you might say we're in the same racket!"

"You got the right time, by any chance?" asked Calvin. "My watch isn't working."

Mr. Harry pushed his sleeve up. On his hairy wrist was a silver watch with a heavy crystal face. Mavity and Calvin moved close for a better look. Under the crystal, in addition to the big disc clock were four dials fitted into the clock's quarters, two black, two red, all with luminous green numbers. The watch itself had a rotating bezel and several winding stems.

"The astronauts have ones like this," said Mr. Harry. "It's eleven-oh-five."

"Time to wake up my wife," said Calvin. "Nice meeting you. Maybe I'll see you around."

"I'm not going anywhere," said Mr. Harry, raising his glass.

"Like I said, neither am I," said Calvin.

* * *

Mira was still asleep when Calvin entered. The room was stuffy with warm morning odors, the humid air that is generated by a naked person slumbering in a closed room. The latched shutters threw down two washboards of light, awhirr with dust specks. A fly was busy on the ceiling. In a dish on the floor next to the bed a smoldering mosquito coil released a thin vertical string of scented smoke. Calvin sat on a stool and picked up a little battery-operated fan, the shape of a flashlight, with a small pink propeller. He clicked it on and played it over his face.

Bailey considered this room the brothel's love nest. So much more classy, she said, than the filthy little knocking shops down the hall. It had a brass bed and more mirrors than a barbershop, and it was trimmed in gilt and mauve. But it was littered, cluttered. This was Mira's doing. She was a collector, and this instinct of hers was apparent. All her things were heaped in the room. Several chairs were mounded with her dresses (closet space was always lacking in a brothel), and there were deposits of other things everywhere, string, shells, ribbons, Calvin's empties, fancy ashtrays, records out of their sleeves. Calvin wondered if this collecting was an assertion of her existence, all the junk as proof.

In February, Calvin carried a box of the Homemakers' Mutual "remembrance advertising" out to the back of the eating house to be burned. He had met Mavity on the stairs, and Mavity had looked in and seen the plastic wallets, the key rings and calendars, the mechanical pencils and ball points.

"Where are you going with all that stuff?" Mavity had asked.

"It's just a lot of cheap crap," Calvin had replied. "I'm chucking it out."

Mavity had picked out a few of the items. He looked at Calvin and said, "Your missis would like that stuff. They love shiny things, the blacks. Little shiny objects. They save them."

Testing Mavity's prejudice Calvin offered Mira the box. She was pleased. She wanted it all. Calvin couldn't explain why.

Curiouser than this was her habit of tacking nude pictures to the wall and taping them to the mirrors. They were big-bosomed girls, ripped from the pages of such magazines as were stocked by the local bookstore. All had blemishless pendulous paw-paw breasts with pale dilated areolas. Most knelt, dimpled buttocks to camera, head thrown back; some lay on their stomachs, pillowed on their paw-paws, one leg crooked back and dangling. Some were preoccupied. They looked out of windows, they splashed in surf, they washed in bubbly tubs, they unzipped their dungarees or felt for buttons on soaked and clinging blouses, they pouted sleepily on rumpled beds.

They made Calvin uncomfortable, at first because they were white, but later more rationally because they were unnecessary. In the room Mira was usually naked, and her breasts were more subtle, her skin and angles finer and smoother than any of those in the pictures. Often she crouched and invited buggery in the same way as that kneeling girl. She lazed more temptingly, she bathed more candidly. It was Mira and not those girls whom Calvin, busy, busy, wanted to tattoo with kisses and bites. The pictures were pointless. They did not arouse, yet they called attention to themselves, from size if not from nakedness. Calvin asked her to take them down. Mira refused.

Calvin's instinct was to discard, and while he only guessed that Mira's reason for saving was to prove that she lived and owned, he knew his motive for discarding was to destroy every trace of his existence. When Mira wasn't looking he packed the wastebasket and chucked things out the window. But it was no good. Mira always won. She tipped out the wastebasket, and if Calvin broke or ripped something she saved the pieces.

Calvin continued to play the little fan over his face. The room was a pigsty, but he forgave Mira her collecting. He needed her. Stronger than love, it was something which made him more thoughtful, more passionate than any lover, and he had none of the lover's selfish hunger. He watched his wife. She slept in the bed under a cone of mosquito netting, a wigwam of billowing gauze, soft and white, suspended from a rafter hook, the bottom edge tucked under the mattress. Her dark smooth shape, nude inside the tent, stretched slowly; she complained in a drowsy yawn, "Let we shift."

"What did you say, honey?" Calvin clicked off the fan and set it down.

"Let we go other place else," said Mira.

"Shopping?"

"No shopping. Shifting."

Calvin strained to hear.

"Here is no good. Girls all time watching you."

Calvin feared conversations with Mira. She was fluent, if illiterate, in two vernaculars, one of which Calvin could understand, though not reproduce. She insisted on English, and Calvin's own English suffered when he talked to her; in order to be understood he used verbs wrongly or sometimes invented new ones, he made Italianate gestures, he simplified, and occasionally, grunting for clarity, he was apt to overdo it. His reply was: "Girls all time watching me who?"

"In bar, one with big bottoms. She looking you."

"She looking *me?*"

"She saying, sure, you promise give baby her."

"I no promise," Calvin said firmly. "Understand?" He stabbed himself in the chest with his thumb. *"Me no promise!"*

"She say."

It was possible. Calvin had slept at one time or another — but always it had been out of pity and charity: it was the only way to get them to accept a few osbongs — with nearly every girl who hung around the bar. One day he entered the bar and looked at the twenty girls who sat in the chairs or played the fruit machines, and he realized he had made love to every one of them — some more than once. But since his marriage he had tried to ignore them. They eyed him from their chairs, they brushed by as he was drinking with Mira; they winked without subtlety, they sucked their teeth and said in the matey hoarseness of familiar greeting, *"Hey Carving!"* Recently, taking an evening walk, he had heard "I love you, mister" — he was not sure whether it was he who was being addressed. It was embarrassing. They were not ordinarily homely, but truly horrible scratching beasts. Several looked like men. And they caused Calvin the discomfort that men who frequent prostitutes always fear, of meeting them constantly on the street in the daytime and forgetting their names.

Calvin bent close to the bed. "Me not," he started. This English had its limitations. He continued on as tender a note as the primitive syntax allowed, "me not promise give baby her."

"You not?"

"Me not," said Calvin sincerely. "No kidding."

Mira pondered this, then said decisively, "You give baby me."

Quailing at the sentence, Calvin clutched at the mosquito netting and asked Mira to repeat it. She did so, without varying her intonation.

"Do you mean," said Calvin; then he paused. He had carefully thought out the sentence, but as soon as he started delivering it he panicked, and lapsed into standard English, "You mean you want me to give you a baby? Or — " He grinned as if with heartburn and clapped his hands on his stomach, "or have you already got one?"

"Got one," drawled Mira. But this might mean anything. In a verbal fog she groped for the familiar. Calvin's hurried sentences had bewildered her and made her echo his final words.

"*Have* you? I mean, are you preg-nant?"

"Preg-nant."

"Because if you are," Calvin attempted a chuckle, "we'll have to make plans — "

"Plans."

" — and *do* something, won't we?"

"We," said Mira.

Now she sat cross-legged in the gauze tent, like an idol in a neglected shrine. Her loveliness bordered on error, it was so generous. But they were barely able to communicate. Even after all Calvin's questions he could not establish whether her gnomic "You give baby me" was a request or a statement of fact. Time would tell, time would tell.

"Guess what happened in Lilongwe," said Calvin.

"Um?" queried Mira.

Calvin looked at her. She was the blackbird, he the grass snake — cousins, but bearing little resemblance. He started to describe what Mr. Harry had told him. Then he broke off. What was the point?

"Bah," said Mira. "Me dress now."

"Me go drink," said Calvin. But he did not rise. He picked up the little battery-operated fan and with a painting motion, as if the fan were a brush, cooled his face. He continued to sit by the bed and look fondly upon his wife.

27

Marais sat solemnly at the bedside of Brother Yatu in a heavily guarded wing of the Lilongwe dispensary. It was late afternoon, the dust of the day was beginning to settle and thicken just above the ground in a tide of pale purple. Marais had been sitting staring in the room since before dawn; he had seen the day flash into brightness and felt the room dry out at midday.

Once in the morning, Brother Yatu had gasped and clenched his fists. But for the whole afternoon he had lain motionless, and it was hard to tell if he was breathing. His fists stayed stiffly clenched. His arms were strapped flat to the bed; in each, a needle and tube was stuck, feeding liquid — in the right plasma, in the left saline solution. Throughout the day the bottles emptied and were changed by the medical assistant, a short studious-looking African who ran the dispensary and who had spoken to Marais earlier. Marais took the emptying bottles as a sign of life in Yatu.

What he could see of the body was burned, all the black skin had been scorched off, gray peels revealed bright pink underneath, some patches were raised with pale blisters. He had been swabbed with ointment, but it was not a medicinal odor that reached Marais — it was roasted flesh and burned cloth. The attitude of the body on the bed, the needles and gauze, only heightened the impression that this was not a human but a luckless animal, a side of singed meat swathed in sheets.

In the hot part of the day Marais closed the shutters to keep the sun out. Now the shutters were open, and Marais looked across the bed and out the window where a streak of sunlight on the road was losing its wattage. At the roadside some men were hammering on what looked like a wooden cart. Marais watched them for a long time. They were huddled around it and knocking erratically at it. Two of the men were his own; Marais studied their movements especially — they were less busy than the rest. Marais had a creeping notion of futility: it was impossible for him to say from its shape or their random bangings what they were doing to it. Most were busy. They levered boards up and clawed out nails, making a sharp hen-screech sound; they tossed slats on top and pounded at them. At five they dropped their tools and drifted away, trailing good-byes after them. Marais looked again at the cartlike thing on the street. It was not whole, nor was it dismantled; it seemed in disrepair. All around it were wood shards and splinters, the shadows of footprints. It did not have a name, but that was unimportant. What troubled Marais was the knowledge that he had watched the men closely for so long, more than an hour, and still was unable to determine whether they had been trying to build or destroy something. He did not understand.

It grew dark, and in the darkness of the small sickroom the smells were stronger. There were faint unfinished shapes, the heavy bars of the headboard, the lyre of a chair back, the small cluttered tabletop with its jug of water and tumbler. The rest was shadow, the furniture appeared legless, and the darkness was dense with the smells of paint and floor wax, dust and soap, and that awful predominating smell of burned flesh. Marais lit a cigar stub and inhaled it, refreshing himself with the smoke as if it were pure air. Then he let the cigar go out. He had promised himself one puff, that was all: he did not want to risk gagging Brother Yatu. No smoking, or as little as possible — it was one of his rules.

The suspense had made him superstitious. All day he had been framing rules for himself. He was not to leave the room, or look too hard at Yatu's blistery face, or ignore him; no loud noises, no direct sunlight, no sudden movement. Patience was needed, and caution. Marais picked out omens everywhere: in a point of sun sliding up the wall, in a twitching cockroach that sniffed at the leg of the bed, in the angles of the cracks in the plaster. Watching that wooden thing in the street he had said in a rushed whisper as if to dispel a bad omen, "Much too big for a coffin."

"Bad burn and bullet wound, too," the medical assistant had said. "My, my." He was young, but Marais felt curiously reassured by his starched white smock, the clean thermometer, the stethoscope coiled in the ample front pocket, earpieces showing. He said that in severe burn cases there was little to be done.

"Can't you graft skin onto him?" Marais asked. He showed the medical assistant his arm. "Here, take some of this if you need it."

"We don't do that here," the man said. He looked at Marais's white forearm; it was very near Yatu's face. "Also from you it would reject. They have to take the graft from the same patient, from his back or thigh. They do this in Salisbury."

"Reject?" Marais pinched the pale hairless skin on the underside of his forearm; he held the flap. "It would reject this?"

"Yes, I think." The bullet wound in Yatu's upper arm was not serious, he said, but the burn covered most of his body and he had lost a lot of blood. And there was always the chance of pneumonia. "Pneumonia. It is terrible," he said. "We always have successful surgery, then *bam* the patient dies of pneumonia. It is hopeless. We need a doctor. We had one but he went away."

"Osbong probably chased him away."

"Maybe. I know he didn't like Osbong. But Osbong never comes here. I think our doctor just got tired. He got tired and went away, back to England."

The medical assistant began to tuck in the sheets at the foot of the bed.

"They say you are the man who captured the town."

"Not only me," said Marais. "There were others, almost fifty men."

"Our electricity was off yesterday. I asked one of your soldiers to please turn it on — "

"They're not all — "

" — and he said no. We had to operate. Strangulated hernia, very serious. No lanterns, no telephone to call the doctor from Blantyre. The man died."

"I'm sorry," said Marais. "If you had asked me I would have given you some help."

The medical assistant smiled. "I thought your soldiers would help. Fifty soldiers," he said, touching the bed. "But not this one, isn't it?"

"What do you mean?"

"It is not me, but some people are saying this one and two others tried to stop you from killing us."

"That's a lie."

"So you found them at the station and killed one, and burned this one, and put the other one in jail, the one they call Mr. Chimanga."

"Who told you that?"

"People are saying."

"We didn't come here to kill you," said Marais. "We captured this town because we wanted to get it away from Osbong. This man here disobeyed my orders. He was in the railway station shooting at us. He killed the ticket agent."

"The people say you killed the ticket agent," said the medical assistant. He did not challenge Marais; he simply stated the rumor.

"They, whoever *they* are, have it all wrong," said Marais. He nodded at Brother Yatu. "This man killed the ticket agent. He would have killed you too if you had been in his way."

"He is not from Lilongwe?"

"No," said Marais. "He's not from Lilongwe. Don't you understand? He's *my* man, one of my soldiers. Didn't you see his uniform there?"

The uniform, what was left of it, a mass of burned and bloody rags, lay in a corner of the room next to a torn pair of boots that had been scissored from Brother's Yatu's feet.

"He is your soldier?" The medical assistant began taking Yatu's pulse.

"Yes," said Marais.

"He knows you?"

"We've been together for the past seven months. He was my friend."

"Then why did he shoot at you?"

"I don't know," said Marais. "Maybe he didn't understand."

"Pulse is very slow. Very faint. Almost cannot feel it."

"Do you think he's going to be all right?"

The medical assistant frowned. Marais thought he was going to say no. He said, "Wait and see."

That was in the morning. Marais kept a fastidious vigil and made his rules from the little phrase *wait and see*. He imagined that Brother Yatu's life depended on his attention; if Marais left the room or watched too closely or made a wrong move, Yatu would die.

His cigar had gone out. He slipped it into his pocket. Outside a radio began to blare. He rose quietly, swung the shutters together and hooked them. Then he sat in complete darkness and tilted his head back until it rested against the wall. He had caught Brother Yatu with his second shot. The first had hit Brother Eddy in the face — he was dead before he fell. Chimanga had taken cover. Yatu was shot after the fire started; he had run past the window and been winged in the arm. Reconstructing it, Marais saw their panic. It had been a mistake to shoot. He had done it for the camera; he had not guessed they were his own men. Had he known he would have smoked them out with the Molotov cocktail. All three could have stood trial and been forced to explain why they mutinied. While dead men were riddles and corpses had to be interpreted, the evidence was always in their favor: the dead always looked innocent, the death itself seemed proof of that. He had been wrong about the trial by ordeal. It was forgotten that Mussa had raped: his death, his smashed head was remembered. Eddy's body was hidden in the coal pile: what were they saying about him or Chimanga? The bottle soared out of Marais's cocktail launcher and through the large window; there were flames, and a frightened shadow leaping past them. Marais fired, driving the shadow back. The sun bore down, and there was shouting.

The sickroom light was on, an unshaded light over the bed. The medical assistant was lifting Brother Yatu's eyelids and shining a small flashlight into his eyes.

Marais had been dozing. He woke quickly, looked across the room and said, "He's dead."

"Yes."

"Goddamn," said Marais. "What do we do now?"

He had looked at the door when he said it, and it was a sighing whisper; but the medical assistant replied to it.

"Now we must make out a death certificate. You can sign it. He has to be buried and — "

"No death certificate," said Marais. "He's not going to be buried yet."

"Government regulations," the man shrugged. "Have to keep records."

"You have a new government now," said Marais severely. "We'll put him in the morgue. Keep this room locked — I'll post a man here. You have a morgue?"

"A small one, but," the man looked concerned, "it's not so cold. It is just for temporary. The body will rot. Smell bad. Even now, you see." He sniffed and made a face. "To bury is better."

"Not now. I'll help you get him ready. We'll move him into the morgue after I send my men off duty. If anyone asks you about Yatu say he's alive."

"No one will ask. They will say he is dead. They know."

"But he's *not* dead," Marais protested. He grasped the lapel of the white smock and drew the medical assistant toward him. "He's not dead, is he?"

"No, he is alive, sir. Alive."

Much later, after midnight, Marais left the dispensary and headed for his hotel. The town seemed ridiculously small and silent. The map was deceptive: it had shown Lilongwe as important, the name had been printed as large as Blantyre, streets were drawn on it that did not exist. But, then, the other places, Rumpi and Fort Hill, had seemed important until they were captured. After the attacks they were hardly towns at all. Lilongwe was one poorly paved street.

Brother George was waiting in Marais's room. He stood when Marais entered.

"What is it?"

"Reporting," said Brother George. "Everything quiet. Men at posts."

"Any sign of trouble?"

"No sign. Radio call from Harry. He says okay. Osbong still doesn't know how many we are, and he will not attack unless we stop the water. Harry says the rumors are going okay. Everyone believes."

"What about the locals?"

"People here?" Brother George laughed. "They don't care. I met one man who didn't even know we captured. He was sleeping when we did it. Silly man."

"They'll know pretty soon. We're having a parade, just to wake everyone up. Find some boys who know how to play the drum — maybe there's a police band. We can put them to work. Everyone will wear a clean uniform. We'll get as many of the locals to march as we can. Indians, too. We've got enough rifles — "

219

Brother George shifted his feet and sighed.

"What's wrong?"

"Parade," said Brother George. "The men will not like it. They are not . . ." He paused. "They are not happy so much."

"You said there was no trouble."

"No trouble. Just — I went out to the roadblock tonight. The ones at the roadblock — asleep. I wake them up and tell them keep awake. But they walk slow-slow, you see? They say to me that *Where is Brother Yatu? What you do to Yatu?* He is okay, I say, but he shot to us. *We want to see Yatu. You killed him and Eddy.*" Brother George looked at Marais for assurance. "Yatu — he's okay?"

"Yes, he's okay. He's much better." Saying so, Marais thought, I don't trust George. He had not known that until he had told the lie.

"Good," said Brother George with relief. "Sometimes it is very bad, burns. My cousin burned. Dead very fast. The men don't — "

"Get this straight," said Marais. "I want any man who makes trouble or drags his feet reported to me. Everyone's going to march in that parade."

"Yatu?"

"Yes," said Marais, "Yatu's going to march if he's feeling better. So is Chimanga."

"Chimanga," said Brother George. "He want to see you. He was troublesome — making noise. We had to beat him."

"I'll see him tomorrow. But you tell the men this. I don't want any fucking around. We've got to get organized before we leave here. We can't march on Blantyre like this. Tell them I said we're not going anywhere until we get organized. I said we were staying here a week, but I'm changing that now. I want discipline, and I'll get it. I'll stay here six months if I have to."

*   *   *

In the compound outside police headquarters the next morning the prisoners' women were cooking over wood fires and passing tin cups of food through the barred windows. It was nine, but already so bright that the cooking fires appeared to be flameless.

The ground-floor cells were full. Most of the prisoners were policemen, some Youth Wingers who had been rounded up the day before, several party officials and a number of worried-looking men who had been arrested as counter-revolutionaries — stoogies, Marais's men called them. The stout government agent was alone in a cell. He wore a shiny green suit but was shirtless, his jacket over a naked torso; he mopped his neck with a hanky and stalked the cell in his bare feet. During the night he had been removed from a crowded cell when three of his fellow prisoners tried — no one knew why — to garrote him with a shoelace. An Indian family of six lolled abjectly in another cubicle. The morning of the attack their shop had been looted and they asked Marais's men for protection. They had brought their own food and spices in sacks; the sunken-eyed wife squatted before a kerosene stove stirring a pot of fragrant vegetables.

Striding into the compound Marais was besieged by appeals from bystanders, the women who were cooking and others who stood as soon as they saw Marais's stocky figure leave the hotel. They knelt and pleaded, beseeching him for the release of their relatives; one tugged at him and offered a bribe, a plug of tightly folded bills. They were like chickens disturbed in a coop, they beat the dust and fluttered and clucked at Marais.

He brushed them aside and hurried into the building, stepping carefully over the rubble of broken glass and the blackened timbers and chunks of cement that littered the entryway. Brother Jaja's name had been daubed large in thick dripping strokes on a discolored rectangle of wall once covered by the gun case, which lay shattered on the floor. Behind the counter, on the cot next to the wall where early on that Saturday morning the obliging duty officer had been sleeping, Brother

Henry lay askew, his feet stuck off the end of the cot, his shirt was open, his peaked cap over his face.

"Wake up!" Marais banged his fist on the counter. Bits of glass on the counter top tinkled.

Brother Henry groaned and sat up, letting his cap fall. He rubbed his eyes and sleepily tasted his tongue, running it over his teeth.

"What the hell are you doing? Get off your ass! What's that *smell* — has the toilet backed up?" Marais looked around in disgust. "This place is a mess! Get out front and make some explanations to those people — and look smart, for Christ's sake. Do you want a riot on your hands? I want to know who they are, some are offering bribes. Write down their names and their complaints. If they don't have a reasonable gripe send them the hell out of here." He kicked at a tin can, then lit a cigar and puffed it to drive out the smell. There were flies everywhere.

Brother Henry made no explanation. He sluggishly responded, slowly buttoning his shirt — yawning a roar as he did so — before getting up from the cot. It seemed deliberate provocation.

"Those people," he said; he sampled his tongue again, looked displeased, and spat. "Too troublesome."

Marais was looking at the littered entryway. He said, "And clean this goddamned place up. Sweep up that glass. What's that big puddle out front?"

"Big puddle," said Brother Henry. "Where the car esplode. Water come."

"Drain it," said Marais. "Scoop it out." He looked at Brother Henry. "What's wrong with you?"

Brother Henry snorted, flipped his cap on and fitted a pair of sunglasses over his eyes. "Chimanga out there," he said, crunching through the broken glass in his heavy boots, his long laces trailing. "Want to talk to you."

Chimanga's was a low narrow cell at the back, sheltered by a makeshift roof of thatch bundles. It had originally been a kennel where the Royal Nyasaland Constabulary kept their Alsatians. Chimanga sat on the floor hunched over, talking to a group of children who crouched before the cell door hugging their knees. They were listening intently to Chimanga. Seeing Marais they got up and — sheepishly, Marais thought — they backed away into the sunlight until Chimanga shouted for them to stop.

"You scare them," said Chimanga. "They are fearing Europeans." He laughed and extended his left hand through the bars in a rude greeting.

The children covered their mouths and muffled embarrassed giggles.

"You refusing to shake me?" said Chimanga, smiling at his own hand. "Well . . . You thinking I am a dog? Putting me in the dirty place?"

"There's no room inside headquarters."

"The Indians will come here. I go inside. No good here, just sitting."

"You'll stay here."

"Uh," Chimanga nodded, "like a dog." He called to the children in Chinyanja. "He thinks I am a dog — woof! woof!"

Marais eyed Chimanga. "What were you telling them when I came?"

Chimanga returned Marais's stare. His face was bruised, his mouth torn, the flesh around his eyes puffed up. There was a welt on his neck, as dark and thick as a leech. He held the bars with both hands showing roughened lacerated knuckles.

"Little story," he said, and smiled.

"Telling them a little story? What story?"

"About General Bang-Bang. You knowing him?"

"No."

"You knowing Livingstone Island, eh?"

"The prison. In the lake."

"Mm. In the lake, Salima side," said Chimanga. "Before,

six-seven years before, was a prison on island, and General Bang-Bang, European man like you, he was the in-charge of prison. A bad man. Had to wake up African prisoners in night when they sleeping and just telling them work-work. In night, eh. Sometimes they saying that we not working in night, and Bang-Bang he saying that okay I cane you twenty-thirty stroke. Too much he cane poor African, all time he cane-cane-cane with bamboos and *sjamboko* too. He like caning African too much. For Bang-Bang it is better."

"You can tell me in Chinyanja," said Marais.

Chimanga looked insulted. "I speaking English." He slid his hands down the bars and nodded. The children had crept closer; they seemed to be listening, understanding. Marais smoked.

"Oh, Bang-Bang was a bad man — *too* bad. He finished those African, kill them, bang-bang-bang with *sjamboko*. That why they name him. And sometime he take their cloths and make them running about just naked. Sure. Always when the government — *British* government — asking that what you doing to these chaps, Bang-Bang he refusing that he finishing them and saying that, well, they all just bloody *Kaffir* shit. Some caught with fever and some they had to fall down from paining."

"That's the story you're telling these little kids!"

"That not the end of story." Chimanga wet his lips. "The end of story is that African prisoners they all hoping, sure, Bang-Bang he too devil and we just have to finish him for God sake, he sinning on us too much." He smiled at Marais. "So one night they making a hell of noise, all African jumping and doing *ngoma*. Bang-Bang he wake up and foot over to prison house and say that, okay, you all have to work just now. And all men saying that, yes, we will work digging, so forth. And they take big *kisu*, shovel, stick, what-not, and they *cut* him in pieces, and they fire all houses, everything and singing — "

The children were very close to Chimanga now, fixed by his steady voice. He looked directly at them and started speaking in Chinyanja. Perhaps, Marais thought, he had interrupted at this point in the story and frightened the children away.

Marais listened, translating to himself.

Chimanga said, "The police in Salima saw smoke rising up from the island and they went in boats. But the African men were not there. The island and all the houses were burning and mocking the police. They could not find the white man, Bang-Bang. They looked very hard and saw blood, then *ah!* They found a piece here, and over there a piece. All little pieces with blood dripping. A dog was eating his leg and he liked it. The white man's head was off, his arm, his foot — "

"Stop it!" snapped Marais.

At his shout the children jerked their heads around and looked at Marais with startled faces. They jumped a few steps back and lifted their puny arms. Then they ran, stamping in the dust, scattering in four directions. Marais turned and saw them regrouping under a yellow thorn tree fifty yards away. He saw them dance; they spun in their loose rags like imps, lifting their legs high and holding their arms above their heads and calling out in bursts, "Bang-Bang! Bang-Bang! Bang-Bang!"

Chimanga smiled, deeply satisfied. He said, "They are knowing your name, eh."

Part Four

28

It might have helped if they spoke the same language, but they didn't. Calvin patted his tummy, put his grin close to Mira's face and grunted, "Unh? Unh?" He cradled an invisible infant in his arms and (saying goo-goo in singsong) pretended to cuddle and burp it. None of this got through to Mira. She buffed her nails and looked blank. Her pregnancy remained unconfirmed.

And yet they were always together, either sitting on the verandah, or shopping in town, or taking an evening walk down Osbong to the clock tower. Her silences did not keep Calvin from talking, particularly in friendly sentences which began, "Did you ever notice how — "

He noticed how whenever there was a grassy plot there were little footpaths crisscrossing it: Africans always trampled their own paths and detours, and after Calvin saw his second one he saw hundreds. Or the clock tower. This was a cement cube on the top of a slightly inclined steel post which grew out of a flower bed. It was (with Osbong's Presidential Palace, Parliament House, Market Day, Lakeside Dwelling with Dhow and Queen's View — the hilly view south from the top of the

escarpment) a favorite postcard subject. Calvin noticed each of
the four clock faces on the cube's vertical sides showed a different time. The difference in the hours shown was so great
they could have told the time in four parts of the world. But
that was not the intention. They showed the wrong time in
Blantyre four times over. Calvin said, "Did you ever notice how
those clocks — " Mira looked away. She hadn't noticed. No
one had. Calvin still began his questions in the same way, but
now he knew that the reply would always be no. Sometimes
Mira said "Yah" but this meant no as often as yes. She was not a
communicative person. They didn't speak the same language;
most of the time she was silent.

The silence made their sex a wholly anonymous pleasure.
Calvin locked the bedroom door and tied up the mosquito net;
they usually made love in the dark, and except for her yah they
did not speak. But it seemed to Calvin that most sex was anonymous anyway — though in the dark with his first wife it
had felt like queerness or incest because it was, or so it felt,
a cozy conspiracy of white people that left him feeling guilty and
sullen. With Mira, the one time lightning flashed and lit up
the bedroom, Calvin saw in the spacious barbershop mirrors
a dozen skinny Americans in their undershirts, each hunched in
a tense gymnastic with a pair of brown cycling legs. This sight,
in the lightning's tumbling instant, took all the starch out of
Calvin. It was better not to see or speak, and the very invisi-
bility of it made them adventurous: the bird beating her wings
in the heat swallowed the snake in gulps. It all bolstered Calvin's confidence, for he had a recurring feeling, fortified every
time he made love to Mira, that he would never go home, ever.

It was strongest on rainy afternoons, with a thrum of drops
on the tin roof of the eating house. People disappeared indoors,
the empty street steamed; all work stopped and would not
begin again until the rain was past. It gave Calvin a sense of
well-being and in this hot place where there was little privacy,
a cool stretch of undisturbed reflection. It was a calming he

needed, for by the middle of the afternooon his head was full of
fizzy beer gas, and with the seven or eight pints he had put away
since morning he felt a sick tingle at the ends of his unreliable
limbs. His head was swollen, his temples balloon tight. Drinking in sunlight took him that way; it tired him but would not
let him sleep; it made his eyes boil and his head ache and swell
like a football straining against its laces. He feared his head
might explode.

But a spray of rain from a black sky eased everything: the
temperature dropped, Calvin's head cleared. He got up
from his verandah chair and passed through the bar, touching
Mira slightly on the shoulder as he passed by her. In the bedroom he lay and waited, listening to the rain's splash on the
leaves and the roof and in the gurgling gutter. Mira understood. She entered the room, active, kicking off her sandals, one
arm twisted behind her back, unzipping, the other unwinding
her headscarf. And soon, smoothly, still braceleted, she was beside him — so speedily from her chair that waffles from the cane
seat were deeply imprinted on her buttocks — pulling his
clothes off. These rainy afternoons there was no hurry; they
made love slowly in the storm's twilight with amazed sighs, as if
each moment of the way had to be invented, and everything they
did happened to be new. Afterward there was all that warmth;
they lay in the rain-enclosed room, in a mist of love. No, he
would never go home. He would stay and not fret; his silent sex,
like any other passion, like politics, like revolt, had a pattern
which comforted — a beginning, a middle, and an end.

This was maybe the middle. After the "You give me baby"
discussion Calvin saw a new dimension to his marriage. Spec-
ulating on the possibility of Mira's pregnancy, he decided that
the most remarkable thing about children and the whole idea
of parenthood was that it had nothing whatever to do with sex.
After all (Calvin's reflection went) sex was fundamentally an
embrace, and a brief one at that — though people tried to
lengthen its duration by devising tricky preliminaries, believing

231

that, prolonged, it was more voluptuous. Naturally they failed: sex had explicit contours, and touching all these peripheries it had to repeat and so, finally, bored. The manageable variations were limited. Invention failed. And man was a sexual weakling — that was the first fact of life; it worried man sick and made him brood sadly over his body. Still man persevered, but not because of the lust only. It was something else; it was a kind of intrigue. A love affair was as close as anyone in his square house got to real cloak-and-dagger suspense, to plotting, conspiring, defeating, to intentional mystification. Most got no closer to mystery; but what people called love was pretty close — almost a complete plot, that rainy afternoon in the bedroom. Parenthood was different, much more serious and companionable than sex, and like insurance in that it made promises, it took luck and it was vaguely morbid.

He hoped Mira was pregnant, or as the vernacular put it, "had something on her person." The childless were paupers — children were insurance in its purest form. Your small deposit, given with thanks and allowed to mature undisturbed, guaranteed a residue of your flesh forever on earth, a kind of immortality for people who found it hard to get through an afternoon. It was possible that your children might fetch and carry for you; more likely they would do nothing. But after your death they had no choice: they were deputized in your image to pass on to other generations that waspish pallor, that yen to laze and drink in the morning, those tooth gaps and long bones, that nailless little toe. Your whole style was bequeathed. In your child, the squat simian version of you was your death — the child was the mortician of man; but this deadly elf, probably less than half human, charmed you with his undertaker's eye, beguiled you with a dimple or a foible of your own endowment, buried you and then carried on, helping you to outlast your death. It was insurance, but no policy could guarantee the drama of those certainties. An example of Homemakers' Mutual futility, the folly of all insurance, was the feeble memory of poor dead Ogilvie living on in the tarnished bangles that Mira kept

232

on the neck of a beer bottle; Ogilvie lived in the clutter of merchandise in the bedroom, the heaps of clothes, the silly pictures. In his way, Ogilvie had paid for it all. And so many other clients had simply piffled off into death without leaving so much as a brat behind. The Africans were right in valuing children. They trampled their paths and ignored the clock tower; they weren't bothered by Osbong, they saw no landscape and had no faith in anything except their children. It was right. Barrenness was the only poverty.

Weeks passed. Mira varied her utterances. One day it was "Let we shift," the next day the ambiguous "You give baby me," both sentences either preceded or followed by "Yah." She spoke without alarm or hurry, her mood was constant, she did not urge. She said, over and over again, "Let we shift" and "You give baby me." Calvin said "okay," "fine," "very good," "if you say so."

A month after that first discussion there was a distinct swelling in Mira's stomach, the half globe of a heavy meal. It stayed. It grew. Now there was no doubt.

"I rather fancied she had a bun in the oven," said Major Beaglehole, when Calvin broke the news to him. "I'm glad you didn't do the dirty on her."

"No," said Calvin. "I wouldn't do that."

"You did the decent thing."

"I married her."

"You married her," said Major Beaglehole. "I say we drink on it. Where is that bloody waiter!"

"There he is," said Calvin, "talking to — say, did Jack introduce you to that guy Harry?"

"A swine," said Major Beaglehole. "He chats up the blacks. Pay no attention to him." The major looked at Harry talking to Jarvis. "Chap could do with a haircut."

It was now May, the wedding present of the double room — the love nest — ceased to be a present: it would have to be vacated or rented. This, Calvin considered, was as good a time as any to shift and have the baby. It was not a question of money — if anything there was too much of that, more than Calvin wanted or needed. There was plenty. Mira's spending had still not exhausted Ogilvie's endowment. Her brand loyalty prevented her from squandering it all: she deprived herself when her brands were out of stock. She smoked only tipped Matinées in yellow boxes of fifty, drank only Manica *cerveja* (*tipo de exportação*) and chewed only Double Bubble (smoothing and saving the waxy cartoons). Calvin's own paycheck was still cabled every month from the National Shawmut Bank in Boston to the Barclay's Bank in Blantyre.

What had he done to deserve any of it? He had not filed a report to the home office or sold a cent's worth of insurance since February. He had persuaded people *not* to buy. The honest thing to do was to resign and stop paying that farcical alimony, to close up shop, sell what Homemakers' called the hard furnishings and ship the files back to Boston. And then shift himself and his swelling wife into the lush cushions of secondary jungle in the highlands south of Blantyre. They could live in a sturdy little hut, tangled and hidden in the high skirtlike roots of the trees that grew there. He could raise chickens, do a little fishing, farm a few acres of peanuts, ride on the motorcycle, go for walks and wait for Mira to pip. Life was simple, death was inevitable, only children had meaning; and there was no inconvenience except pain, despair the only calamity.

*　　*　　*

"We're moving," Calvin told Bailey. "But I want you to know that room meant a hell of a lot to Mira and me. Be seeing you."

"Wait half a tick," said Bailey. She drew her greasy shawl tight and examined Calvin. "You mean to say you're vacating that room there?"

"That's right," said Calvin.

"That cute little room? You're packing it up?"

"Yes. We're shifting — " He didn't want to say *into a hut.* " — out of town."

"Haven't you heard?"

"Heard what?"

Bailey sputtered. "Why there's a ruddy *war* going on! You can't go a half mile out of town without some black sod stopping you and getting you into a punch up."

"I heard there was a little trouble in Lilongwe —"

"A little trouble in Lilongwe!" Bailey showed her spotted teeth. "They blew the bloody place up! All the white people have moved across the border to Fort Jameson — they ran for their lives. The blacks went buzeek. Ask anyone."

"They're not all black," said Calvin. "I know that."

"You know so much, don't you?" Bailey sneered.

"Their leader is a white man. I saw him. He's worse than any of them."

"What's a nice European bloke like that getting mixed up with *Kaffirs* for?"

"He's not such a nice bloke, really. I admit he seems sincere, but he killed Mira's brother. Or his soldiers did — but that's the same thing. Anyway, before that, he showed me around the camp in Rumpi. He's white all right."

"You're quite the pleasure tripper, aren't you, now?"

"I was up there — that was Christmas — seeing some clients."

"I've seen your *clients,*" said Bailey. "Ha!"

Calvin frowned. "Well, I've seen your clients, too, and *they* don't win any prizes."

"Don't be sarky," said Bailey. "I keep a clean house."

"Right," said Calvin. "I didn't mean to be nasty. I just want to move for personal reasons."

"But you know about this here war, don't you?"

"I've heard the talk," said Calvin. At the Zambesi, a week before, the bartender had said *bloodyshed and boochery,* and other listeners had chimed in; but all had returned serenely to their drinks. They didn't care. Late at night they blamed Calvin for the trouble in Lilongwe, as Mavity blamed him for American space travel. All the Africans in Blantyre seemed to know that it was a white man who led the soldiers.

"So I'm right, aren't I?"

"Yup," said Calvin.

"They're going to kill the old man," said Bailey. She tossed her head at the picture of Osbong. (*If I am, then I am a Dictator for the People . . .*)

"That's what they say."

"And take over this whole bally place."

"So they say."

"There," said Bailey, and threw her shoulders back and smiled as if she had just baked a cake and was holding it up for Calvin to admire.

Calvin lifted his glass and drank. He said, "But we're still moving out of town."

"Oh, bloody hell!" said Bailey.

"It's cheaper for one thing. But that's not the reason."

"It's gormless, that's what it is. You're better off here in the house," said Bailey. "You may pig it here, but it's safe. You don't have a lot of *Kaffirs* shaking knives at you."

"I wish you wouldn't use that word," said Calvin.

"Which word?"

"*Kaffir*," said Calvin. "It's disagreeable."

"Listen to *him!*" said Bailey. She put her head down in a butting position. "They was *Kaffirs* before sixty-three, and as far as I'm concerned they're still *Kaffirs*. Maybe it's just my habit, maybe not. But it'll be a long time before they're anything but *Kaffirs* to me."

Calvin felt uncomfortable. He had made her say the word three more times. "You don't like Africans shaking knives," he said. "But Jarvis has a knife."

"Jarvy wouldn't hurt a flea," said Bailey.

"I don't think he likes me," said Calvin.

"Course he don't like you," said Bailey. "He don't like anyone except the bloke in fifteen."

"Harry," said Calvin. "I thought he looked familiar. Now I remember where I saw him. It was out in the garage, they were eating like two cannibals, Harry and Jarvis. I felt like puking. And you want me to stay here!"

"Not good enough for you, eh?" said Bailey. "Well, I'll have you know the U.K. high commissioner came here once with his dolly. It was good enough for *him*. That don't happen to every house, I can tell you."

"We're moving," said Calvin wearily. "And that's final."

"There's a bloody revolution — "

"Fuck the revolution," said Calvin. "Nobody cares."

"That's a fine way to talk," said Bailey. "And here you are grousing about the way people eats and thinking you're the bee's knees."

"Sorry," said Calvin. "Now I think I'll have one more beer and then go in there and start packing my stuff."

"I'll give it to you for fifty osbongs a month," said Bailey. "Take it or leave it."

"Look — " Calvin began.

"Twenty," said Bailey helplessly.

"It's not the money."

"Take it for bugger-all," said Bailey. She turned away. "I don't need it."

"But that's your best room," said Calvin. "Everyone wants to stay in that room. It's got mirrors."

"Used to be number one," said Bailey. This was nostalgia. "Oh, it was very lardy-dardy before the mess-up. The U.K. high commissioner stayed there, and lots of government bods. We had a nice class of gent, I can tell you. Used to hide their cars out back in the garage. Everything was laid on, cheese and biscuits, a little Portugee plonk, the sparkly or that *rosé* in baskets. I had hopes, I did."

"Before the mess-up."

"Before the, yes, the mess-up," said Bailey. "Not much call for that room since. Might as well be frank."

"Since the mess-up."

"That's right. You see, round about the new year, must have been about then, we, you might say lost one of the gents, you see."

"You lost one."

Bailey puckered and coughed. She splashed a little gin into her tankard of beer and said, "I could use a little rain about now to cool things off."

"You *lost* one?"

"Correct," said Bailey. "Lost one. He, you might say, dropped dead on us."

"Who *might say?*"

"You, the police, lots of people might. You know how people are. There was some talk."

"I never heard it," said Calvin.

"*You* don't hear anything, do you? Just go your own way — bugger you, I'm all right, Jack. Well, I suppose that's your lookout."

"Let's get back to this guy that dropped dead, okay?" said Calvin. His fourth pint always made him methodical. "No one . . . ah . . . no one *helped* him drop dead, did they?"

"There was a few what you might call clues. But it don't make tuppence worth of difference now. Because after the mess-up none of them politicians wanted to use the room, if you see my meaning. They was scared and such-like. And they're the only ones with two tickeys to rub together. So I says to myself, I says, as no one's going to use that nice little room, might as well give it to the kids, I says. And you got it, God help us. It ain't much, but — "

"Which clues?"

"Well, there was a sort of knife, if you see what I mean."

"You found a knife?"

"Yes, we did," said Bailey. "Mavity did, that is."

"Whereabouts did you find — "

"Point of fact, it was right in that room, the knife was."

"In the room," said Calvin. "On the floor?"

"Yes, right on the floor."

"Just lying on the floor, right?"

"Not lying. It was what you might call sticking up in the air."

"I see," said Calvin.

Here, Bailey became very positive: "Yes, that there clue was sticking right in that *Kaffir's* shit bag. It was in so bloody far we couldn't yank it out."

"So you didn't. You left it there and dragged him out and wedged him in a drain during the storm."

"You might say that," said Bailey. "Gives the house a bad name if they find dead corpses inside. They found him the next day, of course. Funny, though. It still gave the house a bad name. Didn't make no difference at all."

"He was the minister of defense."

"So they said."

"Maybe the murderer's still around." Calvin looked around.

"Won't be the first," said Bailey.

"But that guy was killed right here, right in my room!"

"Not so loud," said Bailey. "What are you complaining about anyway? You got a free room out of it, didn't you?"

Calvin started to reply. He was going to call them all pigs and fling his glass at the mirror over the bar. But he had not said two words when he felt something warm pressing against his leg. He saw a gold woolly head. It was one of Mavity's children, a little girl; her face was smeared with ice cream. He scooped her up and wanted to kiss her, but he thought he had better not. He was known as a drunk, and drunks were excused for many things; but they were blamed for more. After a minute or so the little girl wriggled off his lap and ran to her father.

*　　*　　*

"Everything," Calvin said, sweeping a pile of papers from the desk with the side of his hand. "Put everything in these boxes. Don't leave a scrap behind. We're clearing out."

Hired for the day, Jarvis slouched about the office flipping wrapped parcels of brochures into crates. He crushed sheaves of paper into file boxes which he bound with string.

Most of the office papers were set aside to be burned. Some

had to be shipped with the adding machine (rust erupting in bubbles under the blue lacquer), the gummed-up typewriter with a piece of headed paper in it and the beginnings of a message (*Dear Sir, I regret to inform you that I haven't done a stroke of work since the middle of February this year, and furthermore I don't think . . .*), stocks of pens, ornate policy blanks with gold stickers on them, a stack of papers headed TABLE OF VALUES PER EACH 1000 FACE AMOUNT, Thompson's *Ready Reckoner* in plastic, empty ledgers and gift calendars (Samuel Chamberlain's scenes of rural New England with *Season's Greetings from Homemakers' Mutual*). Everything was coated in a gritty layer of red dust. Termites had nested in the receipt books.

"All this shit is going back," said Calvin, indicating a pile of papers. But he would have preferred to destroy it all.

Jarvis tidied the pile by nudging it with his toe.

At twelve-thirty Calvin went downstairs to the Highlife for a beer. He was hunched over his glass and thoughtfully blowing a hole into the inch of warm foam when Jarvis appeared beside him.

"Upstairs," said Jarvis, rolling his eyes up to emphasize the direction. "Man says he wants you."

"You might know," said Calvin. "Just when I decide to have a beer. Here, you want to finish it?"

"If I want a beer I will buy one," said Jarvis petulantly. "I don't want your germs."

"Germs," said Calvin. "Jesus, I haven't heard that word in ages." He drank up quickly, gagging on the foam, then wiped his mouth on his sleeve and they went upstairs.

An African man was sitting behind Calvin's desk, leafing through a Homemakers' Mutual appointment book, the Samuel Chamberlain one. He was in Calvin's swivel chair and working it around in squeaking circles. He wore a dark suit, a striped tie, large gold cufflinks and sunglasses. His hair was stylishly uncut, very bushy, a kind of hairy helmet. He did not rise.

"Boy!" he called. "Get over here."

Calvin walked to the desk and said angrily, "Don't you talk to my assistant like that. He's not your slave."

"I'm talking," the African flipped the page of birch trees to one of a covered bridge, then looked up, "I'm talking to you — boy."

"Well, that's better," said Calvin.

"You don't care?"

"If it makes you happy," said Calvin. "Why should I spoil your fun?" Calvin saw that pinned to the African's collar was a Doctor Osbong badge. "Now, if you don't mind, we're busy."

"Doing a little spring cleaning?"

"Nope," said Calvin, "closing up shop. I'm giving up the whole works. Leaving." He saw a clearing in the jungle, dappled by sun.

"No, you're not."

"Yes, I am."

The African smiled and shook his head. "You're not going anywhere, boy. You've just been nationalized."

29

Two weeks ago [Marais wrote] I buried Yatu, taking every possible precaution. I used to be able to make people disappear without a trace. It's a revolutionist's most useful talent, better than bomb-making or a good aim. The art of kidnapping, the murder with no corpse, the vanishing act. I'm sure the PIDE never found the man they sent to hunt me — even on the run I was able to send him into thin air! I know they're still looking for me. The South Africans are still looking for the man who cancelled all their letters with a bomb.

I was going to take Brother George along. There was a marginal risk, but I was willing to take it to find out whose side G. is on. There would be digging. G. would insist on doing it, and then resent the fact that he worked while I watched. I decided to go alone and be done with it. Most of the men seemed to sense a month ago when I hid the body in the morgue that he was dead, that I killed him unfairly and that he'd already been buried. So there weren't any suspicions. I put the body in the van before dawn and drove into the bush pretty far. No one followed. It was still not light when I finished digging the hole. Afterward I covered the freshly turned dirt with boughs and took a roundabout route back to town. Today, out of curiosity, I went back. Had no trouble finding it. The grave was piled a foot high with a mound of boulders. There was a hefty spear wedged upright in the rocks, probably showing that he had been a warrior. In a little clay pot next to the grave there were fresh flowers.

I think it is that shock that made me turn this textbook into a diary. That and the fact that for five weeks we haven't moved. We seem to have lost whatever momentum we had, and I know I'm alone.

* * *

They remember incidents with terrifying inaccuracy. Their version of the march from Rumpi is a slave caravan being stalked by Mussa's ghost, with me as slaver riding comfortably at the lead. A simple maneuver becomes a death march, a gesture a threat. Today three came to me drunk and said that all along I've been hindering them. I got up to explain. They thought I was going to chase them, and ran out of the room.

* * *

There's no one to talk to. They don't trust me. I'm not sure if I trust them. George sulks whenever I ask him about their sneaking treason. He was never much company, none of them were. But I thought it would be all over by now: this was the week I was supposed to go back to Dar. I told G. that I never expected them to be loyal to me, only to each other.

They fight. Fistfights among themselves and with the townspeople. They don't punch; they close their eyes and slap wildly, missing, spinning around, kicking out. They've looted most of the shops. And there's some kind of sloppy, bullying protection racket going on. Yesterday one of them tried to screw some money out of an Indian tailor. The Indian gave him all he had. It wasn't enough, apparently. He was shot in front of his kids. The other day it was an African they killed. I tried to find out what was going on. "Leave us alone," they said. "He's an African — this is our business." They had beaten him to

243

death. The beating victim is the most mangled corpse; they keep at it, never quite sure when he's dead. I have no control over them now. If I have any it's negative. I've threatened to track down and shoot anyone who starts for Blantyre. This has some effect, though they don't seem organized enough to do anything together. If I could kill Chimanga and get away with it I think I could get them into fighting shape. But I'd never get away with that, and now it's impossible to put him in solitary. They won't let me near him. If they weren't so heavily armed I'd leave. They're dangerous with all those rifles. Tonight I saw two having a smoke next to some gasoline drums.

*   *   *

Sometimes they talk to me, a stupid kind of needling that wears me out. If I talk in English they reply in Chinyanja, or vice versa. I can't win. They tell me not to interfere. When I ignore them for a whole day they say I don't care what happens to them. They accuse me of delaying. ("You don't want to kill all those whites in Blantyre!") They don't know anything about my bomb in Jo'burg. I suppose I should stand there and tell them how many white people I've killed; but that would be foolishness as bad as theirs. I never killed anyone because he's white. I never thought about it that way. It was always political. But these bastards are making me into a racist.

"It's not racial," I want to say. "Don't you see it's not?" Perhaps they have no respect for me because I trusted them so much, and they know they were never worth it. It's bad when they accuse me, but it's much worse when they're silent. There are times when I want to wake up black, anonymous, and then seat myself at one of their tables. Maybe Chimanga was right when he said, "No white man can ever be friends with an African. Look at your skin." The only thing that gives me hope is that I know him to be a liar.

*   *   *

It used to be *We, Us*; now it's *Them* and *They*. This bothers me, but I can't write it any other way. *We* is a lie. Lately I've caught myself thinking: maybe there's nothing there when they're silent, maybe they're not thinking anything at all. Maybe they don't care because they can't. I begin to hate them and wonder if it was hate or a kind of revenge that made me torture those prisoners and shoot Yatu and Eddy. In which case they were right to distrust me. Analyzing it is no good. The process of analyzing it makes me guilty, and my guilt in the end makes me easier on them. Then, after these feelings, I walk out of my room ashamed and I accept their abuse. I seem almost to ask for it. I know I'm to blame for most of it.

* * *

It's not one complaint. For some it's that I'm not black, for others that they're not white. A few haven't got over the feeling that I'm a zombie; some can't forgive me for being half-American. Most object, in a very unusual way, to the fact that I led them here. All are unanswerable, but the complaint about leadership is the only one I've looked into.

They insist that they were forced to follow me and do things against their will. Their major grievance was this persuasion. They could not mutiny in Rumpi because I had "medicinized" them, put a spell on them. There was nothing they could do to prevent it: "So we had to kill our brothers." The blame was all mine because I gave the order and worked the spell. I am an enemy, a witch; I have this power, and they see themselves as powerless. But it's a paradox because I'm still with them, still powerful. They hate and accept my power at the same time. They can't do anything except complain. All the while they obeyed my orders they were building up a resentment for obeying them. To them this is a form of exploitation higher than Osbong's. I thought that I was any white man to them, no different from the American from Blantyre we picked up who tried to sell me insurance.

Their racial mutiny might be as simple as this: they needed me; they hated the thought that they needed me and so hated me; but this did not make them need me less.

* * *

245

So they have their own demonology which they obey, and still they keep a kind of order in town. They know it has to be defended. (It is failure that makes them superstitious. They stumble and then see the witch.) They've set up scanning posts on the hills outside town. A few days ago a beat-up Dakota tried to land. Probably the journalists I was told to expect. They let it come in low — I was watching from the roof of the hotel — and then peppered it from all sides. It banked sharply, nosed up and sort of peeled off. They already have a song about this. Tradition seems to come easy.

*   *   *

Today they woke me up early. I had my hand on my revolver as soon as I heard the knock. Told them to come in with their hands in the air. A half a dozen of them, all shouting like hell. "Come see — a spy!" I went expecting to be jumped. They took me to the jail, one of the basement cells: a white man. From the amount of blood on the floor it looked as if they locked him up first, then shot him through the bars. A spy, they kept repeating. I'm sure he wasn't. And not a missionary from the look of his tattoos. They had taken all his valuables, papers, etc. He was about 35-40, not tall, had some old scars, probably from combat. Almost certainly a mercenary looking for work. No idea how he got here. I hate the mercenary code — never shoot at another white man, even if he's on the enemy side. But I felt sorry for this guy. I must be weakening; I think I might have taken him on, if only for someone to talk to. They were very cheerful about the murder, bragging and so forth. They refused to bury him. Dumped him in a field to let the kites pick his bones. There are so many voices they hear that I don't.

*   *   *

There are several alternatives. I can leave or I can sit it out and wait for their own leaders, whoever they are, to let them down. I've threatened to leave a dozen times already. This is the only thing that brings them around. They don't want me to leave, but the threat produces an odd reaction: they want me to stay and yet the threat itself intimidates. They're dependent on me; I still somehow represent their ambition. But in their eyes I'm still an enemy. They hate me more and depend on me more when I say I'm leaving them.

Another possibility: they really don't trust each other any more than they trust me. Their accusations are excuses. After a certain period of time they'll reject whatever leaders they have. But we've been here two months.

Another: I can kill myself.

* * *

People have started to disappear from town. It's emptier during the day, most of the cars are in disrepair, the drains are blocked. The shop fronts aren't as beat-up as I thought before — some are in good shape. But practically all the shops are empty, either looted or locked. I don't think they're secretly massacring people. I'm pretty sure that most of the townsfolk have snuck off into the bush at night. I remember the day of the attack, a market day, the streets were full of people. There was even a kind of euphoria, excitement, with the flags flying and lots of people talking together in groups, wondering what had happened.

The emptiness is not gloomy: it's desertion, and it's made this already small town seem even smaller. Most of the people in the street during the day are in uniform. But I don't recognize them. They're townspeople mostly, young boys and old men in khakis they've found. They are not armed, but at a slight distance they look like a formidable army.

The men have a cowboy image of themselves. They complete the impression I first had of Lilongwe: a cowboy town, the main street with wild-west covered sidewalks and false-fronted shops. The men dress up in extravagant stolen clothes — bright shirts and blue jeans, sombreros, scarves, boots, etc., with beads and bracelets. And they all wear shades — dark wraparound sunglasses. They swagger along, clomping their boots, with their hands jammed into their front pockets. Some take pot shots at cats or stray dogs. Most of them wear pistols slung low on their hips, with full ammo belts crisscrossed on their chests. A lot of them carry shotguns, at slope arms on their shoulders — very casual. Mad black cowboys.

It's almost comic, and safer now that the townspeople have left them to their masquerade. They live by these fantasies, they like this cowboy image. Almost the first thing they asked me was whether I had ever seen a real cowboy. I thought they were joking then. A lot of them have set up house with local girls. Most were billeted in this hotel, but now they've moved out. I think I'm the only one left. From time to time the wind slams a door. I notice its emptiness when I walk down a creaking corridor. The carpet is rucked up. Outside some rooms there are shoes which were put out to be shined on the day of the attack and left behind when the guests ran off. This is the only wooden building in town. I'm on the top floor at my desk most of the day. With a little planning they could burn it down. I don't think I could get out in time. But they won't do that, and I feel safer knowing I'm able to hear them climb the stairs.

*　*　*

She came today for the second time. But when she left she said she would not come anymore. She is afraid they'll find out and kill her for it. I gave her some money.

*　*　*

I thought Osbong was a fool when he didn't rush his army here. We have no strategic advantage. The town is in a kind of depression, enclosed by thick jungle which makes tracking impossible. We have no heavy arms, and after the second day had no discipline. During that first week I expected to be woken by bombs and to hear tanks rattling down the main street. They could have been on top of us before we laced our boots. I was tense then and didn't sleep.

I should have guessed that it's really unnecessary for Osbong

to attack us. Osbong knew it all along. He knows these people
better than I do. He's leaving us alone on purpose — he never
put up a fight. He let us capture our positions. He's probably
laughing up his sleeve. Once in a while he sends his old French
jets, vintage Mirages, I think. We haven't got anything to hit
them with: I can see the pilots — probably Israelis — looking
down at this pitiful little place.

It was a mistake to try and start a popular revolt here. No
one cares. The biggest error was arming fifty men. I made
them dangerous; I made the mutiny possible. The town, like
the exploitation, was imaginary. This is just jungle, with a few
buildings and some voices, all dispensable to Osbong. The
image of order was mine. What I didn't see before was that
the order is tribal, chiefs and headmen, ancestor worship and
bride prices. And no one is angry about that. Politics never
got to this level, I don't think there was any exploitation here.
No one mentions Osbong: he was my demon. It's still a tribal
village, and all we've done is to uproot it and scatter it tempo-
rarily. When we leave, as we must, it will go back to being a
village, slightly scarred with the memory of deaths. It was
always cows and children. Osbong knew that.

*   *   *

I thought it was a rape, but it was a love affair. And now
we're at the worst stage: knowing we don't love we see only
the worst and we know what hate is. We select the worst to
prove that the decision not to love is the right one. Indifference
isn't strong enough to justify our parting. We have to hate.

*   *   *

I spent most of the afternoon looking for her. Some bad
weather has started, dull chilly days and a driving wind, filled
with sleet, that blows sideways into your face. They call it
chiperoni. I was caught out in it this afternoon, *chiperoni* and
thunder, and decided to wait in a shed for it to let up before I
pushed on. I knew she lived in the area. The sleet whipped
the shed and spat through the straw walls. I looked out and

saw a small boy running along the road, dodging puddles, with his head down. He ran into my shed. He was wearing a long yellow shirt drooping sodden to his knees. There was a thunder-crack just as he entered. He grimaced and stuck his fingers into his ears, shuddering under his soaked shirt. Then he saw me and shrank frightened into a corner. There were raindrops beaded on his face. I tried the Chinyanja greeting, saying it softly so as not to scare him. He recoiled when I spoke, but did not take his eyes off me. After several moments he slipped a finger into each ear, carefully, one at a time, and then darted out into the rain and thunder. I watched him go. His dancing yellow shirt bulged and twisted as he ran.

30

Major Beaglehole and Calvin stood elbow to elbow at the sputtering two-stall urinal in what was called the Gents at the eating house.

"You're up early," said Major Beaglehole.

"Yup," said Calvin.

Each was, splashing, intent on his task. Calvin crowded his place, his eyes fixed on a space high on the mossy wall.

"Off to work?"

"Right," said Calvin.

"Bastards," said Major Beaglehole. "I was just starting to trust them."

"No choice," said Calvin. Having acknowledged Beaglehole's presence with the usual polite but brief lavatory exchanges, Calvin fell silent.

Then Beaglehole sighed and said, "Oh, Christ, have a look at this."

"What's that?" Calvin spoke to the wall over the urinal.

"Look over here." Still Beaglehole splashed.

Calvin could not look.

"Here, have a squint."

Calvin's bladder seized, his jet petered out. Beaglehole spattered on, and urged.

"I'm off," said Calvin. "Work."

"Look here." Again Beaglehole sighed.

Out of the corner of his eye Calvin saw Beaglehole nodding downward.

"What have you got there," said Calvin. He did not want to see. But he took a breath, squinted, and leaned.

"That," said Major Beaglehole. He pointed with his free hand.

"I don't see anything," said Calvin.

Major Beaglehole touched the porcelain on the upper part of his stall. Just above his finger, near a leaking pipe, a blue tattoolike emblem showed under sticky grime.

"See that? It's a Twyford Adamant," said Major Beaglehole. "Made in U.K. Christ, do I get homesick when I read that. Don't you?"

"Never saw that brand in the States," said Calvin. "But even if I had," he went on, stepping back and zipping, "I don't think it would make me homesick. Excuse me, I'm late for work."

"Off you go," said Major Beaglehole, looking at the Twyford emblem. "They'll nationalize Bailey next, the bastards."

Calvin walked unsteadily down the street in powerful sunlight, his shirt pocket full of ball points. Swinging his new cardboard briefcase he headed for the Agnello building and his office. He had been back on the job for over two weeks and felt some frustration. Osbong's takeover of Homemakers' had surprised him, as if out of the blue, and just as Calvin had started to sprint away, a dark hand had awkwardly grasped one of his ankles and was holding it. He would not have minded going back to his old routine of rising with the kitchen clatter of pots and spoons, reading the paper in the toilet and perhaps soothing himself with a warm pint of beer in the empty bar before going off to work at ten or eleven. But this was denied him. Nationalized, he was a civil servant and had to keep government hours, nine to four-thirty, with a coffee break in the morning, a tea break in the afternoon, and an hour off for lunch. He missed his session in the toilet, his paper and his beer; he missed napping with Mira on rainy afternoons.

The Homemakers' Mutual sign had been taken down. The new one, a homely signboard from the Ministry of Works, read AFSURE, THE AFRICAN NATIONAL ASSURANCE COMPANY. The Commission to Nationalize Vital Industries had thought up that detestable name as well as the testimonial on the Afsure stationery: "The only assurance company in Central Africa owned and staffed *by* Africans *for* Africans." It was partly true: the commission had given Calvin an African trainee.

A peanut vendor had set up his boxes of shelled nuts and paper cones on the stairs of Agnello House; he dozed, his head against the handrail. Calvin stepped carefully over the boxes and went up to his office.

The once-vacant office across the hall from Calvin's was now occupied. A man in white shorts and kneesocks stood at the door and greeted Calvin with a snort. He asked, "Any post?"

"I don't know," said Calvin. He unlocked his office door and pushed it open. Some letters lay on the floor where they had fallen from the letterslot.

Seeing the letters the man said ruefully, "The stupid bugger didn't bring *me* any post."

"Maybe tomorrow," said Calvin. "The mail's slow."

"Not a hope," said the man. "I think the post boy's pinching them. I'd report him, but that wouldn't do any good. They're all the same, aren't they? They raised the rent on the British Council downstairs. They nailed you right enough I heard."

"I'm training someone to take over the business," said Calvin. "After that I'm cutting out."

"Back to the States?"

"I don't know," said Calvin. "Some quiet place."

"I've had it. I'm packing it up and going back to the Republic. They're turning communist here, and when the old man goes — "

There were footsteps in the hall: Mwase, Calvin's trainee. The man in the white shorts looked at Mwase, cursed, and entered his office. The pane of glass on his office door was still rattling from the slam when Mwase said good morning to Calvin.

"Hi," said Calvin. "How's every little thing?"

"I'm late," said Mwase gloomily. "I was getting that hawker off the stairs."

"The peanut man?"

"He was in the way," said Mwase. "Hawking."

"You shouldn't have done that," said Calvin. "He's been here for years."

"It looks bad selling groundnuts there."

"I don't mind," said Calvin. "He doesn't bother me."

"Others will come, selling sweet potatoes, maize cobs, cigarettes, what-not. You don't know Africans. If you give them an inch they take more."

"Let me ask you something," said Calvin. "How would you like to be out there selling peanuts on the street?"

Mwase shrugged and put his briefcase on a side table. It was a Japanese briefcase, fiber glass, with a plastic name tag. Mwase said, "I've done my O-Levels."

"You've done your O-Levels," said Calvin. "So no peanut-selling for you! You mind if I ask you another question? No? Okay, who got you this trainee job?"

Mwase unsnapped the briefcase. "I applied," he said.

"A pig's ass you applied! Who was it, your uncle? Brother? Second cousin?"

"I applied," said Mwase. "I've done my O-Levels."

"You know what?" said Calvin. "I'm going to check on that. Yes, I am. I don't have anything against you personally, Mwase — I know all about extended families. But the least you can do is be honest about it."

254

"I am not telling lies."

"We'll see," said Calvin. "I'm going to check. If I find out you got this job because of family connections or something, I'm going to put that peanut man right at your desk, right there."

Mwase opened the briefcase. It was empty except for one small pamphlet, a correspondence lesson perhaps, which he took out and placed on the blotter. He snapped the briefcase again and seated himself. With his fists clamped over his ears and his elbows on the blotter he studied the pamphlet.

Calvin phoned the Commission to Nationalize Vital Industries and asked to speak to the head of the personnel section. There was a buzz and then a British voice: "Harris here."

"This is Calvin Mullet of . . . Afsure," said Calvin. He hated the name so much he could not say it well. "I've got a question, so I thought I'd call you up and ask you. It's about my trainee."

"Go right ahead, Mr. Mullet."

"Well, what I was wondering," said Calvin, "is how do you go about picking them?"

"Is he making a nuisance of himself? Because if he is, you can send him straight — "

"No," said Calvin, "he's okay. But how did he get picked? I was just wondering."

"Yes. We have an absolutely rigid selection board, a written examination and an interview. Your chap has his O-Levels, which is more than most of them have. It's a pretty ropey lot."

"Thanks," said Calvin. "That's all I was wondering." He replaced the receiver and said softly, "Mwase, how would you like a beer?"

"I'm not supposed to drink on duty," said Mwase, looking up briefly from his pamphlet.

"You're the boss," said Calvin. He found an air-mail envelope in the stack of mail and slit it. He pulled out the letter, unfolded it, and held it up and snapped it several times.

"Mr. Calvin?"

255

"Yes?"

"I am thirsty."

"*That's* the spirit!" said Calvin. He threw down the letter and got up from his desk. "There's a bar right downstairs."

They stayed in the Highlife until after lunch. At one-fifteen Mwase struggled up from the table and said to Calvin, "I cannot stand it. I must refresh myself with that pleasant girl," and he disappeared out back with the waitress. Calvin waited, drinking, until three, and when he was certain Mwase would not return, went upstairs to read the letter he had opened at nine-thirty.

He was sweating, three-quarters drunk, and had to pinion the letter to his desk with his two palms in order to read it. It was from Homemakers', regretting the nationalization but giving in to it. Calvin was offered his plane fare back to Boston. In the previous weeks several letters and cables had been exchanged between Homemakers' and the Nationalization Commission, and all had been crosscopied to Calvin. He opened the file.

The commission had notified Homemakers' of the decision to nationalize the agency. The value was being assessed so that full compensation could be made. It was hoped that Mr. Mullet would stay on long enough to train someone to take over.

Homemakers' wrote a shocked reply to the commission saying that it had been promised that there would be no nationalization. A great deal of capital had been invested in setting up the agency. But, the letter said, it looked as if they were being offered no alternative. They wanted compensation in American dollars and not in osbongs. On Calvin's copy of that letter, Wilbur Parsons wrote in a P.S. that he was sorry it had to happen like this but that maybe everything would turn out all right: "We were forewarned. Reliable sources say the Malawi government is going to be overthrown in the very near future, and the thrust of our information is a very real possibility that the new regime will take more kindly to an H.M. agency, allowing normal operation to resume. Are you interested in playing ball?"

Calvin wrote to Parsons. He didn't, he said, know where H.M. got their information, but the so-called new regime was just a bunch of bullies kicking the slats out of a little town in the central province. He had already tried but failed to sell these creeps a policy. He wouldn't make a deal with them even if he was paid to do same.

The commission wrote again to Homemakers' informing them that Mr. Mullet had agreed to stay on and that assessment had shown the agency to be heavily in debt; no compensation could be made.

Calvin clipped the latest letter from Homemakers' into the file marked *Nationalization Correspondence*. Then he wrote to Parsons: "I wasn't given much choice but I'm staying here just the same to train the new man whose name is Mwase. I forget if I told you I got married again and she's having a baby and I'm sorry if I put you to any trouble. Longer letter follows." But he knew as he wrote the last sentence that there would be no more letters. He wrote his letter again, improving the punctuation and omitting the last sentence.

And the next day, with Mwase's approval, the peanut vendor returned to his place on the stairs.

31

His absorbed secretiveness with his little pamphlet and his occasional fits of melancholy aside, Mwase was a busy, usually cheery soul and, once Calvin was certain Mwase had forgiven him his blunt accusation of having used pull to get the trainee job, became a good friend, though for many days Calvin repeated his apologies. Their chief pleasures were drinking beer during the breaks and reading *Boom* comics. *Boom* was a weekly magazine of photographic sequences illustrating the serial adventures of The Lance, a half-caste detective in Johannesburg in one section, and a Zulu Tarzan named Samson in another. Samson loped through jungle and low veldt in a leopard skin, doing good and shouting gibberish to wild animals. For a while Calvin was The Lance because he owned a hat; Mwase was Samson. This was the way they introduced themselves to the girls in the bar downstairs. Mwase said to Calvin, "I like you. You are not the same with other Europeans."

On the last page of *Boom* there was a pen-pal corner, thumbnail sketches, with photographs and addresses. Mwase wrote to the girls who advertised and, while still keeping his pamphlet to himself, showed his letters to Calvin for correction. They usually opened, "Well, here I am writing to you this missive" and went on, "I am a strong healthy boy of 22 years, brown of complexion, Chewa by tribe, and I collect stamps, coins and Elvis records. I like dancing, sports and games of all kinds." He offered visits, promised vigor, and hinted broadly at marriage. He ended each letter, "Hoping for your prompt and favorable reply . . ." He was an industrious letter writer. He had won a two-rand prize for a letter condemning spitting; it was published in *Boom*. Much of the morning mail which so irritated the man across the hall was Mwase's. He used the Afsure stationery and diligently taught himself to type with the office portable; he frowned down at the keys, hovering and selecting like a berry picker, licking his lips when he was successful, sucking his teeth when he bungled a key.

Over his desk Mwase hung his framed O-Level certificates, a pale green diploma from the Emmaus Bible Correspondence College in Salisbury, and a first-aid certificate issued on the completion of a course given by the St. John's Ambulance Brigade. He added an old photograph of a very black man wearing wire spectacles and a suit buttoned to the knot of his cravat. He was seated outdoors in a stuffed chair, and he had a Bible on his knee.

"Looks like a clergyman," said Calvin, wondering who the man might be.

"My father," said Mwase. "A good preacher, but a stooge of the British."

"You shouldn't say that about your father," said Calvin.

"Crucifixes can't help us," said Mwase. "You don't know him."

On Mwase's birthday Calvin presented him with an Afsure policy, paid up for a year. It was the large Homemakers' Mutual policy certificate with that firm's name smudged out by a block of ink and AFSURE overprinted at the top. This, Mwase framed and hung.

Mwase's policy was the only one Afsure sold for some time. The interest in insurance which Calvin had noted months back had fallen off. Mwase had an explanation: no one trusted the government, no one liked Doctor Osbong, so no one would insure with a company that had been nationalized. It was a boycott. There had already been, Mwase said, two go-slow strikes, Posts and Telegraphs and Public Works.

"The post office was on a go-slow strike?"

"Oh, yes," said Mwase, "for a month. Didn't you know?"

"I didn't notice," said Calvin, "no."

Other strikes were planned, said Mwase. Everyone knew that the government was going to be overthrown by the soldiers who were in Lilongwe.

"If everyone knows that," said Calvin, "how come *I* don't?"

"You don't eat rice," said Mwase.

"No," said Calvin, "I don't eat much of anything."

"Because if you ate rice you would know that there hasn't been any for three months — anyway no number one, just cracked. Most of the rice comes from the northern region, but it has to pass through Lilongwe to get here. No rice has come to this side."

"So what?"

"That means the soldiers are strong. They cut off the supply. It always happens. When the Portuguese raid their villages, hungry people escape and start a famine on our side. It's the same. If you cannot buy a stick of cassava you know there is trouble somewhere."

"So you ran out of rice and you guessed there was a revolution? Maybe it was just a bad harvest — ever think of that?"

"Not only rice. At first it was maize. That grows in Fort Hill. Maize was short in November. Trouble in Fort Hill. Then a shortage of sweet potatoes. That's Rumpi. Trouble in Rumpi District."

"I had a little trouble in Rumpi myself," said Calvin.

"December."

"Right," said Calvin. "Around last Christmas."

"The rice stopped in April. Trouble in Lilongwe. Each town is closer, so we know the soldiers are coming this way. Their leader is a European. They say he is as strong as Samson in *Boom*. He talks to animals, too, and he can even change himself into an animal if he wishes. He can sleep under trees or go for a month without eating. He can — "

"Stop," said Calvin. "Don't believe that. I know the guy you mean. He wears shades and carries a gun. He's just a bully, a tough guy with a big cigar. He picked me up in Rumpi. I wasn't afraid."

"Some people are afraid," said Mwase. "Bullets bounce off his head."

"Mwase, who tells you this crap?"

"It's true," said Mwase. "People know."

"It's not true."

"You think I am telling lies, Mr. Calvin?"

"No, of course not. But, look, it's just a bunch of soldiers. I saw them myself. Just some troublemakers in Lilongwe."

"They are not all in Lilongwe," said Mwase, forcing mystery into his voice. "Some are here."

That day Mwase did not drink with Calvin. He sat in the office and said he had work to do. But Calvin knew there was no work. Mwase had withdrawn into melancholy; he studied his pamphlet, holding his ears.

* * *

It was June, cold in Blantyre; the flower petals rotted on the grass, and a stiff wind blew down from Soche Hill and rattled the eating house shutters. The days were misty. For much of the time the hill was hidden from view. Some days whole bluey-white clouds sat on the town. In the Gents on one of these chilly June mornings Major Beaglehole said to Calvin, "Queen's birthday tomorrow. We're having a little do at the Moth's. Like to come along?"

"Sure," said Calvin. "No objections if I bring an African?"

"Certainly not," said Beaglehole. "We're multiracial now." He chuckled and nudged Calvin's elbow with his own.

"What's *he* doing here?" demanded Beaglehole in a loud voice the next night. Mwase stood petrified by the silence created by his entering the Moth's Club with Calvin and Mira and his own girl friend. Many eyes were upon them; a song was in progress when the four appeared on the verandah. The song ceased as suddenly, as awkwardly, as an interrupted adultery.

"You said it was all right," whispered Calvin, hoping that Beaglehole would whisper too, and that the music would start.

"Balls," said Beaglehole. "I thought you meant your wife."

"He could join. I bet he's been shot at in anger," said Calvin.

The people in the Moth's clubhouse, among them Mavity, Bailey and Mr. Harry, started singing again, joylessly and with some defiance. Major Beaglehole joined them.

"He hates me," said Mwase.

"No, he doesn't," said Calvin. "Here, let's find a seat and have a beer. What does your girl friend want to drink?"

The girl did not speak English. She was not like the other girls Calvin had seen Mwase with. She was from a village; she might have spent the day in a cornfield hoeing; she had a dusty brown face. She kept her head lowered and did not seem comfortable in her chair. She squirmed and cracked her finger joints, the sound of twigs snapping. She had a gin, and gulped it, and had another. Perhaps she was Mwase's reproach to Calvin, as Mwase himself was Calvin's reproach to Major Beaglehole and the Moths.

Mira did not take to her; Beaglehole and Mavity eyed her severely. Mavity had left his own wife at home. Bailey ignored the girl, but Mr. Harry, who was standing with Bailey near the tiger skin, smiled at her and came up to Calvin and murmured: "You know what? I bet she's hiding a fantastic front porch under that get-up." He offered Calvin and Mwase cheroots, and winked at the girl.

She wore a faded blouse with old-fashioned puffed ruffled sleeves trimmed with a carelessly stitched border of white wiggly ribbon. A washed-out sarong was drawn up and tied tightly at her midriff. She kicked at yellow plastic sandals. She had fine ears, her hair was knotted into narrow plaits, her skin was smooth and seemed an inch thick. She ventured to speak only once. She asked Mira in Chinyanja, "How many months."

"September-October," said Mira, and sniffed.

A record was put on; the machine was cranked. Everyone stood and sang. Calvin knew the tune and sang "My Country 'Tis of Thee," the rest sang "God Save the Queen." When it was over, Aubrey stood on a chair and rapped for silence. He raised his glass to a picture of the Queen, bemedalled and wearing a blue sash and a diamond tiara. Aubrey shouted once, "The Queen!"

"The Queen!" shouted everyone in reply. And they all drank.

Mira sat back into her chair; her knees were apart, her big arms folded over her baby. Pregnancy, ruinous to some women, had given Mira a peaceful glow. She was rounder, and when she walked did so with a slow flat-footed gait, considering her steps, one hand on her hip, the other pinching a hanky. The heavy-meal bulge in her stomach had swelled to the size of a pumpkin, and her face, arms, and ankles had grown too. Her yen was for Settlers' Oats with melted margarine, sprinkled with sugar. She was solid, and the motherly roundness of her new size made her seem very reliable, with a look of serene contentment in her eyes. Calvin was proud of her. He said, "If it's a boy we'll call him Mwase."

Mwase nodded.

"No," said Mira.

"She's right," said Mwase. "The midwife has to name the baby. That is how we do it."

"No midwife," said Mira. She raised a trembling arm and said, "Doc-tor, hosipital!"

Major Beaglehole came over. He looked at Calvin as if Calvin had behaved traitorously and said, "Well, you're here, damn it. Take a pew. You're going to see a very old tradition. Keep your eyes on that door."

Seated beside Mwase at a long banquet table Calvin asked, "By the way, what color are African babies when they're born?"

"Some are almost white or gray," said Mwase. "But after you wash them," he said, sipping at his water, "after you wash them they turn . . . black."

"Interesting," said Calvin.

Mwase was watching the door gloomily. A man appeared in the doorway dressed in a velvet hat and a cape, kneebreeches, and square-toed shoes with silver buckles. Mwase's girl friend said *"Eee!"* when the man blew his trumpet. He stood aside.

Wine was poured. Two Africans, one of them Old Willy, carried a large plank through the door. There was a side of beef on the plank, roasted black, basted shiny.

"Before you drink," said Calvin to Mwase, "there's just one thing I want to say. All that business about the soldiers sleeping under trees and the bullets bouncing off them — let's forget it, okay? You got your girl friend here, and I've got my wife. That's the important thing, isn't it?" He smiled, hoping to inspire a smile in Mwase.

Mwase did not drink, or smile.

Aubrey got to his feet and thumped the table with his knife handle. Cupping his hand to his mouth he shouted very loudly, *"What ho! Is that the meat!"*

"Isn't it the important thing?" repeated Calvin.

"We have worries," said Mwase. He looked at the carcass on the plank.

"Yes! It *is* the meat!" the man with the trumpet was shouting back to Aubrey.

The Africans tottered with their burden; the side of meat swayed.

"We suffer," said Mwase. "You can leave if you wish and go back to America. But where can we go? Even Osbong says it.

God punished us with this useless country. God hates us, everyone does. These people here. You have chances. We have no chances. We are hopeless. Hobbies — have you read Thomas Hobbies? He was right, life in Africa is nasty, British and short."

"And is it good meat?" shouted Aubrey.

"Indeed!" said the man with the trumpet. *"It is the baron of beef!"* He picked up a carving knife from the plank and slashed off a hunk of meat. He nibbled it. "And it is a *good* baron, m'lud!"

"You don't know," said Mwase. He put his wine to his lips and drank. He said ominously in words he might once have used in a school debate, "But I put it to you, Mr. Calvin, that I do know and I do possess information. Not one information, but many. I like you, Mr. Calvin, but you are a white man and you do not know what is going on in my black head. I have worries."

"Serve it to all and sundry," yelled Aubrey. "Let not a scrap be wasted. God save the Queen!"

The side of beef was carved and dished out.

"You think I don't have worries?"

"Not like mine," said Mwase. "I am a prisoner. This country is a jail and Osbong is the in-charge. These people want to kill me and cut me up like they cut their roasted meat."

"It's the Queen's birthday," said Calvin.

"Not for black people," said Mwase. "I will tell you something I learned. Yellow is a color, so is red. White is *all* colors. But black — it is not a color at all." He paused, groping for something more. Finally, he said, "You think my girl friend is a savage."

"No, I don't," said Calvin.

"But she is," said Mwase. "That's the trouble."

After the banquet, on the pretext of showing them the cricket pitch, Calvin fled with his guests.

* * *

Calvin scratched on his blotter with a sharp pencil, pretending to write. Through his very dark sunglasses, with growing curiosity and diminishing patience, he watched Mwase studying his pamphlet. It was not a correspondence lesson. Mwase did no writing. He read, and what he read caused gloom. He remained bent over the booklet, regarded closely by Calvin. At ten Mwase shifted his feet and looked up at his framed certificates. Calvin continued scratching with his pencil. They did not break for beer.

At half-past twelve Calvin dropped his pencil into his plastic pen tray and said, "How about lunch?"

Mwase shut the pamphlet and put it in his briefcase, snapping and locking the chrome hasps. Lately, Calvin noticed, Mwase had taken to eating with his hands. He went to wash them.

Calvin heard the washroom door click shut, heard the bolt shot and water being run. In a flash the briefcase was under his arm, and he was prising off the hasps with a scissor blade. They came off easily, the case was open, the pamphlet was in his hands.

The title, ketchup-colored, was UNITE, BROTHERS! Calvin riffled through the pages; it was badly printed in a tiny antique typeface, unevenly inked, with faulty margins and blots. It was bound with one staple which had worked loose, freeing the center pages. No author's name was given, and for a moment, holding the stained pamphlet and standing over the damaged briefcase, Calvin felt all his curiosity disappear. Wearily he thought of a bad excuse for his prying — no! he would take all the blame.

His eye fell on the first sentence. *Would you insure me? I have been beaten, robbed and nearly killed a thousand times. I live at the worst end of a bad world* . . . Calvin flipped to the last page. The ending was unchanged: *never hold my head up high,* even to the trailing dot-dot-dot. The epigraph from the poem by the late vice president of the Hartford Accident and Indemnity Company had been expunged, and so had the name Jigololo.

Presently, Mwase returned from the washroom. Wiping his fingers with his hanky he walked only part of the way into the office. It was not the broken briefcase gaping open on the floor, the hasps twisted off — though that gave him pause, he had valued it and had saved to buy it; it was not the disorder which had visited the room, but that was new. What made him freeze in his tracks was the look on the face of Calvin who stood with big accusing *bwana*'s eyes, and who held the pamphlet out to him, a ripped half in each raised fist.

32

At the Rumpi camp, the men had told Marais of a lunatic in the hills, an old Portuguese who, marooned by a failed love affair, went about naked in a pair of ragged sandals. He brandished an ancient shotgun at strangers. He had lost the gift of speech; he was dirty, and his hair was wild. He would have starved long ago but for some African women in a neighboring village who regularly left food at his hut door, the way they left pennies on the gnarled roots of witch trees, a token against the possibility of wrath.

Marais thought of that poor man whenever he strapped on his pistol and went for a walk. He heard his men whispering behind him. Often he heard laughter. No one spoke to him. Many watched; he felt their curious eyes. Perhaps they had decided that whatever powers he had were now dispersed. He wasn't feared, he knew. He was left alone. He had not heard from Harry or Brother Jaja for months, which was unusual, but no disappointment. The men might have been intercepting messages and keeping them from him. Or maybe Harry and Brother Jaja had changed, like the men; or maybe they were dead. Marais did not know. He seldom thought of them.

He had privately resigned his command: he did not think of revolt anymore.

In that captured town he felt slightly absurd, as if in walking he was acting out a meaningless routine, like the man gone foolish, the local figure of fun who is allowed his eccentricity because he is harmless. The town had been his, and he had made the whole place tremble with a bomb. But the eccentric often made those claims. "Do you know who I am? See that deep crater in the street and those burned-out buildings? I did that. I am Marais." He had said that to puzzled strangers in Lilongwe, speaking in English, though he was not sure they understood. One man had walked away before Marais told his name.

He spent less time walking in the town. Normally, feeling watched, he turned off the main street — named Brother Jaja — and took deserted paths. On wet misty days he looked for land crabs, glossy black and touched with scarlet, scuttling on high legs and holding pincers — so odd there, a thousand miles from the ocean. At dusk flocks of small wild hens nested on the sun-warmed paths: he saw men on speeding motorcycles hunting them by running them down. If a figure approached on the path Marais hid himself. He did not want to be seen. It was said that the naked man in the hills preferred solitude and in his own mad way was armed. Marais understood. He felt as naked and as hunted. A person gliding easily through grass intimidated him; another presence seemed a judgment on his sanity, or a jeer. He wondered what version they knew of his failure. They made him uneasy. But in solitude there was no madness; alone, the lunatic was just a naked man who had been loved once.

He wanted to go on with his diary. He sat with it open before him. The only whole thoughts that came to him were of ingratitude and mutinous betrayal. He hated: he thought of revenge, of a punishment so elaborate it required help and apparatus. One evening he scratched in his notebook, making small doodles; he shaded and enlarged them. He began to write with a word hinged to a doodle. He darkened the word, tracing and retracing the letters, as if waiting for dictation. Then anger broke over him and shook a sentence out of him: he cancelled the first halting words and his handwriting quickened and changed character as his mood turned and turned. He wrote for hours, the sentences sloping into abuse, the wavering candle flame making his pages jump as he stabbed excitedly at them. He stopped, exhausted, but slept badly. His half-ignited brain still smoldered behind his eyes, composing, erasing, appealing. He fingered pages in his dreams.

In the morning his pages accused. There was a time, not distant, when he killed men who wrote such things. There was no anguish in the handwriting; it had all been written easily, speaking with eagerness of vendetta. Marais tore them out and burned them, noticing that as he did a handful of corresponding leaves at the front of the notebook, some details of revolt scribbled somewhere else, fell free. He burned those, too.

He wrote no more. On rising, he crossed that day off the calendar. (Once he had habitually done this at the end of the day; now he knew in advance that the day held nothing for him.) He opened his notebook to a clean page, but he did not write. He felt something savage in him, something unlovely that stank, like a rat in his room. Always with a sigh he slammed the notebook shut, and he walked. Walking was all he could do; it simulated action and helped the time pass.

But he came to fear even that.

On a walk late in July, the clammy month, he saw small boys huddled in grass, smoking mice out of holes in the ground. Some roasted the skewered mice over fires. The mice sizzled and burst like sausages. To Marais it was a moment from prehistory: naked black children carrying embers from fires and cramming them into holes, driving the mice out and killing them by tramping on them or swatting them with sticks. He watched one boy chase a mouse and kick it to death against a stump, and peel its skin off and begin to cook it. Busily they hunted and ate. The crude method worked, but that was not so frightening to Marais as the boys themselves. They were not playing at cruelty any more than their fathers who in brown ragged overcoats hunted bush pigs with torches; locating a bush pig the men scattered and lit the grass, building by degrees an encircling fire. They waited, scowling at the fire's fringe, and when the pig stumbled through the flames, all its bristles alight and sparking, they clubbed it to death. Marais had seen them. They were hungry.

It was hunger that made the boys so busy they did not notice Marais at first. They mutely tended their fires. Marais was fascinated: the sight revived much of his old disgust, and for a moment he understood all his bombs — it was this degraded hunger he had tried to eliminate, though he had not imagined it so bad. Those boys, forced to practice savagery, justified all revolt. Marais was composing a new paragraph, finding words for what he saw, after three idle months feeling his despair diminish and blur in his surge of indignant longing to make another bomb.

He got no further with that paragraph; it collapsed in his head and his despair came back and cloaked him with a chill. The scene he was witnessing — the naked boys hunting mice in a windy field — was happening in what he used to call a liberated area. The children, like those men hunting pigs with torches, lived within sight of the bombed police headquarters and the room on the top floor of the hotel where he slept. They had been free since April. He watched them eating the mice and he realized that he was speaking his thoughts, narrating the scene in a distressed whisper.

The children looked up, but they did not move away from the fires. Their bodies were streaked with dust and gray ashes, and they knelt, hiding their penises. They were not cowering or begging for mercy; discovered in their meal, they were protecting their food, a small pile of limp rodents.

Marais took a step toward them. One muttered and picked up a stone and showed it. The wind shifted, blowing smoke into the boys' faces, then into Marais's. It whirled an ungainly acrid cloud about and gave the illusion that the little boys squatting in it — headless in one gust, disembodied heads in another — were actually moving about in jerks and hops, and swinging their arms. Marais thought he felt a sting on his thigh, a pain that could have been a stone or his unsettled imagination: it may have been the deception of the wind-whirled smoke, or the uncomfortable itch of its bitter smell. Another stone seemed to strike his boot. But he was uncertain. He saw nothing thrown. He backed into the grass rubbing his eyes, and he turned down the path. A moment later five black boys ran before him clutching their food. While Marais watched them a sixth dashed by, bumping and startling Marais as he passed. This one swung a glowing stick he had dragged from the fire.

For a time (he did not know how long; he was impatient in crossing days off the calendar) Marais stayed in the hotel and kept himself busy. He did not want to see those children again and, even more, did not want to be seen by anyone. He was the jilted lover, to whom people can be as cruel in their indifference as in their curiosity, and who knows enough of hurt to keep to himself and not risk hitting back. He shined his boots and took his pistol apart and cleaned it; he noted temperature changes and weather in his diary, and did his tiny dark drawings. He did not move out, not even when one day his window was shattered by a shotgun slug; he swept up the glass and moved his desk away from the window to the center of the room. Most days he cooked his meals in the room on his Primus. Occasionally he used the wood-burning one, a black cast-iron stove in the hotel kitchen; and on those days he rummaged through the larder. He found gallon cans without paper labels, though each was stenciled with the name of what it contained, baked beans, pineapples, syrup, cooking oil, soup. They had been left untouched by his men, who opened a can only when the label pictured the contents, assuming all else was motor oil.

Marais carried the cans he could use up to his room, saying nothing to the men who sat drinking, dressed in cowboy clothes, in the broken chairs of the hotel lobby. Earlier he had looked through all the rooms. The walls were pissed on and scorched, there was shit in the corners of some, and broken bottles and crockery; in others there was moldy food that even the rats that infested the place refused to touch. (At night Marais heard rats pattering across the top of his ceiling, vaulting the rafters.) He never looked in the hotel bedrooms again. The men seldom came upstairs; having fouled a room once they did not return to it, a habit of village hygiene that demanded space. What hours Marais did not spend on the roof searching the town and the surrounding jungle with his binoculars, he spent in his bare room — orderly because it was so empty — at his desk facing the door, with his loaded pistol and his notebook.

He did not fire the gun, or write. He thought constantly of doing both; but each was so final.

*   *   *

Stocking up on cans in the larder one afternoon, he caught sight of a dog outside the kitchen door. It pawed a pile of rubbish and lapped at papers. A wild mongrel, very skinny, with a patch of mange on its neck, it fumbled and glanced nervously around, shaking its broken tail, as Marais walked to the doorway. He wanted the dog, he felt pity for the scavenging outcast. He had some spare food to fatten the dog; it would keep him company. He opened a tin of stew and splashed some at it, pitching it with a spoon.

The sound of the stew hitting the ground scared the dog; but it turned, moaning, and looked at the food and at Marais.

"Here, boy," Marais coaxed. He displayed the open can. The dog appeared interested. Marais walked a few feet, edging toward the dog, and said, "Take it."

There was a loud bang behind Marais, a gunshot. He winced, stunned by it, feeling his brain wither; he started to fall. But the dog's piteous howl checked him. The dog jerked forward, as if kicked, and fell on its side. It struggled, its eyes popping, and rolled and whimpered, leaking blood. Then painfully it rose to its forelegs and dragged its dead hind end into the tall grass.

"Where you going?"

Brother George, in cowboy hat and bright shirt, leaned against the gray clapboards of the hotel, holding his rifle waist high, aimed at Marais.

"You shot that dog," said Marais, walking up to Brother George. The gunshot had deafened him: he did not recognize his own voice. Brother George stopped Marais with the rifle muzzle; he pushed it into Marais's stomach and nudged. Marais said, "If I had my gun with me I'd kill you," and he slapped Brother George's face hard.

Marais ignored the rifle stuck against his stomach, which made him slap at arm's length. Brother George slid away from the wall and backed to the kitchen steps. Marais stayed with him, a rifle's length away, and slapped Brother George on one side of his face, then the other, saying, "Stupid, stupid," with each slap. Brother George squinted and made his smarting jaw big, and he prodded Marais with the rifle and fumbled with the bolt; but he did not shoot. His nose began to bleed.

"He tried to escape!" Brother George said suddenly, looking behind Marais.

Marais turned and saw four men behind him with rifles leveled at him. They were silent, and looked not ugly— though they could repel—but brutish, their faces clumsy and unfinished. It was something in their features Marais had never seen before. Chimanga stood at the head of the group.

"Who let you out of prison?" Marais asked. Marais had blood on his fingers. He wiped them on his shirt.

"I have been out of prison for long time," said Chimanga. "You in prison now, *bwana*."

"What do you mean?"

"We arrested you last week."

"You're crazy. I've been going for walks anywhere I pleased."

"But not outside hotel, eh. Not for one week," said Chimanga. "We know. We guarding. Special orders."

"Jaja wouldn't tell you to do this. Who gave the order — Harry?"

"Secret," said Chimanga, and he laughed, opening his mouth and unrolling his wide tongue and wagging it, stuck out, as he laughed.

"I have a gun," said Marais.

"One only," said Chimanga. "We having plenty guns. If you try to escape we will kill you." He laughed again.

"Why don't you kill me now?"

"We wanting you," said Brother George.

"You are my prisoner," said Brother Henry in Chinyanja, "*Iwe wam' jigololo wanga.*"

"We not your monkeys now!" said Chimanga.

"You're not Lumumba," said Marais.

"Take him upstairs!" said Chimanga. "Bye-bye, Bang-Bang!"

Three of the men accompanied Marais to his room. They nailed the door shut, but badly, all but splintering a door panel with a wild swing of the hammer. Marais heard two men descend the stairs.

The door was frail; he knew he could kick it to pieces, or cut through the wall into the next room and sail down the stairwell on a rope. There were half a dozen exits in the hotel, and on two sides fire ladders that ran from the roof to the ground. He knew he could get out; he had known it all along, and so he had kept it unconsidered.

For Marais, escape was ingenuity, always simple; it was staying that pressed him, because that measured his hope. But in the time he had stayed willingly they had declared him their prisoner: *Iwe wam' jigololo wanga.* He had been satisfied to stay and test himself and them; and he might have done for weeks more if they had said nothing. Now everything was changed. With the knowledge that he was their captive he thought only of escape.

33

In the end Calvin decided against going to the police about Mwase. You didn't report someone for stealing your porn or your zip gun, so why make a fuss about the theft of your subversive literature? Malawi had an instructive precedent. In Calvin's first month in the country a case was heard at the High Court of a man suing for breach of contract. The man (his name was Odrick Chipandale) was a witch doctor. He had been hired for a fee of four pounds, ten osbongs, to turn into a crocodile and kill a bewitched girl who was provoking a drought in a village near Blantyre. Half the money was paid in advance. Shortly after payment the dead girl was found by a riverbank; she was punctured with long rows of teeth. It rained for days. Satisfied with the deluge, the villagers saw no need to pay the balance. The witch doctor Chipandale took them to court. He was awarded the two pounds, five osbongs, tried for murder, and hanged.

Calvin heeded that lesson. He would get his pamphlet back, but he would be shot for treason or imprisoned with the three thousand others in the political detainees' camp on the lower river. Osbong was not gentle. But Calvin's decision gave no assurance of safety. What if Mwase turned *him* in? The manuscript in Calvin's incriminating handwriting was missing. Mwase had all the evidence. Calvin would swing for treason. Osbong had hung one man publicly in Zomba.

Mwase was no help. He went remote again and demanded his copy of the pamphlet from Calvin, with swallowed insults. He stuck the torn pages together with tape and, as before, studied it at his desk.

Calvin got plastered for courage. He winked, and said as light-heartedly as he could, in a joshing singsong voice, "I know where you got that thing."

"I don't care," said Mwase. His eyes were red, troubled.

Calvin saw criminal arrogance, the killer witch doctor. But he attempted conciliation: "Shall we have a beer and talk it over? We'll kick it around for a while — what do you say?"

"There is nothing to talk. I want a new briefcase."

"Take mine," said Calvin eagerly.

"It is cardboard. Mine was fiber glass, washable, Japanese model."

"I'll get you a nice one, really. But, Mwase, the pamphlet," said Calvin. "It's all lies."

"Of course you think so."

"I *know* so! And I know where you got it. Not that one," said Calvin, "but *another* one, right? Written in black ink, by hand. Huh?"

"It was given." Mwase wouldn't budge.

"You stole it!" said Calvin, his anger released. "I know you did. You can't kid me. That's the trouble with you people — you think everything is public property."

"I know you hate us."

"I don't," said Calvin. "Anyway, what do you mean *us?*"

"Well, we hate you," said Mwase. He glared and said, "Would you insure me?"

"I would, I *did!*" said Calvin. "You know I did — there's the certificate on the wall, all framed. I gave it — "

"I have been beaten and robbed," Mwase went on. "The white man treats me like rubbish because I am black. I am poor."

"You have your O-Levels," said Calvin. "And this job. You're going to be the fucking manager of this agency!"

"I slave."

"Bullshit! There's no business, no one wants insurance. You don't do a thing here."

"I go to meetings," said Mwase mysteriously. "You don't know."

"You write letters to pen pals, I know that."

"Not at night. At night we are invisible because we are the color of night."

"I know where you read that."

"Someday we will rise up."

"Please," said Calvin, "stop saying that." Words he had scribbled on boozy evenings were being shoved down his throat. They choked him. He pleaded, "I'll make a deal with you."

"No deals with white men."

"Just one?" Calvin's voice was small.

"None. You hate us." Mwase turned and looked past Calvin to the window and intoned, "On the banana leaf of life we hang like hungry worms."

"Cabbage leaf! That's in the book."

"It's our old proverb."

"It's not; it's a fake."

"Our old fathers taught us this wisdom."

It was impossible. Mwase knew the pamphlet by heart. Calvin tried again, with care, in a soothing voice, "Mwase, the whole thing's forgotten. I'm not going to tell anyone about this. You don't have to worry."

"I do worry," said Mwase. "And suffer."

Calvin continued, conceding: "What you steal is your business. Just like," he implored for assent, "what *I* do is my business. Right? So . . . everything . . . is okay . . . isn't it?"

Mwase did not reply. He sat at his little desk before his certificates, with his smashed briefcase and his patched pamphlet, holding his ears. He was undersized, quite black; and lately, probably because of meetings or doings at night, he had begun to look frazzled. His name could have been A. Jigololo.

"What are you going to do?" Calvin asked at last.

"Rise up," said Mwase, without taking his eyes from the pamphlet.

*   *   *

The mood in town had changed, with Mwase's. Africans sidled up to Calvin and abused him with unexpected malice. The malice was new; it was uninformed, a raw kind and full of fright. It pinched Calvin's heart. The Africans followed him, prancing. They cawed at him and honked him off the road. They knocked off his Panama hat and called him "the giraffe." It happened everywhere in Blantyre, on the side streets, St. George's, St. Andrew's, St. David's, and at the market, on Osbong and Livingstone and Hanover. The baggers at Kandodo Supermarket were rude and dented his purchases, pressing their thumbs into the items Mira had a yen for, *naartjies,* nutbars, slabs of chocolate. In the drink shops and the post office, blacks jumped the queues, crowded him, assaulted him with bone-sharp elbows; he was shoved aside. It happened to other white people, too: the Greek brothers who ran the coffee shop, the Italian tea planters and their children, the queer Maltese barber on Henderson Street, the fat Rhodesian ladies from the bookshop — people he had never taken any notice of before. Now Calvin saw them, confused foreigners who had stopped in the wrong place to trade, who didn't belong, and whose faces were damaged, set in new and not natural expressions by the strain of humiliation which, in addition to altering their faces, made them grovel or bluster unreasonably. Calvin thought he disliked them, but he felt sorry for them. They moved slowly, these old expatriates, not comprehending the city, as if the place had overnight become populous and strange with villains; they were often rude to the Africans, and for this provocation, at night, they were jumped and struck with clubs, and they got their shins kicked. For sarcasm and their funny color they were hit: the violence was the African's reply, the savagery his denial that he was a savage.

Returning one evening to the eating house after a film at the Rainbow (*On Moonlight Bay* — he had last seen it in the early fifties at the Hudson Roxy), he was stampeded by a dozen black boys, and one had whispered hotly: "You a white sheet!" Calvin tried to protest, but there were so many of them, and they were so angry. He said nothing, lest they be pushed to murder. He even allowed one to claw the inside pocket of his jacket.

You a white sheet. Calvin didn't mind being called that. But later the veil fell from the mild abuse when he heard *keel* for "kill." "Keel new boat," a black man had said to Calvin and Mira, nowhere near a shipyard. Mira hurried Calvin away to translate, "Kill you both." On other occasions he was a bloody sheet, a useless sheet, a stewpeed sheet. The Africans were sinisterly equipped to abuse; their English was no good, but their mood was dark. Calvin was worried. It was as if all of them had read his awful little book. And after a time he saw loose copies of it in town, the ketchup-colored title was unmistakable.

His unborn child worried him most. The place was becoming unsafe for children: what would they do to a half-caste child, a brown and gold one with green eyes? At night he lay beside his large wife. Threatening noises and shouts kept him awake. He feared arrest, and worse, feared mob violence — feared it most because it was just: a mob inflamed and inspired by his own words. He wanted to throttle Mwase. Each time he dozed the pamphlet was shaken in his face, and once in a dream he was made to eat it. He dreamed of the prison island Major Beaglehole had described to him. Calvin was the governor, Aubrey's brother. He looked up from his desk and saw a pack of muttering inmates trotting toward him, armed with shivs and machetes. "Stop! Sort yourselves out, chaps!" Calvin screamed. "I will insure every one of you!" He woke himself with his pleading.

But that night the muttering jungle voices did not stop when he woke. He sat up in bed and listened. He heard grunts rising to a bawl of accusation, and dropping low in threats that seemed to scratch the bedroom wall. Calvin wondered for a moment if he was deranged. But no: Mira murmured, she shifted to her side and protected her big belly with her arms; she heard.

Calvin got out from under the mosquito net. It was like so many other voices. Everything in Malawi spoke: the little scurrying dust devils, the rain on the leaves, the breezes patting and smoothing the grass; drains grumbled and belched when they were full, cooking fires munched branches. And now the house itself was alive and gabbing in what sounded like English.

He put on his clothes and crept into the hall. The sounds were loudest in the bar. Calvin entered on all fours, by the side entrance, his teeth clenched for fear of noise. He slid behind a stack of beer crates, pulling his knees after him. The beer crates obstructed his view of the bar and the men.

"Wait, wait!" said a bass voice. "That's all you can say."

Calvin snared his face in a cobweb and immediately began wondering if it was a spider web, and if so where was the spider now? He picked strands of web from his eyes and mouth and unthinkingly sucked some of the dusty filaments into his nose.

"It's not my fault. He's delaying, I told you. You want me to sing it?"

"Every week you say that. It's late. Osbong should be dead by now, but he's not!"

"Not so loud. You wanna wake everybody up?"

There were only those two voices; both were thick, drunken. They argued in the dark.

Calvin tried to identify the voices. There was something in the conscious grammar and finished word endings of the bass voice that indicated a person who had learned English late; a slur in the other's disclosed the impatient familiarity of the native speaker. But Calvin was so close that it distorted instead of clarified, and he could not link the voices to faces.

"It is not the job of the president to fight," said the bass voice slowly. "If I have no choice, of course I will fight beside my men."

"You're not the president yet, don't forget that."

"Don't threaten me. You have not been paid yet; remember that."

"That's another thing. If you want action you gotta pay for it. Nothing for nothing." Liquid was poured, the bottle neck chinking the rim of the glass twice. After a breathy swallow, the same voice continued, "I have to do all the dirty work."

"You expect me to perform all the dirty work?"

"I didn't say that."

"Who stabbed the minister? That was a big job. He had a gun."

"I said thanks, didn't I?"

"I do not want your thanks. I want Osbong dead. I want this country."

"You drive me nuts with all your I want."

"I want results."

"You got some."

"We have been fighting for almost a year. You tell me what results."

"For Christ's sake, half the country is yours."

"I don't want half!"

Someone was slapped, someone muttered.

"Slaps, that's all I get."

"You deserve worse."

Worse? Calvin tried to leave. He wiped what remained of the web from his face, and started to back out. There was a noise at his heel. The plump-backed bar rat was nibbling at sawdust in a pool of moonlight. Calvin drew his legs up and made himself as small as possible. He had to sit it out. The rat was stupid and moved noisily; to scare it was to give himself away.

"I deserve a medal for all the shit I've been through," the slurring voice said. "Who sends all your messages? Who runs his ass off around town delivering your pamphlet? Who *printed* the lousy thing! I had to set the whole thing by hand. Damn near went blind doing that."

"So you think it is a lousy pamphlet? Do you realize that my pamphlet is the only thing we have to show for a year's struggle. The people read it and now they listen to us."

"It was a corny title. I could have done a better one."

"You are wrong. No white man could have written that."

The thief. And it wasn't Mwase.

"I did a nice little book in Angola. It was called *Now*, but in Portuguese. 'Give us our land, take off our chains, listen to our crying voices,' and so forth and so on."

"They're still fighting in Angola."

"Marais said the same thing."

"Because they don't know anything about revolution. You don't know yourself."

"Revolution! Don't talk to *me* about revolution, you twerp. I know the old way, a few bombs, a few arrests, some snipers on the roof. Riot, strike, riot, strike. You don't have to start a whole goddamn war against one man. You want a big army to come here and blow the place to bits. That's not a revolution, you fathead, and I told Marais that, too. You're both new to this game. So don't tell me what I know."

"It will happen here whether you help us or not."

"When it's supposed to happen, it happens. You don't have to push all the time. People help. If they don't help you, it's no go."

"It sounds to me as if you don't want to work for us anymore."

"I look and what do I see? A couple of people knocked off.

No one cares. A little town captured. No one cares. You have a strike and no one notices. Just a few black people turning nasty, but no riots, nothing like that. Sometimes I figure why not go back to Addis or Dar and have a cold beer and forget the whole shebang. No one gives a shit, why should I?"

"That's what you think!"

Feet scraped.

"Get your hands offa me! If you're so full of piss and vinegar why don't you go kill Osbong?"

"I will!"

"I mean, why should I? I got a wife and kids."

"Bugger your wife and kids."

"You get so British all of a sudden."

Someone spat, a table was bumped. Calvin pressed himself between the wall and the beer crates and hoped that they wouldn't chase into him. Or shoot! What if they began shooting? He put his head between his knees and tried to shut out the noise of the two men cursing each other in the dark.

"This is a knife."

"So is this. Now back off!"

There was a scuffle; chairs were cracked and tipped over, and Calvin could hear the men panting and dragging their feet sideways.

"I'm going to kill you first, then him in Lilongwe. Then Osbong. I don't need any of you."

"Yes, you do, you gutless bastard. You need us to fight your battles."

"We were doing all right before you came."

"Sure you were! Shitting in the grass — "

A crash of glass. One swore.

"Come one step more, jungle bunny, and you'll be so much dead meat."

Quick steps were followed by a short pause, then a thump. Calvin imagined a lunge. He closed his eyes and heard bodies rolling on the floor, upsetting the wooden furniture in the bar and smashing glass. Then the hurrying bumps of a person crawling swiftly on hands and knees. This stopped with another struggle, puffing and blowing, and an insistent but muffled punching, each punch producing a groan. One was dying, making the sounds of a mourner, sighing down the scale in a kind of grief. That slowed, and soon was gone; one man breathed heavily, making snorelike sounds.

Calvin opened his eyes. Through the bottles in the beer crates he saw a feeble swinging light at the far end of the barroom.

"Get out of here or I'll ring for the police!" This voice was Bailey's. "And take him with you. If he's dead I don't want to hear about it. Filthy bloody sods," she gasped, and then the light was gone.

34

After that night Mira produced some early pains. Calvin thought they might be her response to the fright of all that noise: idle trees in Hudson orchards sometimes blossomed and bore fruit when their trunks were whammed by a big farmhand swinging a pick haft.

She woke turning with cramps. They went away for minutes and she got up; then they surged back, and she had to sit. Calvin put her back to bed. She started to tell about them in her halting English when the pains were gone, but when they were on her she switched into her own language: she remembered it in her distress. Calvin didn't know a word of it.

They had shared everything before and had managed tenderness without speaking. From the pain Calvin was excluded. It was private, she labored with it alone. He wheeled the tea trolley into Bailey's kitchen and piled it with food, bananas and boiled eggs, oatmeal and a jug of orange squash. The sight of it seemed to make Mira dyspeptic and knotted her cramps. Calvin got on the Matchless and flew to the Queen Elizabeth Hospital; he reported the pain and the cause to the Israeli doctor in Emergency. The doctor put a few extra tools in his black satchel and rode cheerfully on the groaning rear saddle of the motorcycle, still wearing his white coat. He said, as they crackled over leaves near a vast fence of gum trees, what a lovely day it was, so fresh.

At the eating house the doctor wrinkled his nose. "This place give us a lot of headique."

"She's in the back," said Calvin.

They passed through the bar. The furniture was still tipped over from the night before; the room looked bombed. On the bar counter stood a tray of dull unwashed glasses. The doctor regarded them. He said, "*Lot* of wee-dee."

Mira crouched on the edge of the bed at the raised fly of the mosquito tent. Her arms were folded, dismay made her face small.

The doctor picked his way through the untidy room. He was white haired and plump and had rosy cheeks, and he looked to Calvin like a benign mayor visiting a slum.

"And here is the little mother," he said, and smiled.

The exclamation was a comfort to Calvin. He thought of Mwase; he owed Mwase an apology; he would find him and explain.

The doctor felt Mira's forehead with the back of his fingers. He timed her pulse and tapped her back and took her blood pressure.

"Tell me where is the pain?"

"She doesn't speak — "

The doctor bent and elaborately cradled her belly, the whole harvest in his hands. He pressed gently with his thumbs and inquired, "Here? . . . Here? . . ."

Mira shook her head.

"They come and go," said Calvin. "Maybe they're gone."

The doctor asked Calvin to leave the room for the rest of the examination. Calvin shuffled into the hall. The eating house was strangely quiet. It was just past nine and usually at this hour rumpled clients would be slipping out, Bailey would be cursing the cooks, Beaglehole spattering the Gents, Jarvis polishing glasses, a sound of frying. But there was no stir. Without movement and people the eating house seemed very squalid, almost derelict.

Mira dozed on the bed, tucked in neatly, when Calvin was recalled to the room.

"My diagnosis is false alarum," said the doctor. "If they come back, give me a tinkle, yes?"

"There's no phone," said Calvin. "I'll come and get you if she has the pains again."

"Best thing is to time contractions," said the doctor pushing up his sleeve. "How many minutes pain, how many minutes no pain. Like that."

Calvin was staring at the doctor's wrist. "Pardon me for asking, but why two watches?"

"You remind me!" said the doctor appreciatively, slipping off the large silver one. "This morning I must go to the police and give this."

"Can I see that watch?"

The doctor handed it over. It was still ticking.

"Astronauts have ones like this."

"Was the property of a man they bring in this morning dead. Poor fellow, full of wounds. No identification, only this nice vache."

"African?"

"No," said the doctor.

*   *   *

The office door was unlocked, but Mwase was not inside. Calvin searched the hall and the washroom and even the broom cupboard, preparing his introduction and detailed apology each time he flung a door open. He looked everywhere; he found the peanut vendor sneaking a drink. But no Mwase. Entering his office a second time he noticed the doorknob was loose. The lock had been yanked out.

"Come in and shut the door." The voice came from behind the file cabinet.

Calvin pushed the door shut.

The man appeared. Calvin recognized him instantly as Marais. He wore the same khaki fatigues, but they were faded; his hair was longer and it was pushed, rather than combed, straight back over his ears and showed the round indent of a cap. His sunglasses were the same and so, Calvin thought, were his boots; but the boots were chafed and covered with mud. His face was thinner and very sunburned, his mustache ragged, and on his chin was sun-bleached stubble.

"What do *you* want?" It was meant to be sharp, but it caught in Calvin's throat.

He was shorter than Calvin remembered him. Calvin towered over him, feeling awkward and badly arranged. He tried to do something with his hands that would not alarm Marais. But he could think of nothing; he let them wander.

"Just want to talk to you," said Marais. There was no threat in his voice. It was, if anything, apologetic.

"Where's your gun?"

Marais patted a lump under his shirt.

"You the president now?" asked Calvin, giving the sarcasm a cautious edge.

Marais shook his head slowly. "Let's sit down," he said. "My back aches. I walked from Lilongwe."

"What happened to your fancy car?"

"I want some life insurance," Marais said, ignoring Calvin's taunt. He sat in Mwase's chair and took a taped block of bills from a haversack at his feet. He placed the money on Calvin's desk. "I'm willing to pay."

"Why come to me?" asked Calvin, seating himself at his desk but not looking at the money. "There are lots of insurance companies in town."

"I've got reasons," said Marais. "I want it from you."

"Well, you're wasting your time. So you can walk back to Lilongwe for all I care. I'm not going to insure you."

Marais moved his chair closer to Calvin's desk. He said, "Here's the money."

"I see it," said Calvin. "Stick it."

"What more do you want?" Marais asked quietly.

"I don't want anything from you," said Calvin. "You killed my brother-in-law."

Marais looked at the floor, then at his palms. He nodded. "I'm sorry."

"*Sorry! Sorry!*" Calvin repeated in unbelief. He rapped the desk. "That's what you say when you bump into someone — not when you kill him! Do you know the difference, pal? He was a harmless little guy, he didn't give a sweet shit for politics, and you knifed him in his own house. Sorry! Jesus Christ, you got a big nerve."

"The men were punished," said Marais. "What do you want me to say?"

"Nothing," said Calvin, "but don't tell me you're sorry when I know you're not. I don't want to see you. Get out of here and leave me alone." A sob dragged itself through Calvin and he thought he might cry. He didn't want to cry in front of Marais.

"A favor — " Marais started to say.

"Wait a sec," said Calvin. The sob passed and left him lucid. "You called me an exploiter, you remember? And I used to worry about that. But I don't worry anymore, because you know what I think now? I think *you're* a fucking exploiter! You and all those ass-kicking bastards of yours! You killed my brother-in-law and you scared the hell out of my wife! You cheesy two-bit bastards — " Calvin had risen and was shouting down at Marais. " — All the lies I've had to listen to! You're bulletproof, you're big and strong, you're going to save everybody — "

Calvin was still burbling and blinking, but he was not saying words. Marais had removed his sunglasses. He faced Calvin, who stood over him.

Marais's faded clothes and muddy boots had suggested effort, and the voice out of his thin face had been strained; his eyes confirmed that and said more. They were the eyes of a casualty, lifeless, sunken in patches of yellow flesh the shape of lenses, set off and framed by the sunburn. The hollow eyes were on Calvin but did not focus or register his presence. It was as if they had seen something terrible and had been stunned and emptied by that sight. The sunglasses had masked them. The doomed had those eyes.

A tirade had been building in Calvin for months, and he wanted to continue, to make up for the anger and shame at the thought of his stolen book being passed around and crazing the Africans, for Ogilvie beheaded in his hut, the rumors of attack, Mwase's accusing fantasies and the still-vivid memory of the knife fight in the darkened bar. He wanted to shake Marais, spit threats at him, wound him.

The eyes revealed hurt deeper than any he could inflict. They had suffered the calamity of despair. Calvin could accuse, but he knew that whatever he said, whatever abuse he offered would be accepted. The murderer was wounded and was himself a victim. Calvin saw this and forgave.

"Please leave," Calvin said at last. "And don't ask me to insure you. Look at me — "

The ruined gaze was terrifying.

" — I sell the stuff and I'm not even insured myself. That sounds nutty, I know, because I'm an insurance man and if I don't have it, who does? I used to have a lot of coverage, but after we got nationalized I let my policies lapse and said screw it, it's no use. I mean, what's the sense?"

"Who nationalized you?"

"Who else?"

"Did he rough you up?"

"Osbong doesn't rough people up," said Calvin. He was about to add *not like you do* but he stopped himself. "He just nationalizes them. You never see the guy — he might be out of the country. You never know. I'm not saying I like him. He wrecked my plans. I suppose I should complain, but who to?

I'm not ambitious, and this isn't my country. Jesus, I don't even think it's a country."

"No?" The voice was empty, like the eyes. "What is it, then?"

"It's a little parish, sort of," said Calvin. He thought a moment. "If you got the faith it's okay. If not, not."

"The only thing worse than having it," said Marais, with fatigue, "is losing it."

"I used to have it," said Calvin. He was surprised to hear himself say it. But he meant it. "Now . . . I don't see the same things or hear them. They still do. I guess I don't really fit in."

"I don't either," said Marais. "But I envy you."

"Come off it," said Calvin. "You're in *charge* of them, for Christ's sake."

"Not anymore," said Marais. "I gave it up."

"Really? You gave it up?" Calvin smiled briefly, then asked, "But what about *them?*"

"They're still at it."

"That's worse, you know that? Why the hell didn't you stop them?"

"I couldn't," said Marais. "I didn't try."

"That's worse," said Calvin again. But he had no blame for Marais. He thought of his book, his little pamphlet: it screamed at him. He had given that up, but men studied it. It was a voice he would always hear.

"I know."

"What are they going to do?"

"Everything I taught them," said Marais bitterly.

Calvin rose and went to the door. He fought with the bolt, jiggling it, and finally, by lifting the door, shot it. He pulled the shade down over the frosted pane of lettered glass.

"I wasn't going to tell you this," said Calvin, seating himself. "But last night I heard a thing or two. My wife and I live — "

"At the hotel on the upper road," said Marais. "I know."

"Well, it's a cathouse, really." Calvin went on, "Late last night, after midnight, I was having a bad dream. I woke up and heard these noises in the bar. I got scared. The thing is, if I hear something like shouting at night and I don't see the person actually doing it, I start to think *maybe he's shouting at me*. So I went to have a look . . ." Calvin described what he had heard, the voices, the threats, the brawl.

Marais did not ask Calvin to repeat anything, and when Calvin said, "I think one was an African," Marais accepted it with a grave nod.

"One was killed?" Marais asked. In his fatigue his concern sounded like pleading. "Are you sure?"

"Positive," said Calvin. "I didn't see the body. I heard it hit the deck, though."

Marais's face was anxious. "One said he was going to Lilongwe, the other said he was giving up. But one was killed." He looked away. "It's hopeless."

"You know who they are?"

Marais nodded.

"Tell me."

"It doesn't make any difference to you," said Marais. "What matters is who died. If I knew I could make a move."

"Was one a man called Harry?" Calvin asked.

"I thought you said you didn't see them."

"I didn't," said Calvin. "But a doctor at the Q.E. did. See, my wife is going to have a baby pretty soon . . ." Calvin told about Mira's pains. He repeated the doctor's story and described the watch. Marais listened motionlessly, as if hearing of a great catastrophe, not a stabbing in a bar, but something perhaps as awful as that which had stunned his eyes. He folded his hands and seemed to pray.

"The other one was Brother Jaja," said Marais in a strained voice. "Harry and he were friends. I didn't think they'd ever fight. Besides, Harry was good with a knife."

"But the other one killed the minister," said Calvin.

"So you know about that, too." Marais breathed deeply and said, "I didn't count on Harry and Jaja fighting."

"Like I said, they were fighting over a pamphlet of some kind," said Calvin, his voice dropping.

Marais put on his sunglasses. "I need a car."

"Where are you going?"

"Lilongwe," said Marais.

"To stop them?"

Marais waited, then said, "I don't know."

"I've got a motorcycle," said Calvin. "Take it."

"How much do you want for it?"

"Nothing," said Calvin. "But bring it back."

"Okay," said Marais quickly. He grasped the block of bills. "There's a grand here. How much insurance can I get for that?"

"For a thousand bucks?" Calvin snickered. "A mint. If you died we'd be bankrupt. I mean, not me, but Osbong." Calvin smiled. "We'd have to close the damn agency!"

"Make me out a policy," said Marais.

"Are you serious?"

"That's what I came for."

"But for that amount of cash you have to have a medical check-up. I mean, you don't look like the healthiest person I've ever seen. You've got to have a check-up. It's the rules."

"You're the agent," said Marais. "You can fix that."

"I can fix it," said Calvin. He opened a drawer and took out a thick application. "Okay, sign here where I make a check mark. Just your name and address, date of birth and that stuff. I'll fake the rest."

Marais signed the forms.

"Montreal," said Calvin, looking over Marais's shoulder at the form. "Well for Christ's sake!"

"You from Montreal too?"

"No," said Calvin. "But we've got a fantastic Homemakers' agency there. One of the fifty-six." I'm still a company man, thought Calvin. "Actually, I'm from Hudson, Mass. There are quite a few Canucks in Hudson — hey, the beneficiary, you forgot that."

"Did you say your wife was going to have a baby?"

"Yes, but — "

"When she has it, put the baby's name there."

"*My* kid as *your* beneficiary?" Calvin started to smile, but Marais's frown stopped him. "He's not even born yet."

"Put your name there for the time being. Afterward you can put your kid's."

"What do you mean *afterward?* After what?"

"After your wife has her baby."

"I don't even believe in insurance," said Calvin.

"No, but your kid might," said Marais.

35

The night sky over Lilongwe glowed red. A deep lighted cloud appeared through a mesh of black branches as Marais came near. Holding the Matchless stiff-armed like a plow, he plunged off the road into grass and made a wide circle around the border of the town on narrow tracks, rocking the motorcycle over the knuckles of roots and entering the way he had escaped, in the dark, by the north end, where the roadblock was abandoned. He leaned the motorcycle into a ditch and walked the last half mile.

Voices came toward him on the road — muttering, and hurrying feet. He pulled himself behind a tree and saw, in the red glow from the town, people — the first he had seen since before nightfall — families sneaking off. The men pushed squeaking wheelbarrows stacked with belongings, some women carried cloth bundles on their heads. Certain they were not soldiers, Marais started again, and the line of people passed by him, walking in the rain trough at the side of the road. They scuffed the gravel with invisible feet; most were merely shadowy torsos, the children were small heads, the bundles the women carried were highlighted pink. They fled like scared beasts from a blaze of grass, without looking back, calling out, crying to those ahead of them; the straggling line continued to pass Marais, and then the last lighted shirt vanished into the blackness.

Closer to the town the color of the sky altered: the crimson cloud was laced with gold, sparks lifted and died in the dark after a wobbling flight, and buntings of blue smoke like yards of silk rose slowly wrinkling as if unfolded from bolts on the ground. Not the lantern it had seemed from a distance, it was a ragged nimbus, and at its edges steady sheep, pink and orange, led off in flocks, becoming tiny lambs, then rose-colored wisps, before they disappeared altogether.

It was fire, the dry season again, a whole year had passed since that first blaze on the frontier where the hills had been spectacularly alight, the whole province a furnace. Marais had stood alone, enclosed by fire; he had faced south down the dirt road, a lane of steaming dust which led through waves of sloping flame. He recalled the roar of the burning, the hot cloth of his shirt, the gusts of the sweeping draft, grass crackling and the sputtering hiss of sap. Some trees had fallen muffled, as if into fathoms of water, and he had woken to skeletons, the black spikes of trees, his black soldiers marching through the black meadow.

Lilongwe was burning. Marais hid at the corner of the last shop in town. A tall bonfire swayed in the middle of the street, at about the place the bomb had gone off, near the police headquarters. It was a pyramid of flaming crates of the sort Marais had seen his men hammering in the street the day Yatu died; he had watched from the dispensary, unable to guess what the men were doing. But it seemed inconceivable that they planned the fire so far ahead — that was April. Or had he been unfair? He had charged them with never planning. Maybe, he thought, they've had their own plot all along and kept it from me.

Beyond the bonfire, on the far side of the street, a row of shops was alight. There were men near the shops in a long snaking line. Some held gallon jugs, others sticks and axes. Led by a big man with a thick four-foot torch, the line wound toward a shop front. A broken sewing machine stood on the verandah. Men with axes smashed the shutters of the shop and broke the door down; they were followed by others with jugs who first sprinkled the liquid over the shutters, then threw full bottles into the shop. It was gasoline: the big man touched his torch to it and there was blossom of orange flame. When that shop was burning more gasoline was thrown. The men cheered and knocked their sticks together, and on their way to the next shop, they sang.

They burned the shops one at a time, stopping at intervals to run back to the bonfire for fresh torches. Marais heard bells, and saw the men wore strings of them on their wrists and ankles; some blew low notes on gourd horns and others rattled shallow drums to a monotonous three-beat chant. Marais thought he heard his name screamed — but he was not sure, for the men were coming up the street and closer to him, and the roar of the burning shops drowned their words.

It should have been a devilish sight, or at least unusual, but it wasn't to Marais. It was methodical holocaust, an annual reflex. Every year in that season there were fires, Marais knew, for he had been in the country now a year and had been through the whole cycle of seasons. The Africans believed that unless every dead plant was burned and every field blackened nothing would grow. So they lit fires. They lost their dry houses sometimes, and always in those months the sun was shrouded in a haze of gray smoke which only the heavy rains dispersed. The soldiers were burning the town with the same ritual energy they used on acres of brown corn shucks. One season was finished; only fire could renew. Marais wondered who had given the order that night. It may have been just a coincidence, the bonfire and the hysteria prompted by his escape and the death of Harry; but if it was not an accident, it was genius.

He was surprised by their number. The people on the road

leaving the town with their belongings had prepared him for a deserted place, for though fires were not unusual, people near them were. The burning frontier had been empty, no man stood nearby with a torch, Marais was the only witness. But here in the snaking line there were many more than fifty men — there were hundreds.

They wore the khaki uniform and visored cap; they wore cowboy hats and bright shirts and cartridge belts. Most were dressed in the baggy shorts and torn collarless shirts of the villager; a score were in clerk's garb, dark trousers and white long-sleeved shirt with the cuffs buttoned. The majority of these last, the clerks, wore ties. It was the only incongruity, these men in neat ties and billowing white sleeves pouring gasoline on shops and shrieking when it was lighted. Their ties flew to their shoulders when they ran to a new shop. Marais recognized some of his men: Brother George, Henry and Chimanga were near the head of the line; they were busy, but not giving orders.

The leader was a man Marais had never seen before. He guessed it was Brother Jaja, the man Marais had avoided meeting personally. He fitted the description Harry and Gbenye had given. He was a fat giant, the biggest African Marais had ever seen, impressive not only for his height, but also for his broad shoulders, and with it all, his fatness, a rare bulk. He had a bellowing laugh that rang above the crackle of the fires, and he led the line with a big man's rolling walk, swinging the torch he held in his fist in wide circles. It was obviously heavy, but he twirled it like a matchstick, at times singeing his men and making them scatter about his legs like pygmies. He was agile, in a tight black suit of a material that glistened in the firelight, and he wore boots which reached to his knees and also gleamed. Around his waist was a waiter's red sash, but he wore it with casual pride, like a campaign ribbon.

Why didn't you stop them? Marais heard Calvin's question again. He watched the men; he was satisfied that his reply was true: he couldn't, he didn't try. And he began to think that there had never been a time when it was possible. He wished he had always known that. Now they were just across the street. Marais held a loaded pistol in one hand and a full clip in the other. He could kill a dozen or more right there, drop them in the line, and the others might pause. It was no good. Death and grief made men silent, but it never cowed; on the contrary, it waked their revenge: men smoldered with the memory of a death. Death was the beginning, grief was anger. And no less for his own death. He smiled at the illumination, the flames.

It was then, as Marais stood dreamily by the shopside watching the opposite building burn, that they saw him. His name was distinct, it stopped the chanting song. He turned to them.

Chimanga ran halfway across the street, fired two shots from his revolver, and hesitated. He had missed, but he seemed to understand it differently. He ran back to the line. Others left the line and pointed. There were more shots. Another man skittered into the street crying out at Marais who remained, dazed, with his arms at his sides. All the men were shouting and blowing their horns, but they were still separated from Marais by the wide street. Except for the one man halfway across the street, wincing at Marais and trying to move forward, the men showed no inclination to mob him.

Brother Jaja roared at the men and stalked to the center of the street, jabbing his torch at Marais. He waved the men on. The men held back.

Marais had not counted on their cowardice. They would have to move. He took a step toward Brother Jaja. Brother Jaja flung down his torch and pulled out a revolver, and still bellowing, he shot repeatedly at Marais. Marais took aim.

Brother Jaja screamed and fired at the ground near his feet. He shuddered, and held himself with his arms and sank to his knees, going down with a crack, as the shop behind him caved in and blew cinders and splinters of flaming wood on the men. He steadied himself with one arm, holding his heart with the other, and he screamed his angry disappointment, not at Marais or at his men, but down the empty smoke-filled street.

"Kill him!" a shout went up, two voices, then many. The line of men broke and crowded past Brother Jaja.

Marais spun and ran behind the row of unburned shops on his side of the street. He knew where he was going. He saw the dull gleam of a trash-can lid and leaped in the dark, tripping and falling in a clatter of metal. He rolled, discarding his pistol and clip, and looked up. Torches bobbed toward him; he heard feet and shouts. But he saw no faces: they could have been any angry men.

"Shoot him! Shoot him!" the wall echoed. He climbed the high fire ladder on the clapboard side of the Great Northern Hotel. They were in the yard, under him, shaking the ladder. A bullet hit the ladder and made the rungs vibrate in his hands. He continued climbing. He looked down one last time before he vaulted the lip of the roof. Now he could see their faces. They were shining at him.

Crossing the roof to the stairwell, he got a glimpse of the single row of blazing shops. From the ground it had seemed the whole world was burning, and he had felt some exhilaration: the night sky red as a sun capsizing in it, heat against his face, and the whole town lighted. But at this new height he saw it differently, without the exaggerated distortion of closeness. From the roof the faces in the mob had no names; the bonfire was mostly black and flickering out, and on the opposite side of the street from the hotel the row of small shops was in flames. Long, but regular and narrow, from one end of the street to the other, it was like a row of children's toy blocks, set alight in an immense and darkened room.

It was a trivial blaze, it burned noiselessly and without spreading; beyond it was night and jungle, all of Africa, and stars he had not seen from the ground. The darkness confined the flames, and at one end it seemed to smother them.

Marais's room was brightened by the fire at the window. The

room had been ransacked, the bed tipped over and the mattress torn apart. The desk was on its side, the drawers dumped out, the mirror over the dresser smashed. Marais went to a corner and lifted a floorboard; he removed his notebooks. He considered their covers, then broke their bindings. And his own face shining in the flames which brightly curtained the windows, he hurriedly dealt the loose pages onto the floor, like playing cards.

The following morning a charred skeleton was found in the smoking rubble of black beams and plaster that had collapsed into the basement. It was seated in a burned-out chair, but no one could tell whether, alive, it had righted and chosen the chair, or whether it had been dumped into it when the floor gave way. Even so, it may not have been Marais, the men digging had decided, for it was impossible to establish from what remained of the body if it had been white or African, man or woman.

36

The birth, Calvin thought, should have followed promptly upon Marais's death, or at least the news of it which Major Beagle-hole, flustered, brought back from a stroll in town. It would have eased his grief, making a logical sequence of the sort that helps to compensate, a nice surprise coming after a bad shock, like the neat comfort insurance was supposed to be. It would have been a pattern achieved in all that outlandish confusion — celebration of success with a little lesson bringing a finish to all his suspense. The insurance money was no solace to him; he mistrusted that amount, it broke the agency, it wasn't his. He looked for relief. It happened in the smooth push and pull of popular fiction; and even the old ballad which claimed its hero in stanza eight, produced a powerful infant in ten.

The death prepared him, but the birth didn't happen. The only events were disappearances: the girls decamped, the eating house emptied, Mavity went to Beira, the baby stopped kicking. There were closures, the bars and shops were shuttered. What a terrible place it was without drink. The weeks went in jerks and reverses, and Calvin lost track of time; but it was hot again, and cloudy with smoke haze, so he knew it was the hot season, October perhaps, a month he hated.

In the evening noisy black soldiers came to play the fruit machines. They jammed them with flattened bottle-cap slugs and demanded beer from the diminished stock. Jarvis was gone; Bailey served. Mira and Calvin sat with Major Beaglehole, who had yarns and rumors. The most violent caused Mira pain, but it was always simulated labor, false alarm: they timed the pains now. Sometimes Bailey said, "He was a lad, was Mavity" and Beaglehole shushed her and turned up his hearing aid, raised his eyes to the plane he heard and said, "It's them. They're coming, by God. I can hear them . . ." He meant the British, but it was usually the DC-3 from Salisbury with the mail. Major Beaglehole was vulnerable with the volume up; one evening when it was on loud a soldier booted a fruit machine and knocked the old man to the floor.

Calvin's eyes were on Mira's bundle, so intensely that he saw nothing else: the bundle was still, and nothing moved in the periphery of his vision. He was jumpy in an agony of waiting. He offered no stories. He showed no surprise when told of Jarvis, Brother Jaja: the king of spades, as Bailey came to call him.

"I twigged it, you see, when he dressed up at night," she whispered in a voice full of gravel. "If he had taken over I'd have closed the place and got one of those really swish knocking shops in Bulawayo or Jo'burg."

Aware that he too might have to leave soon, Major Beaglehole spoke of the discomfort in cold countries, and his feeble blood, thinned by a life in the tropics. He obsessively described the effects of English weather on his elderly body: "It gets me in my toes and fingers. They ache and sort of die on me. And would you believe it," he would say, grimacing and showing a finger, "a frightful stabbing pain in the tip of my old man." He had seen soldiers camped near the radio station, near the High Court at Chichiri, at the Queen Elizabeth Hospital and the clock tower and on the grounds of the presidential palace. Siege recalled to him many stories; he told them all, and said Durban was the place for him.

Calvin was with Mira all day now in the bare eating house. The office was closed: Mwase had left, seemingly for good — maybe, as he had warned, to rise up. Though Calvin hoped not. Calvin's only consolation about *The Uninsured* was that if he had not written it, someone else would have; but he was still annoyed by the thought that the someone would have had to be a stranger to the parish, like himself or Marais.

Mira was soulful, staring at the floor through her hooded eyes; and Calvin came to believe that the baby had died. Mira was terrified by the soldiers, of any man with a gun, as she had been just after the marriage. She held Calvin's arm when the soldiers were present, and she would not let go until they left.

But one night after the soldiers had all tramped out, Mira still held on. It was a loose grip; she was reassuring herself rather than enduring a pain. She looked across the empty bar with a wondering face, at the fruit machines, widening her eyes, then squinting, while Calvin looked at her.

She stood abruptly, as if inspired to march across to a machine, feed in an osbong and pull the lever for a jackpot. She murmured and held her dress and put her knees together and said, "Goodness."

She splashed from under her skirt. Beneath her chair was a small dune of flooded sawdust. The waters had broken. But there was no pain. She began to speak in her language, a familiar signal, but no more comprehensible to Calvin than the first time he had heard it. She tried to run.

"Get her to the bedroom!" Bailey cried. "Quick!"

Mira was carried to her bed.

There was no motorcycle to reach the doctor with; and there were soldiers on the street watching for enemies. Calvin knew panic. But Bailey pushed him aside and brought a basin, and threw off her greasy shawl. She scrubbed her arms and then comforted Mira with a show of such gentleness that Calvin permitted it and stayed apart.

"Here?" he asked.

"Won't be the first," said Bailey. She started to tell of the deliveries she had performed on her girls, right there in the eating house. "Oh, I've delivered so many kids for my girls," she said.

"Hosipital," said Mira. "Doc-tor."

"Now you just lie there," said Bailey. She handed Calvin a rag and told him to wipe Mira's perspiring face.

Major Beaglehole tidied the room, muttering about disorder. He found a chair and, overcome by tiredness, slept.

Bailey was nimble and clean; she spoke to Mira in Chinyanja and was busy in her midwifery. She calmed Mira and told her when and how to breathe and push. The baby was six hours coming. It arrived after a great struggle, in the darkest hour of the morning, giving a gasp and a yell as soon as its head protruded.

"Boy it is!" said Bailey, snipping the cord and swinging him up. It was a packed, colorless little child, covered with gore. Bailey laid him on the bed. He shrieked and shot out his arms, and immediately he took color.

"A boy," said Calvin, stunned. The infant was amazing: he had a full head of thick black hair, and a very wrinkled gray face. His fingers found his mouth, and he sucked them loudly.

Mira raised herself on her elbow and watched Bailey bathing it. It pissed a thread of spray in the air. Bailey washed it and said, "That's funny," and washed it again, and repeated her perplexed remark. She scrubbed it thoroughly and poured a pitcher of water over it. The baby started to cry. Bailey dabbed its pudgy face with a towel and looked puzzled. She closed one eye and studied the baby's face; she shook her head and tried to hand it to Mira.

Calvin intercepted it and wrapped it up. He cradled it carefully in his arms. And Bailey, with the expectant look of someone remembering something, a look she often got before she coughed, left the room and closed the door.

Mira's hands were out. Her eyes pleaded.

Calvin held on. The baby's chipmunk face was folded,

his eyes were shut tightly. Calvin lifted him and kissed the wet wool of his head. The baby seemed very black. But Calvin's imagination had fooled him before: he had simulated miseries in his black book, and there had been times when he himself had felt black, like the king of spades or Mr. P. Lumumba, grumbling under vines in the wet stillness of jungle. It had been an unusual feeling.

But Mr. Bones was dead, and lately Calvin knew that he would surely go, now with a whole family. And he saw himself planted in Hudson or elsewhere, walking down a clean sidewalk in squirts of sunshine, a breeze stirring the poplars: he would stroll past hedges and lampposts, while people gawked amazed in cottage windows at the black woman he loved on his arm. He hoped they would be able to see, in the carriage he wheeled, the tar baby kicking and gurgling, his son.

The baby woke and wailed again, furiously changing color, going darker.

"I knew it," Beaglehole said, without waking himself. "It's them . . . they're coming . . . I can hear . . ."

Outside in the hall Bailey was breathing. The cough took her and held her. She hacked and panted and sawed the silence of the empty house with her sobbing cough. She coughed without letup again and again, as if she would drive out her very life.